ADVENT

Book One of the **RED MAGE** Series
Written by **Xander Boyce**

Table of Contents

Acknowledgments

There are a ton of people who I should probably thank for their efforts, and I'm sure I will miss some people in this. Know that I'm still very appreciative of your influences in my life, I'm just terrible at expressing my appreciation.

First, I'd like to thank my family. My mother for forcing me to read as a child. My father for showing me the wonders of Science Fiction. My youngest sister for showing me online serials and being my editor and sounding board throughout the creation of the book. My dog Dewey, the best puppy in the world.

The teachers that told me to keep writing even when I stopped for a few decades: Mrs. Kelsch for telling me I could do better. Dr. Booth for making me read my poetry in front of 150 of my peers. Mr. Park for showing me that anyone could write a book. Mr. Tenny, for kindling a love of the written word in my young mind.

Last of all, I'd like to thank you. For giving me a chance.

Prologue

We know the stories of the Heroes of the Advent: how Jason the Destroyer felled the Dark Titan and brought us to the Greater Age, the tale of Anna the Kind's creation of the Tree Bountiful, Boris the Belligerent's breaking of the Green Tide, Sung Min the Prognosticator's ride through the night to save New Boston, and Francois the Flippant's famous taunt of the Consumer that bought the forces of Destin their final minute. These tales and ninety-five more you have learned from your First Level.

These are not the stories of the Hundred Heroes. This is from the time before, of the souls that laid a sure foundation upon which the Heroes built. These are the tales of the Advent itself, but a tale for the bright day, as the dark shadow stalks its margins and the Bright Corridor has stolen all but their names.

Taryn Hollingshead, Seer of the First Gate.

I have seen the creation, the first day of Advent. A voice with enough power to shake the sky whispered, "Begin." It commanded, and creation obeyed. People collapsed, praying to the forgotten god. Others froze as the world they had known crumbled into memory. This is the story of Drew Michalik, one of those who stood.

Chapter One — Tutorial

"Begin." The word echoed throughout his skull. The large room, which had previously been lit by dozens of monitor screens and lights, went completely black. An image appeared before Drew, staying in the same place as he turned his head. New words scrolled underneath the first set after a short delay.

> Mana accumulators have reached initialization charge.
> Dimensional split commencing.
> Dimensional split complete.
> Operational capacity in 200(+/-15) local days.

Drew blinked the messages away. Had he fallen asleep? The room was completely black. He waited several heartbeats for the emergency lights to come on, waiting for the numerous fail-safes on the electronics in the room to energize.

"Fuuuu." It wasn't the complete blackness that scared him. It was the silence. The ventilation systems, uninterruptible power supplies, and fans had all stopped. The only sound to be heard was his pounding heartbeat. From the tests and drills, he knew it usually took about two or three seconds, tops.

Six seconds, ten, then twenty passed.

"What the actual f–" His words cut off as another line of blue text appeared in front of him, his entire body going rigid as an electric surge swept through his frame.

> Citizen scan commencing.
> Citizen scan complete.
>   Citizen status: Healthy.
> Citizen Evaluation:
>   Physical: Common.

Resistance: Basic.
Pain Threshold: Intermediate.
Speed: Undeveloped.
Mental: Advanced.
Mana Receptivity: Intermediate.
Mana Discharge: Rare.
Mana Charge: Advanced.
Xatherite node potential: 73.
Xatherite node Balance: 24 Red, 13 Orange, 14 Yellow, 4 Green, 6 Blue, 2 Indigo, 3 Violet, and 7 White.
Xatherite node Structure: Constellation.
Xatherite node Links: 68.

As soon as the scan was complete, his body unlocked from its rigid state, and he reflexively took a deep breath. "Well, that makes sense; whiskey tango foxtrot is going on?" He was five floors down in a bunker that apparently no longer had power, having video game style pop-ups appear in his vision. "This is just a dream. I must have fallen asleep." It didn't sound like him, but he couldn't think of any other realistic options. The building had enough backup power options to survive pretty much anything but a direct blast.

There hadn't been an explosion, no ground shaking, and no loud noises. Well, minus that voice saying, "Begin." He reached for the landline that was used for emergencies like this. Even an EMP shouldn't affect that line. He knew before he picked it up that it wouldn't work, but it was just something he had to try.

He slapped his cheek. "Wake up Drew." Nothing changed. He slapped himself again, harder this time. "Wake up."

Citizen geolocation acquired.

*** Warning: citizen is in near proximity to primary nexus. ***
Citizen is awarded an additional 5% (rounded down) of their
total nodes in intermediate grade xatherite to assist in survival.
Citizen compatibility tool initialization.
Citizen is awarded 7% (rounded down) of their total nodes in
beginner grade xatherite as an initialization bonus.
Citizen compatibility assessment concluded. Available xatherite:

        Red – Fireball (Intermediate)
        Red – Storm (Intermediate)
        Red – Cone of Frost (Intermediate)
        Red – Minor Dancing Sword (Common)
        Red – Major Spark (Basic)
        Orange – Major Refresh (Basic)
        Yellow – Major Mana Guard (Basic)
        Red – Minor Acid Dart (Primitive)
Citizen, please slot at least one node to continue.

What followed was a map that appeared to be a large
grouping of constellations. From the earlier messages, Drew
assumed it was his xatherite node structure. There were many
small, multi-colored constellations ranging from two to six nodes
each. Some were connected by thick lines and others by smaller
lines. He assumed the larger connections were the node links
mentioned in the assessment. Most of the slots were dimmed.
However, a point near the bottom was pulsing white, and the
nodes within two connections of it looked usable. In all, only
three red nodes, two orange, and a yellow node looked to be
available for immediate insertion.

"What's going on?" Drew asked the darkness, his voice
bordering on panic.

Warning: To facilitate an adequate survival rate, citizens will not
drop xatherite for 100 days.

> You have been selected to view the tutorial; you may view the tutorial prior to slotting a node.

"Okay, some answers." He turned his head around to see if there wasn't some small amount of light. "Well, I'm either crazy, or it's really happening... Either way, might as well get some information. Now, how do I start the tutorial?"

Saying that was enough to activate it. The darkness around him changed, shifting from absolute darkness to a deeper darkness while simultaneously illuminating the nearest section, giving him the sense of vision. A moderately attractive woman appeared in front of him.

"Greetings, citizen. I am the artificial intelligence assigned as Earth-3's Tutorial guide. You may call me Aevis. I am authorized to instruct you on basic system interface, xatherite, xatherite nodes, and your rights as a citizen of Earth-3 in a newly initialized system."

"What's going on?"

"Your system was claimed and settled by the Human Protectorate in galactic year 17,543. As such, mana accumulators and humankind were seeded on the third planet, designated Earth, in preparation for full citizenship integration when ambient mana reached sufficient levels to support full functionality. This is the third successful split in Earth spacetime. As such, your dimension has been designated Earth-3. During the activation process known as Advent, Earth-3 will undergo a series of radical shifts to bring it more in line with Protectorate development standards. Did that answer your question?"

Drew's mouth opened and closed a few times as he tried to parse everything that he'd just heard. "What's the Human Protectorate?"

"Before I answer another question, you must affirm that I have adequately answered your previous question."

"Why does that matter?" Drew asked, walking towards Aevis who turned to keep him in front of her.

"Before I answer another question, you must affirm that I have adequately answered your previous question," the image repeated.

"Fine, yes, you did," Drew growled.

"Very well, which of your questions would you like answered first? The Human Protectorate, or why I cannot answer a second question until I have completely answered the previous question?"

"The Protectorate one. Ignore the second question." Drew sighed. This was worse than Alexa.

"I will ignore your second question. The Human Protectorate is a collection of humankind whose stated goal is the advancement and protection of Human life within the portions of what you know as the Milky Way, Andromeda, and Triangulum galaxies. The full scope of the Protectorate consists of more than eight thousand Earth-like planets across twenty-three dimensions. That is all the information I am authorized to divulge about the Protectorate at this time."

Drew nodded his head, trying to comprehend just how big that made this Human Protectorate.

"Please respond with a verbal confirmation," Aevis stated.

"Yes, that answered my question." Drew sighed with some amount of exasperation. "What sort of changes will happen to Earth?"

"As a result of higher concentrations of mana, Earth-3's natural flora and fauna will develop more aggressive tendencies. Additionally, excessively high concentrations of mana will spontaneously create additional organisms. These manaborn creatures will assist in the advancement of Earth-3 citizens by developing their combat capabilities. Additionally, mana constructs designed to train and test the citizenry of Earth-3 will be implemented. Does that answer your question?"

"Are you telling me that there are going to be monsters that you want us to fight?"

"That is an accurate interpretation of my response. Does that answer your question?"

"Why?"

"Before I answer another question, you must affirm that I have adequately answered your previous question."

"Yes, it does. But why?"

"Your question is ambiguously worded; please clarify."

"Why are there going to be monsters? Why do you want to improve our combat capabilities?"

"Both questions are interrelated. All dimensions of Earth have been designated as combat training facilities due to their high mana potential. As such, all citizens become de facto members of the Human Protectorates Naval forces. The monsters created have been deemed appropriate training systems. Does that answer your question?"

"Yes," Drew answered out of habit as he considered everything that he had just heard. He was already a member of the U.S. Coast Guard, but he had switched from doing boardings to military intelligence after he picked his rate eighteen months into his contract. He didn't particularly like the idea of being shanghaied into some alien naval force.

"Your time inside the tutorial is limited; I suggest you go through the basic xatherite node tutorial prior to beginning your training," Aevis interjected into Drew's thoughtful silence. Apparently taking his silence as permission, she began.

"Xatherite is crystallized mana and comes in seven different colors. These xatherite crystals also come in nine different grades. Each color of xatherite focuses on a different type of active skill or spell. For example, the low-grade, red xatherite crystal, Major Spark, you were given will allow you to summon a single damaging spell to deal lightning damage to a single foe because Red is the color of attack xatherite. The color designations are as follows:" As she said this, a projection of the different colors of xatherite appeared next to her.

Red-Attack
Orange-Enhancement
Yellow-Defense
Green-Psychic
Blue-Creation
Indigo-Deception
Violet-Alteration

"You will note, in addition to the seven colored nodes, there are also white nodes in your structure. These white nodes can accept any color of xatherite. Individuals are identified by the majority colors in their node structures. With low physical stats but high mental stats and a major concentration of red nodes, you would be designated as a red mage or assault mage."

"The major color of your nodes, its structure, and how many nodes you have are all directly related to your personality and capabilities as an individual. Your node and link count are both higher than the mean for Earth-3, and it is recommended that you exercise discretion when communicating their values with your fellow citizens."

"What was the average?" Drew interrupted the AI before it could continue.

"I am not authorized to divulge that information," Aevis said before continuing with her lecture. The image of the starmap structure that made up Drew's xatherite nodes appeared next to her.

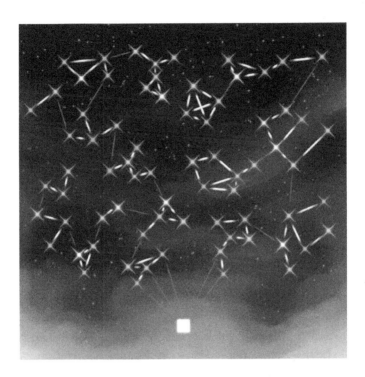

"As you can see, you have a constellation-class structure, which means that your nodes are arranged in subgroups. You can only use a xatherite crystal after it has been inserted into a node. After you insert a crystal into a node, you must then attune to the crystal, which involves using the crystal in combat situations."

"Once you have attuned the crystal, you can begin the process of upgrading your crystals. Low-grade crystals will upgrade through use as excess mana crystallizes within the node, amplifying the power of the crystal."

"What about higher grade xatherite?"

"Higher grade crystals will usually have additional requirements to upgrade them, but that is beyond the scope of this tutorial," Aevis responded before pointing to the pulsing white square at the bottom of the grid. "This is your origin node. You may place a crystal into any node within two connections of the origin or any already inserted crystal."

Four nodes next to the origin that were all linked by heavy lines began to glow. "This is a constellation. As you can see, it consists of two red, a yellow, and an orange node. By filling this constellation with attuned crystals, you will create linked skills. For example, if you were to place your intermediate grade storm and your undeveloped grade minor acid dart xatherites in a constellation and attuned both, you could create the linked ability: Minor Acid Storm. The grade of the crystals in the linked ability will be averaged to determine the grade of the linked ability. However, not all xatherite combinations will create a linked ability."

"What is the hierarchy of grades?" Drew asked, falling back into his old gaming habits.

"Xatherite grades are as follows: primitive, undeveloped, basic, common, intermediate, rare, advanced, master, and legendary. Those same grades are used for all equipment, statistics, and evaluations within the mana system."

"That answers my question. How do I see what combinations will create linked abilities?"

"Only trial and error. It is also important to note that you cannot remove a placed crystal; you can only replace it, destroying the original. Unfortunately, your time in the tutorial has elapsed. *Humanity prevails.*"

The last words Aevis said were in a different language, but he somehow knew that was what they meant. Humanity prevails. The question was, who do they prevail against?

Chapter Two — Xatherite

The tutorial faded, and Drew was back in the darkness of the watch floor. He turned his head from side to side, looking for any source of light, but he didn't find any. The oppressive gloom added weight to everything he had just heard. He was here in a world that wasn't anything like the one he had known before. Reaching behind him to find the chair he had been sitting in, he sat down with a heavy sigh.

Citizen, please slot a xatherite node to continue.

Grateful to have at least something for his eyes to focus on in the darkness, Drew accessed his node structure with a thought, and it sprang into being before him. To the right of the map was the list of xatherite he had available.

Focusing on them one by one, he pulled up the info screens on each crystal.

Xatherite Crystal Name: Fireball
Xatherite Color: Red
Xatherite Grade: Intermediate
Type: Magic
Effect: Convert mana into a high energy blast of fire that will travel in a straight line until exploding, causing major fire damage in a 1m radius around the blast.
Mana recharge time: 10.5 seconds.

Xatherite Crystal Name: Storm
Xatherite Color: Red
Xatherite Grade: Intermediate

Type: Magic
Effect: Create a localized storm around a target. The storm will have a radius of 10m and will cause significant wind, water, and lightning damage within its radius.
Mana recharge time: 1 minute, 17 seconds

Xatherite Crystal Name: Cone of Frost
Xatherite Color: Red
Xatherite Grade: Intermediate
Type: Magic
Effect: Creates a cone of cold energy which causes significant freezing damage, originating from any part of your body. Has a chance to partially enclose the target in ice, slowing them down considerably. Cone will extend 4m and has an arc of 1/4pi radians.
Mana recharge time: 16.8 seconds

Xatherite Crystal Name: Minor Dancing Sword
Xatherite Color: Red
Xatherite Grade: Common
Type: Magic
Effect: Creates a mana construct of a sword that lasts for 30 seconds. The sword will move on its own and attack any target designated for the duration of the attack.
Mana recharge time: 1 minute, 45 seconds

Xatherite Crystal Name: Major Spark
Xatherite Color: Red
Xatherite Grade: Basic
Type: Magic

Effect: Creates an arc of electricity, dealing minor lightning damage from any body part to a target no more than 3m away.
Mana recharge time: 4.2 seconds

Xatherite Crystal Name: Major Refresh
Xatherite Color: Orange
Xatherite Grade: Basic
Type: Magic
Effect: Infuses mana into the target to reduce fatigue and lactic acid buildup.
Mana recharge time: 22 minutes, 24 seconds

Xatherite Crystal Name: Major Mana Guard
Xatherite Color: Yellow
Xatherite Grade: Basic
Type: Magic
Effect: Creates a shield of mana around the caster. This shield will absorb moderate amounts of energy and kinetic damage.
Mana recharge time: 4 minutes, 33 seconds

Xatherite Crystal Name: Minor Acid Dart
Xatherite Color: Red
Xatherite Grade: Primitive
Type: Magic
Effect: Creates a small globule of acid from a finger that travels in a straight line until it impacts a target, dealing minor acid damage.
Mana recharge time: 16.1 seconds

He was a little confused by the damage amounts he was given since they didn't match up with the hierarchy he had been told to expect in the tutorial. He assumed minor was smaller than small, which was in turn smaller than moderate, but was significant higher than major? Also, Minor Dancing Sword didn't list a damage at all. Did it not do any damage, or was it because it dealt kinetic damage while all the others dealt energy damage?

He glanced back over the units used. Meters and radians, really? He should have paid more attention in calculus. He was pretty sure 1/4 pi radians was approximately forty-five degrees, and meters were easy enough to convert into feet. "I guess this means the system is more interested in math than politics."

Also, judging by the weird recharge times, his stats must play some sort of effect on how long it took before he could cast the spell again. He also realized that there was no cast time. Did that mean they were all instant effects? Or was it a hidden value that he would have to figure out for each spell?

Glancing at his node structure, Drew realized that he wasn't going to be able to insert all his xatherite currently. Well, he could, but it would spread him out around his constellations and prevent him from fully populating any constellations. He would need to use the yellow and orange xatherite he had to bridge the locations to the other red nodes. This meant he needed to decide if it was more important to complete a constellation or to place all his xatherite.

There were obvious pros and cons to both. If he placed them all, he would begin the process of upgrading all of them, and there was a clear difference in value between his intermediate quality xatherite and the lower grade ones. Getting those lower grade crystals upgraded would make him significantly more powerful, but at the same time, completing a constellation or creating linked skills would do the same thing, giving him more power and hopefully a better survival rate.

Also, where he put them was important. Did he put his good crystals in the four-constellation node so that he could complete it or in the six-constellation that required a blue and violet xatherite? He had no idea how common xatherite were; the only reference he had for getting more was that apparently killing other humans would allow him to get their xatherite in one hundred days, after the restriction was removed.

That was a worrisome prospect. It meant that xatherite was rare enough that killing another human for their crystals was part of the process, which meant that it could be a long time before he got the purple and blue xatherite he needed in order to fully complete the six-node constellation. Perhaps he could trade with other people? Obviously, only ones that he didn't have slotted, which would be another reason not to slot all his xatherite immediately.

He stared at the nodes in front of him. He simply didn't have enough information to make the best choices. The gamer inside of him wanted to push him to make optimal choices, but what if he needed all those high-level xatherite to get away from the primary nexus? That was why he received them in the first place, because being near it was so dangerous. He didn't think the world had suddenly given him multiple lives, so he needed to focus on the options that would give him the most immediate survivability while still not severely hindering his future growth.

His stomach rumbled, and he realized it had probably been a few hours since he last ate. He could probably crawl his way over to the snack bar, but the problem was the darkness. He couldn't see anything, and if that continued, getting a light source was probably his highest priority.

Glancing over his options again, he looked for any options that would provide light. All his attack spells would probably create small bursts of light, but they would also create quite a bit of damage in the area around him. Spark would probably damage considerably less than the higher-grade fireball. He wasn't even sure if cone of frost would create any light at all. Storm seemed like a bad idea in an enclosed area like the bunker he was currently in, but he really wanted it to start getting attuned.

The short cooldown on spark would also be helpful, but he just wasn't sure how much light it would produce.

On the other hand, dancing sword and mana guard may or may not create light; it all depended on the game. In some games, mana shield would create a nimbus around him, which would give him at least a small amount of light to work with, but it could just as easily be an invisible effect. Dancing sword was in a similar category; it could be made of light, or it could be like a normal sword and not help at all. The same could be said of major refresh; there could be a light effect when he cast the spell, but the nearly half an hour cooldown on major refresh made it unlikely for that to be very useful.

He decided that his best bet would probably be dancing sword. Most games would create an object of light for an effect like this. He didn't anticipate it being very bright, and the gap during the spell being active to when he could recast it meant that he was going to spend about two thirds of the time in darkness. The question was, which slot was he going to put it into?

Looking at the other xatherite, then at the map, he decided that he needed to place cone of frost, fireball, minor dancing sword, major mana guard, and major refresh at least. That meant he could complete the easy constellation if he wanted. He could also get four out of six in the larger one or put some in the larger one and then slot more into the six-slot constellation that had two reds, two oranges, a yellow, and a white.

With a heavy sigh, convinced that he was making the wrong choice but unsure what would be better, he put dancing sword and major mana guard in the first constellation on the right. He then put fireball in the white slot and major refresh in the orange before putting cone of frost and storm in the red slots of the six-slot constellation in the bottom right of the starmap, leaving minor acid dart and major spark unslotted for now.

Satisfied that he had made the best choices available to him according to the knowledge that he possessed, Drew confirmed the changes.

> Congratulations, citizen, you have taken your first step on your training. Fight well, survive, and prevail.

Drew grasped his skull as information suddenly flooded his brain. The correct actions to cast six spells burned paths into the neurons in his head. Then his eyes rolled up, and he slumped down into the chair, unconscious.

Waking up an unknown amount of time later, Drew groaned, a hand rubbing his temples as a massive headache prevented him from thinking straight for several minutes. The pain receded slowly, gradually allowing room for more coherent thought. As soon as it was at a manageable level, he cast his first spell. His fingers twisting in familiar patterns he had never made before, implanting the xatherite.

There was a flash of orange light, the first color he had seen in the real world since the voice had said, "Begin." His headache reduced to a much more manageable level, the pain in his neck from his abrupt collapse earlier disappearing as well.

"Guess that answers the question on cast times." He felt like he had just woken up from a good night's sleep as he stood up and stretched. Looking around at the darkness, he muttered, "Well, here goes nothing."

His fingers twisted to form a circle between his thumb and pointer finger, then made a strange jerking motion. Then there was light. A translucent gladius, made of what appeared to be glass, came into being about two feet in front of him, floating in midair and glowing with a faint red light. It wasn't bright, but it was enough for him to see a few feet around him, which was all he needed. He turned towards the snack bar and made quick work of finding a bag of chips before the sword, following behind him over his shoulder, disappeared, plunging him into darkness yet again.

At least now it was darkness with a bag of chips. He ripped the bag open and began to stuff his face. He wasn't sure how long it had been since last he ate, but his body certainly knew that it was hungry.

Six bags of chips, a soda, three candy bars, and two bags of peanuts later, the edge of his hunger was gone, replaced by a faint craving for something more substantial, which he had a feeling he wasn't going to get in the near future.

Now armed with some light, his belly mostly full, and his thirst temporarily abated, his immediate issues had been solved. Now came the hard part... getting out of the bunker.

Chapter Three — The Door

Of course, to get out of the bunker, he first had to get out of the room. The watch floor, or rather the former watch floor, was about one hundred feet wide, eighty feet long, and had large, vaulted ceilings. There was a small changing room off to one side and then a heavy-duty metal door that required a key code to open. The door didn't require a code to leave, a safety measure he was glad had been implemented. It did mean that he wasn't going to be able to get back in without breaking down the door.

Not willing to risk leaving anything inside that he was going to need, he worked in short bursts. Waiting for the light from the sword to appear, he would then rummage through the various lockers and desks looking for anything of value. Throwing his civilian clothes in a duffle, he kept his uniform on; it was sturdier and would be able to protect him better from the monsters he expected to encounter. After all, the bunker would make a perfect dungeon.

He was filling up the two duffle bags that he found in Marsh's locker. They had Marsh's distinctive smell—the larger man sweated even in the climate-controlled watch floor. He stuffed one with extra clothing and other supplies he thought might be useful; the other had all the snack bar food shoved into it. It also had the box of organic pop tarts that he found in Marsh's locker; he'd tried one and determined that they were as disgusting as they sounded. He also grabbed the fire axe it was the most effective melee weapon he could find.

Now with the two duffles at his feet and the shaft of the fire axe leaning against his hip, he stared into the darkness. A fear deep within him stirred, trying to pull him down to inaction. He was before the door but sensed that as soon as he stepped out of the quiet darkness of this room that all of this would become real. He was going to have to face monsters, more darkness, and who knew what else. The world had kept on moving while he had been in the tutorial. His partner hadn't returned, he was five floors down in a bunker near the primary nexus, and he was alone.

Wallowing in the fear that threatened to swallow him, Drew let that wash over him, let it eat away at his resolve. Then he pushed it away. He had acknowledged his fear, had experienced it in full. It would not control him. "Out of the night that covers me, black as the pit from pole to pole, I thank whatever gods may be for my unquenchable soul." He quoted Invictus to himself as his fingers formed the seals and pushed down, activating major mana guard, the yellow light flashing briefly before disappearing into his skin.

He lifted the axe, holding it in one hand as he pushed open the door, the red light of the dancing sword sending strange shadows around the antechamber.

Drew paused for a moment, looking around the small room. Then he slung both duffles over his shoulders and stepped forward. The silence here was the same, comfortingly without any of the wheezing breath or the clack of claws on cement that his brain had imagined monsters would be making.

He didn't look up.

The only thing that saved him was the dancing sword responding to threats automatically, slashing up at the chitinous mass that clung to the ceiling above him.

It was impossible to see in the darkness. The sword's quick movements sent dark red shadows throughout the room. However, the creature had fallen to the floor a few feet away from Drew, knocked off course by the sword's blow.

There were no floating damage meters. There wasn't a floating HP bar above the creature's head either. So much for the system being like the games he used to play. With a thought, he struck out with cone of frost. The air immediately around him turned frigid instantly, but the creature reacted with a harrowing scream as it seemed to curl up around itself.

The sword's duration ran out, and he was plunged into darkness yet again. But his axe was already swinging towards the body of the thing that had managed to sneak up on him. He could feel the blade bite into it deeply, and then it stuck when he tried to pull it out, the sound of metal grating against chitin. He lashed out with his boot, kicking at the thing while his other hand tried to cast another dancing sword.

He wanted the light; he needed it. The creature under his boot continued to thrash against his leg, long and hard legs or arms grasping at the thick fabric of his uniform pants. Yellow light flared every so often as mana guard protected him from damage. The spell's cooldown wasn't over yet and wouldn't be for more than a minute. The thing was too close to use fireball. He should have slotted spark; it's low recharge and single target nature was perfect for this sort of fighting.

Drew pushed the ax down, trying to drive it deeper into the creature, simultaneously causing damage and keeping the thing away from him.

Suddenly, the mass under the axe twisted, a chunk of chitin bouncing off his shin as it was torn free by the action. Another shorthand movement and he thrust a finger in the direction of the thing, another blast of cold erupting into the room.

The creature screamed again, and judging by the sound, it was attempting to retreat. Shifting the shape of his hand slightly, a massive bloom of fire streaked towards the other side of the small room. Drew's eyes were focused on the creature he was fighting. The burst of light from the Fireball had been enough to give him a good look at it for the first time. It was a massive spider, its body as thick as a soccer ball. It was dripping blue ichor from the axe and sword wounds with three of its legs encased in ice, while the main body just happened to be directly in the path of the blast. He could see the chitin melting as the ball passed through its body and then exploded against the far wall.

The reverberating force threw him back against the wall, and he felt a sharp pain in his lower back from a shelf he had been smashed against. Mana guard's energy spent; he could feel the air around him loosen as its protection disappeared, but it was over. There was no way the spider had survived that.

The door behind Drew clicked closed, denying him the safety of the former watch floor. His limbs were shaking from adrenaline; the aches and pains from impacts he hadn't even realized had happened during the brief fight began to make themselves known. He quickly cast major refresh on himself.

The pain receded immediately as he took stock of the situation. One of the duffle bags still hung around his shoulder; the other had been dropped sometime during the fight. The axe haft still hung in his trembling hands. He quickly pulled up his node structure and slotted minor acid dart and major spark in the constellation to the left of his origin node and confirmed the change.

As the pain began, he realized he'd made a horrible mistake. If he lost consciousness again here where it wasn't safe, there was a good chance he wouldn't survive. His fingers tightened around the wood of the axe handle, turning white as he fought against the pain that burned throughout his entire body.

Instantly, he could tell that it wasn't nearly as bad as the first time. Six xatherite of higher grade clearly imparted more information into his brain than the two low-grade spells he'd just put in. Still, the pain was intense, and he started to see lights dancing in the darkness.

Drew slumped back against the wall, not caring if the shelves dug into his back. His legs were shaking too hard for him to stay standing.

He had escaped relatively unscathed from the ordeal, but at the same time, there were no notifications popping up in his vision telling him how much experience he had acquired. There was no level on the spider indicating how hard it was compared to other monsters. No system generated loot from its corpse. Everything was the same as before, except now there were monsters, and he could cast fireball

Sitting in the darkness, Drew tried to catch his breath, the headache dissipating as he tried to collect himself. Casting dancing sword again, he grabbed the handle of the axe and pushed himself back up to an upright position. He groaned again, feeling where the sharp corner of a shelf had dug into his back when he collapsed earlier. He walked over to the remains of the spider and nudged it with the axe, then looked around the room for any loot.

Monsters dropped loot, and they guarded treasure chests. That was just how games worked, and while he was becoming more and more convinced that this wasn't a game like the ones he was used to, his brain kept telling him that there were more game elements in the world now.

The only thing he found was a bunch of spiderwebs in the corner above the door. Small dark spots in the webs were remnants of the spider's previous meals. If this were a game, he'd collect the webbing and use it to make some rope or some super strong cloth, but looking at the sticky stuff, he shivered slightly, having no desire to go about gathering it.

Miraculously, both duffles had landed on this side of the door, but he realized that carrying both would make fighting extremely difficult. He would kill for a bag of holding or a magic system inventory. Or heck, a Tenser's floating disk.

With the duffles in a slightly better position on his back and the fire axe in hand, he cautiously moved to the next door. He pressed the side of his head against the door and listened for a moment. This little vestibule wasn't soundproof, and the spider had screamed quite loudly. If something was out there, it probably would have heard the fight. But maybe the explosion would have scared anything off?

Cracking the door open just enough to send a cone of frost into the hallway beyond. The tension of wandering the dark hallways was already making him a little on edge, and since the only 'cost' associated with casting his spells was the cooldown as far as he could tell, he figured it wasn't a big risk.

Nothing screamed on the other side as he closed it and leaned in to push his weight against the door, listening again. He waited for dancing sword's cooldown to be up so that he would have some light, then opened the door again, glancing around at the dark hallway.

To the left was the less secure facility where all the unclassified work was done, and to the right were offices of some of the chain of command. The way out was to the left, but the realization that he didn't have a plan for how to leave the bunker caused him to close the door again and back up as he considered his options.

He could follow his normal route out, which would take him across half the building and up and down eight flights of stairs. The bunker was built to house thousands of office workers. Granted, the only people in it when the Advent began were the two people on his watch floor, the security guards, and the other night watch.

They were in the commandant's plot room and had a couple people stationed there at all hours of the day. This meant there were four or five people in there; if he could meet up with them, he wouldn't be alone.

He considered his options. The building was massive. He had explored some of it, but he still got lost in the unmarked corridors. His best bet was to follow his known route, which would take him out to the ground level near the parking structure. There were a couple of vending machines along the way that could be raided for additional foodstuffs. That was assuming they didn't have spiders guarding them.

The plan was to head to the commandant's plot, see if they were still in their watch room, and then escape the building along his normal route. With a nod of his head, he stood up again, his next few actions determined.

Chapter Four — Logistics

Stepping out into the hallway again, he had mana guard back up and the faint, red light of the dancing sword was illuminating the hallway for a few feet either side of the door. The glow wasn't even enough to penetrate to the far side of the hallway. "Frak, this isn't going to work."

He needed more light. He'd acquired a few flammables from his raid on the locker room, but he needed a better option than dancing sword. He turned left into the large, open space that was the cube farm. He stepped as quietly as his boots would allow. The sound of the cloth duffles rubbing against his uniform jacket reverberated loudly in his ears as he strained to hear anything.

With a grunt, he swung the duffles down onto the floor, his fingers gripping the axe handle as the dancing sword blinked out of existence. He stood there on the threshold of the cube farm, his eyes peering into the darkness and his ears straining to hear the skitter of another spider.

He waited a minute and then, on a hunch, he pointed his finger to the leftmost corner of the room and launched a fireball in that direction. The bright ball of flame moved quickly but still lit up the room better than the blade had. It revealed the dark shapes of massive spiders before exploding with another loud scream as two of the beasts were caught in its area of effect.

Drew's free hand was already moving in the pattern that would allow him to resummon the dancing sword. Meanwhile, he clumsily swung the axe one handed in a circle around him, as a deterrent against the now swiftly approaching forms.

He hadn't seen any of them that were any larger than the one he had already fought, so hopefully, that meant there wasn't a boss type monster here. As soon as the axe had finished its arc without meeting any resistance, he dropped it. The hand that was previously holding it began casting cone of frost. The spider screams that followed told him that he'd scored at least a partial hit. His other hand beginning to cast major spark already.

The flash of electrical power that surged from his left hand arced to a nearby spider that curled up on itself with a twitching motion. His right hand was already throwing a minor acid dart at the same location. His left hand moved to form another fireball. The pattern repeated, lighting the room in weird flashes of burning flame, arcing electricity, and red shadows as the sword attacked any spiders that came close enough to him.

When it was over, there were a couple of small fires throughout the room as paper and fabric burned. Using the firelight, he could see half a dozen spider bodies; some were half melted, others still twitching as electricity arced around holes eaten away by acid darts. The carpet around him had clumped bits of frozen blue ichor and sliced off spider legs.

The adrenaline that had caused the full fury of his spells to erupt in bright flashes faded again, and he felt a weakness in his knees. The curious thickness in the air around him proved that the few spiders that had gotten close enough to be killed by the sword hadn't even managed to deal enough damage to break his mana guard spell. The air smelled thickly of ozone, smoke, and burning spider flesh. "That...... that wasn't even that bad," Drew said to himself, looking around the room. Open spaces were much easier for him to lay out the hurt. He leaned down to pick up the axe from where it had landed a few feet away from him.

Congratulations, citizen, you have attuned your first xatherite. Minor Acid Dart will now begin to level up.
Congratulations, citizen, your Minor Acid Dart has reached level 1. Damage has increased.
Congratulations, citizen, your Minor Acid Dart has reached level 2. Damage has increased.
Congratulations, citizen, your Minor Acid Dart has reached level 3. Damage has increased.

> Congratulations, citizen, Major Mana Guard has been attuned.
> Congratulations, citizen, Major Refresh has been attuned.

The blue screen appeared in Drew's eyes as he finally calmed down after the fight. He willed the blue message away, and taking advantage of the newly lit room, he left the duffles near the entrance as he advanced on the two side doors along the right side of the room. He was really hoping that there was a janitor's closet in the storeroom area. He had some ideas for a more permanent light source. Or at least one that worked more than a third of the time.

As he waited for the cooldown on dancing sword to end, he put his ear to the crack between the doors and listened. Hearing nothing, he tried the doorknob. Upon finding it locked, he threw a quick acid dart at the lock. The pop fizz of dissolving metal echoed through the room, and then the door lurched slightly, the latch no longer keeping it closed. Pushing it open all the way allowed some of the light from the still burning fires to illuminate the room. Drew couldn't help but laugh, the adrenaline of the fight coupled with the absurdity of his situation suddenly hitting him. He grabbed the mop and a couple of spare heads from the corner and then looked around for any other supplies that might come in handy.

The problem was carrying capacity. He could only carry so many things, and he had to keep his hands clear and be relatively unburdened to fight. In video games, this would have been solved for him by a magic backpack, a bag of holding, or the GM would just waive the weight restrictions as being too much paperwork. The reality of the situation was significantly different from those idealized versions he had spent so much time in before. He already had his hands full with the axe and the duffles. Adding a torch on top of it all meant he was going to have to give something up.

He was reluctant to discard the axe. While he hadn't used it during the second fight, if anything got in close, it was imperative that he be able to use its weight and reach to keep his opponent away from him. His defensive and healing spells didn't seem like they would hold up to a major barrage, especially if he came up against something that had anywhere near the firepower he did.

He looked around. The room was moderately large, containing several shelves with cabling and other electronics. All of which were now useless since nothing with electronics worked, but standing in a corner was a two-tier AV cart. Walking over to it, he pushed it a few times to determine how sturdy it was. Made of thick plastic, it couldn't hold a ton of weight, but it was probably enough for the duffles. Also, as the round posts in each corner were hollow, he could put the mop turned torch in one of those and have light without sacrificing his casting and the axe.

Sliding the once expensive laptops off the cart, he cleared the cart of everything but the wire and the toolkit. He looked around and grabbed two more unopened boxes of cabling, then some other cleaning supplies that looked flammable.

The squeaky wheels of the cart wouldn't help much for his stealth, but by the time he was back at the duffles, he had something of a plan. First, he set to coating the mop head in the shoe polish that he'd found in the locker room. He then soaked it in some of the cleaning chemicals that were labeled as flammable. While he waited for the mop to soak them up completely, he cut off several lengths of cabling and braided them together, giving him eight feet or so of stronger 'rope' he could use to pull the cart.

Tying the cabling to the cart and then putting everything on it only took a few more minutes, but it was enough for the scattered fires to begin to die down, their fuel consumed. Looking around quickly, he thrust the mop through several of the spider webs for good measure, coating it in the thick webbing. He lit the whole thing on fire with a quick spark into some steel wool. Mana guard prevented the resulting cascade of sparks from hurting his hands too much. He waited a few seconds to see how his new torch would work, then slipped it into the hole at the front of the cart, pleased with the height of the torch and how much light it gave off.

Pulling the cart with one hand and holding the rope in another, he could easily drop the rope he was using to pull the cart if combat started.

"Not perfect, but it's better than I was hoping to get," Drew said to himself as he surveyed his handiwork. He pulled a bag of chips from his supplies and munched on them while he did another quick raid of the desks, hoping to find more food, a candle, or something.

He found a few candy bars and lots of nonfunctional electronics that he couldn't think of a use for. "Lots of metal here. Would be nice if I found someone who knew how to make weapons or armor." He shook his head. The lack of system generated loot meant that, eventually, humanity was going to need to make their own weapons and armor. However, how many people in DC knew how to use a forge, grow crops, or butcher a corpse?

He glanced at the various spider bodies in different stages of burned, melted, frozen, and shocked. He had the three-inch folding blade he had started wearing after he joined the coast guard. The blade had been dulled by years of opening boxes and cutting rope (or line as all the 'real' sailors used to call it) when he was on the cutter, but it would probably work for a field dress.

He probably should try to get something from the bodies; poison glands, chitin, and meat were all things he had harvested from spiders in games. But he wasn't a doctor; he'd never taken an anatomy class, and he had hated dissecting the frog in biology. In truth, he had no idea where to even start butchering soccer ball sized spiders. So, he just left them there, in favor of moving forward and escaping the bunker.

His next stop was the bathrooms. He wasn't entirely sure how long it had been since the Advent—a problem that kept nagging at the back of his mind—but as soon as he saw the stick figures, he realized he needed to use the facilities

"This is where the zombies kill me when I've got my pants down..." Drew muttered to himself as he looked around. The bathrooms seemed clear, no signs of spider webbing. He propped the door open and inspected each of the stalls. Finding that they were empty, he brought the cart into the bathroom and spent a few minutes attending to some bodily functions.

He reached for the bar to flush the toilet out of habit. Nothing happened. "Right. No pumps to make running water a thing." Human waste management was going to be a big issue, particularly if there were any large groups of humans around. This also meant he couldn't wash his hands. "No running water; tons of people are gonna die from bad food alone." He shook his head. "This is gonna suck." He raided the bathroom for toilet paper, adding it to the cart and then moved on to the objective at hand.

The next few hallways were uneventful. There were just a few lone spiders that he could handle from a distance with his newly expanded light source. The only things of note were blue boxes informing him that he had attuned major spark and received another level of minor acid dart.

That's when he got to the stairwell. He left the loud cart behind, opting instead to hold the mop ahead of him while he scouted to make sure it was safe. Opening the door was simple; the electromagnetic locks that had kept it closed were no longer functional. The smell of iron immediately filled his senses.

Looking down, he saw a thick trail of some sort of brown substance on the stairs leading down. Frowning, he leaned down and looked at it more closely, the red glare of the torch casting weird shadows. Then it clicked—the smell, the color.

Blood. It was human blood.

Chapter Five — The Stairs

The stairwell served six double tall floors. It consisted of twelve switchbacks with two concurrent staircases with a wide gap between them. Drew had never attempted to figure out where the other staircase went; he just knew that he had to go down a flight of stairs here. He was on the second of the six floors. The trail of blood led downwards, the direction he intended to travel.

"Well, shit. If horror movies have taught me anything, it's that I'm going to get jumped by something big and scary right now," Drew whispered to nothing, the torchlight reflecting off the concrete and casting orange shadows. He put his back against the wall and then glanced up, having learned his lesson from the first spider.

Nothing loomed above him. "Well at least my life isn't a penny dreadful." He glanced back down to the boot prints scuffed through the dried blood. "Please don't be Lovecraftian. Please don't be Lovecraftian."

Holding the mop high, he advanced to the edge of the stairwell. The stairs on the other side didn't seem to have any blood on them, but as far as he could see on his set of stairs, the red streak marred the floor. He shifted his grip on the mop and looked up again. Then moving to keep one shoulder near the wall and away from the central chasm of the stairwell, he descended.

In his brain, he mentally prepared himself for the most obvious monsters. "So far, it's just different kinds of spiders. Probably just mutated versions of the ones that already existed in the building, so odds are this is either a spider, a centipede, or something similar." Drew's habit of talking through his problems out loud was manifesting. His steps reverberated throughout the echoing chamber, a comforting sign to him, since it meant that anything creeping up on him would probably also make some noise.

One landing down, and the blood trail continued. He glanced at the doors that were his typical egress but opted to continue to follow the path of blood. Rob, his partner, had been out on his lunch break when the Advent began, and the only other people that could be in this portion of the building during the Advent was one of the security guards. Either way, if there was a chance that the person was still alive, Drew owed it to them to try and help. He wouldn't be able to live with himself if he didn't at least find out what had happened to them. He continued down the stairs, a white-knuckled grip on the mop.

The next landing was a grislier tableau; a large pool of dried blood covered the floor. The doors on this level had been bashed in. They were bent and lying broken on the floor along with hand sized chunks of chitin that looked to have been smashed away from a large beast. A dismembered hand lay among the other viscera. Hardened blue ichor caught the light and threw it in prismatic shadows across the floor, the rainbows adding a disconcerting gaiety to the morbid scene. Drew's eyes fixated on the hand, his brain going into overload trying to suppress his instinctual reaction to run screaming.

A furred claw swiped at him from behind. A puff of yellow light flashed as mana guard's energy was spent blocking a single blow. The shield saved his life, but the force sent him flying forward; the mop dropped from his nerveless hands. He tucked his shoulder and rolled past the broken doors, trying to open the distance between him and whatever it was that had attacked him from behind. Dazed, Drew rolled to the side and raised a finger as he tried to get a look at the thing that had attacked him.

It was hard to tell with the limited light, but whatever had attacked him had a bipedal form and looked like it would tower over most humans. He got the vague impression of thick fur that made it look even bigger than it would have otherwise. The creature compressed its lips and growled in Drew's direction, a low and dangerous sound, its weight shifting into a combat stance. Before he could think to cast a fireball, the beast was gone, jumping back over the railing and out of his sight. Confused by the strange behavior, he turned his head to look behind him.

Now that he was on the other side of the doorway, he could see a faint, sickly looking, yellow light coming from hundreds of small orbs in the rather large atrium on this side of the landing. It took him a moment to realize why there seemed to be a gap in the otherwise densely clustered orbs. Something large blocked the orbs' light about twenty feet further into the room. Raising a shaking hand, he pointed his finger at it, summoning the power of the xatherite. The fireball bloomed in the air between him and the creature, streaking towards its massive form. The light shed by the fireball illuminated the room to some extent. It resolved the shadowed mass into a man-sized black spider with its abdomen displaying a crimson, four-foot-tall hourglass.

The fireball spell hit the spider near where its abdomen and thorax connected. Two of the legs on its left side were burned in the blast, hindering the monster's movement considerably. Drew pushed himself to his feet while the spider struggled to maneuver its body towards him. Its bulk and injuries prevented the normally rapid movement it used to hunt down prey. He held one hand low and flat, the other pointing at the spider, waiting for a shot at a vital spot. Minor acid dart's damage wasn't high, but if he could hit an eye or two with it, he might be able to keep on the spider's injured side long enough for fireball to eat through its health pool.

The spider raised its two front legs. Wickedly sharp blades became evident even in the dim lighting, with the front left leg notably lower than the right as it tried to compensate for the damage he had already caused it on that side of its body. The ambient light was just barely enough for Drew to get a sense of what the much larger creature was doing. When the spider had finally managed to shift to face him directly, he flicked the fingers on his left hand, and an acid dart shot towards the left side of the spider's head. Drew was hoping to disable an eye, but the darkness prevented him from being able to see if it scored any damage. One of his hands immediately began the series of seals to summon a dancing sword while his other hand was still held flat and ready. Drew edged to the right, hoping to stay on the weak side of the spider, who was beginning a slow and painful looking shuffle towards him.

Opting to close the distance with the spider's weak side, Drew dashed forward. His cone of frost raked the arachnid's flank, encasing the left front leg and a considerable portion of its body in ice just as it tried to slice at him with its leg. The sound of ripping cloth and the burning feeling in his arm told him that he hadn't dodged quickly enough. He mentally cursed the heavy boots he wore that made his already slow movement speed even worse. Still, he had managed to avoid being impaled on its sharp leg

Dancing sword flashed into being and immediately sliced towards the last good supporting leg on the spider's left side, hacking a deep wound through the chitin and causing blue ichor to spray into Drew's face and mouth. The nearly crippled beast took another burst of damage as an arc of electricity was emitted from his elbow, colliding with the already damaged leg. With a crack of protest, the leg gave out, sending the hundred-pound spider crashing into the ground near him.

Drew stumbled, spitting out the vile tasting ichor. The uneven ground and heavy impact combined, causing him to trip. His chin bashed against the cement floor as he crashed, rolling into several of the orbs lining the room. Fighting through the pain that seemed to fill his entire body, he stumbled to his feet again. The spider was thrashing around in the middle of the room but was unable to get close enough to him with its good legs to do any damage. Drew warily backed away, casting his long-range spells that weren't on cooldown for the next half a minute. The third fireball he launched managed to finish the beast off. As the red glare of the spell faded, the spider twitched once, twice more and then went still.

Casting his eyes around to see if there were any other hostiles, he put his back against the wall, keeping an eye on the door. He was waiting for the furry biped to reappear now that the spider was dealt with. His breath was coming in ragged gasps, and his good hand began to form the seals for refresh. The seconds it took to cast the yellow spell seemed like an eternity to Drew, whose head was still ringing from the hard impact of his chin against the floor. Blood trickled from the two major wounds on his temple and shoulder, mingling with his sweat and causing his uniform to stick uncomfortably to his body.

Refresh did its job. Drew felt his mind and body renew, recovering the dangerously flagging energy levels to which the fight had reduced him. However, it did nothing for his open wounds, and this didn't seem like a place where he could tend to his injuries. Immediately after finishing refresh, he began to cast mana guard, not wanting to take another blow from the hairy beast without its protection. Dancing sword disappeared, and he pressed his hand to the wound on his shoulder, worried about bleeding too much.

Inspecting the orbs now that he wasn't under obvious threat, he realized that they were eggs. He was standing in a nest of thousands of spider eggs. He shivered, his mind and training fighting against the shock that his body wanted to succumb. Refresh could only do so much for him; his vitality had been bolstered but was draining away just as quickly with his blood. He needed somewhere safe, and he needed it soon. He took a step towards the stairwell. His only hope now was getting to the other watch floor, where hopefully someone was still alive. As he edged past the spider's head, he realized that the eggs weren't the only thing glowing in the room. An intricate crystal in the shape of an X had formed between its eyes; it glowed a soft green that seemed reassuring when compared to the sickly yellow luminescence of the eggs.

Some instinct caused him to reach down and touch the crystal. As he did, the gentle light intensified within it, filling the entire room with a brilliant emerald color before fading away. The crystal crumbled into dust, and a blue screen appeared at the edge of his vision, which he ignored for now; he could worry about the messages later.

He stumbled out of the nest, picked up his torch, and made his slow and laborious way up the stairs. The palm he pressed against the wall for support left a bloody smear. His eyes were focused on the open space in the middle of the stairwell, watching for another attack.

Afterward, when he thought about it, he couldn't remember how he'd gotten up the stairs, through the door, or the hallway beyond it. Pain and the need for safety pushed any other thoughts from his awareness.

The large metal door, like the one he left a few hours ago, filled his vision. He kicked it twice before collapsing against the wall, letting out a muffled grunt as his shoulder met the rough bricks. The last thing he saw before he lost consciousness was a brilliant, white light.

Chapter Six — How long

Awareness came slowly. The dream he had been having seemed more like a nightmare than anything else. Spiders and crystals, blood and fire. One hand reached out, trying to find the warm form of Zoey sleeping next to him. Drew's hand found hair, and he stroked it gently. He loved her curls.

"Normally, I'd ask a guy to at least buy me dinner before letting him paw at me like that." The unfamiliar voice was female, which caused all sorts of alarms to go off in his head. Drew's eyes shot open. Sitting next to him was a moderately tall brunette. She had an oblong face with brilliant, light blue eyes. Her hair had been let down, clearly against the military regulation her uniform dictated she should be following. She looked to be in her early thirties or late twenties and was wearing a disheveled dress uniform, the insignia on her collars designating her as a first-class petty officer with a name tag that read Sabin.

"Ensign, he's awake," the woman before him called out to someone beyond Drew's field of vision. He tried to stand up, but the pounding in his head slammed him back down with a grunt. "Woah, steady there, don't try to move just yet. You took quite the beating out there. I'm glad the Ensign was able to heal you up... but I don't think you're back up to ops normal quite yet." The brunette grabbed his shoulder and helped him back down, moving the pillow behind his head to ensure he didn't bang it on the hard floor.

Drew's eyes closed again, and he realized that it had not been a dream. He turned his attention inward; the pain he remembered was mostly gone, but small aches and pains remained. His clothing was still stuck to him, the blood and sweat not having been washed off. With his eyes closed, he could still see the flashing blue box in the corner of his vision, but he opted not to give it any credence until he was surer of his current situation. "Lights? How?" His voice felt raw and dry. The blanket covered his hands, and he began the process of casting major refresh on himself, wanting more clarity for the situation.

"Easy there shipmate, just hold up a minute and you can talk to the Ensign. She's in charge," the brunette said. He could feel a hand on his shoulder trying to comfort him. "Ensign Rothschild?" She made the question, with her voice tilted away from him. Drew was aware of other sounds in the room, cloth shifting and footsteps sounding as they approached him. Major refresh went off, and he breathed a sigh of relief. His eyes opened, and he moved to sit up again, the headache no longer affecting him.

"Alright, I'm up." The Ensign came into view. She was young, early twenties at best, about what Drew would have expected from an Ensign. She looked him over. "So, Petty Officer Michalik," her pronunciation of his name was horrible, with the emphasis on the ch rather than the second i. "You show up at the door, mostly dead, covered in blood and who knows what else. Care to tell me who you are and what's going on?"

Drew laughed. "Ma'am, I have no clue what's going on. I'm IT2 Michalik and I'm... no, I was the Cyber Security Operations Command mission lead. When the lights went out and the blue boxes appeared, I left the watch floor and went looking for my partner, who was on his lunch break." Drew scratched his forehead, flaking pieces of dried blood falling onto his hand. With a grunt, he shook his hands, causing the flakes to fall onto the ground. "I ran into a six-foot spider that almost killed me and then came here hoping you all were still here and alive." He shrugged and looked around the room for the first time. He was sitting in a corner. The two women standing next to him weren't the only people in the room; he could see the prone shapes of two more people sleeping in the far corner. The room was lit with several small, stone-like, white lights that were scattered around the room.

"Have you had any contact from the outside? All my lines were dead," Drew asked the junior officer

"No, we've... been here for the last couple days. Same situation. All the lines are dead, the power is off, and every time we've ventured outside, something has attacked us," the Ensign replied.

"Days?" Drew asked, confused, "How long was I out?" He moved to stand up, the first class helping him, and he smiled at her in thanks.

"An hour or so... We haven't had much sleep, and healing you took a lot out of me," the Ensign responded, and Drew frowned. He hadn't ever really felt tired after casting spells. Then again, after pretty much every fight he had cast major refresh, which would theoretically have removed all the negative effects of the casting.

"That... doesn't make sense. It's only been a couple hours since the voice said 'Begin' and all this craziness started."

Sabin shook her head. "No, IT2, it's been a couple days. Why don't you tell us what you remember, and we'll figure out what happened?" She gestured to the polished cherry wood table where the higher-ups of the coast guard had their daily briefings and the very nice seats that surrounded it.

"Alright. So, me and Rob were on night watch together this week, Rob... that is IT2 Omondi was on his lunch break, and suddenly the voice said 'Begin' and the blue boxes appeared. They told me my stats and then gave me some xatherite for being close to a central nexus or something. Then I went through the tutorial, which only lasted a handful of minutes."

"Wait, tutorial?" Ensign Rothschild interrupted him. "What tutorial?"

"Uh, the Aevis lady appeared in front of me and gave me a rundown on the whole Human Protectorate, slotting xatherite, linked skills, and all that stuff. Not a ton of information, to be honest." Drew looked between the two women, taking in their blank glances. "I mean, I guess it said I was selected for it, so I suppose it isn't ubiquitous. Must have got lucky there. But anyway, then I slotted a bunch of xatherites and lost consciousness for a bit, no idea how long."

"Two questions. What is the Human Protectorate, and exactly how many xatherite did you slot? Caballos is the only one that lost consciousness after he slotted all five of his at once, and even then, that was only for a few minutes."

"All five? I did six that first time—three intermediates and a couple of commons and basics. Wait, you guys only got five? That means you have like... fifty nodes? The tutorial said I had more than average, but I didn't think it would be that much higher." Drew looked between the two women as they stared at him with slightly agape mouths.

"Three intermediates? The first time? I have thirty-seven slots, Katie and Mitch are in the mid forties, and Juan has fifty-five. How many did you get?" Ensign Rothschild asked him.

"Uh, seventy-three," Drew said a little embarrassed.

"Holy shit-dogs!" Sabin exclaimed. Rothschild shot her a glare for her language as she considered the ramifications of his words.

"And the Human Protectorate?" Rothschild prodded.

"Oh uh, they own Earth and like eight thousand more planets, and they installed the mana accumulators and, uh, humans here. Earth has been split dimensionally—is that a word?—a couple times; this is Earth-3, but all the Earths are a military training facility, and we're effectively shanghaied into their Navy," Drew answered, just now realizing how crazy that all sounded as he watched Rothschild and Sabin's faces.

"I'm sorry, what? I already signed one dotted line to join the military. I'm not okay with being force conscripted into another." Sabin's voice had a hard edge.

"Hey, my contract is up in a year so I get that, but I don't really see it affecting us much. They want us trained first, and unless they have a way to modify the collective memory of humankind and created a massive fake human history, I get the feeling that this whole thing has taken thousands of years. I don't imagine those of us here now will have to go out to space."

"Did you say food?" Rothschild asked, clearly changing the subject.

"Yeah, I guess I left it at the top of the stairs when I began to follow the blood trail."

Rothschild asked, "Blood trail? You didn't mention a blood trail."

"Sorry, hadn't gotten to it yet. Where was I? Oh yeah, it was super dark." Drew looked around the room. "Where did you guys get all the light by the way? I had to make a torch out of a mop and shoe polish."

"Ahh, one of my xatherite is major glowrock. I've been casting it as soon as the cooldown comes off." Sabin seemed somewhat mollified by Drew's words and the more pressing matters at hand. She picked up one of the rocks off the table and tossed it to Drew, who caught it and turned it over in his hands, amazed at how simple their solution was.

"Well, dam-ng, that's handy," Drew responded, and seeing Rothschild beginning to wince, he managed to say what he was going to say before offending the officer. "Ahh, sorry, ma'am, I'm a little out of sorts with this whole..." He trailed off, his hand gesturing towards the metal door that denoted the entrance. He shrugged again and then continued, "Anyway, as I was saying, I left the watch floor and scavenged a few more things, made a cart that I could pull along and a torch so I could actually see what was going on. Oh, and I killed about a dozen of the little spiders." He snorted. "Well, little compared to the queen. They were about soccer ball sized. Anyway, I got to the stairs, and I found a trail of blood leading down. I left the cart there and followed the trail, hoping I could find Rob or one of the security guards."

He then described the fight with the spider queen and the strange, furred creature and how he ended up at their door.

"That's amazing," Sabin said, and Rothschild nodded her head in agreement. "We had a little food, same situation as you, just a snack bar, but we finished it off a while ago. We tried to go scavenge from the break room outside, but we got attacked by weird, little, green guys, goblins I guess, and the knight got destroyed. Mitch is the only one with any red xatherite, and they always came in larger numbers than he could handle."

"I'm sorry, did you say the knight was destroyed?" Drew asked.

"Oh yeah, I've got mostly blue slots, so one of my intermediates was summon knight. It's just a suit of armor that protects me, doesn't even have weapons," Sabin answered his question.

"Well, I think we need to wake up Windsor and Caballos and send a couple of you out to grab those supplies," Rothschild said with a bit of a frown.

"We need to kill those spider eggs too. Don't want to think about what would happen if they hatch. I should be able to do it quick, just need someone to watch my back while I set off the big guns," Drew answered while standing up and wincing as more dried blood and ichor flaked off his body. "Also, it might be helpful to know what xatherite we're working with here." As he said that, he realized that he hadn't looked at the blue boxes that appeared after the fight with the spider queen. "How about you wake up the other two, and we can talk strategy?" Both women outranked Drew, but that didn't seem to bother them as they deferred to his experience on this.

Drew willed the waiting blue boxes to show their contents.

Congratulations, citizen. Your Minor Acid Dart has reached level 4. Damage has increased.
Congratulations, citizen. Your Minor Acid Dart has reached level 5. Damage has increased.
Congratulations, citizen. Your Major Mana Guard has reached level 1. Amount of damage absorbed has increased.
Congratulations, citizen. Your Major Refresh has reached level

1. Recharge time has been reduced.
Congratulations, citizen. Your Major Spark has reached level 1. Damage has increased.
Congratulations, citizen. Minor Dancing Sword has been attuned.
Congratulations, citizen. Fireball has been attuned.
Congratulations, citizen. Cone of Frost has been attuned.
Congratulations, citizen. Storm has been attuned.
Congratulations, citizen. Linked skill: "Frostfire Ball" has been obtained.
Congratulations, citizen. Linked skill: "Cone of Frostfire" has been obtained.
Congratulations, citizen. Linked skill: "Firestorm" has been obtained.
Congratulations, citizen. Linked skill: "Icestorm" has been obtained.
Congratulations, citizen. Linked skill: "Frostfire Storm" has been obtained.
Congratulations, citizen. Linked skill: "Minor Refreshing Rain" has been obtained.
Congratulations, citizen. Linked skill: "Minor Bladeshield" has been obtained.
Congratulations, citizen. Your Minor Acid Dart xatherite is ready to upgrade.
Congratulations, citizen. You have found your first wild xatherite.
Rare grade Major Blink Step acquired.

"Holy shit," Drew whispered under his breath before calling up the information on each of the new skills.

Linked Skill Name: Frostfire Ball
Xatherite Color(s): Red

Linked Skill Grade: Intermediate
Type: Magic
Effect: Convert mana into a high energy blast of frostfire that will travel in a straight line until exploding, causing major frostfire damage in a 1m radius around the blast.
Mana recharge time: 13.1 seconds

Linked Skill Name: Cone of Frostfire
Xatherite Color(s): Red
Linked Skill Grade: Intermediate
Type: Magic
Effect: Creates a cone of frostfire, which causes significant frostfire damage, originating from any part of your body. Has a chance to partially enclose the target in burning ice, slowing them down considerably. Cone will extend 4 meters and has an arc of pi/4.
Mana recharge time: 21 seconds

Linked Skill Name: Firestorm
Xatherite Color(s): Red
Linked Skill Grade: Intermediate
Type: Magic
Effect: Create a localized storm around a target. The storm will have a radius of 10m and will cause significant fire, wind, water, and lightning damage within its radius.
Mana recharge time: 1 minute 45 seconds

Linked Skill Name: Icestorm
Xatherite Color(s): Red
Linked Skill Grade: Intermediate
Type: Magic

Effect: Create a localized storm around a target. The storm will have a radius of 10m and will cause significant ice, wind, water, and lightning damage within its radius.

Mana recharge time: 1 minute 45 seconds

Linked Skill Name: Frostfire Storm
Xatherite Color(s): Red
Linked Skill Grade: Intermediate
Type: Magic
Effect: Create a localized storm around a target. The storm will have a radius of 10m and will cause significant frostfire, wind, water, and lightning damage within its radius.
Mana recharge time: 1 minute 45 seconds

Linked Skill Name: Minor Refreshing Rain
Xatherite Color(s): Red, Orange
Linked Skill Grade: Common
Type: Magic
Effect: Create a localized storm around a target. The storm will have a radius of 10m and will infuse mana into all creatures within its radius, reducing fatigue and lactic acid buildup.
Mana recharge time: 1 minute 45 seconds

Linked Skill Name: Minor Bladeshield
Xatherite Color(s): Red, Yellow
Linked Skill Grade: Common
Type: Magic
Effect: Creates a barrier of blades around the caster. This barrier will parry 3 melee attacks before disappearing.
Mana recharge time: 5 minutes 41 seconds

```
Xatherite Crystal Name: Major Blink Step
Xatherite Color: Green
Xatherite Grade: Rare
Type: Magic
Effect: Move up to 12m without traversing the intervening area.
Leaves behind a mental afterimage that lasts 2 seconds.
Mana recharge time: 31.5 seconds
```

Drew was stunned. There was nothing in here saying that the cooldowns were shared with their linked xatherite. Did that mean he could chain cast five storm spells? Unfortunately, this didn't seem like the place to try it out, but if he could cast fireball and frostfire ball back to back, then his damage output had increased exponentially.

He glanced at the last message; acid dart was able to be upgraded. He pulled the spell up and clicked yes then looked at the new spell.

```
Xatherite Crystal Name: Acid Dart
Xatherite Color: Red
Xatherite Grade: Undeveloped
Type: Magic
Effect: Creates a small globule of acid from a finger that travels
in a straight line until it impacts a target, dealing minor acid
damage.
Mana recharge time: 16.1 seconds
```

"Well, that was anticlimactic." The name and grade changed, but the damage upgrade, if any, wasn't enough to even register. Cabellos and Windsor were getting up.

Chapter Seven — Party Formed

While Drew was sorting through the notifications, Windsor and Cabellos had been roused. He vaguely recalled hearing one of them grumbling about wanting a steak while he did so. The thought hit him hard. Without power, every steak in DC was spoiled by now. Meat, in general, was going to be hard to come by; there just weren't a lot of animals around here. Not unless you want to eat manaborn spiders, cockroaches, or squirrels. Drew didn't really look forward to that. Thoughts of food made his stomach rumble. It had been a couple of days, and he hadn't had anything more filling than a bag of chips and some nuts—a couple of days, which meant Zoey hadn't been cared for in days.

It used to take fifteen minutes to walk from his car to the watch floor. It had taken him a couple of hours to walk the first hundred feet of that walk. In no traffic, he could be home in Arlington in fifteen minutes. Something told him that the cars wouldn't work anymore, though, which meant he would need to find a way to travel miles on foot through a monster-infested DC, cross the 14th street bridge, and then make his way through Arlington to his apartment. At his current rate of travel, it would take weeks.

Even if he made it back, there was no assurance that Zoey was safe. In fact, odds were she was already dead, and Rob was also most likely dead. He had family all over the country; his sisters were in New York and Seattle, and their parents were in Nashville. His parents were probably a little better off than him, as they were on the edges of those metroplexes. His other two siblings were in Idaho and were likely in the best spot—more natural creatures around and probably no nexus nearby, so the mana warping wouldn't be as bad... He hoped.

The sheer weight of these realizations hit Drew, and he buried his face in his hands, his elbows making smudges on the cherry wood table. He felt a hand on his shoulder, and he jerked up, not having heard anyone approach. "You alright there, bud?" Sabin asked.

"Yeah, sorry, it just hit me there for a minute. All this." Drew gestured towards the glowrock in front of him. "It's never going to go back to normal again. My family is thousands of miles away, and I'm most likely never going to see them again. Zoey is probably dead, and I'm stuck in this gods-damned bunker fighting spiders." Drew kept his voice low, decades of societal reinforcement telling him that he should be acting manlier in front of this beautiful woman. He looked up and saw the other three eyeing him out of the corner of their eyes from the far corner of the room. They were clearly waiting for Sabin to calm him down from his mild freak out before they began.

Sabin laughed softly. "I'm sorry, I shouldn't laugh, it's just... it's nice to know I'm not the only one barely keeping it together." She gestured to Drew's uniform. It was covered in dried blood, blue ichor, and ripped in half a dozen places that he had no recollection of. "Shit, you walked in here like a goddamned Spartan dripping blood and talking about killing dozens of spiders like it wasn't a big deal. We haven't even been able to leave this room, and there are four of us. IT2, I know we don't know each other, but with what you've done... you've got to be one of the strongest people I've ever met." She settled into the chair next to him.

"Drew."

"Pardon?"

"Drew, my name is Drew. If the world is over, then I'm not going to go by the designator the coast guard assigned me. The 'slave name' as someone I knew once called it."

"Kathryn or Katie, take your pick," Sabin said with a smile at Drew. "I think we all had our come to Jesus moment a little earlier, the benefit of not being a lazy ass and sleeping the last two days away." They both laughed, each of them understanding that the other was forcing the laughter. They were in a terrible situation, but at least they were in it together.

"Thanks, Katie, I'm sorry for losing it like this."

"Hey, no apologies. As far as I'm concerned, you're my knight in filthy ODUs come to bring this damsel out of this—what did you call it? —gods damned dungeon." Katie winked at Drew and stood up, "Need another minute? I think I can hold Mitch off for a bit, but we're all a bit hungry, and we're sort of counting on you for dinner."

Drew laughed again, a little less forced this time. "No, I'm good now." He reached out to grab her elbow, squeezing slightly. "Thanks." Katie just gave him a smile and nodded.

"Alright, let's do this thing," she said loudly enough that the other three could hear. They all made their way over to the table. Drew stood up as they came near, reaching out a hand to shake with the two men as he introduced himself.

"Hey, I'm Drew."

"IS3 Juan Cabellos. It's good to have you here, Drew," the younger of the two men replied. He was short, a few inches over five foot on a good day and had the dark hair and skin of a Latino. Drew guessed he was probably Puerto Rican. The Coast Guard attracted a lot of the islanders.

"OS2 Mitch Windsor. I hear you know where some food is?" Mitch was taller than Juan, and he possessed the thick forearms of a man who did a lot of weight lifting.

The Ensign elbowed Mitch. "We'll get to that. Sorry about not introducing myself earlier. I'm Sarah Rothschild."

"No problem, ma'am," Drew said as he shook her hand as well.

"Well, shall we? We're on a bit of a timeline before Mitch here hulks out from hunger." Sarah took a chair, and everyone else followed. "I guess I can start. First thing we need to do is recover the food and supplies IT2 gathered before he was attacked by the spider queen. They shouldn't be far." She glanced around. "Drew, I know you said you wanted to destroy the eggs? How long do you think that's going to take?"

"Ahh, well, I have a couple of really large AoE spells that I think should be able to take out the eggs in a few seconds. Problem is I haven't really had a chance to cast them yet, so..." Drew shrugged.

"Sorry, I'm not familiar with that term, what does AoE stand for?" Rothschild asked.

"Oh sorry, it's a gaming term, it means 'area of effect'. The ones I have are a ten-meter radius, all based around a storm xatherite."

"What do you mean based around a storm xatherite?" Mitch asked.

"Oh, right, you guys didn't get a tutorial. When you attune your xatherite and they're linked together, then you can unlock linked powers. The ones I got are fire and ice linked in with the storm, and it just increases their damage and changes the damage type to include fire and ice," Drew explained. "Guess I'll just tell you all the rest of mine. I have two versions of fireball which is a... ranged explosion, really. Another two versions of a cone spell, the different storm spells I mentioned earlier. Uh, I also have a couple of defensive buffs, a spell called dancing sword which summons a sword that attacks on its own, two more reds that are my only individually targeted ones—one is a long-range spell called acid dart, and the other is a short-range one called spark that does electrical damage—and last is a slow recharging buff that gives me the equivalent of a good night's rest after I cast it. Oh, and I got a green xatherite from the spider queen that I can't slot yet."

The four of them just sort of stared at him. "That... is a lot of spells," Juan spoke for all of them. He looked at the other four and then with a shrug. "I guess I'm next. I'm mostly indigos. There are two spells that might work well with you. One called illusory fire that allows me to pretend to throw fireballs, but they must believe them for it to do any damage, and with you around that might actually work. The other is a fake dart projectile with the same limitation. Another is a buff that, well, hulks a guy out, makes him look bigger, and causes their melee attacks to do extra damage. I can also summon a lesser earth elemental, which doesn't seem to be very effective in combat. My last is a violet that allows me to repair clothing." He gestured to Drew's uniform. "I can fix that for you, haven't really had a chance to use this one yet."

"Oh, that's great. Does it clean it at the same time?" Drew asked. He was filthy after the fight with the queen. He started to unbutton his blouse so that Juan could fix it.

"Guess we'll see," Juan said with a smile as he took the blouse and, holding a hand over the rips in the uniform, began muttering under his breath.

"I'll go next. You already know about my knight. I can also create walls; I have a green spell that allows me to move super light stuff with my mind and the glowrock one. The last one I would have killed for before this whole thing, but it's worthless now. It allows me to cast an illusion on clothing to make it appear to be something else," Katie said matter of factly.

"Nice. Trust me, you're worth it for the light alone. These things are gonna be amazing when we get out there," Drew said, pointing at the glowrock in front of him. His enthusiasm for not being in the dark anymore was obvious.

"I'll go next; it's short. I've got a bunch of random colors. The first one is 'group cure which heals all allies within seven meters of my target. The second is a buff called mana jump, which increases the target's mana charge stat by three. The last is a green called mind sense, and it allows me to form connections with up to four people, and I can sense what direction they are from me." Sarah offered her part, and Drew could tell she was upset about her lack of skills compared to everyone else.

"Well, you just became the most important person in the room," Drew said with an encouraging smile at the younger woman. "You are going to literally keep us together and alive. What's the cooldown on your heal spell?"

Sarah seemed to perk up at Drew's words. "It's pretty long, fifty-seven seconds."

"Okay, so once or twice in a fight, unless we get really unlucky." Drew nodded again and then turned to Mitch.

"Last is me, I'm a red like you... well, except I'm not a spell caster. I have a bunch of reds that allow me to do some interesting things to my melee strikes, but mostly, they just make me hit harder. I've got an orange buff that redirects some of the force from attacks away from me and a shield that blocks incoming kinetic damage."

"Alright, so, we have a healer, a tank, a support class, and two ranged damage dealers." Drew looked around the group. "Honestly, that's a far more balanced a party than I was expecting. We might have to take it a little slow and heal up between fights, but I think we should be fine." He looked over at Juan, who had finished mending his uniform, and he gladly put it back on, even if it was still covered in blood and gore.

"You guys do look a bit rough, though; I want to try casting my refresh spell on someone else... Ma'am, you look like you've not slept in a while. Mind if I try it on you?" Drew asked Sarah. She just nodded. Drew reached a hand out to grab hers, his other hand forming the seals to cast the spell. When it was done, the bags under Sarah's eyes disappeared, her shoulders relaxed from the invisible tension she had been carrying, and she stood up, stretching.

"Man, I would have killed for *that* back at the academy. That's better than a dozen cups of coffee. Gosh." Sarah beamed at Drew, and he realized that a lot of her sourness was just plain being tired. He tried to imagine how she must have felt being responsible for the group despite being one of the youngest members of it.

"How did you do that? You didn't say a word," Juan asked, staring at Drew incredulously.

"Do what? Cast the spell? I just formed the seals for it with my other hand. How do you cast your spells?"

"We all have to say a bunch of weird words," Katie offered. Drew finally realized that Juan hadn't been muttering; he'd been casting the spell under his breath. "Even Mitch has to say his xatherite's name to active them."

"Oh, well, yeah... the only ones that really need much more than a thought and a point are the buff spells and maybe the storm spells. Like I said, I haven't actually tried to cast those... the three longer spells take a couple of hand seals each."

"Wonder what the difference is. It'd be really nice if I didn't have to say Illusory Fire when I tried to damage people. I have a feeling they aren't going to believe that it's going to hurt them if they understand English."

"I dunno, try activating them by just pointing and thinking of the spell. That's what I do with all my attack spells." Drew hadn't realized just how individual the system was. Now that he thought about it, they could all have different types of xatherite nodes other than the constellation type he had. "Mitch, try using yours with a thought. Swing your fist around a bit; I don't want to be throwing imaginary fireballs around in here."

Mitch adopted a fighting stance and looked away from the rest of the group, then threw a punch, his hand crackling with lightning as he did. "Hah! It works," he crowed, "That'll help a ton with my breathing while I fight."

After a few more minutes to sort out the division of labor, Sarah cast her mind link and buff on the four of them. She and Juan would stay back to let them back into the room and prep all of their things for the trip. Meanwhile, Katie, Mitch, and Drew would go recover the supplies and kill the spider eggs.

Chapter Eight — Storms

Chanting words of power, Katie began the process of summoning the knight. Drew watched as a dark figure slowly began to appear. The dark shape slowly gained substance; the knight was seamless. The figure was solid, made of a dark metal shaped like a set of full plate, the articulating points defying physics as matter seemed to disappear and reappear to accommodate the change of shape. The entire ritual took just under two minutes.

"Wow, that's really cool!" Drew exclaimed. Katie grinned back at him.

"Yeah, some perks of living in the end of times, eh?" The brunette reached down and tossed some light rocks at Drew. "Keep a couple of these in your pockets. It might be useful to throw them down a hallway for your long-range stuff."

Tucking the rocks into the various cargo pockets in his pants, he kept one in his hand. "Good idea, probably should get a mount for these so we don't have to keep our hands full. You know... when we have a bunch of downtime needles and thread, and probably a bunch of other stuff we don't have." Katie laughed as Drew put the final light in another pocket.

Mitch just shook his head as he picked up this room's fire axe. "Let's do this," Mitch said, nodding towards the door.

Drew stood a few steps away, casting both his shield buffs and causing three small swords to begin rotating around him. He then took a ready position, both hands pointed towards the door, motioning for Mitch to open it. Juan stood to the other side of him, both of them ready to throw their spells through the door if there was anything waiting on the other side. "Don't forget to look up," Drew cautioned, but nothing seemed to be lurking in their little alcove. The knight moved through the door; instead of the clank of metal on metal, the knight's movements were only distinguishable by the heavy footsteps.

Again, nothing attacked the knight, so Mitch followed him out. Drew was a few feet behind him and Katie behind him, both hands holding lights above her head.

As Drew glanced around the atrium, he caught a flash of movement in the distance. He immediately reached into his pocket, grabbing a light rock and throwing it down the hallway. It bounced several times before coming to a stop eighty feet away, a circle of light in the darkness. "Possible contact," he whispered to the others. His hands held in front of him ready to cast spells. "It's far enough... let's try this." The atrium was long, three hundred feet from end to end but only about eighty side to side with fourteen-foot ceilings. He put his hands together and began performing seals. "Crap, it's a two-handed cast." The spell also wasn't instant but took about five seconds to perform the rather tricky finger movements.

When it was over, the boom of lightning echoing down the hallway was nearly deafening. The wind blew debris around too fast to see. The glowrock itself was caught up in its turbine-like effects, sending chaotic white light echoing around the storm while lightning flickered an angry purple-white, reflecting off ice chunks and water droplets. Rain lashed the ground, and solid chunks of ice smashed against the concrete, breaking off small rocks with their impact that in turn would fly around in the storm, obliterating themselves to pieces against the walls, floor, and ceiling. The panels of the dropped ceiling were long since stripped away, exposing pipes and cabling.

The silence that followed the thirty-second-long ice storm was as deafening as that initial boom had been. The three stared wide-eyed down the hallway. Katie finally blurted out, "Ho. Ly. Shiiit." The individual syllables were stretched out in amazement.

"Please tell me that was your biggest gun," Mitch whispered into the silence.

"Second or, uh, or third probably," Drew said, staring at the remnants of the atrium as dumbstruck as the others.

"Well, that's bullshit. I get the ability to make a lightning fist, and you get Zeus's fucking lightning bolt." Mitch looked around. "Well, I think that probably scared away whatever it was that you saw. Let's get some food."

They all turned away and headed in the other direction. Another door received the same treatment as the one outside the safe room. They entered the stairwell on the third floor, the blood trail leading down. "Down or up first?" Drew asked, his eyes focused on the chasm in the middle, afraid of whatever that furry beast was reappearing.

"Up. I'm starving," Mitch said with a grunt.

"Hold up, let's leave a glowrock here. I'm pretty sure I can cast it again." She uttered a few short words, and another glowrock replaced the one she had dropped before casting the spell. "Alright, let's go."

They followed the blood trail up the stairs. "I can't believe you did this in the dark," Katie whispered to Drew.

Drew snorted. "Wasn't completely dark; I had the mop. Besides, what else was I going to do?"

He couldn't see it, but Katie looked at him and shook her head, incredulity written on her features.

The group reached the top without incident. The cart was still there, untouched. Mitch ran over to it and grabbed a bag of chips; they seemed to disappear into his mouth without touching his hands.

Drew looked around; it didn't seem like anything had been here. It was weird to think that he had only left the cart here a few hours ago. So much had happened since then.

Katie was eyeing the restroom, though. "I don't suppose you cleared the ladies' room too?" she asked Drew. He shook his head.

"No, but give me a minute, and I can. Wait, what were you guys using in the...? Never mind, I don't want to know." Drew nodded and walked towards the door.

"It wasn't pleasant. I made some walls for privacy," Katie responded.

"We can take turns watching," Drew said, opening the door while tossing in a glowrock. The light showed the small room to be empty. Clearing the bathroom took another few seconds, and he left, nodding to Katie. "Ladies first. Not that Mitch is going to care." The tank was on his third bag of chips, a soda in one hand and an opened bag of peanuts in front of him. "Easy, big guy. We gotta bring some back for the Ensign and Juan."

Mitch nodded but didn't slow down on the stuff he had already opened. Drew watched the hole, worried about the furry beast. They rotated through using the facilities, Drew and Katie taking the chance to eat some food while they waited. Then Katie and Mitch carried the cart down the flight of stairs, both insisting that they wanted Drew's hands-free to cast when he offered to take Katie's spot.

They left the extra ax and cart on the third-floor landing. Katie threw up some walls around it to prevent any scavengers, explaining that she could dissolve any conjured wall at will and that the spell had a really short cooldown.

They got to the queen's room, and both stopped in their tracks. In the much better lighting of the glowrocks, the room was even grimmer. Red blood—both from whatever had been dragged here and Drew's fight with the spider—mixed and blue ichor covered the entire floor. The body of the queen herself was easily seven feet long and three feet tall.

"You killed that thing alone?" Mitch asked, a hint of awe in his voice.

Drew nodded his head once. "Mitch, watch the stairs. I don't want to get ambushed again." He and Katie advanced on the spider queen, doing a visual inspection. Drew saw something shiny on the ground and bent down to pick it up. "Bullet casings," he said, holding them for Katie to see. "Must have been a guard...looks like he got off a few hits on the queen before he died." He looked the corpse over again, the bullet holes now obvious. "She must have already been injured. Don't see a body, though."

"Me neither... maybe she ate it?" Drew glanced at the queen's mouth, which was too small to fit a whole human being into it.

"I don't think she could have, not that quickly. Spiders normally web and drain their prey, not consume it whole." He looked around at the room that was free of webbing. "This is weird, no webbing anywhere near here; the little ones had lots of it." He kicked some of the clutter on the floor away and then saw the black matte shape of a SIG Sauer P229 pistol. He picked it up, checking the chamber and then sliding the magazine. "Empty," he spoke, showing the gun to Katie. He slid the magazine back into the gun before handing it to her. She shook her head.

"I don't think we're gonna get any answers here. We should destroy the eggs and go back."

"No, I'd like to try and harvest her forelegs. They were sharp, and we could use some more weapons. Maybe make them into spears; that's probably the easiest thing to use," Drew said as he walked around to the front of the queen. Both legs seemed to be in good shape. "Hey Mitch, come use the axe on the queen's front legs. I'll guard the rear."

Mitch and Drew changed positions. He didn't watch, but the sounds Mitch and Katie made were enough to convince him that the whole experience wasn't fun. It took about twenty minutes to break the legs off, the thick chitin resistant to damage even in death.

"Any ideas on how to carry this? They're gonna cut through anything we have," Katie asked Drew, who took off his blouse again and handed it to her.

"Guess Juan will just have to repair that again." They wrapped the legs up as best they could. "Alright, I think we're done here," Katie said, putting a hand on Drew's shoulder. He nodded, his eyes never leaving the stairwell.

"Okay, let's get back up the stairs, and I'll do another storm and kill the eggs." Everyone retreated, and Katie managed to convince the knight to hold the lights while she took the legs. About halfway up the stairs, they hunched down. The memory of the earlier storm was enough to keep them as far back as they could make it. Drew, partially hidden by a new wall Katie made on the stairs, leaned over and began to create seals with his hands.

Again, it seemed to take forever, his fingers flashing through the movements before the room they had just been in caught fire.

Massive fireballs rained down amidst the storm, electrical pulses flashing around them. The rain did nothing to stop the fires from starting, and the eggs were apparently quite flammable. Wind stoked their fury and the conflagration spread. The raw ozone and smoke reached them even as far away as they were, the occasional furnace blast of heat erupted out as the wind caught it and flung it out into the stairwell. The crackling sound of flames died down in an instant as the storm ceased its fury. Scorch marks and the lingering fires of masses of eggs thrown together into large piles in the corners of the room were all that was left.

"I don't think I ever want to be on the receiving end of one of those," Katie said, shaking her head again.

They both began to climb for a moment before realizing that Drew wasn't following them. He stood staring into the flames, whispering under his breath:

"Beyond this place of wrath and tears
    Looms but the Horror of the shade,
And yet the menace of the years
    Finds and shall find me unafraid."

After a few minutes, he turned. Nodding to them, they walked up the stairs to the cart.

They returned to the safe room without incident. Juan and Sarah, sensing the group's somber mood, didn't say anything; they just took a portion of the food and began eating it. Drew seemed lost in thought, and the other two had an edge to them. The sheer destruction of what they had seen the former Information Technology Specialist do had made them realize just how dangerous this world was now.

This was the power of spells in the new system, and these weren't even the most powerful level. What would happen when they were upgraded up to legendary? What other monsters did this world have that would need such levels of destruction?

Chapter Nine — Breakdowns

The pistol landed on the table with a thud. Everyone eyed it before Drew began talking, "The queen had already been injured when I fought her. If she had been at full speed, I probably would have died. Whoever emptied the magazine into her probably did." He looked at the other four. "That said, we didn't find a body or even a trace of a body, and the Spider couldn't have eaten it that quickly. She may have cocooned it and stashed it away somewhere; we didn't search around too much."

"Could they still be alive?" Sarah asked.

"It's unlikely, ma'am," Katie answered, "If they were able to empty an entire magazine into the spider, and she was still able to fight through Drew's attacks for a while, then survival... I don't think that's possible."

"I think we should send another group out to raid some of the close vending machines. With careful rationing, that should last us a week or two." Sarah's words were met with incredulity.

"I'm sorry, Ma'am, but did you say you want to stay here for another two weeks?" Drew asked, looking around the table to gauge everyone else's opinions. Katie looked as confused as him, while Juan refused to meet his eyes. Mitch looked between Drew and Sarah but kept his face relatively impassive.

"That's right, IT2," Sarah emphasized his rank, "we're going to stay here until we are properly relieved of the watch."

"Sarah," Drew emphasized her name, "no one is going to come for us. If they were going to come, they would have been here already. The phones are dead, and the power still hasn't come back on. Heck, the backup generators that should have kicked on immediately didn't even work. If they were going to come for us, they would have done it days ago. The only thing that sitting here is going to accomplish is to give the dungeon time to spawn more monsters and make our eventual escape that much more difficult."

"Petty Officer Michalik, you are dangerously close to insubordination." Sarah stood up, trying to intimidate Drew by physically looming over him.

"Quite frankly, ma'am, no, I'm not. I swore to defend America from threats both foreign and domestic. Look around you. We aren't helping anyone in here. Our jobs, my job? It doesn't exist anymore. There are no more computers to monitor, no more risk of being hacked. You guys? You're supposed to be coordinating the intelligence efforts of the commandant. You can't do that here. You have nothing to report, no one to report it to. But there are bound to be a lot of scared people out there, and our oaths require that we render that aid. You most of all because I promise you that there are injured people out there, and if you sit here safe in this little room, you are refusing to help them." Drew had stood up in the middle of the speech, glaring down at the shorter woman.

"Ma'am, I think Drew is right. We need to get out of here." Katie stood next to Drew as she looked at the Ensign. Juan and Mitch stood up as well, supporting the two more senior enlisted.

"We can't stay here. Drew's right, the longer we let those monsters grow, the worse it's going to be," Juan offered.

"We can't put up much of a fight on half rations of potato chips and soda. We need supplies, and this place is just going to become more and more of a death trap."

Sarah looked between the four of them, her mouth opening and then closing again.

"Look, ma'am, our responsibility, our duty, isn't here anymore, and I for one have no intention of abandoning that duty. If you feel like you need to stay here, then I understand. But I'm not going to be coming back here, and your best chance of getting out of this place is going to be with us."

"I could order you to stay." Sarah's voice was soft, the fear in her eyes obvious.

"You could, ma'am, but that would be an order to abandon my duty, and I'm not at liberty to obey unlawful orders." Drew's voice lost the edge that it had previously. He understood that she was afraid, afraid of the darkness on the other side of the door as well as the gore, the blood, and other viscera he had arrived in earlier. "Don't worry, ma'am; we'll keep you safe."

They all nodded, and Sarah folded. Drew walked over to the cart to get it situated, while everyone else gathered up the few items they would be taking with them. Katie had stopped after the three men left the table, whispering something to Sarah that Drew intentionally tuned out.

Having the least amount of work to do, Drew considered how best to utilize his time. The confrontation with Sarah reminded him that the two youngest members of the team, Juan and Sarah, hadn't had the conditioning he had out in the fleet arresting drug runners and human traffickers. Making his way over to where Juan was picking through the things on a desk, he asked, "Hey, we haven't really had a chance to talk. How you holding up?"

"Hey, Acho. Honestly? I'm glad that we're finally getting out of here. But man, I thought se fue al garete[1] for a bit there." Juan tipped his head up towards Sarah to indicate he was talking about the conversation earlier.

"Yeah, me too." Drew leaned against the desk, looking at what Juan was putting away. "This whole thing has been a bit of a nightmare."

"Yeah, I was thinking about that. You know the bible?" Juan asked, and Drew nodded, "Well, you don't think like... this whole thing was Armageddon? Like, the rapture happened, and we didn't get picked, and now we're in hell?"

---

[1] se fue al garete literally translates as: the rudder has gone adrift. It is equivalent to the English phrase "has gone to hell" in Costa Rican slang.

Drew laughed slightly. "I'm not super religious anymore, but I think there were a whole bunch of signs that were supposed to happen before the rapture. I'm pretty sure that this isn't God's handiwork."

"So, do you think that means God isn't real, that if we die like that guard did, we just gonna cease to exist?"

"I don't know if there's an all-powerful being out there, Juan, but from what I was told during the tutorial, Humankind immigrated here. Maybe the blue boxes are God, finally talking to each of us on an individual level. As for death, I don't know about you, but I don't plan on finding out in the near future." Drew clapped the younger man on the shoulder. "Don't worry about it; as long as we stick together, I don't think there is anything here that the five of us can't handle."

Drew looked over at Mitch, and the two exchanged a nod. Katie had finished talking to Sarah, and the two women had split up to finish getting ready. Drew frowned to himself before walking over to Sarah. "Ma'am?"

She turned around and looked at him, and he could see the faint redness in her eyes indicating that she had been crying before she looked away. "Look, I just wanted to say I'm sorry."

"No, it's... it's fine. You're right; we can't stay here." Sarah didn't meet his eyes as she picked through her desk.

"I'm terrified too, you know. The darkness out there? It scares me more than I care to admit. Heck, it almost killed me once already, and you saved my life. I never properly thanked you for that. So, sorry for not doing that earlier." Drew paused as he looked at her. "I know you can handle this, and most importantly, we need you; I have a feeling we're all going to bleed a little bit before we get out of here."

"Thank you IT2... Drew." Sarah sniffed but didn't look up. "I don't know what we would have done if you hadn't shown up."

"You would have figured something out; you're a smart woman. Me showing up just makes it a little bit easier." He smiled at her again and then turned to leave. He didn't have anything to pack up, but he rearranged the duffles on the cart.

Juan and Mitch each took a fire axe, while Sarah would grab the cart. Katie would be in charge of the lights and making walls for the ranged folk to duck behind if things turned dicey. Buffs were reapplied, and after double checking that everyone had everything, they left the safe room. Sarah locked the door and flipped the magnet from "Open" to "Secured." When she turned around and saw everyone looking at her strangely, she shrugged. "What? It's not like we'd be able to get back in without breaking the door anyway, might as well let anyone who comes know that we aren't in there. Now, let's get going before we get ambushed by goblins or whatever the heck is out here."

"Aye aye, Ma'am," Mitch said before doing an about face, leading the way towards their egress down the hallway. Following him were Drew and Juan side by side, then Sarah, with Katie and the knight bringing up the rear. Juan's earth elemental was following behind him.

They passed the point where the ice storm had gone off, Sarah having to maneuver around the pits in the floor.

Juan whispered to Drew, "You did all this?" His earth elemental seemed to be inspecting one of the pits, poking it with a stubby rock hand.

"Uh, yeah," Drew said, scanning the area for any sign of a creature struck by the spell, hoping to find some evidence of the shape he saw moving in the darkness here.

"Dios mio," the Puerto Rican whispered, crossing himself while looking around at the rubble.

Forging ahead, Drew glanced back at Katie and Sarah, who were having some trouble getting the cart over the uneven terrain. Katie helped her pick the cart up for a moment after concrete rubble got stuck in one of the wheels. He nudged Juan, who was staring at the damage, and they moved forward. They were almost to the stairs now.

Catching up with Mitch, he said, "I'm not going to be much help in the stairs. It's too small an area for me, so I'll only be able to cast my weakest spells."

"Which of course means that's where we're going to get attacked, doesn't it?" the ever-hungry man said with a grimace, but he glanced back and gestured for Juan to join them.

"Yeah, probably. What do you think? Send the elemental in first? See if it can see anything?" Drew asked.

"You're just going to sacrifice the little guy?"

"Better it than one of us."

"Yeah, I guess." Juan gave some instructions to the elemental, and it wandered forward towards the door. The girls had caught up again, the knight bringing up the rear.

"Checking the stairwell with the elemental," Drew answered Katie's raised eyebrow at the unplanned stop.

With a nod, Katie leaned against the wall. There was a sudden sharp whistling sound and then a loud clatter as something impacted the wall right next to her head. With a cry of pain or fear, she immediately collapsed. Drew and Juan immediately sent two fireballs streaking into the darkness around them.

"Kill the red mages!" The shout was followed by a strange, snapping sound. Drew and Juan both dropped to the ground, a blast of cold energy flying into the air above them as Drew cast a cone of cold. Sending the bolts off course, a short wall appeared between the group and their attackers, Katie giving them some cover from the sudden attacks.

"What's going on?" Mitch shouted from where he too had fallen to the ground.

"Ambush," Drew said, throwing a glowrock over the wall like a grenade.

Chapter Ten — Ambush

The knight was the only figure still standing. Drew watched as the second wave of projectiles smashed its helmet to pieces, the knight's body dissolving in a manner similar to how it had appeared. He poked a finger over the top of the barrier and launched a blind frostfire ball in the same general direction he had heard them coming from before.

"Can you make part of the wall glass?" Drew asked Katie as more barrages fell around them.

"I can try," Katie said, concentrating on the wall in front of them. Drew threw another glowrock from his pocket over the wall, hoping to distract the attackers. As he did this, the wall in front of him added a foot-tall section of glass to its height.

"Perfect," Drew said, popping his head up a little so he could get a look at whatever was attacking them. It was difficult to make them out through the thick, cloudy glass, but he guessed there were seven or eight figures standing back a few dozen feet away from where they had emerged from the branching hallways.

"Katie, put up a wall behind us. I don't want to get flanked," Drew said, glancing behind him. They couldn't have known about the walls, but any good ambush would have them defending against multiple avenues of attack.

The brunette glanced back as well, chanting a quick spell to create another long wall, this one slightly taller than the one in front of them. "Got it," she said before ducking reflexively as another clatter hit the wall behind her and shattered, showering them with slow-moving shrapnel. Drew glanced down the line. Juan was poking his fingers over the wall and launching projectiles blind, not doing much, but hopefully, it reduced the number of projectiles coming their way. Sarah was curled up with her hands over her ears leaning against the half wall, and Mitch crouched next to her, axe in hand, unable to attack anything.

Drew peeked his head up again and began the hand signs to cast a storm spell. However, a projectile cracking the glass in front of his face caused him to duck down reflexively, losing the cast.

Pinned down, Drew poked his fingers over the wall and cast fireball and frostfire ball towards the larger group he had seen. The rate of fire slowed for only a second before the glass above him shattered as two projectiles hit it at the same time.

Glass bounced off his mana guard harmlessly, but Katie, who was next to him, wasn't so lucky. Sharp bits of glass embedded themselves in the exposed flesh of her neck and face as she cried out in pain. "Sarah, heal Katie!" Drew shouted, covering her with his body to prevent any further damage as projectiles rained down on the pinned down group.

Mitch shouted back, "She's in shock. We need to stop that barrage!" Drew glanced back and saw that Sarah was still curled up in a ball. Cursing under his breath, he popped up long enough to target an acid dart at one of the attackers. A shout of alarm originated from where he had aimed, but Drew had already ducked back behind cover. His quick, long-range options were all on cooldown for a few more seconds. He pulled Katie away from the glass section of the wall towards the outer edge and away from the rest of the group.

As Drew rapidly considered his options, Juan launched his attacks, which elicited another grunt of pain from the attackers. "Mitch, get ready, this would be a great time for them to charge the barricade." Drew poked his finger up and launched a cone of frost blindly towards the floor, hoping to dissuade them from making a charge by creating slippery terrain. With the enemies' numbers, they would easily overpower the group if they got into melee.

Having finally made his way to the end of the wall, he glanced around it. He saw three figures dashing toward him, another finger came up, and cone of frostfire exploded out, catching all three of them in its blast. They immediately dropped their weapons, screaming in pain as ice-encrusted their flesh and began to burn them. Beginning the cast of a storm spell, he leaned out at the last second, launching his most deadly spell at the ranged attackers that continued to pelt the wall behind them, showering them with shrapnel and filling the ground between the walls with sharp pieces of what looked like bone.

He watched as the spell tore the remaining attackers to pieces, their projectiles stopped by the wind and then turned into additional debris. Their lack of cover from the large chunks of ice and fire that circled within the storm was devastating. Lightning crackled in the tempest, bouncing between their forms.

Drew looked away from the doomed attackers and back down the line. Katie and Sarah were now both huddled against the wall, and Juan lay on the floor, red blood pooling around his body. Another unfamiliar green humanoid was lying next to him, an axe buried in its chest. Mitch was repeatedly punching a second, unresisting, green humanoid. "SARAH! Cast heal now!" They were all within her radius. Drew dove towards Juan, heedless of the sharp bits digging into his legs as he knelt beside the youngest member of their group.

The source of the blood was obvious—a thick dagger protruding from his chest. His eyes were lifeless as Drew checked for a pulse, shouting Juan's name over and over. He felt the air change as the storm spell dissipated, and when he looked up, Sarah was staring at him and Juan with wide eyes, her lips moving silently.

"Sarah! Cast the fucking cure!" Drew cursed at her again, "Now!" He added, making eye contact. He could see her shake out of the shock she had been in and begin to cast the spell, yellow light illuminating Drew, Mitch, and Katie. Drew looked over towards Mitch, who had finally stopped punching the dead attacker. He slumped away from Juan, his hands bloody.

The fight was over, blue boxes in the corner of his vision indicating that the mana system had good news for him. He numbly concentrated on it, pulling up the notifications.

Congratulations, citizen. Your Acid Dart has reached level 1.
Damage has increased.
Congratulations, citizen. Your Acid Dart has reached level 2.
Damage has increased.
Congratulations, citizen. Your Acid Dart has reached level 3.
Damage has increased.
Congratulations, citizen. Your Major Mana Guard has reached
level 2. Amount of damage absorbed has increased.
Congratulations, citizen. Your Major Refresh has reached level
2. Recharge time has been reduced.
Congratulations, citizen. Your Major Spark has reached level 2.
Damage has increased.
Congratulations, citizen. Your Major Spark has reached level 3.
Damage has increased.
Congratulations, citizen. Your Minor Dancing Sword has
reached level 1.

Drew dismissed the screen, standing up to survey the battlefield. He slipped on the blood and had to put a hand on the wall for support. The enemies caught by the storm were destroyed; he could see portions of them in various locations throughout the hallway.

Mitch approached him. "They jumped the wall behind us. They killed Juan before I realized what was going on." Drew glanced down at the bodies, studying Juan's killer.

Thick, green skin covered a squat, thickly muscled frame. It looked like a typical orc from any game he had played, except for the two, inch-long horns protruding from either side of its forehead. Thick pelts covered most of its body, a crude form of armor that looked more suited to a cold climate than DC in April. Drew kicked the body a couple of times, spouting nonsensical curse words in half a dozen languages.

Katie finally stopped him, putting a hand on his shoulder as she spoke softly, "Drew, we can't stay here."

She was right, they were exposed. He looked around, only to see that Sarah was crying into Mitch's shoulder as she watched them both. "Right. Grab the weapons. See if any of them are growing xatherite." He reached down and picked up another dagger that lay near where he had cast the storm spell, this one smaller and thinner, made for throwing. It was only then that he realized that his mana guard was gone, having saved his life from the dagger that he never even knew had targeted him. Sarah sniffed a few times, then picked up the dagger that the orc Mitch had brutalized had been using. Mitch recovered the axe Katie picked up the half dozen lights that had been spread around during the fight and searched for xatherite, shaking her head when she came back to indicate she hadn't seen any.

Drew glanced at Juan's body. It would be nearly impossible to bring with them. "Katie, can you make walls around Juan? We're gonna have to leave him here." Katie nodded, causing two small walls to appear near his head and foot with two more sloped walls that met in a point above his chest, sealing the body inside.

"Alright, let's go. There could be more of those things around." Drew turned to leave, but Katie put another hand on his shoulder. He turned to look at her, and she nodded towards Sarah. "We should say something."

"Right." He glanced at the others. He had known Juan the least of all of them. They had worked with him for months at least.

Sarah spoke first, "I'm sorry, Juan. I'm so sorry." She began crying again, and Mitch put his arm around her to comfort her.

"You were a good shipmate, always going above and beyond to make everyone happy," Mitch offered from where he comforted the Ensign.

"You were a good kid, like OS2 said, always willing to help people and eager to learn," Katie offered her portion and then turned to Drew.

"I didn't know you for long, and I'm sorry I didn't protect you like I said I would. Looks like you'll figure that God thing out before me." Then he nodded, and they all turned away from the bodies, leaving the orcs for whatever spiders or other scavengers came for them. No one had the heart to wade into the scattered body parts torn apart by the storm spell to look for their weapons.

Drew did take a last glance around. The ambush felt off to him somehow. It was executed perfectly, and the pincer attack would have killed them all if it weren't for Katie's wall spell. The question he had was, why? Was it because of his first storm spell? The only words that he had heard were 'kill the red mages'. Was that just good practice or a response to the spells he'd cast? He frowned again, looking at the others. "We should use a different stairwell." He ushered everyone to a branching hallway and away from the main elevators. Grabbing the rope for the cart, he pulled it behind him, the wheels bouncing over the bone shards that littered the floor.

The building was organized strangely, built into the side of a hill. The 'ground floor' was the highest floor, and they counted going down from there. They were currently on the third floor but going up meant being on top of the hill with more buildings surrounding them and no real way off the hill. There were exits on floors five, six, and seven that opened onto the parking structure and the road off base. The closest exit was on the sixth floor. The fifth- and seventh-floor exits would require traveling through the building either more to the west or east, as they exited on the slope of the hill. This was the main stairwell and allowed access to all nine floors of the building. The problem was that it was the only stairwell that went all the way up and down, and the rest of them only spanned three to four floors each.

They were currently headed towards the stairwell that would probably get them to the fifth floor. The problem was that

Drew couldn't remember if it went down all the way to the fifth floor or if it only went to the fourth floor. Sarah was a mess, the knight was gone and on cooldown, the cart had been damaged by some of the stray projectiles, and Juan was dead.

He pushed that thought away. "Katie, can you make walls behind us? Block off pursuit?" She looked up at him and nodded.

"Oh yeah, good idea." Her short chant created a six-foot-tall barrier. It would take another casting to fully close the area off, so they waited the slow seconds before she could cast it again and then moved on, stopping three more times for Katie to erect barriers behind them.

They took a ninety-degree turn in the hallway, and Drew nodded Mitch towards the little breakroom on the side. "Let's hole up there for a bit. We can raid the vending machine and get some rest." Drew could keep them all awake forever with his refresh spell, but all of them needed some time to process Juan's death. Katie erected a few more walls as they all entered the break room. They hadn't seen any monsters since the ambush. The air smelled stale with no wind or ventilation present to push fresh air in.

Sarah was curled up in one of the corners, and Drew opted to give her as much space as possible. Abandoning the cart in the middle of the room, he sat in the opposite corner which also gave him a good line of sight on the entryway. Katie sat down next to him, leaning against his shoulder. A part of Drew's mind told him that the contact should be weird; they had only known each other for a short time, after all. Instead, the comforting warmth on his shoulder reminded him of Zoey, and he slung his arm around Katie and pulled her closer.

"Well, that sucked," she said softly.

Chapter Eleven — Interlude

Drew nodded his head. Not wanting to say anything, his fingers began the process of casting refresh, but the brunette recognized the cast and put a hand on top of Drew's, effectively stopping the spell. "I just... can we just pretend everything is normal again for a few minutes?" Katie had turned slightly so she could look at his face as she asked.

"Yeah. Yeah, sure," Drew responded, and Katie curled her fingers around his, leaning back into his shoulder.

"Where are you from?" Katie asked.

Drew answered with a quirked eyebrow. The question was so normal, it seemed incongruent with the current state of things. The habit of answering these small talk questions had become routine to him since arriving in DC a few years ago. "Boise, you?"

"I'm from a little town in Vermont you've probably never heard of. Wait, Idaho? How did you join the Coast Guard from Idaho?" Katie responded, looking over at Mitch and Sarah who were in the other corner. The other two weren't talking, but Mitch was there for when Sarah was ready.

"It's a weird story, actually. I had finished college and was sort of just drifting, I guess. I went on a road trip with a bunch of friends to the Bay Area. We were heading to the Point Reyes Lighthouse, and we passed a sign saying, 'Coast Guard training facility'. I thought... I could do that. About a year later, I was the oldest guy in my boot camp company." Drew shrugged.

Katie turned to look at him. "Wait, you joined the Coast Guard because of Petaluma? Are you crazy?"

Drew laughed softly. "No. I loved Petaluma. Horrible duty rotation aside, it was great being so close to Point Reyes. I must have gone out to Alamere Falls every other weekend the entire six months I was there."

"You and I clearly had different A-school experiences," Katie said with a grunt, "Man, do you remember how terrible the food was?" Her stomach rumbled in response, the thought of food reminding them both how long since it had been since they'd had a real meal.

"Yeah, I remember all the OSes getting off of watch so they could do their normal school work while the rest of us that had been there twice as long had to clean the toilets after doing eight hours of schooling," Drew said with another chuckle which earned the pair a glare from Mitch.

The glare cut off any reply Katie might have been about to make, and the two sat in comfortable silence. After ten minutes, Katie asked, "So, who is Zoey?"

Drew grunted slightly, "She's my dog. I got her as soon as I moved to DC. She's helped me deal with some stuff."

Katie glanced at Drew again, a small smile on her mouth. "Well, I think I can deal with a dog as my competition."

Drew quirked an eyebrow at her. "Competition?" Drew wasn't exactly a lady killer; he spent most of his time playing video and board games or at the dog park. "Uh, yeah... no, she's uhm, you know, she's just my dog." The realization of what Katie had said made the normally self-assured Drew stammer a bit.

Katie's smile grew larger as Drew stumbled over his words. "Finally! There is some human under that machine face you've got going." She laughed softly before resting her head on his shoulder. "You should really talk to Rothschild, you know. She's going to need your approval."

"My approval? Why would she need my approval? I'm just an IT2." Drew latched onto the change of topic as a way of ignoring where the conversation had been going.

Katie blinked and pushed away from Drew again. "You don't see it, do you?" She studied his face for a minute and then shook her head. Drew couldn't help noticing how nice her hair was, and he had to mentally shake himself. This wasn't the time to get twitterpated; they were still in the middle of a dungeon during what was probably the apocalypse.

"See what?" Drew asked.

"Drew, you're in charge here... none of us would have left that room if you hadn't shown up. We're all relying on your strength to get us out of here. The Ensign is going to need you to tell her that she didn't just get Juan killed." Katie's voice was quiet to ensure that it didn't carry far enough for Sarah to hear her.

Drew looked away from Katie, unable to meet her eyes. "Don't you think she might have, though? If she hadn't frozen..." He trailed off, not wanting to fill in the gaps on that sentence.

"Maybe. Or maybe he was killed immediately, and she couldn't have done anything. But that's not the point. We need her and telling her that she might have saved him is going to destroy her."

Drew frowned, looking down at his hands, "Maybe you should tell her. I'm... I'm not good at this stuff. I was never a leader. I'm too critical, too exacting."

Katie reached up and turned his head so that he was looking at her. "Drew, we all believe in you. She needs you. She needs your strength and your approval. You may not consider yourself a leader, but we all do. We all followed *you* out here. She's still a kid, and she's in way over her head here."

Drew bit his lip in frustration. Looking across the room at Sarah. "We're all in over our heads. I don't recall 'how to deal with an apocalypse' being in our training manuals." He paused, considering. "It's just... I've never been very good at this emotion stuff." In truth, the only person he really confided in was Zoey, and while a great listener, she was hardly the greatest conversationalist.

Katie shook her head, looking at him again, "Well, time to get better." She squeezed his hand before leaning back against his shoulder. She sniffed, "You know, you smell horrible."

"Yeah, getting coated in blood and guts on a regular basis will do that to you." Drew had gotten used to the smell; the lack of other options made it a necessity. Sarah was the only one in the group that was still relatively clean. Everyone had been wearing the same clothing for a few days, but the other three were colored in various amounts of red, blue, and green blood. He leaned forward, careful not to disturb Katie too much. "I... have an idea for this actually."

Standing up with a grunt, he grabbed the trash can in the corner and removed the liner. Then, poking his head out of the room for a minute, he put the can in the furthest corner and then walked back away, putting as much space between him and the area as possible. He then began the linking together hand seals to do the five-second cast of refreshing rain. When he was done, the gentle patter of rain sounded in the hallway, the wind and lightning of his other versions of the storm absent. With a shrug, he walked into the rain, holding his hands out to the side and letting the refreshingly warm water wash over him. Katie, who had followed him, also stepped into the rain, her face turned up towards the ceiling.

Thirty seconds wasn't long, and Drew didn't start in the rain, but he managed to clean the worst of the gore off him. He walked over to the bin and frowned. The water inside was evaporating at a visible rate, and by the time he had picked it up, only a few traces were left. His clothing and hair were also mostly dry already, despite having been soaked through previously. His energy levels were greatly increased, but not as much as if he had cast refresh on himself.

Coming back in slightly cleaner, Drew shrugged. "Well, it's not a perfect solution, but at least we know I won't be flooding anything. I'll cast it again in a few minutes if you two want a bit of a shower." Both Mitch and Sarah looked up at his words, excited for the idea of being a little bit cleaner.

"I think I have an idea for these spider legs too, might as well work on them for a bit while we rest." He pulled the legs off the cart and put them on the table in the middle of the room. Then he climbed on top of the counter and began popping the dropped ceiling up so he could look at the pipes and wiring hidden within. "I figure we can attach it to some pipes. There might be a bit of a draining issue if the pipes still have water in them, but it shouldn't be too bad."

Selecting two five-foot sections of piping, he used acid dart to eat away at the metal, causing a half a cup of water to fall to the floor as he did so.

Using another couple careful application of acid dart, he ate away holes in the metal that he could use to keep the legs in place. Then he jammed the pipes into the spider legs and began to awl holes in the chitin using the daggers they had acquired from the orcs.

Katie and Sarah both came over and began to help him while Mitch began cutting strips of wire. They worked in near silence, everyone glad to have something to keep their hands and minds busy.

It took about an hour. There were several breaks for showers in the rain, to eat more of their food, and raiding the vending machine. By the end of the hour, they were cleaner, rested, sated, and they had two finished spears. They were crude, and Drew wasn't convinced the wire would hold up to the stresses of combat for long, but at least it gave all of them weapons.

The rain had wrecked the drop ceiling though, and several tiles had warped and fallen, only to be speed dried shortly afterward. They all felt a little less safe when they realized just how much space there was above them that was difficult to see through. A spider could easily be hiding above them, and no one would be able to detect it.

Finally, as they were getting packed up and ready to go, Katie nodded to Drew, who frowned at her but nodded his assent. Katie pulled Mitch out into the hallway, while Drew sat down at the table next to Sarah, who held the spear level, staring at the spider leg on its tip.

"How do you do it?" she asked, having seen Katie and Mitch leave the two of them alone.

"Do what? Kill the spider? A lot of luck and a bunch of fireballs." Drew peered at her, curious.

"Spider is part of it... but you left alone. You were safe, and then you got attacked by stuff, a lot of stuff. You came and found us, and you were almost dead, but then you went right back out after I healed you." Katie looked up from the spear to Drew, "How do you keep going? What's the secret?"

Drew chuckled slightly. "There isn't a secret. I'm just too stubborn to sit down and die. Look, you couldn't have saved Juan. He was already dead. You couldn't have known what was going to happen."

Sarah's face tensed up as Drew mentioned Juan, but she just nodded slowly. "I think I knew that, but I just... I hate this. I hate how powerless I feel. All four of you were contributing to the fight, and I just... I couldn't do anything. I was so scared." She shifted the spear around in her hands; it was too big for her small frame, but there was something in her eyes as she shifted the polearm around, getting used to its weight.

"I don't want to be scared anymore. I don't want to be the only one who can't contribute."

"You are contributing. You healed us all after that fight, and trust me, I really appreciate not being dead after the spider queen." Drew smiled at the girl. "And now we have weapons, so you can do something while your heal is on cooldown."

Sarah looked behind him, her eyes narrowing before she leveled the newly crafted spear and pushed it past him with a grunt. A squeal was the last thing he expected as he pivoted to the side to avoid Sarah and then saw what she was attacking.

A rat at least five feet long had just dropped from the ventilation shaft and onto Sarah's spear, impaling it through the chest. Still, it wriggled, unable to do more than scrabble at the spear shaft. Drew launched an acid dart and a spark at the head of the beast before it stopped moving. It was over before Mitch and Katie could get back into the break room, where everyone eyed Sarah, who was breathing heavy.

"Well, I don't feel quite as safe here anymore," Mitch said, looking around. "Nice thrust. You pinned it perfectly." He helped Sarah pull the spear out of the rat, the serrated spider leg making removal difficult.

They rebuffed, everyone eyeing the dropped ceilings warily as they gathered their things, and then they headed out once more.

Chapter Twelve — Backtrack

Mitch led them forward. Drew was next pulling the cart, while Sarah and Katie walked together with spears in hand and the knight behind them. It didn't take long for them to reach the stairwell. Six massive rats had been wandering the hallways. Each appeared alone, and Drew merely double cast fireball and frostfire ball as soon as their beady, little eyes began to reflect the light in the distance.

They quickly checked that the stairwell was clear and then descended. The cart's weight made it a little tricky, but gravity did most of the work for them. Drew kept it steady as they slowly lowered it down the stairs. Unfortunately, their luck ended there; the stairwell only went down to the fourth floor.

"Well, crap, anyone ever been down this way before?" Drew asked from within the safety of the stairwell.

"I had a meeting down here once. I think I remember there being another stairwell a couple hallways down on the back side of the cafeteria," Sarah offered. She had recovered some of her spirits after killing the rat.

"Well, that's better than nothing," Mitch said with a shrug that seemed to be the consensus.

Stepping into the hallway, they saw a few placards giving directions to the cafeteria and some of the offices that had been on this floor. Sarah thought the stairwell was to the left, so they followed the Ensign's half-remembered directions.

The first cockroach landed with a thud in front of Mitch. Two hooks that had grown from his foremost appendages scored red lines along his arm, his shield preventing a significant amount of the damage, and one leg even bounced off to the side, deflected away by the magic protecting him.

Before anyone else could react, Mitch's axe had already taken on an electric buzz as he used his skill on the axe head and then used it to push the cockroach away from him, opening a distance between them. Drew launched an acid dart at the beast, though Mitch's push caused the projectile to go wide and the acid sizzled as it impacted the wall. Katie and Sarah advanced around Drew, the weaponless man unable to help due to the close quarters of the combat.

Each of the two women stabbed at the cockroach, but the sharp spider leg tips simply bounced harmlessly off its armor. The cockroach swiped at Mitch again, the sharp claws attempting to rip at his legs. Mitch refused to allow that though, stepping back before shifting his grip on the axe, bringing the blunt side of it down with an audible crack on the cockroach's carapace. Another of his skills came into play as a gust of wind caused his blow to impact both harder and in a longer range than he could physically achieve.

The two women continued to thrust their spears at the cockroach, but their attacks didn't seem to be doing any damage. They did, however, keep it occupied so that Mitch could get in close enough to swing his axe. Drew ducked in close enough to cast spark on the beast, but it didn't seem to affect the bug at all. He dodged back, not wanting to get in his group's way. His fingers moved in the motions that would allow him to cast another acid dart, but the spell was still on cooldown. He looked down the hallway. "Katie, walls! There are more of them." He could see another half a dozen cockroaches making their way down the hallway, the noise of combat having alerted them to a potential meal.

Katie backed away from the cockroach, shifting over to the other side of the hallway and casting a wall to block off the reinforcements.

Mitch took a step back, then shifting his grip on his axe again, he brought it in underneath the cockroach, flipping the bug up onto its back. It immediately began trying to right itself, but Mitch's follow up blows—hard overhand swings with the blunt end of the axe on its underbelly—kept the creature from doing anything. Katie and Sarah shifted their attention away from trying to do damage and instead started sweeping their spears at any legs that appeared to be getting traction, helping to keep the creature defenseless.

Drew watched the wall, and when he saw the first cockroaches begin to crawl over, he cast a cone of frost, which encased some of the bugs in ice along with the top of the wall but didn't seem to do any damage. Another cone of frostfire added a little damage and more slick ice. Drew angled a fireball to explode on the other side of the wall, hoping the kinetic energy of the explosion would keep them from making their way over the top of the wall. His spells damage didn't appear to be affecting the cockroaches, but their secondary effects had made scaling the wall difficult. With the seconds that bought him, he began casting ice storm, centered as far as he could see down the hallway.

Mitch had cracked most of the underbelly of the bug, and blue ichor was leaking out of it slowly, but it had taken a dozen heavy swings. He switched to the sharp side of the axe now that the shell had been cracked and began cutting deep impacts into its flesh. The bug was mostly dead, which gave Sarah a chance to back up and cast a heal. Katie glanced behind her, and seeing Drew in the process of casting storm, prepared to cast another wall on top of the current one as soon as she felt the wind.

The storm exploded around them, the small confines of the hallway channeling it beyond its normal radius, and Sarah ducked an ice chunk that bounced off the wall above her and sent razor-sharp shards of concrete and ice raining down around her. Katie threw the prepared wall spell out, and the impact of the storm lessened, although they could still feel and hear its fury through the small gap at the top of the ceiling.

Mitch finally killed the one cockroach he had been hitting for the last minute straight and grunted, his breath short. "Back to the stairwell, we can't fight these things," Drew said as he pushed the cart back the thirty feet they had managed to come down the hallway. Everyone else following behind him, casting glances behind them to ensure that none of the cockroaches managed to climb the wall and make it through the two-foot gap left at the top. Once back in the stairwell, Katie created a wall behind the door to prevent it from opening. Mitch and Sarah collapsed on the floor, the adrenaline wiping their energy reserves out.

The short fight and retreat from the cockroaches had taken a lot out of them mentally. Drew cast refresh on himself and kept watch while the other three slumped against walls.

"So what do we do now?" Sarah asked, looking towards Drew while carefully picking ice and concrete out of her hair.

"We have a couple of options," Drew said after a few seconds of thought. Ticking his fingers down, he listed them for the group, "First, we can head back to the ambush spot and use the main staircase. We've already cleared the path, and with the walls in place, it should be relatively safe until we get there..." He trailed off, everyone filling in that they had been ambushed by the orcs there once already and would have to deal with whatever else they had prepared for them. "Two, we could go up to the second floor and head over to the western stairs and head down those."

"We'd have to break through the clinic, and even then, I'm not sure there's an exit to the far side of the stairwell. I tried coming up that way to get to the clinic once and got stuck behind it," Mitch offered. Everyone groaned; the joke before the building had turned into a dungeon was that whoever had designed it was trying to make a maze. It was clear that it was working against them now. The building was massive, meant to be the headquarters of the entire Department of Homeland Security. Movement through the building was far more complicated than it needed to be.

"Might not be a bad idea, might be able to grab some medical supplies while we're up there," Katie offered.

"But probably not worth getting stuck if there isn't a back door, especially since we have healing magic," Drew said with a shrug, "Anyway, our last option is going up to one and trying to make our way down the hill. Either way, with options two and three, we run the chance of running into more cockroaches or something worse."

The group considered their options in silence. "I think we need to do option one," Mitch offered, "We've already cleared that path, and with OS1's walls still in place, it's going to be the safest trip we have, and it gets us to where we really want to be. The other options are potentially riskier for worse results."

Sarah nodded her head in agreement with Mitch. "I agree. We could run into another bunch of cockroaches the other two ways and end up having to do option one anyway."

Everyone looked at Katie. "I don't really want to go back that way, but I guess it's better than the other options we have."

"Alright, back the way we came then," Drew said with a shrug, giving Katie a hand up while Mitch and Sarah picked up their weapons.

They made their way back to the central atrium, Katie unsummoning the walls as they went to clear the path. As they got closer, everyone fell silent, the site of the ambush weighing on their psyches. When the last wall came down, Drew held up a hand. A faint thumping could be heard echoing through the space.

"What is that?" Sarah whispered. She was near the back, behind the cart. Mitch and Drew were in the front, Drew holding the rope of the cart since it was the easiest for him to drop if they got into combat because everyone else carried a two-handed weapon.

"No idea." Drew motioned for Mitch to check it out.

Mitch peered out and then looked back, shrugging. "Nothing out there."

They left the cart there, no one wanting to drag it around when there might be a fight pending. The pounding echoed through the room, making it difficult to tell the source. "I think it's coming from..." Drew frowned, advancing on the tomb they had made for Juan. Sure enough, the pounding got louder as he put a hand on the wall. He could feel the faint vibrations as something pounded a dull rhythm against the inside.

"It's Juan," Sarah said, her voice tight and shrill.

Katie moved to dispel the walls, and Drew raised a hand to stop her. "That can't be Juan. There's no air in there. The pounding is constant, no breaks for rest." Realization blanched everyone's faces as they stared, horrified, at the tomb.

"What do we do?" Katie asked the silence.

"Leave it," Drew said with a shudder, tearing his eyes away from the tomb to glance around the room. He hissed; there at the edge of the light were three forms—impossibly tall, bipedal, and covered in thick fur. The others looked up at Drew's wordless alarm and raised their weapons, backing up reflexively. The light shifted with them, and the figures advanced, seemingly unwilling to come into the light, they nevertheless stalked forward as the light allowed. They appeared menacing, but not overtly hostile.

"Hello?" Drew called out, his fingers pointing at the figures ready to cast fireballs.

The biggest of the three walked slowly into the light, nearly eight feet tall and covered in thick, black fur. Scraps of clothing seemed to cling to its torso, stretched near to the breaking point. One hand was shriveled and small, like you see in movies when something has been cut off and is slowly growing back. The last clue to its identity was the name tag "Omondi" on the ripped ODU scraps still clinging to the body.

"Rob?" Drew asked, backing up with the others as the big figure approached. "Rob? Is that you?" The creature was taller than Rob by several feet, and Rob had been a larger guy already. The creature growled at him, baring fangs the size of Drew's fingers. Sarah let out a soft scream, dropping her spear. The group continued to back up until the light barely illuminated the tomb where the thing that had been Rob stopped and pounded on the tomb's wall. Shards of concrete went flying from the impact. He continued to hit the surface until he had chipped away enough mass for a hole to appear.

Sticking the fingers of his good hand into the hole, the creature roared, and with a loud crack, more concrete went flying. The walls Katie had made apparently didn't have rebar support within them, as he was able to tear out chunks of the stuff. Feral light shone in Rob's eyes.

The group watched stunned as it dug Juan out, but what emerged from the tomb wasn't the Juan they had interred. Juan had been short at five and a half feet. The thing that stood up in its place was just under seven feet, similarly covered in thick, brown hair and powerfully built, his clothing shredded to account for the increase in size. The newly risen beast shrank away from the light of the glowstones. All four of the creatures retreated away from Drew's group, dragging the two orc bodies with them as they disappeared into the gloom of the hallway from where Drew had originally come.

"What the fuck?" Mitch asked after the strange scene had ended.

"Another 'gift' from the Advent," Drew said shakily. "Looks like human corpses turn into..." he paused, searching for the right words, "wereghouls."

"What the fuck is a wereghoul?" Sarah asked, picking up her spear now that the threat was diminished. No one thought it unusual for the normally clean mouthed officer to curse; what they had just seen warranted the profanity.

"Nothing. Nothing that should exist. A lycanthrope like a werewolf but combined with a form of intelligent undead called a ghoul," Drew answered, his mind coming up with a solution from his days of playing Pathfinder and Dungeons and Dragons.

"Fuck, you're telling me that these things are intelligent undead werewolves?" Mitch asked, and Drew simply nodded his head.

"Why intelligent? They could be zombies?" Katie interjected.

"No, if they were zombies they would have attacked us. They were just coming to gather their new packmate and had plenty of food with the two orcs. We weren't worth the risk. They seem to be photosensitive. Although the one I saw earlier didn't seem to mind my torch, maybe just mana created light?" Drew mused, glancing around. "We should move. I don't really want to be here if they come back hungry." Drew nodded towards the stairs they had been too afraid to go down last time. It now seemed like a much better option than dealing with these wereghouls.

The group followed him, staying closer together than they had before—no one wanted to be near the edge of the light. Katie blocked up the door to the stairwell after they got in. It had taken the wereghoul that had been Rob several minutes of pounding to break through. It hadn't been quiet or quick, and all of them were happy with a little bit of time and warning before having to deal with the wereghouls again.

They descended two flights of stairs, ending up on the sixth floor. Only a few hallways and they would be out.

Drew sensed that it wouldn't be that easy, though, and as soon as they exited the stairs, he looked around. The coast guard paraphernalia that had decorated the floor had been trashed. In its place, scrawled on the walls in what looked to be blue blood, were strange symbols, angular and harsh with difficult to read words intermixed.

"Shit," Katie said when she saw them. "We're so fucked."

Chapter Thirteen — Deathweaver

They had only traveled about sixty feet before they heard the clapping. From somewhere up ahead in the darkness, the sound of a slow and heavy clap rang out. Everyone pointed their weapons towards the sound and halted, focusing their eyes on the edge of the light. The voice that followed was rough and guttural.

The words had a strange guttural quality to them as if English was not his native tongue, "Congratulations. You almost made it out of the dungeon alive. I was surprised that you were able to defeat ten of the brethren we sent to kill you, but the survivor informed us that their mission was successful. Your Deathweaver is dead. It is no wonder you could not progress through the other paths. Without his aid, you are clearly lost."

The speaker came into view midway through the speech, an orc that was nearly a foot taller than the ones they had killed before. He wore what appeared to be cockroach chitin plates that covered the vital areas of his body and wielded a massive battle axe made from scavenged spider parts.

On either side of the tall orc stood two massive beasts. They had the same basic shape as a dog, except without any fur. Thick grey skin covered their sides, while the ridge along their spine sported thick red spikes and skin the color of rusty iron. Their ears were pointed and large, reminiscent of a bat's, framing an angular face with small eyes that glowed red in the reflected light. Sharp fangs protruded from a heavy underbite in an elongated muzzle, while each foot contained four toes that were topped with an inch and a half long claws.

Behind the two beasts and the lead Go'rai stood another dozen Go'rai like the ones they had seen earlier, all armed with bone javelins and atlatls, as well as bone clubs. Several of these smaller Go'rai also wore armor made from cockroach chitin, although of inferior quality.

"Put down your crude spears. You are no match for the Go'rai. This is a new world; I can sense the mana is raw and primal. Your Deathweaver was potent but inexperienced. His life would not have been risked with so few defenders otherwise. Still, for your victory, I, Chakri of the Go'rai, give my word that my brethren will let you pass. Just leave the females here, and we will not harm you until you return again to our land."

"I don't think we can do that," Mitch said, his grip shifting on his own axe.

Chakri gave a short, barking laugh. "Of course not, you humans." He spat on the ground next to him. "You think yourselves better than us because of your Deathweavers. You are all the same, weak hangers-on that ride the coattails of your War Gods. But we have killed your mage, and you are not a match for the lowliest Go'rai bloodling. Leave now before I rescind my offer." The Go'rai behind Chakri had chuckled with him but were now fitting javelins to their atlatl.

Drew realized that these atlatls were what the orcs above had used to pelt the party in their first encounter. He took a step behind Katie, attempting to hide his hands as he began casting a frostfire storm. Mitch held the Go'rai's attention by responding to Chakri's taunting with one of his own. Drew paid little attention to his words, focusing on his spell as Katie moved to shield him with her body. "Get ready to cast a wall," he whispered.

The whisper was a mistake. One of the lesser Go'rai looked in his direction and could see enough of his hands to know he was casting a spell. "Mage!" it shouted as it moved to launch its spear at Drew. Sarah jumped, pushing Drew down just as he completed his last gesture. The storm went off behind the main line of the Go'rai, only catching half their number in its wrath. An instant later, Katie's wall went up, just in time to block half a dozen javelins aimed at the trio.

They weren't the only targets, though; Mitch, who had been standing just far enough away from Drew and Katie that he wasn't immediately behind the wall, took a glancing blow from a javelin that hit his shields and then deflected off, shattering against the wall to his right.

Chakri shouted, "Ravagers, attack!" The clack of javelins breaking did little to drown the sound of claws ripping carpet or the beast's shrill growls of excitement.

Drew looked up from where he lay on the floor, Sarah's slight frame on top of him, and pointed his finger at the edge of the wall, waiting for the lanky beasts to come into view. Katie, meanwhile, commanded the knight to assist Mitch on the far side while she waited impatiently for the five seconds to be over, so she could create another wall. The first ravager beat the cooldown and got a face full of fireball for its efforts.

Scorching heat ate away at half its face before consuming the grey flesh of its shoulder and half its chest. It lay whimpering on the floor; Drew wasn't sure if it was dead or not, but it didn't get up before a new wall blocked his vision of it. Sarah had been trying to extricate herself from around Drew. Her spear was tangled in his legs, making the process more difficult, and she elbowed Drew's sternum in her haste to rise. The blow momentarily dazed Drew, but she managed to stand up and retrieve her spear.

Mitch and the knight were trying to fend off the other ravager but were not having anywhere near as easy a time of it; the limited space behind the wall made maneuvering difficult as he ducked under the airflow of another javelin launched at him. The relatively short range of his axe was somewhat remedied by using his wind slash power, but he was only just keeping the beast away from him.

Drew, finally recovering his breath and standing, poked a finger over the six-and-a-half-foot tall wall and launched a cone of frostfire down towards where the ravager had been. Its shrill cry of pain was expected, but the orcish cries were not. "They're coming around!" Drew shouted.

Sarah had gone to help Mitch, her longer spear allowing her to score several hits on the beast while Mitch and the knight protected her from retaliation. The ravager's blood was the same green as the orcs they had killed and began to cover the floor around them, soaking into the carpet.

Katie created another wall behind them, enclosing the group on three sides, narrowing the approach paths but also trapping them inside.

"Don't kill them; I don't want to deal with the wereghasts!" Chakri shouted from somewhere on the other side of the wall.

Drew launched a shocking bolt and an acid dart at the ravager, neither of which did much damage. He cursed under his breath. He couldn't risk a fireball; the chance of hitting one of his allies was too high, and the space was far too small for a storm. He considered casting dancing sword, but he was too far away from the front line for it to be effective.

The walls were six and a half feet tall, but to get that height, Katie had needed to sacrifice length. They were only about nine feet wide, which meant that the group had three melee fighters in a space slightly wider than the radius of his fireball spell. The distance to the wall they had funneled their enemies into was only another ten feet. He couldn't cast anywhere near the frontline without risk of hurting his allies.

Drew jumped up, thinking he could cast a fireball at some of the approaching Go'rai.

Javelins whistled past his head, impacting behind him and shattering against the inside wall of their U. He ducked back, poked a finger over the wall, and shot off a fireball blindly. Drew wasn't sure if the lack of screams meant he had killed them immediately or missed completely. He hopped up again and saw the three orcs he had targeted were still standing. More javelins rained down, and Sarah cried out in pain as one of the fragments buried itself in her shoulder.

Katie increased the height of the walls in response, all three sides growing another two feet. Sarah cast her healing spell before returning to the fight. Drew was helpless, his spells useless in the small confines of their shelter. Mitch was fighting off the ravager and another orc that had joined the melee. Sarah and the knight were positioned on either side of him, darting in to stab or block an attack whenever there was an opening. He could see another Go'rai standing behind the melee, waiting for a chance to join in.

Drew considered the situation. The Go'rai clearly wanted him dead more than the others. They seemed to have something against red mages or 'Deathweavers'. If he could draw them away, the others might be able to take on what was left, and he could use his spells without fear of hurting his allies.

Unfortunately, he was also trapped in the U-shaped box, and he wouldn't survive trying to dodge past the ravager. Helpless, he recast his buff spells, knowing he would need them at their peak for what he was about to do, throwing another acid dart with little effect.

They couldn't keep this up much longer; fatigue and numbers were against them. Drew needed to change the game.

He pulled up his star map, and with a thought, he inserted major blink step into the available white node and clicked accept, and immediately his head seemed to explode. The xatherite instantly formed billions of new connections as he dropped to his knees with a groan, struggling to stay conscious through the pain. Wave after wave of agony seemed to eat away at his mental resistance, but he clawed his way through it, knowing that if he passed out now, he likely wouldn't live long enough to wake up.

The pain diminished enough that he could see again. Katie was shouting at him, but any attempt to comprehend what she was saying sent lightning bolts of pain through his skull; he just shook his head. Immediately, the warm feeling of Sarah's cure spell filled his extremities.

The pain in his head subsided to the point that he could think again, and he put a hand to the conjured wall next to him, pushing himself up. How long had he been out? The last thing he remembered was that Sarah had just cast heal, but apparently, the cooldown was already up? He could feel liquid trickling from his nose, but he forced himself to ignore it and take stock of the situation.

Mitch and Katie had managed to drop the ravager while he blacked out; it looked like the knight had jumped onto it and restricted it enough for the axe to cleave a gaping hole in its skull. The knight's form was still trapped under the ravager's body. The two Go'rai had moved in, clubs out since their javelins and atlatls were useless in the narrow approach path that was available to them. Chakri wasn't visible, but it was only a matter of time before he arrived.

Drew didn't think Mitch had much of a chance against the battleaxe he possessed. He needed to pull Chakri and as many of the orcs away from the group as possible. The direction he needed to pull them was easy enough; the orcs seemed to be able to see in the dark, an ability Drew did not share. If he could make it to the entrance, there would be light, assuming it was daytime, but it was better than wandering deeper into the darkness.

He shifted, moving closer to Sarah who had re-joined the fight on Mitch's right side. He needed to be able to see as far out of the box as he could. "I'm going to try and draw them off." His shout reverberated painfully in his head before he blink stepped past the melee.

Out of the box, he turned around to survey the battlefield. Five Go'rai were visible, the three from before standing in a loose cluster and aiming javelins at the wall, waiting for Katie to dissolve it, Drew assumed. Taking advantage of their split attention, Drew sent a frostfire ball exploding against the middle one, sending all three to the ground, hopefully dead. The sound drew the attention of the other two Go'rai that had been fighting Mitch, and the closest one shouted, "Deathweaver!" before turning back to his fight with Mitch.

From behind him, he heard a rush of air as someone swung a weapon. The blade barrier blocked the attack, and yellow light shown from around him as his mana guard blocked a secondary effect he couldn't see. Drew immediately cast a shock bolt, the blue energy shooting from his shoulder to whatever had attacked him from behind. Meanwhile, he turned and began running away from the group, another hand casting cone of frost behind him to slow down whoever had swung at him.

Drew didn't risk a glance backward, but he could hear the grunt of pain as the Go'rai was hit by his spells.

Turning a corner, he barreled into two Go'rai that were moving to join the fight. He pushed one down, elbowing past the other. They both carried atlatls; he needed to get around the next corner before they could recover and target his back.

Ahead, he could just make out the next turn, some light ahead illuminating it. He might be able to launch another couple of spells at his attackers as they came around the bend—if he could get to it first. He pushed himself seven or eight more steps, and he turned around, his hands held high. Chakri was charging towards him, angry burn marks on his left side, and Drew launched the fireball he had been preparing at him.

With surprising agility, the Go'rai stopped his forward motion and dove away. The fireball exploded, throwing the orc into a cabinet, his leg hitting with a loud crashing sound. Drew turned and began running again. It was a mere forty feet to the last bend and the exit. He wanted to shout a taunt, but his breathing was already ragged, and his head felt like it was on fire.

He heard a whistling behind him and dove to the left, trying to avoid the javelins he knew were coming. His shoulder hit hard against the floor, and for a second, his vision greyed out from the pain. He managed to force himself into a roll, pushing up off the ground with a moan. Only twenty feet to the corner. He clenched down on the pain, running harder than he had ever run, his heavy boots making him feel clumsier and slower than normal.

Ten feet left, then another telltale whistling. This time he tried to pivot off his left foot, sending him into the wall with a loud grunt, but the javelin passed him. He pushed against the wall, every part of his body feeling like it was on fire, but he couldn't give up now.

Then he was around the corner. Ahead, for the first time in days, he saw the bright beam of natural light. It illuminated the thing he should have been expecting but hadn't—a barricade. Cube farm walls and desks had been piled six feet high, forming a wall that would take several seconds to climb, several seconds where he would be completely exposed to the javelins behind him, not to mention the three Go'rai who were sitting around a small table, their weapons close at hand. He charged forward, hoping to get close enough to cone of frostfire them before they could get their weapons out.

Chapter Fourteen — Chakri

The look on the three Go'rai faces was one of surprise. They were all holding cups and dice; Drew assumed it was some form of gambling. He made it halfway to them before they understood the situation well enough to respond. Unfortunately for them, Drew only needed a couple more steps by then. His cone of frostfire engulfed them and froze two in place, but the third was partially shielded by the closest orc's body and went down clutching his face and screaming in pain.

Drew swerved slightly to avoid the treacherous terrain created by his most recent cone. He launched a shocking bolt at the screaming Go'rai and then for good measure, cast acid dart, the glob of acid landing on its forehead above the unburned eye. Drew hoped that was enough to keep it out of the fight as he pivoted, facing the hallway he had just come from.

Using the break to take a quick mental inventory, he realized he was down at least one block from blade barrier and some of the strength of mana guard from that unexpected attack after he blink stepped. He thought frostfire ball was available again, but the feedback he experienced last time he had cast a spell before its cooldown was up scared him away from trying it. All his storm spells but frostfire were available, and he'd love to cast refresh, but he didn't dare take the time to cast it. Dancing sword fell into the same category. Blink step was probably halfway off cooldown at this point, while both cones were still recovering.

The pursuit still hadn't rounded the corner, but he could hear them coming. Drew made a quick decision to begin the cast for firestorm, hoping to catch all three of his pursuers within it as soon as they came around the bend. He elongated the last few hand seals, delaying the five-second cast by a precious second and a half. He finished the cast right as the first of the three orcs rounded the bend, the dry heat of the firestorm blowing past him as it raged into existence.

A bone club whistled past his shoulder; the last remaining Go'rai sentry had made its way over to him while he cast the firestorm. His blade barrier caught the blow, and Drew twisted so he could see the sentinel. A shock bolt expelled with a thought from his elbow, blue light illuminating the ugly face near him.

Drew backpedaled, trying to open some space between him and the orc. He then launched a fireball over the orc's shoulder, aiming for the explosion to take it in the back while missing him. The shockwave from the explosion knocked him back and to the ground, sliding across the carpet. The scent of burning flesh filled his nose as he sat up with a groan. His head dazed, he looked around. The firestorm was still raging, but otherwise, he was alone in the hallway. He cast refresh, which didn't seem to renew him as much as he would have liked, before standing up with another groan.

His head still pounded from slotting blink step. In all, he was pretty battered from the fight, and he sensed it would take a few more castings of refresh and another cure or two to get him back to normal condition. Suddenly, the air went quiet, firestorm's energy spent. He studied the darkening gloom carefully. He took another glowrock out of his pocket and held it up as he advanced towards the corner. The mad rush had been in darkness, using the faint light from the party behind him and the blockaded entrance to guide him. He paused and cast dancing sword, unsure of what would be waiting for him around the corner.

He bounced the glowrock against the far wall, extending his vision further into the hallway as he drew the last one from his pocket. He edged around the corner, a frostfire ball ready to target any waiting Go'rai. He saw two silent forms on the floor, burned by the storm he had conjured.

"You will pay for their deaths, red mage," Chakri's disembodied voice echoed through the hallway.

"You started this. You attacked us first." Drew's eyes flickered back and forth, looking for the charging form of the orc.

"Your kind has hunted the Natren for millennia, the War Gods of the Iron Fleets bring only death and suffering in their wake." Drew thought Chakri's voice came from the left. In the space, there was a large cube farm, much too big for his small light to illuminate. He briefly considered launching his last glowrock, but Drew couldn't be sure he was on the left; the echoes made it hard to determine Chakri's direction.

"I haven't hurt any Natren; we're just trying to leave this accursed hole." Drew edged forward, heading towards the glowrock he'd thrown earlier.

"Foolish child, the Natren are all the clans. We cannot allow another Deathweaver to ascend. You are skilled, particularly for one so inexperienced. Allowing you to live would be to abandon numberless children of the Natren to their deaths. I will hunt you through your world like your kind has hunted mine through the stars."

Drew realized how stupid he was being. The others were possibly dying, and he didn't need to know the orc's exact location; he dropped the glowrock and then began casting frost storm. Chakri, seeing the mage begin his casting, bellowed and charged, his large form a darker black to Drew's right.

Drew dropped the frost storm cast, immediately double casting frostfire ball and fireball, both streaming towards the orc, who was limping still. Chakri was still fast enough to pivot, a skill flaring as a yellow glow surrounded him, protecting him from the blast as he lunged away from the explosive magic.

Drew launched an acid dart at his prone figure, which also raised yellow light as Chakri's shielding spell blocked the damage. The orc grunted and stood up, wiping green blood from his mouth with a backhand while the other grabbed his dropped great axe. "You are all out of tricks, Deathweaver. How you have so many spells so early, I am not sure, but I will destroy you." He had stalked forward as he said this, Drew backing up at the same time.

Drew's last few spells needed the orc to be closer, but the length of the ax made him leery. Dancing sword had a small amount of time left, and he had one more block from blade guard. He stopped his retreat and waited for Chakri to come to him. When he was about fifteen feet away, another cone of frost coated the ground between them, the orc stepping back in time to avoid getting damaged by its blast.

"Come, Human, my ax will taste your blood!" His heavy feet stomped through the ice, which cracked under his weight but didn't cause him to slip.

Drew waited until the orc was within ten feet this time, cone of frostfire catching his legs and burning away at the exposed skin it encased in ice. With a grunt-filled with equal parts pain and anger, the orc lurched forward, his axe flying straight for Drew's midsection. The dancing sword struck at Chakri's shoulder, though the cockroach chitin blocked any damage.

A piece of debris caught under Drew's foot, and he stumbled, the ensuing axe barely blocked by his last remaining blade barrier charge. A shocking bolt connected his palm to Chakri's face. The orc merely grunted again and reversed the swing of his axe. Drew watched the axe descend, but he already knew he wasn't going to be fast enough to dodge this one; in a close combat fight, the orc had all the advantages. So instead, he blinked away.

"Goodbye, Chakri," he said, as his fingers formed the seals of ice storm. The slowed orc bellowed in anger as his axe split the head of Drew's afterimage. Chakri attempted to cover the distance between them, but it was a futile gesture, as his haste caused him to slip on the ice and land sprawled on the floor. His eyes glared at Drew with utter malice before disappearing into the storm.

Drew turned, his energy spent again. The adrenaline that had kept him moving quickly disappeared as he saw the blinking notifications at the edge of his vision—the system telling him he was out of combat. He ignored them, hurrying back to where he had left the others.

The area near the summoned walls was deathly silent. Two Go'rai corpses lay before the visible portion of the walls, and he picked up the pace. Limping around the corner, he was sure he had landed on his ankle wrong when he stumbled; it burned with pain, but his boots had prevented any serious injury.

Turning the corner, Drew nearly impaled himself on the spear Katie thrust at him, averting it at the last moment when she saw who it was. Her face was pale, and Mitch and Sarah lay unmoving on the floor. Another Go'rai lay dead between them. "They're all dead."

Katie took a moment to process his words and then dropped the spear, heading towards Sarah. The brunette dropped to her knees, her fingers feeling for a pulse. Meanwhile, Drew did the same for Mitch. The fight was strangely devoid of red blood, although there were plenty of green stains on the carpet. The clubs the orcs wielded more often did internal damage and broke bones rather than cut flesh. Drew pushed his fingers against Mitch's carotid artery, leaving it there for a few seconds, but there was no pulse.

Looking over at Katie, he saw she had been doing similar actions to Sarah. "She's alive!" Katie exclaimed. Drew shuffled over to her, pushing the body of the orc off Sarah's legs where it had fallen. One of the Ensign's legs was bent in the wrong direction, and there were a couple of lesions visible where her clothing had been torn by the blows.

"What do we do?" he asked Katie, who had been checking for breathing.

"I... I don't know, she's got a pulse and is breathing. I think she hit her head." Katie began slowly feeling around Sarah's head for any wounds, trying not to move her spine as she did so. Her hands came back clean.

Drew sat back on his heels. "Mitch is dead," he said, looking at Sarah's immobile form.

Katie leaned back as well, glancing over at Drew, a pleading look in her eyes. "What do we do? I don't know how to help her," Katie echoed his words while Drew looked around and cast replenishing rain. The warm water was refreshing, but the Ensign remained unconscious.

"Maybe Chakri has a healing xatherite?" he said, realizing that he hadn't stayed around long enough to see if the orc had grown any crystals. "Stay here, put up another wall so nothing can get in, and I'll be right back." He stood up with another groan and trudged back to where he had last seen Chakri. The storm had not been kind to him.

The cockroach armor he wore had cracked in several places, while several particularly deep wounds looked like shards of ice had dug into his body. Drew flipped the orc over, a difficult prospect given his mass. Growing up from his chest were four xatherite. The yellow, violet, and orange glows were dim compared to the white crystal that grew from his sternum.

Drew touched all four, too tired to do more than blink at the white xatherite. They flared with light and then disappeared as he did so. He turned, heading back towards Katie as he willed the notifications to appear.

Congratulations, citizen. You have defeated the first Manaborn dungeon boss on your world. As a reward, you will receive a white xatherite.

Congratulations, citizen. You have reached level 1. Due to your membership in the Navy of the Human Protectorate, you have advanced to the rank of Seaman Apprentice.

Congratulations, Seaman. Due to your designation as an Assault Mage, you have been inducted into the Knightly Order of the Dragon. Since there are no senior Knights in close proximity to your location, the accolade ceremony has been deferred.

Congratulations, Seaman. As a member of the Order of the Dragon, you have been promoted to the rank of Midshipman. Due to your rank of Midshipman, new interface options are available to you.

Condensing xatherite level ups, only the highest level obtained will be listed.

Congratulations, Midshipman. Your Acid Dart has reached level 5. Damage has increased.

Congratulations, Midshipman. Your Acid Dart xatherite is ready to be upgraded.

Congratulations, Midshipman. Your Major Refresh has reached level 5. Recharge time has reduced.

Congratulations, Midshipman. Your Major Mana Guard has reached level 5. Amount of damage absorbed has increased.

Congratulations, Midshipman. Your Major Spark has reached level 5. Damage has increased.

Congratulations, Midshipman. Your Minor Dancing Sword has reached level 4. Duration has increased.

Congratulations, Midshipman. Your Cone of Frost has reached level 2. Damage has increased.

Congratulations, Midshipman. Your Fireball has reached level 2. Damage has increased.

Congratulations, Midshipman. Your Storm has reached level 2. Damage has increased.

Congratulations, Midshipman. Major Blink Step has been attuned.

You have acquired wild xatherite!

Basic grade Major Heat Shield acquired.

Rare grade Major Mana Sight acquired.

Master grade Major Gravitas acquired.

Primitive grade Metallurgy acquired.

Xatherite Crystal Name: Major Heat Shield
Xatherite Color: Yellow
Xatherite Grade: Basic
Xatherite Rarity: Widespread
Type: Magic
Effect: Reduces temperature based environmental damage by up to 15°C.
Mana recharge time: 31m 30s

Xatherite Crystal Name: Major Mana Sight
Xatherite Color: Violet
Xatherite Grade: Rare
Xatherite Rarity: Uncommon
Type: Magic
Effect: Allows users to see external mana flows within 15m and all ley lines within 10km. Effect can be toggled at will.

Xatherite Crystal Name: Major Gravitas
Xatherite Color: Orange
Xatherite Grade: Master
Xatherite Rarity: Uncommon
Type: Magic
Effect: Reduces or increases gravity on user or inanimate objects within 1m by 1.5G. Effect lasts 20 seconds.
Mana recharge time: 59.5s

Xatherite Crystal Name: Metallurgy
Xatherite Color: White
Xatherite Grade: Primitive
Xatherite Rarity: Scarce
Type: Crafting

Effect: Grants access to the Metallurgy skill.

Drew was too tired to pay attention to the new flag he saw on his xatherite or to worry about his promotion and induction into a knightly order. He instead sat down next to Katie, who had erected walls all the way to the ceiling, leaving only small gaps for air to come in and out.

"No healing spells." Drew looked at Sarah's pale face and frowned. Then he looked over at Mitch. "I need to burn his body. He wouldn't want to be a wereghoul." Katie nodded tiredly, then helped him move all the bodies out of their little shelter. They piled the orcs on top of each other but laid Mitch off to one side.

They burned Mitch first, tears carving white lines through the dirt on their cheeks. They didn't say anything, both too spent for words.

Chapter Fifteen — Scavenge

They didn't bother to burn the other corpses. He just went back in with Sarah and sat down as Katie recreated the walls that surrounded them and Drew cast replenishing rain on cooldown. He wasn't sure if the spell did any healing or increased the body's own ability to heal but didn't think it would hurt. He thought Sarah looked a little bit better after every casting, so he kept doing it.

Katie conjured more glowrocks, but the two just sat there for an hour listening to Sarah's slow breathing, too mentally exhausted to do anything else. They sat with their backs to a wall, close together but not touching.

Drew thought to break the silence a few times but stopped. In his mind, he was going over the fight, trying to figure out if he had made the right decisions. If he had stayed and fought here, would Mitch still be alive? What if he had run the other direction or even just circled around the box instead of heading for the entrance? He pictured a hundred ways that the fight could have gone differently. He tried to think of any way he could have been able to contribute in the close quarters fighting. He had the dagger still, not that it would have been very useful during the fight. Could he have thrown it? Would that have done anything? He didn't know how to throw a dagger.

With a sigh, Katie stood up and Drew looked at her curiously. "We can't stay here," she said, looking around. "We need to find a way to move Rothschild." Drew put his self-recrimination aside and stood up easily, the rain having kept their muscles from stiffening.

"Right, we'll grab some more pipes, see if we can't find something to make a litter with." Drew waited while Katie re-summoned the knight—who must have been crushed sometime after he pulled Chakri away—and then opened the way out. It didn't look like anything had been scavenging the bodies of the orcs or the ravagers yet, but Katie sealed Sarah back in and began to explore the orc encampment.

The camp was spartan with dirty clumps of bedding piled in corners and what looked to be communal work areas. Drew leaned down and picked up a leather vest that had half a piece of cockroach chitin attached to the stomach. It looked like it would fit him, so he shrugged out of his ODU blouse and tried it on. The fasteners gave him some trouble at first, but he eventually got the hang of it. Amazingly, the armor fit well, albeit a little short in the torso, but then again, he had been half a foot taller than most of the orcs.

There were three other vests in various stages of completion. Katie, seeing what he was doing, tried on a vest of her own. The first two she tried on were obviously much too big for her slight frame. Drew moved over and helped her get the third one on, which was the best fit of the three, although nowhere near appropriately sized for her. Katie pulled away as soon as it was on her.

They also found chitin pauldrons that were one size fits all; the leather used to tighten it would be easy enough to make additional holes in so that it fit them better. For now, they hung loosely, but it would be a simple fix the next time they were in a safe place.

Drew turned away and frowned. Again, they were working in a silence that he didn't know how to break. Did she blame him for what happened? Was she just mourning? He dug around at the various items, lifting what looked like rat hide lid off a cockroach shell. Inside were chunks of blue-tinged meat. "I think I found some food." He wrinkled his nose at the smell.

"Oh god, that's awful," Katie said, putting an arm over her mouth and nose. Drew replaced the hide and put it back.

"Oh, shit," he said, glancing back towards the stairs. "We left the cart up near... up on the third floor." Drew didn't want to remember what had happened to Juan, and he didn't want to remind Katie about it.

"I don't want to go back up there," Katie said after a few seconds of contemplation.

"Yeah, I don't really want to either," he looked around, "but we're gonna need food and water."

"Well, we can't eat that stuff," Katie said, pointing at the recently covered meat. "Maybe if we could cook it." She glanced around, but there wasn't anything to burn.

"Probably too bulky to carry anyway," Drew said, once again wishing for a video game's magic inventory. They resumed their search for things to assist them and found several bone clubs and javelins. Drew put on one of the quivers, putting an atlatl and several javelins in it. They were heavier than he would have liked, but he didn't want to complain. They hadn't seen any movement or monsters during their search of the camp. When they got to Chakri's corpse, Katie kicked it a few times, and then with a strangled cry, she seemed to collapse next to it, head buried in her arms.

Drew knelt next to her. He raised a hand to put on her shoulder but then thought better of it and sat there in silence, her quiet sobbing echoing through the chamber. Drew, afraid he would say the wrong thing, stayed silent, waiting for her to be ready to talk.

"What the fuck are we supposed to do, Drew? I feel so goddamn helpless. Everything we try just ends up killing someone, and now we have no food, no place to go, and who knows what is out there? What if it's worse? What if this is the safest place on Earth now? What sort of fucked up psycho did this to us? What if Sarah never wakes up?" She looked up, and Drew could see the pleading in her eyes, waiting for him to tell her it was going to be alright, that he was going to be able to fix everything.

"I don't know, Katie. I don't have a clue what's out there. All I know is that there's light, and I'm so gods damned sick of the darkness." He looked down, breaking the eye contact, "I don't want any of this; I didn't ever want to be the one that kicked down doors and shot up the bad guys. I joined the Coast Guard so that I could hack drug lords' computers. I don't know how people deal with this, the violence and the death. Maybe there aren't any safe spaces anymore, maybe there never were. But what do we do?" He paused, looking around. "We keep moving because otherwise, I know we're going to drown here. We keep moving until we can't because otherwise, that's letting this, all this," he gestured towards Chakri's corpse, "win."

Drew looked up again, meeting Katie's eyes. He wasn't sure what her expression meant. He had never been good at interpreting other people. She reached a hand out to hold his, squeezing it tightly. "Alright, let's keep moving." She stood up and grabbed Chakri's axe; it was heavier than she could easily handle, but she added it to her pile of things and then turned back towards the safe room.

Drew shook his head, unclear as to what exactly had just happened, but he stood up as well, eyeing Chakri's equipment. The chitin was still in good shape, but all of the leather had been ripped or burned. He didn't relish trying to pull it off the dead, so he left it there.

Katie had found a fleece blanket in one of the cabinets. With the blanket, two more pipes that Drew cut out of the ceiling using acid dart, and a couple of the uncut leather pieces, they had enough material to build the litter.

Drew also built a splint for the obviously broken leg, hoping that treating it would help Sarah wake up faster. After binding the leg and getting Sarah onto the litter, they prepped to set out again. Katie shooed Drew away from picking up the litter, "If—no, when we get attacked again, you need to have your hands free to cast." Drew nodded, the look in Katie's eye telling him that arguing wouldn't help him.

"Did you level up?" Drew asked, remembering he still hadn't upgraded his acid dart.

"Yeah, I did," Katie said as she stared at nothing. "The human protectorate has demoted me to Seaman Apprentice."

Drew snorted. It was the first thing like a laugh either of them had done since the break room. "Oh yeah, I got that message too. You get the one about the knights?"

"Knights? No, just the one about the level one thing. What did the knight one say?" Katie asked.

"It said because I was an assault mage, I was inducted into the Order of the Dragon and promoted to Midshipman."

Katie quirked an eyebrow. "Am I supposed to salute you now?"

"Hah, no." Drew shook his head, "It did say I got more interface options though. I haven't taken a chance to check that out, actually." The only interface he could think of was his xatherite map. He pulled that up and realized that there were two options off to the side—SA Sarah Rothschild and SA Katie Sabin. He focused on Katie's name, and a new map appeared in front of him.

Katie's map was three concentric circles, but there didn't seem to be anywhere near as many links between the nodes as there were on his, even accounting for the smaller number of nodes.

"I can see your xatherite map, Sarah's too." He focused on Sarah's name, and her even smaller map appeared. It was hard to tell at first, but the nodes and lines were roughly in the shape of a blossom.

"They look different," he said, comparing the three maps. "How so?"

"Well, mine looks like star constellations. Yours is a bunch of circles, and Sarah's looks like a flower," Drew answered, flipping between the maps in front of him. "Also, you both have fewer links than me. And smaller groupings."

Katie had pulled up her map as well and was looking at it curiously. "Yeah, before you came, we discussed it. Mitch said his map looked like a human, and Juan said his was stars like yours. How big are your groups?" she asked.

"Well, I have a bunch of five and six links." He looked through Katie's map, but the largest linked set he saw only had four links in it, and there was only two that large.

"Well, that explains why you have so many linked spells. I was wondering how lucky you had to be to get a perfect grouping. They aren't even full yet, are they?" When Drew shook his head, she frowned, "Did the tutorial tell you anything about how the maps are generated?"

"Not really; the only thing it said was that I had more nodes than average." Drew flipped through the nodes and focusing on the various xatherite, saw that the new value of rarity had been added to all his xatherite. "When you look at your xatherite, do you see the rarity?"

Katie pulled up an individual xatherite and then shook her head. "No, just name, color, grade, type, effect, and cooldown. What are my rarities?"

"Well, all of your xatherite are widespread, except for the knight, which is common." Drew looked over his xatherite too, and all his old ones but storm were likewise widespread, with storm being common.

"Let me see if I can give you some of these new wild ones."

He sent selected Major Heat Shield and then tried to trade it to Katie.

You are attempting to trade the basic grade, yellow xatherite "Major Heat Shield" to SA Katie Sabin. Are you sure?

He confirmed it with a thought, and it disappeared from his map. "Yeah, I got that, major heat shield? Is this one of the ones you got off the bastard with the battle-axe?"

"Yeah, the other three are major mana sight, a violet, major gravitas which is orange, and a white one called metallurgy.

The first two are uncommon, heat shield is widespread, and metallurgy is scarce."

Katie glanced them over. "I can only slot the violet and yellow; my whites are pretty far away, but I think you should probably do the mana sight one and maybe this heat shield one. Those both sound like they'd be more useful for you. What does gravitas do?"

"It allows me to change the way gravity affects either myself or an object near me. I can make it either heavier or lighter."

"Damn, that sounds cool. You think you can use that to fly?" Katie asked, and Drew shrugged, trading it to her.

"I dunno, you can look at the effect."

"Ugh, master? I don't think we have the time for that headache." Katie frowned for a minute. "Did you slot that teleporting xatherite in the middle of the fight?"

"Uhm, yeah. I couldn't think of a way to get out so I could use my spells without slotting it," Drew answered before Katie hit his arm under the pauldron.

"And it was rare, right?"

"Yeah."

"You idiot, I thought you said you couldn't slot it," she said with a glare.

"Well, I had to use a white slot for it, which I was hoping not to do."

"Drew, you have to tell me stuff like this! You could have slotted it before the fight, and then you wouldn't have blacked out for a minute when we needed you." Katie hit his shoulder again.

"I know, I'm sorry, I didn't... I didn't think it was that important."

Katie shook her head and looked back at her xatherite. "I can upgrade create light. Have you upgraded anything?"

"Oh yeah, it's fine, doesn't hurt like slotting it does," Drew said, again remembering that he could upgrade acid dart. He clicked over to the red and upgraded it.

Xatherite Crystal Name: Major Acid Dart
Xatherite Color: Red
Xatherite Grade: Basic
Xatherite Rarity: Widespread
Type: Magic
Effect: Creates a small globule of acid from a finger that travels in a straight line until it impacts a target, dealing small amounts of acid damage.
Mana recharge time: 16.1 seconds

Well, it finally upgraded its damage from minor to small amounts.

Chapter Sixteen — Planning

Drew had to fireball a hole in the barricade. They weren't going to be able to get Sarah through otherwise, but when they were finally through and out in the sunlight again, both of them stopped and just soaked in the light.

For the first time in who knows how many days, they could see further than the glowrocks could shine, and it was like a weight had been lifted from them both. It was only when they could feel the warmth of the sun and wind on their skin that they realized just how oppressive the closed darkness had become. By unspoken accord, Katie set Sarah down, and they simply stood there for a moment, drinking in the outside world again.

They were on a small road that traveled around the base; across from them was the parking garage for the building, and on the other side of the garage, just barely visible through the walls and pillars, was a forest. To their right and down the hill was the exit from the base. The road ran alongside the beltway before rejoining the rest of the Anacostia neighborhood of DC. To their left and up the hill were a few more Coast Guard and Department of Homeland Security buildings, while beyond them was the abandoned mental hospital and its replacement.

Either way, they were in the middle of Barry Farm, one of the most dangerous places in DC pre-Advent. How the Advent had changed that, Drew had no idea, but he didn't really look forward to finding out.

"We need to figure out where we're going." Drew broke the silence, looking at the sky. "I think it's around 1600, so we've probably got a few hours of daylight remaining. Water, food, and shelter are the priority in that time."

Katie nodded her head as she looked up the hill. "Base Exchange then? It's the only place nearby that we're going to be able to take Sarah."

Drew followed her gaze up the hill as well. The exchange was only slightly larger than a small convenience store, but it would have food, drinks, and spare clothing. "Other option would be to see what we can grab from cars." He gestured towards the parking garage next to them. "It's closer, and we wouldn't have to move Sarah as much."

"We could, but I think it's a better long-term move to go to the exchange. We might not find anything in the parking garage, especially with how few people were in the building when it happened." Katie turned again and sized up the hill; it rose a couple hundred feet, and the grade was steep.

Drew glanced at the garage—there were only a few vehicles within, mostly from people that found it easier to store their extra vehicle here than somewhere within the district. The odds of them finding food beyond their own vehicles was minimal.

"Well, I have a gallon of water and a 72-hour kit in my car, but you're probably right, we're gonna need to raid the exchange either way."

About halfway up the hill, they switched and Drew carried Sarah. The open nature of the terrain made them feel more comfortable that no pressing attacks were forthcoming. "It's weird. It's been a couple of days now, and yet... everything looks like nothing happened. There are no crashed cars, no burning buildings. Look at Arlington; it's the same as it always was, just quiet." The hill they were on afforded a decent view of the Potomac from the Woodrow Wilson Bridge to the 14th Street Bridges, centered around the Reagan Airport.

"What's been happening out here while we were inside?" Drew mused as he pulled Sarah up the hill.

"Do you always talk when you exercise?" Katie asked with a half-smile, but when Drew glared at her, it morphed into a full smirk. "Who knows?" She looked out at the quiet city so different from the loud, busy five o'clock traffic that normally beset it. "Holy shit," she exclaimed as a turtle surfaced in the river. It was hard to tell from this distance, but it looked to be as big as some of the airplanes near it.

It pushed itself along the river for a few seconds before sinking back down under the water. Now that she was looking, she could see several other gigantic turtles. She had previously taken them for hills, but they were sunning themselves on the riverbank. "Well, that's... disconcerting," Drew said as he caught sight of the creatures as well, drawn to look by Katie's exclamation.

It took them thirty minutes to crest the hill and make their way around to the other side of the building, where the entrance to the exchange was. The building itself was four stories, but the exchange only took up a portion of the bottom floor, and Drew had no idea what was on the upper floors. A barber shop and dry cleaner took up a portion of the lowest level of the building, completing the three staples of military shops.

The front doors were locked, but a single hit from the new and improved major acid dart was enough to eat away at the lock and allow entry. Katie set Sarah down and built walls around her, protecting her while they went off to ensure it was safe.

The inner section of the building had a small landing before turning left into the barbershop. To the right were bathrooms, and straight ahead was the exchange itself. Katie summoned a new glowrock, this one being much brighter than the earlier ones, and handed it to Drew, both of her hands returning to grip her spear.

Drew held it up high. The exchange only had a few windows, and in the dying light, it was filled with shadows. He had never realized how dark it was without the ever-bright fluorescent lights to illuminate everything. The doors into the exchange were locked by a chain. Another acid dart opened the lock and the clanking sound of the chain being pulled off the door and dropped filled the noiseless atrium ominously.

"Probably more rats or cockroaches if anything; hopefully, it's rats," Drew said as he pulled the door open.

Without a weapon and without Mitch's enhanced melee blows, there wasn't much they could do against cockroaches.

The exchange was somewhat large and divided into four different parts. Directly in front of them in the front right section of the store was the electronics and hardware section. Going clockwise around the store was the coast guard branded civilian clothing section, the uniform item section, and then the convenience store area. Glancing around the room, Drew threw a couple of the old glowrocks into the various corners, waiting to see if anything responded to the intrusion of light into the semidarkness.

With a glance at Katie, who shrugged, they moved forward, heading to the food area. Finding nothing, they began moving less cautiously until they had cleared the entire exchange. Drew found a broom and took a moment to knock the dropped ceiling tiles down so that nothing could be hiding up above them. They did find several regular spiders, which Drew killed with the broom handle, not wanting to take any chances on them becoming mana twisted while they weren't watching.

The next hour was spent clearing, using the toilets, and then eating what Katie sarcastically called, "a very nutritious dinner" of jerky, nuts, and warm Sprite. Then they began the process of fortifying the area. Katie summoned walls to block off the windows and door, while Drew raided the clothing area for bedding. They made a spot for Sarah on the most comfortable bed they could make for her. Drew had cast refresh on both of them again, and they both changed into clean clothes, giving them a sense of revitalization they hadn't had since the Advent.

Katie moved to block off the last window at sunset, the hill providing them with a great view to the west where the dying light tinted the city in gold. When it finally set and the city turned dark, Katie started to block the window.

"No, wait. Let's see if there are lights anywhere." They stood at the window and watched for thirty minutes before Katie shook her head.

"Nothing." She raised the wall, and they retreated to the two chairs they found, placed near Sarah, Drew casting refresh on her sleeping body.

"So, what do we do next?" Katie asked. Sarah's state was still pretty much the same... slow, shallow breathing. They had given her some liquids earlier while they ate, but they didn't have any way to give her more substantial nutrients.

"Well, we need to find where the rest of the people are. I think our best bets are going to either Bolling or McNair," Drew answered, glancing towards the now-blocked window. Fort McNair was hidden by the slope of the hill they were on, but Joint Base Anacostia-Bolling was across the freeway from Coast Guard Headquarters where they were, and it was one of the places that had remained dark.

"Either way, we're going to need a better way to transport Sarah. Or wake her up," Katie responded, looking at her silent form. "I don't really feel like dragging that litter all the way to McNair."

"Yeah, but I guess that leaves another question: what do we do if there's no one there?" Drew didn't say it, but both were thinking it. What if there was no one anywhere? "I need to check on Zoey. I know logically that she's probably dead, but I need to make sure either way."

"I don't have anything I really need to do, but I'd like to go home and get some things..." Katie trailed off with a shrug. "I live in Kingstown."

Drew nodded. "I'm right near the Air Force Memorial in Arlington." Sort of opposite directions. To get to Katie's, it would be better to go south and take the Woodrow Wilson bridge west into Alexandria, whereas for Drew's, it would be faster to go northwest across the Frederick Douglass Bridge and into DC proper before crossing the Potomac on the 14th Street Bridges. Both were on the other side of the Potomac, though.

"Well, what are our transportation options?" Katie asked, trying to break the problem down.

"We can try to find an old car, something from... I dunno, the seventies or earlier? I'm not sure when they started using electronics, but an older car would probably still work. The other alternative is a cart? Maybe we can find a horse?" Drew shrugged. "And what do we do with Sarah while we are out looking for transportation?"

"The commissary on Bolling would have shopping carts, but the loading dock here might have something better than that media cart you used," Katie offered.

"Commissary would be a couple hours there and back at least, while the loading dock is a possibility. That would be a short trip."

"But not one with a guaranteed result. Worth a stop though since it's on the way." Katie was using a brush to untangle her hair as they talked; days of fighting with only the replenishing rain to clean had left it a tangled mess, but she paused for a moment. "I'll have to stay here with Sarah."

Which meant Drew would have to go out alone. "Yeah, we'll need you to seal it up again, and we shouldn't leave her alone, just in case she wakes up."

"Here, slot the gravitas. It'll help you get over the highway faster," Katie said, pulling up her interface and giving the xatherite to Drew. "Should probably slot that and the mana sight. Might help you see anything dangerous."

"You sure?" Drew asked, looking at the two xatherite. He then traded metallurgy and heat shield to Katie. "Here, take these. That way we each get two. We'll owe Sarah." If she woke up—otherwise, they couldn't risk losing the xatherite.

Katie said, "Wait, where are you going to slot them?"

"Gravitas in the constellation with storm; hopefully it will give me a gravity storm spell. It's the only linked skill I can think of," Drew said, glancing at the grid. "Maybe something with mana guard, but I don't think that's really likely."

"As for mana sight... I can combo it with either blink step or mana guard and blade barrier. I don't see any of those last two creating a linked skill. So, it's kind of a tossup, I guess. Whether I want to try to complete a constellation or go for an improbable linked skill with blink step."

"You're probably right for gravitas; gravity storm sounds useful. I can't think of anything for mana sight either." Agreed on his course of action, Drew cast refresh on Katie again. "Bedtime." He laid down next to Sarah and slotted the two xatherite, confirming the prompt as everything then went dark.

Chapter Seventeen — Sight

Drew awoke to a world vastly different from the one he had previously known. He remembered the day they'd bought his father color correcting glasses, allowing him to see the reds and greens that he had never been able to see before. He had been in sheer awe at what he had been missing, and this was like that.

He spent seconds just looking around him, amazed at all the things that he'd been missing. His jaw was slack as he watched the ebb and flow of mana in millions of different colors that he had no names for.

Katie laughed behind him, and he turned to look at her. Lines of color were radiating away from her, creating an aura or nimbus around her. He stared, not really seeing her, just the light around her. The colors were present everywhere, but they seemed to twist when they got within a few feet of her, pulled into her body as they disappeared. Her body seemed darker and less real than he remembered. Most of her aura was blue, with different shades of purple and green acting as secondary colors.

"You look like you've never seen a girl before," Katie said with a grin.

"I'm not sure I have. Everything is different," Drew said, looking away from Katie to glance at Sarah's prone form next to him. Her aura wasn't as bright as Katie's, and the predominant colors were different: oranges, yellows, and greens all swirling in equal number, but like Katie, her body itself was devoid of the color granted by his new vision.

"How long was I out?" Drew continued to look around; underneath them, he could see massive, white lines of mana flowing through the Earth. The movement was like watching rivers flow, several of them converging and creating a glowing light directly under the building they had just escaped from. Another, larger line surged out of that node, and from there into DC proper, joining with other lines and then splitting chaotically. It created a vast, intricate web. Every point seemed to fill with light and then when it was full, passed it forward into other lines and nodes. As he looked, he realized that sitting in the middle of all the various webs was a single node that didn't have an outlet. He couldn't tell exactly where that node was, but it was many times deeper than any other node he could see.

"A long ass time. Sun rose awhile back. What the heck are you staring at?"

"Mana, I think. I can see these lines under us. They converge under the HQ building and then head into DC, and there is one massive node there. I'm guessing that whole knot is the central nexus, and it's huge." Drew stood up with a groan, his body stiff from hours of inactivity.

"Cool. Well, your turn to be on watch. I'm going to slot heat shield." She laid down on the spot Drew had just vacated. It was only as she did so that Drew realized she had changed clothing again, out of the ODUs she had been wearing and into a pair of gym shorts and a t-shirt. She had been pretty in uniform, but she was beautiful in normal clothing. He blinked at her. "You know, it's really not polite to stare," she said with a grin and then grabbed her head in pain.

"Mother fucker," she grunted but remained conscious. "Cast refresh on me please. I don't think I'm gonna get to sleep, just feel like I have a migraine." Drew wisely kept his laugh to himself while he created the hand seals to cast the spell on her.

Katie grunted and sat back up. Then she smacked his leg.
"Hey, what was that for?"

"Because of how stupid you were to slot blink step in the middle of a fight," Katie replied, "How did you even stay awake?" She rubbed her forehead and shifted a few feet back so that she could lean against the wall.

"I don't think I did," Drew said as he went in search for food. "You want anything?" he asked, grabbing a bag of chips.

"Chocolate, dark."

"Nuts?"

"God no."

Drew laughed, and he grabbed some M&Ms and candy bars for Katie while he grabbed three ravioli packages in a microwaveable bowl and a spoon. Not that he had a microwave, he just wanted something more solid than snack food. Handing Katie the chocolate, he popped the top on his ravioli and began to eat it cold.

Katie gave him the weirdest look. "Men are so gross."

Drew shrugged. "First real food I've had in a week, even if I have to eat it cold."

They ate in silence for a few moments, Drew getting lost in the new colors around him. His eyes never really stopped moving as he tried to take in everything. He glanced over at Sarah, then back at Katie, who just shook her head with a sigh.

"I can tell what colors your xatherite are with this sight. Well, I have a hard time distinguishing between the indigos and violets, but I think that's just my refusal to acknowledge they both aren't purple."

Katie frowned slightly. "Well, that will be helpful if we encounter any other humans, and it might hold true for the other stuff that has been mana twisted as well. Oh, I know." She hopped up to the wall with the window looking out to the southwest, unsummoning it with a thought. "Can you see the turtle's aura?"

Drew looked out the window and frowned. "No, I can see the ley lines, but anything past about fifty feet, I can't see the mana around."

"Right, there was some sort of range limit on it right?" Katie asked.

"Fifteen meters, yeah." He looked around again. Outside, the mana seemed to flow in a normal pattern, pulled slightly towards the node in the basement of the HQ building, but he realized that the sun was already a quarter of the way through the sky. "Let me try out gravitas a bit, and then I'll head out. I'd much rather do this with lots of light to spare."

He shifted to a spot where there were no pipes in the ceiling and then activated the spell. Unlike all his other skills that were always at full power, he could sense how to change the potency of this one, and a slight change in his intention turned it from negative to positive gravity. He also realized that he couldn't change the direction the gravity was pulling from; it was all either straight up or straight down towards the center of the earth, and thus his hopes of being a windrunner met an early death.

Drew's first mistake was using it on himself instead of an object near him; his second mistake was that he activated it at full negative power, which meant he fell to the ceiling at half speed. It didn't hurt him, as he slowed himself with his hands and then rolled into the ceiling. A feeling of disorientation overcame him as he looked down at Katie with his back against what felt like the floor. He frowned; he needed to get to the floor before the spell wore out or he'd fall at full speed the entire ten-foot distance.

Changing the force of the spell to negate all gravity on him, he floated down away from the ceiling for a moment, lost in freefall. He pushed gently against the ceiling and floated down parallel to the floor until he was eye level with Katie.

"Having fun?" she asked with a grin.

"A little," he said, reaching out a hand to her. "Hey, hold me against the floor for a second." Katie grabbed his arm, and he shifted his body so that he was oriented with gravity again and then let the spells manipulation equal zero. "Okay, more than a little," he said with a grin. He had just flown on his own, eat that, Wright brothers! Well, technically, he had fallen and floated, but that was close enough.

"You wanna try?" he asked Katie.

She laughed and shook her head. "No thanks, maybe if we find another one and I can control it."

"Yeah, that's fair. It would've been much scarier if I wasn't in control." Drew frowned, pulling up the spell again. "Oh, can't use it on other people anyway, only me and inanimate objects."

"Try making my shoes heavier," Katie said. "That would be a huge advantage in a fight if you could make it so Chakri couldn't dodge or make a weapon twice as heavy to wear them out faster."

"Hmm, can't switch to something else while the spell is still active, and I can't cast it again for a minute." Drew looked around waiting for the spell's cooldown to allow him to recast it.

He had Katie take the walls down long enough for them to relieve themselves in the bathrooms; these toilets thankfully had tanks, so they could be flushed. When they were both done, he cast gravitas on her boots, sticking them to the floor with two and a half times the normal gravity. She stumbled but was able to adjust after a few seconds, her movements much slower.

"That's a workout," Katie said, slightly out of breath just from walking back to Sarah.

"Yeah. It'll make it a lot easier to stop things from chasing me. Unless it's a spider or something else that doesn't wear shoes." Drew grabbed one of the backpacks and began filling it with food and water.

"Planning on being gone a long time?" Katie asked with a frown as he packed.

"No, but who knows how common food is out there? If I find someone else who hasn't been able to get food recently, this may give them enough of a boost to follow me back." Drew looked around and then grabbed a couple of the knives on display and several of the spare glowrocks; Katie had made a whole bunch more while he had been passed out. "Just in case they're injured and can't be moved... having some light will be good for morale," he answered her unspoken question.

After he had put back on his armor and tightened the pack down, he turned to look at Katie. "We could all go together, you know."

She shook her head. "No, we already decided on this. You'll only be gone for a few hours, and when you get back, we'll be in a much better spot." She forced a smile and then hugged him. "Just don't go dying on me. I don't want to be alone."

Drew hugged her back, not letting go until she did. "It'll be alright, Katie; I'll be back before dark."

Katie nodded again but didn't seem to be about to add anything else to the conversation.

She removed the walls she had placed, and they both locked eyes one last time before she put the wall back up. Turning, Drew headed down the hill. He looked back at the shop when he was about halfway down and could see Katie watching him from the window. He waved to her and smiled again as she shook her head and waved back. Her lips were moving, but it was impossible to tell what she said at this distance.

The loading dock was near the base of the hill, not far from where they had left the main building the day before. Built under the road he had been walking down and situated between the parking garage and the building was a ramp that led down into it. Drew stopped one last time to look up the hill, where he could still see Katie's figure standing in the window. He then took out a glowrock and descended into the darkness of the loading dock. His new vision painted the area with a brighter color than the exterior had been, showing more ambient mana in the area.

"Does that mean the building really is a dungeon? If so, what does the node mean?" he asked himself rhetorical questions to keep his mind occupied while his eyes scanned the area, looking for auras and movement. The bay was large, several hundred feet across and thirty or forty feet tall. There were no vehicles, of course, and all four of the receiving doors were closed. There was a small access door on the far side of the building that he made his way towards.

From the corner of his eye, he caught movement and suddenly went into high alert; a human-shaped aura was all he could see in the darkness. It was mostly purple in color and about his height.

Chapter Eighteen — Release

Both Katie and Sarah's auras had ended when it touched their actual bodies. This aura continued into the body, morphing from mostly indigo to a dull violet, allowing him to see the figure's face and body. It was difficult to make anything out, like looking at a negative of a picture.

The aura caused Drew to stop. The figure was crouching down and didn't seem to be aware of him. Considering he was holding a bright glowrock, that meant they were either blind or physically prevented from seeing him. The bright circle of light emitted from the glowrock ended about twenty feet and dimmed until it reached the limit of mana sight, where it was nearly impossible to make anything out. Focusing into the darkness, he was able to see what he thought was a wall.

The lack of immediate threat reminded Drew to cast his buffing spells, unsure of their status over the past few days and having completely forgotten to recast them before he left the exchange. It was a bad practice that Drew had no intention of allowing to become a habit.

Blade barrier and mana shield surrounded him briefly in their comforting, yellow light before fading away. He realized that he couldn't see his own aura and had no idea if mana sight would allow him to see buffs or not. Filing that thought away for later investigation, Drew considered his options.

He was sure that the aura wasn't human; the fact that the body emitted a violet light led him to believe that it was probably a wereghoul. They had been human and were transformed into another shape, plus the orcs had been built stockier and shorter.

Frowning to himself, Drew considered his options; he had killed a lot of things since the Advent started, but they had either been trying to kill him or they were giant spiders, and giant spiders probably deserved to be killed anywhere they were found. He shivered involuntarily at the thought of the spider queen that had almost killed him. He didn't like the idea of killing another human or something that once was human.

From experience, he knew that the carts that he was looking for would be in the hallway just past the normal sized door. The problem was that he was pretty sure that was exactly where the wereghoul was. He wasn't sure how he felt about killing something that had once been someone he might have known.

Rob and Juan were gone. He understood that logically, but how much of them was retained when they had changed? Rob hadn't attacked them when he had come to recover Juan from his tomb. But was that because they were only coming to get Juan or because he was still Rob underneath all that and he remembered Drew? What about the one that had attacked him right before the fight with the spider queen?

A dozen other questions along the same vein popped into his mind, but he realized that he didn't have a way to answer any of them. He looked around and didn't see any other auras. This was the best chance he had of getting one alone and maybe getting some answers to his questions.

His shoulder twitched; the last time he had started a fight on his own, it had been ripped apart. He pushed forward, careful to keep his steps as quiet as he could. He realized his hands were shaking and stopped about ten feet from the door.

Breathe in, hold, breathe out. Drew's heart was beating wildly as he gripped the glowrock tighter, looking at the bright red flesh between his fingers. Breathe in, hold, breathe out. He could do this; Katie and Sarah were depending on him being able to do this. But his shoulder twanged again, and though the pain he had felt was fleeting, that was because Sarah had been there to heal him. That wasn't currently an option.

He tapped the half-attached piece of chitin on his chest. He had armor now, more spells, and he could escape much easier if he needed. The shaking slowly stopped as he regained control of his body. Katie and Sarah were counting on him; he couldn't fail now.

Stepping forward, he paused to listen at the door. He couldn't hear anything through the heavy-duty metal, nor could he see anything through the glass pane. He braced himself and turned the handle, or at least, he tried to turn it. It was locked and wouldn't budge. "Right, that makes sense. No point in leaving the door unlocked when no one's here," he said to himself before casting acid dart.

He waited a moment for the spell to eat through the door and into the latch. The shaking returned, less severe than before, as he was forced into idleness.

Drew ran a hand through his hair. Then he tried the knob and, feeling no resistance, pulled the door towards him. Stepping carefully into the dark hallway beyond, he looked to the left, and not seeing anything with either normal vision or mana sight, turned right towards the figure and where he remembered the carts being.

His footsteps were slow, quiet. "Hello?" he called out when the aura appeared in his vision again. It stopped all movement except for its head, which turned to glance at him, its lips pulling back to reveal sharp teeth. Up close, he could tell it was a wereghoul, the faint wisps of mana that infused its hair mingling with the rest of its aura had made it difficult to tell before.

The strange effect of mana sight made it difficult to make out many of the wereghoul's facial features. It seemed to consider him for a few moments, but it's lack of movement gave Drew some courage. He took a few steps forward, looking behind him and wishing he had Katie with him to block off the back.

"I'm not here to hurt you," he said in his best calming voice, approaching the wereghoul like he would a strange dog. "I'm just here for the cart. I need it to carry my friend who's hurt." He continued talking, having learned that it wasn't so much what he said but the tone of voice he said it in that most animals responded to. The wereghoul took a step back as Drew approached, ceding territory to the human.

Drew glanced behind him again, afraid that something was going to ambush him from behind. When he turned back, the wereghoul had used the momentary distraction to jump towards him. With a thought, a fireball rose to meet the wereghoul's form. It exploded on contact about ten feet from Drew, and the concussive force of the blast in the confines of the hallway washed past him, causing him to stumble. He already had a cone of frostfire moving to fill the space.

The aura around the wereghoul disappeared, the green mana within it slowly darkening. Drew carefully walked towards it, the frostfire ice underneath him giving a strange sizzle he had never noticed before as he stepped on it. Drew cast dancing sword as he went, wanting a melee weapon at hand. He was unsure what exactly it took to kill an undead were-creature.

It was clear that it wasn't just playing re-dead by the lack of aura, but Drew nudged it with his foot just in case; it didn't move. He attempted to turn it over so he could look at its face. It had landed on its stomach, but he only got a handful of hair for his trouble. He shook the hair free of his hands in disgust rather than fear this time, then pulled more carefully, grabbing the softening flesh, which squelched unpleasantly as small bits of it came loose under his fingers.

Once he successfully managed to turn the body over, he realized that whatever magic had been keeping it from decaying was rapidly fading. The hair covering its body was rapidly falling off and flaking away. He brushed the fur away from the face, wanting to see if he knew who it had been. With a few seconds of work, Juan's face became evident.

Drew rocked back on his heels. "I'm so sorry, Juan." He looked over at the carts; both had been struck when the fireball killed Juan. He examined them and found the blast had broken a wheel on the first, and the second had three flat tires. They were both different makes, so it was impossible for him to trade them out without a significant amount of effort.

He stood up with a sigh, glancing over at Juan's body. He arranged the arms in a cross over his body, then crossed himself. "I hope there's life after this, Juan. You deserved better than this. We all do." He clenched his fists, looking around for something soft he could hit but didn't find anything. He cursed under his breath. He cast fireball on Juan's corpse to immolate it, not wanting any of the scavengers to get to it.

Turning away, Drew walked slowly out of the loading bay, up the ramp, and down the street. He cried then, letting the drops hit the ground without wiping them away from his face. It wasn't fair; he didn't ask for any of this, he didn't ask for people to look up to him, to depend on him. If he was in a safe place, he had a feeling he would be a mess, but instead, he locked it away in that dark corner of himself and moved forward.

Looking up at the exchange to see if Katie was still watching, he saw that the wall had been replaced. He turned towards the freeway, for the first-time in... a week? Maybe more. He wasn't sure about time anymore. He was going to leave the base, and he wasn't sure what he would find, but he doubted it would be anything good.

He passed the guard shacks; there were no bodies, blood, or signs of violence in any of them. There should have been at least one guard out here. When it went dark, what would they have done? Go into the building or try to go home? He looked around but couldn't find any indications of what would have happened to the guard.

Another eighty feet of walking had him across the street from the freeway. The wall that divided them was only about four feet tall at this point and made of unadorned concrete. He climbed on top of it, looking out over Anacostia Freeway. There were a couple of car wrecks on the road, not many though. The Advent had happened at some time between two and three a.m.; most people had been off the streets at that time.

The other side of the wall had a thirty or forty-foot drop down into some trees and grass that served as a sound barrier for the freeway itself. Lines of girders separated the three lanes of northbound and southbound, as well as blocking the road from the frontage road on the other side of the freeway. On the other side of that was Joint Base Bolling. Studying it in the morning light didn't give him much hope—there was no movement, and the only sound was the occasional animal cry.

The world felt strangely isolated and empty. He had become used to the constant hum and buzz of modern-day city life, and the silence unnerved him. He finally wiped his face; the sun and exercise had calmed him enough to stop his tears, and he didn't want to encounter anyone with streaks down his face.

"Stupid toxic masculinity," he muttered to himself. The world had ended, and he still felt the need to appear strong. With a jump, he pushed himself off the wall, casting gravitas to lighten the gravity enough for him to pass over the trees and grass below. He landed roughly. His legs pretending to run in midair and keeping running after he landed wasn't enough as he hit the ground hard, rolling into the fall.

He lay on his back on the asphalt and stared up the sky. The joy he felt in jumping eighty feet without injuring himself felt hollow, not quite enough to lift the oppressive silence of the world around him. This was the world now—a silent death trap. He sighed and closed his eyes. "This fucking sucks."

Chapter Nineteen — Squirrels

Something hard digging into the small of Drew's back forced him to sit up. He glanced down the freeway; to his left were several motionless cars but no signs of life. To his right was the emergency turn around and more abandoned vehicles. Only a few people had been on the road so late at night, and it looked like most of the cars had pulled over when their lights and power steering died.

He began walking towards the turnaround, looking in the cars he passed on his way. There wasn't any broken glass or other signs you would typically assign to an accident; they simply looked like parked cars.

"Where did everyone go?" he asked himself. There weren't any bodies. Thinking back, he realized that the only sign of a human's death he had come across was the blood-streaked hallway and severed hand near the spider queen. He looked at the base and frowned. Bolling was a bigger base—they had people living on it. Where would everyone have gone?

Crossing over the freeway and frontage road, he looked dubiously at the woods running alongside the road. It looked impenetrable with thick foliage and smaller trees that were about fifteen feet tall while being wide enough that he couldn't see the far side. He headed south along the road; something about the liminal space being empty felt surreal to him, like reality had been warped in an inexplicable way.

Twice he stopped, having heard some large animal moving in the small, green space next to him, but he couldn't identify its source with either mana sight or his regular vision. He quickened his pace as the feeling of being watched unnerved him.

It didn't exactly surprise him when the black squirrel jumped down onto the road, but he wasn't happy about it. Another one followed the first, and he turned to glance behind him and saw that one had blocked his retreat as well. Originally a gift from Canada to America in the early 1900s, the caretaker of the national zoo immediately released the animals into a park, and they had spread throughout the DC metro area over the next hundred years. These squirrels were obviously mana twisted; they were about three feet long from nose to the base of their tail, which then doubled that length. They were also far more aggressive than they should be, and their auras were a faint mixture of green and red.

Drew shook his head. It wasn't the time to think about history lessons when he was likely about to be attacked by squirrels. The two in front of him were spread out enough that a fireball wasn't going to hit them both, and he really didn't like not being able to see all three at the same time. He glanced behind himself again and cast an acid dart at the one there, trying to force it to advance. He didn't count on how fast they would be as it nimbly dodged out of the way of the projectile while chittering angrily at him.

He had never not hit his target with that spell before. This was bad.

The two squirrels that had been south of him had begun rushing forward when he turned his attention to the one behind him. Great, pack tactics. Drew didn't have time to curse out loud, but he pointed a finger at the two squirrels and began running towards them.

Mana may have twisted them to make them more aggressive, but it hadn't been long enough that the natural prey animal instincts didn't take over for a moment. They both diverted away from Drew, who charged past them and then fired a cone of frost blindly behind him.

The angry squawk he heard told Drew that he had made at least some contact. He blink stepped the full fifty feet the spell allowed down the pavement and then pivoted, launching a fireball at his afterimage. The fireball exploded near the first one right as it jumped to attack the image. He detonated the fireball with the squirrel within its blast radius, singing its black fur. The blast caused the already airborne beast to change direction abruptly, impacting the tree line with a crunch. The other two were unaffected by the blast but seemed confused by his disappearance.

He took the time to begin casting storm, assuming they would see him and attack sooner rather than later. He was correct; two seconds of disorientation was all the time he was given. With three seconds left on the cast, he wasn't sure if it would be enough time. He aborted the cast a second later to launch a cone of frostfire with one hand and a frostfire ball with the other. They were too close to dodge, and they took both spells full on. One of the squirrel's face was cut into shreds by the ice shards while the other rocked back on a leg that had frozen to the ground, bending in an unnatural way.

He launched a spark at the one squirrel that still had a face and then backed up, not sure if any of them were still alive enough to pose a threat.

Something hard impacted into blade barrier behind him, and he turned around to find a fourth squirrel. It tried to bite his leg again before he could respond. He kicked as hard as he could, none of his close-range attacks off cooldown yet. His hand searched for the dagger he had picked up from the first orc attack as he jumped onto the last squirrel, trusting in mana guard to keep him alive while he stabbed it into the thing's flesh.

The squirrel was a lot harder to keep a hold of than he had anticipated. Wriggling around, he could see flashes of yellow light where its claws raked against his mana guard. He pulled the dagger out and then tried to stab its chest, but it rolled, and the blade glanced off a rib, doing only minor damage.

Slamming his body weight into the thing to keep it from wriggling, he stabbed again, and this time the blade pierced it between the ribs. The creature let out a wild scream and then bucked, throwing Drew off. It tried to move away from the human, but the blade hindered its movement to a crawl. Drew cast another bolt of electricity and then followed it up with an acid dart to its head. It twitched a few times and then collapsed, still.

Drew heaved himself up, looking around for any other threats in the area but found himself alone again. With a sigh of relief, he went to stand up, only to realize that somewhere in the fight the squirrel had scored a five-inch-long, relatively shallow gash down his calf.

"Fuck," he cursed, sitting back down. He pulled the backpack around in front of him, grabbing a bottle of water. He drank a gulp or two and then poured the rest of it on the wound, wincing as the liquid encountered his torn flesh. He then ripped off portions of the spare shirt he had packed and used it as a bandage before casting refresh on himself.

Standing up again, he gingerly put weight on the leg to test it. "Well, that's fucking amazing." It could support his weight, but he wouldn't be fast. He was about halfway to the commissary but was heading into unknown territory when he could no longer effectively run. This was a bad idea. However, if they didn't get help for Sarah soon, she might never wake up. He looked at the squirrel corpses around him, their auras having already faded to leave them colorless and weighed his options. Then he slung the backpack over his shoulders again and began limping south, towards Bolling.

The slow walk down the frontage road was otherwise uneventful, for which Drew was grateful, as his leg was beginning to ache more and more. About a mile down the road, the tree line ended and there was a slight bank down to an eight-foot-tall wall. Standing next to the wall and staring up, he considered his options. If his leg wasn't injured, he could probably jump up and climb over the wall.

Casting gravitas, it took almost five seconds to float up to the top of the wall and another ten to make his way down the other side, landing with a grunt when his bad leg took the weight.

Crossing the wall, he'd landed on a field surrounding a parking lot. Directly ahead of him was the Defense Intelligence Agency or DIA building. He had attended a few trainings there, and if he recalled correctly, it was the tallest building on the base.

That probably made it the safest place for him to go. If he gravitated to the top of it, he could get a good view of the base and hopefully avoid any more mana twisted predators like those gods damned squirrels.

"Stupid fourth squirrel," he muttered to himself. As he crossed the parking lot, he considered the building in front of him. The nearest portion was only two to three stories tall, rather low compared to the eight-story portion of the building he was headed for. If he took his time, he could blink step up the building easily and then make his way across the roof to the taller sections.

Between them were a few guard posts and parking lots. The DIA complex's parking garage was due west, but like everywhere he had seen, it was mostly empty. The overnight guys must have parked somewhere else.

He stopped at the vehicle checkpoint where there were no guards. And again, no sign of blood. What had happened to everyone? He was in the middle of one of the most important buildings in DC. Thousands of the movers and shakers in the nation's capital passed through this building daily. Yet there were no guards, no signs of life. Would they have evacuated already? How long had it been?

His mind turned over the possibilities as he made his slow way through the abandoned fortifications. He failed the timing on his second blink step, landing with his weight at the wrong point and tripping, falling over the guardrail and getting small rocks embedded in his hands when he stuck them out to break his fall.

"Fuckity fuck," he cursed as he sat up and began digging rocks out of his hands. Several of them were deep enough that he had to pull out his pocket knife and cut them out. He then pulled out another bottle of water. He only had a few more bottles, he realized with a frown, but he suppressed his groans and washed out the dirt and grime, then wrapped his hands with what was left of the shirt he had used to bandage his leg.

That's when he heard the noise.

It was a dull thudding, like a drum. He frowned. It seemed to be coming from the other side of the building, and he quickly advanced the last couple hundred feet and cast gravitas on himself again, floating up the side of the building. He shot past the top and then reduced his gravity until he was floating free in the air. Casting blink step, he landed on the roof, not wanting to worry about controlling the landing properly with gravitas.

He could hear the throbbing better now; it was coming from the open area on the south side of the DIA building. When he finally reached the corner, he caught sight of his first human life since Katie.

The public entrance of the DIA building was adjacent to several parking lots and a couple baseball fields off to the west as well as a well-maintained soccer field to the south. Moving around on the soccer field about half a mile away were a few dozen humans. They appeared to be dragging other humans to a large stack of wood they had built up in the center of the field.

The source of the throbbing sound was indeed a set of drums. Three figures were seated and beating on a single drum that must have been at least a meter in diameter, although it was hard to tell at this distance and it might have been much bigger.

He watched entranced as they dragged half a dozen people—or were they bodies? They weren't moving—over to the pile of wood, carefully placing them on top of it. Once all they had all been placed on the wood, the figures all stood in a circle around it, except for one who stood closer and began gesturing with his hands. He could hear words being shouted, but it was difficult to make them out over the wind and the drums.

The one in the center then pointed at the woodpile, and a crack of lightning descended from the sky, catching the wood on fire with a thunderous boom. That's when he heard the screams. The people in the fire were crying out in pain and fear. They were still alive.

Drew slumped back down onto the roof, his face turning white as he realized that he had just witnessed people being sacrificed.

Chapter Twenty — Ashes

He kept telling himself that there was nothing he could do against twenty people. He almost believed it. Could he cast a storm out that far? None of his spells listed a range he could cast them at. They all originated from him, but how far could a fireball fly?

Spending however long it had been in the close confines inside of HQ, he hadn't had a lot of opportunities to try out how far away he could cast his spells. He peeked back over the wall, studying the figures standing around the circle. Each was clothed in robes that covered their entire body. If he cast storm on them, they would die, and he would be a murderer.

He had already killed sentient beings before. Was he already a murderer? There was something comforting about the fact that the orc blood had been green, inhuman. Some part of him was convinced that because they weren't human, it was alright. He frowned, realizing how slippery that slope could be. Just because they weren't human didn't mean that they deserved death. Or did it? Humanity was locked in an eons-long fight against someone. What if that someone was the orcs? Didn't that mean they were at war? Plus, they had attacked him first, had killed Juan and Mitch. Even if they claimed that humans had killed their people, they were still the aggressors in that fight.

Had he been shanghaied into an intergalactic Hatfield and McCoy scenario without realizing it?

Shaking his head again, Drew cleared his existential crisis thoughts away. He could deal with them later. Besides, he knew it was just his mind trying to find an alternative to thinking about that ash filled morning five years ago. There was no way for him to save those people on the pyre. Or was there? He began casting refreshing rain. He felt it was unlikely that they would be able to pinpoint his location; he would just be another minuscule dot on the roof half a mile away. Unless they had a skill to see where the spell was coming from or something...

After five seconds, the rain appeared; he could indeed cast it from this distance. The blaze had only been burning for just over a minute. However, they had clearly used some sort of accelerant, as the rain didn't seem to have any effect on the blaze. The robed people around the fire had a very different reaction; the drumming stopped, and everyone ceased to move or chant.

Had they been sacrificing these people to some form of weather god? The thunderbolt they used to light the fire made that likely. If so, did this mean their god was angry at them or happy with them? Drew's fingers were already tracing another casting. He aimed for the figure that had called the lightning bolt, whom he designated as the head cultist.

He couldn't save these people; they were already as good as dead, but he could at least give them a quicker death than suffocation and bring some vengeance on their tormentors. Frostfire storm formed slightly off center of the pyre, encompassing the head cultist and several additional cultists in its blast radius. Without stopping, he began to cast firestorm, which then caught an additional four cultists. By now, the cultists had broken ranks and begun to run, their sense of self-preservation forcing them into action. Drew smiled grimly as the majority of them made a break towards him, bunching up enough for him to hit them with his spells a few more times before they could reach safety.

After finishing the cast on firestorm, he immediately began to cast ice storm on those that were running towards him. He had contained all but a handful of the cultists that had scattered to the south and west within his stormy vengeance. He turned his attention to the frostfire storm that was about to expire. He was ready to cast his last storm spell if there was anything still standing, but the storm cleared, and all that remained were motionless bodies on the ground.

The storm had ripped their clothing, revealing their dark skin. But what caused the hard lump in his throat to go away was that several of them had pools of blood around them. Green blood.

A notification popped up in the corner of his vision, so he figured that meant he was out of combat. Glancing at them quickly, he didn't see gravitas mentioned, so he ignored them for now. He waited, wanting to ensure all the cultists were dead and that no reinforcements were going to arrive. Once satisfied, he made his way to the west side of the building and then jumped off it. His stomach lurched from the fall, responding to his instincts telling him he was falling to his death, despite his brain telling it that he would be safe. Casting gravitas halfway through his fall, he slowed down until he was free floating a foot or two above the ground and then lowered himself slowly to the grass.

Limping again, he skirted the road, eyeing the houses that were between him and the commissary. Base housing wasn't large, but he didn't really want to come across a mana twisted dog. He also wanted a better look at the cultists. He avoided the houses by walking through the field.

The first clump of dead cultists he came across were torn to shreds, sharp hail, wind, and lightning having done a number on them. The smell was horrible. He covered his nose and mouth with his shirt as he approached. He counted three heads. The first two spells had caught the clear majority of them. These three had just been either lucky or faster than the others.

Their faces were clearly not human; a flat, pig nose, feral, red eyes, and sharp fangs made up most of their facial features. Their skin up close was a green so dark that it was almost black, without any hair on their bodies. It was hard to say if there was an analogy to any mythological creature he had ever seen in a game; he certainly couldn't think of anything.

None of them had xatherite growing out of them, and their auras, if they had had one, were long gone by the time he inspected the corpses. But he did find a couple of wicked looking knives. Well, more like kris, since their blades were wavy. He tried to remember if there was a length requirement for a kris. He couldn't remember but felt like these were too short.

"So much for knowing how to find that information," Drew muttered, his brain having discarded tons of useless information in favor of knowing how to find it on the internet.

The next group was in a similar state. He counted seven bodies. Although it was difficult to tell, they seemed to be extra vulnerable to fire, their burns rather more extensive than the orcs had been after frostfire. He decided to call these new creatures trolls since that was the only creature that looked even vaguely like them that was vulnerable to fire that he could think of now.

"Why would they sacrifice people by fire if they were more vulnerable to it?" Drew asked himself as he made his way through the rubble and towards the third group. The sacrificial fire still smoldered, and none of the bodies within it moved. He counted another six troll bodies here. None of them looked any different, but he couldn't imagine the head cultist surviving. And none of them had xatherite.

He frowned. That head cultist should have been a 'boss' and should have dropped xatherite. He looked around him—there was no sign that something had gotten away. A shield spell and a teleport maybe? Or was it because he wasn't in the dungeon anymore and xatherite was rarer out here?

Delaying as long as he could while looking at the dead trolls, he then walked towards the pyre. He smelled burned, human flesh. The scent of the burnt trolls had been more... bitter, more like charcoal, but human flesh had a sweet scent to it; his fingers clenched into fists as he flashed back to that night in the Caribbean all those years ago.

Black smoke marred the morning light. The fire had been put out quickly but not soon enough. Sixteen bodies... Doc said they had suffocated from the smoke in the cabin rather than the heat, that the fire had only begun burning them after they were already dead. He looked down, and his hands were covered in ash. It was the smell he knew he would never forget.

He reached out for Zoey; she always came to him when he had the flashbacks. There wasn't any barking, though, and then he remembered where he was. He had fallen to his knees, bad leg forgotten as the memories surfaced. He gulped air; the wind had shifted, coming from the northeast now, and he welcomed the switch to sewage and distant rain. The base had been built adjacent to the district's treatment plant, one of the reasons it could be allowed to be as big and sprawling as it was while still being in DC.

Shaking himself out of his memory, he pushed back to his feet. None of the sacrifices moved, but they were clearly human. He wiped his hands clean of the imaginary ashes, fighting off another flashback as he turned away from the scent and limped away.

"Hello," A voice sounded in his head, and he looked around, his hands ready to cast more spells.

"Hey now, calm down! I'm human; I'm not here to hurt you." The voice was masculine, but as Drew turned his head looking for the source, he didn't see anyone. Then at the edge of his vision, approaching slowly was an aura like the one around Sarah or Katie but made of indigo, violet, and green. He pointed his fingers at the aura.

"Woah, woah, don't shoot!" A thin black man appeared within the aura; he looked to be in his mid-twenties and was wearing blue jeans and a jacket. "I just saw your fireworks show. We're on the same side."

Drew narrowed his eyes. "Who are you? Why couldn't I see you?"

"I'm Daryl. You couldn't see me because I have an invisibility xatherite." Daryl paused, waiting for Drew to ask any questions. "How did you know where I was?"

"It's a secret." The two stared at each other. Drew was still shaken from the flashback and knew he wasn't in a place to make good mental calls.

"Look, we can do this whole spy vs. spy thing later. We need to get inside before the mana storm hits." Daryl turned to point with his face towards the northeast.

Drew frowned. A massive storm cloud had appeared in the last few minutes and was moving towards them at a visible rate. Instead of the normal black clouds, it held the seven colors of the xatherite in all their darkest variations. "What the fuck is that thing?"

"I call 'em the mana storms. They really mess everything up, though. Their water isn't safe... and it's gonna hit soon, so we need to get inside." When Drew nodded, he lowered his hands. "Come with me, I got a spot where I've been laying low."

Drew followed Daryl, who clearly wanted to walk faster than Drew could with his limp, but neither of the two said another word as they headed for the housing area to the northwest of them. Daryl turned into the third house, looking around. "Don't see any green skins, so we should be fine." He unlocked the front door, and they went in. Drew took a moment to let his eyes adjust to the sudden darkness. Outside, he could hear the wind picking up as the edge of the storm started to hit the area.

Daryl waited until Drew was in and the door was locked before turning back to him and saying excitedly, "Man, how did you do that? We tried to fight them when they first showed up, but they just shrugged off the guns like they were nothing."

"I guess that reaffirms my troll theory; they seem to be vulnerable to fire," Drew said. The room was dark because all the blinds had been pulled shut, but he could see through the hallway into the kitchen where tinfoil lined the window over the sink.

"Nice, now if only we could throw fireballs at them, we'd be set," Daryl said, laughing as he led Drew up the stairs. "I found this place on the second day after the green skins came marching out of the DIA building and rounded everyone up. Key was under the mat." The upstairs had been barricaded; desks, chairs, and nightstands had turned it into a narrow walkway that zigged and zagged through the hallway, ending in the master bedroom.

"How did you escape capture? The only reason I'm still out here is that I went invisible and slipped out. Been looking for other people ever since."

"Just made my way here from CGHQ," Drew answered after a moment of thought, now that the stress of his flashback was over. He could tell he had been acting weird, but Daryl had a friendly way to him that was quickly putting Drew at ease. "You stationed on the base?" Drew asked.

"No, I've been out for a few years now; my wife is stationed here," Daryl answered as they finally made their way into the room. The bed had been set up near the wall, and a table of food—mostly canned—and paper plates sat in the other. The rest of the room's furniture seemed to have been commandeered for the barricade.

"Your wife?" Drew asked, looking around for another person.

"Yeah, she was herded with the rest of them into the DIA building," Daryl answered.

"That where the sacrifices came from?"

"Yeah, she hasn't been burned yet. They've only done that twice now, both times right before a storm."

Chapter Twenty-One — Daryl

Drew had been peering out of the corner of a window, enraptured by the beautiful colors of the storm around the house. The rain seemed to catch different colors as it fell, looking like oil-slicked water, the different blasts of lightning changing the colors in a captivating, rippling mosaic of colors. He turned away from the window to look back at Daryl, who he realized had clenched his fists together. Obviously, he had missed some sort of reaction from the other man.

"I'm sorry, I didn't mean to upset you," Drew said, realizing how heartless his questions had been.

Daryl seemed to be quickly regaining his composure, and with a shrug, he sat down on a nightstand. "It's okay; you didn't know."

Drew sat down on the only chair in the room; it was positioned near the window, and he assumed Daryl used it to watch what was going on outside. Both men took a few moments to collect their thoughts. "Thanks for telling me about the storm, by the way," he said finally, not knowing how to breach the massive elephant in the room.

Daryl nodded his head. "It's the least I could do in return for you killing all those green skins." Both men had so much they wanted to ask, but no real idea how to start talking.

"I was in a bunker for the last couple... days? Since the Advent anyway; it was hard to tell how much time had passed down there without light or watches. How long has it been?" Drew asked, figuring that was the easiest way to open the conversation.

"It'll be a full week tonight," Daryl answered. "That first day was crazy, everyone got woken up by the voice. Mae, my wife, and I both slotted our xatherite immediately and lost consciousness. By the time we woke up, it was morning. The general had organized everything fairly well by then. They had people going around finding out what xatherite everyone had and keeping order."

"The attacks started happening around noon—squirrels, rabbits, turtles, a few dogs, and cats, pretty much every creature around. They would only attack small groups, though, so the general had everyone bring all their stuff to the commissary and implemented battle buddy rules," Daryl said, his eyes going distant.

"The green skins appeared midway through the third day. They must have taken out the sentries and then stormed inside. They took all our non-combatants, and then the General surrendered. I managed to escape as they were herding everyone into the DIA building. Went invisible and followed along as much as I could. But I couldn't get into the building."

"How many people do they have in there?" Drew asked.

"I'm not sure, three, maybe four hundred at this point. They sacrificed ten people both times before the mana storm."

"Any of them healers? We had to fight our way out of the bunker; only three of us made it out alive, and one of them is badly hurt. We have no idea what's wrong with her." Drew glanced outside, frowning. He needed to get back to Katie before dark, but the storm was a complication he hadn't considered.

"If we can get them out? Yeah, probably. They had me mostly out patrolling around the base, but I think we had some healers. Does that mean you'll help me get them out?" Daryl asked, leaning forward on the nightstand.

"Yeah, of course. I'm not just going to let the trolls kill them. I just told my people I'd be back by dark. How long did the last storm last?"

"A couple hours. Hard to say really, but I doubt you'll be back before dark. I wouldn't recommend traveling at night either. The really scary shit comes out at night."

Drew turned from the window to look at Daryl. "What do you mean the really scary shit?"

Daryl shivered slightly. "The bugs. They're almost all nocturnal, but you can hear them even through the windows."

Drew looked outside again and then frowned. "Well, shit. We almost died when we had to fight the cockroaches." There were only a few hours until dark as it was, so there was no chance he would be able to get back today. If he could get a healer and be back in the morning, though, that would be worth the delay. "Well, what about the trolls? How many of them are there?"

"Uh, hard to say. Another fifty? Most of them don't seem to have ranged weapons, though, so we could have taken them, but," Daryl frowned, "they didn't really seem to be affected by bullets. I mean, they got hit, and it would stop them, but it didn't kill them like what you did. They just got back up. It was more a war of attrition than anything else; I don't think we really started to hurt them until they got in close and some of the guys that had red skills started attacking."

"And you haven't been in the building at all? No idea where they're being kept?" Drew asked.

"Nope, I imagine it's underground though," Daryl said with a shrug.

Drew ran a hand through his hair. "Well, shit." He made to stand up and pace the room, but his leg hurt too much, and he sat back down, thinking. In the close confines of the building, it would be suicide to go in there, especially without knowing where they were.

Daryl took a jar of applesauce off the table next to him and began eating it. He held one up to Drew, who took it without thinking.

"I don't think I can kill them in close quarters like the building; we need a way to draw them out," Drew finally said, leaning back in the chair and beginning to eat the applesauce. Then he looked down at the sauce in his hands, "What are the trolls doing for food? Are they raiding the commissary?"

"Yeah, they send a couple humans out every morning to bring back a bunch of food, with about twenty gre-trolls to guard them," Daryl said. "I wasn't ever able to get too close, not sure what sort of senses those things have. And I don't have any red xatherite."

"What do you have?" Drew asked, curious if there was a solution there.

"Well, you've seen the invisibility, that and a kind of weird one called necro alchemy are my two intermediates. And then I have the telepathy, another type of invisibility, and a self-cleaning spell," Daryl said with a shrug. "Nothing that's likely to help you much."

Drew had noticed that Daryl was clean, which only surprised him when he realized just how filthy he was. Daryl's cleanliness was like what the world used to be, back when laundry machines and showers were a thing. "What does necro alchemy do?" Drew asked, frowning as he dug his finger into the applesauce, trying to get the last of it out. His stomach was reminding him that he was hungry.

"It allows me to harvest a corpse of its goods, like fur or meat, without having to actually touch it," Daryl answered, grabbing a tin of pears and popping the top off before holding it out to Drew. "You guys didn't get much food up there?"

"Not real food, just gas station food, chips, jerky, and stuff," Drew said. Looking at the contents of the food table Daryl had, he realized it was all fruit, crackers, and other vegetarian options.

"Vegetarian?" Drew asked after a moment.

Daryl laughed. "Yeah, trying to get rid of the animal cruelty aspect of food preparation. Seems a little silly now that people are getting eaten by rabbits, but," he shrugged, "habit, I guess."

Drew nodded with a shrug, pulling out some of the jerky from his pack, "Do you mind?" He wanted something a little more solid than fruit. Daryl just shook his head and began eating the pears.

A particularly loud crack of lightning struck near the house, and both paused for a moment, glancing out the window before returning to their conversation.

"So, what's the difference between the two invisibilities?" Drew asked between chewing jerky.

"First one blocks the visual spectrum. I use that and the cleaning to remove my scent and try to stay quiet. The second one is supposed to block the magical spectrum, but I have no idea what that means. I use it occasionally, doesn't seem to make much of a difference," Daryl answered.

Drew pondered that. It was probably a lower level xatherite, which meant that mana sight, as a rare xatherite, was more powerful and made Daryl's spell ineffective?

"Cool, and the telepathy thing, what are its limits?" Drew asked. He had already opened the grid and found that Daryl was not listed as someone whose map he could investigate. He wondered why, but then figured it must have to do with how they viewed each other. Sarah and Katie thought of themselves as a group, but Daryl clearly still had reservations about him, just like he had concerns about Daryl. Juan had been a good kid, but Daryl's aura was still mostly indigo, which meant he was practiced in deception.

"I can only do one target at a time, and I have to be able to see them and be pretty close, within fifteen meters," Daryl answered, looking at Drew expectantly.

"I've got the storm spell, which you saw, and then it linked with a fireball and cone of cold spell, both of which are area effect, to make the other variants of it." Drew considered how much he should tell Daryl. "I've also got a few more single target spells and a spell called dancing sword, which allows me to conjure a sword that fights on its own."

Daryl whistled. "Damn, that's a lot of red. You must be an angry guy."

"Angry?" Drew asked, confused. He didn't consider himself an angry person.

"Yeah, we realized that what xatherite you got was pretty well based around your personality. Me, I was always just trying to keep out of trouble, and I got a bunch of stuff that would allow me to remain unseen. The hothead eighteen-year-old kids got reds that made them able to hit stuff. Angela, who was always trying to improve herself, got a bunch of orange spells. Stuff like that," Daryl explained.

"Well, I don't consider myself angry," Drew said with a frown. He'd had an anger issue when he was younger, but he'd learned to control that a long time ago.

"Anyway, I think I have a plan for how we can ambush the food group, and hopefully, we'll get some more combatants out of that," Drew said, and then he explained what he wanted to do. Daryl nodded slowly as he followed along.

"Well, it's a long shot, but probably our best chance," Daryl said when he was done. He excused himself to use the restroom, and Drew took a moment to fully view the messages he had ignored after killing the trolls.

Congratulations, Midshipman. Your Major Refresh xatherite is ready to be upgraded.

Congratulations, Midshipman. Your Major Spark xatherite is ready to be upgraded.

Congratulations, Midshipman. Your Major Mana Guard xatherite is ready to be upgraded.

Congratulations, Midshipman. Your Major Acid Dart has reached level 3. Damage has increased.

Congratulations, Midshipman. Your Cone of Frost has reached level 3. Damage has increased.

Congratulations, Midshipman. Your Fireball has reached level 3. Damage has increased.

Congratulations, Midshipman. Your Storm has reached level 3. Damage has increased.

He clicked to upgrade major refresh and winced as a headache immediately came over him. Unlike his other upgrades, this one hurt—not as bad as slotting it would have, but still quite a bit. Giving it a moment to subside, he then upgraded the other two to similar results.

Xatherite Crystal Name: Minor Lightning Bolt
Xatherite Color: Red
Xatherite Grade: Common
Xatherite Rarity: Widespread
Type: Magic
Effect: Creates a bolt of electricity from any body part to a target no more than 15m away. Deals Lightning damage and stuns the target for 2 seconds.
Mana recharge time: 4.2 seconds

Xatherite Crystal Name: Minor Energize
Xatherite Color: Orange
Xatherite Grade: Common
Xatherite Rarity: Widespread
Type: Magic
Effect: Infuses mana into the target to reduce fatigue and lactic acid buildup. Improves the target's natural healing by 2x normal for 24 hours.
Mana recharge time: 20 minutes, 39 seconds

Xatherite Crystal Name: Minor Mana Shield
Xatherite Color: Yellow
Xatherite Grade: Common
Xatherite Rarity: Widespread
Type: Magic

Effect: Creates a shield of mana around the caster. This shield will absorb moderate amounts of energy and kinetic damage. It also creates a slowing effect around the caster.
Mana recharge time: 4 minutes, 33 seconds

After looking at the new descriptions, he realized that there was a qualitative change when you moved from basic to common that caused the pain, but boy, was it worth it.

Spark had upgraded to lightning bolt and could reach five times further! Its damage had also been upgraded, and it had gained a stunning component. That moved it from one of his less used spells to a spell he could use on a regular basis to great effect. Refresh had also greatly improved, becoming able to help him heal faster. He immediately cast it on himself. Looking at his leg, twice as fast wasn't that much, but it meant he would be just a little bit better off than he would have been otherwise. Of course, the new mana shield also made it easier for him to dodge things, as they would move slower near him, giving him a bit more survivability.

Chapter Twenty-Two — Night Watch

Drew watched Daryl sleep. He hadn't told the other man about his energize spell, but they had agreed to take turns and Drew opted to go first. He had no intention of waking Daryl up. The other man was asleep and invisible on a bench he hadn't seen behind the door. He shook his head as he glanced at the bed, where blankets in the form of a person sleeping under the covers lay conspicuously. Daryl had prepared his safe house by making navigating the hallway difficult enough that they would make some noise in the dark, which should wake him up. He then hid where he slept behind the door.

"There's probably some sort of long-term negative effect of not sleeping," Drew mused to himself as he looked out the window.

Glancing towards the HQ building, he hoped that Katie and Sarah were safe during the night. He should have been back already, and being held up unexpectedly by the storm made him nervous for the two women. They were probably fine; Katie's walls would allow them to hold off any attack until he got there tomorrow afternoon. After a few minutes, he was able to dismiss his unease.

The storm had passed with the sun, the multicolored water leaving no trace that it had ever been there. It led to some interesting questions about how physics and mana interacted.

As far as he could tell, the energy and mass created by casting his spells came from nowhere, affected the world for as long as it was designed to, and then returned to nowhere. For example, all his water and ice spells created matter, but as soon as the duration of the spell was over, that matter disappeared. That broke the first law of thermodynamics unless it was pulling energy from a plane of existence or type of energy that humans currently had no sense for.

For that matter, what exactly was he seeing when he looked at the ley lines and auras around him? Was he piercing the veil into some alternative energy plane of existence that overlapped this one? Or was it just a type of energy that existed normally, and humans simply hadn't been able to detect it until now? What exactly was mana?

Drew realized that he only kind of understood electromagnetic force, one of the four—five?—fundamental interactions. Even then, he hadn't been anywhere near an expert in understanding it. He probably wasn't going to be making any major breakthroughs on the principles of mana.

He ducked back from the window as a particularly large bug flew by, holding still lest it sense him somehow. The glass seemed like a flimsy defense against such things, and after waiting for it to move on, he stood up, limped back towards the bed, and sat down next to the fake person on it.

What did all this mean? Electronics ceasing to work and spells that caused energy to be created and destroyed in an instant. What was the connection there? He felt like it was relevant, something that would help him in the upcoming fight, but he dismissed it as something he couldn't really make any progress on currently. His eyes drifted around the room, and he saw a family photo on a wall—a father, mother, and two kids. Were they still alive?

The base had been relatively protected and well organized, and even then, Daryl said the monsters had killed fifty percent of the people before the end of the first day. They hadn't even sent scouts off the base, the general having considered it too dangerous.

Was this all because they were close to the primary nexus? He stared at the ley lines glowing under the ground and concentrating in DC, considering the nexus as he pondered what exactly it had done to the humans in the region. Were the enemies stronger here? Or just more numerous? Did the extra and more powerful xatherite they had gotten put them in a better spot, an equal spot? Or had it not even compensated them for the extra danger?

The problem was the lack of information. Drew had spent his high school years at the cusp of the mobile phone revolution. He remembered the days where you would knock on your friend's door without knowing if they were home and called the house phone of a girl you liked, having to talk to her father before you could ask her out. He had also grown accustomed to the instantaneous information stream modern society had allowed and the sheer depth of knowledge contained on the internet, all accessed through a device you carried with you into the bathroom because it was convenient to look at memes while you used it.

That world was gone; he couldn't even get accurate information from outside the walls of the base's gates. Daryl had gone out a few times, but only after the fourth day, looking for survivors. They had either been gone or too well hidden for his cursory search. However, he had also been too afraid to start shouting for fear of attracting monsters. Could they all have hunkered down in their houses to hide from the world? What about the loss of life due to the storms, people who got stuck outside and then just disappeared? Daryl had told him about the one person he had seen out during a storm; he had been dragging belongings into the commissary but had dissolved before he could reach safety.

He shook his head away from that grisly image. Even if humanity did survive, almost an entire generation had been killed. Xatherite apparently didn't activate until sometime after puberty. All the kids younger than about fifteen had been told that due to their maturity, their personalities hadn't developed enough to determine the state of their grid, and their beginning xatherite allowance had been deferred. It made the children even easier targets to the monsters, and the loss of life of those under fifteen had been almost absolute, even before the trolls had appeared.

How does a society recover from that, especially when it likely wouldn't be safe to raise children for years to come? He ran a hand through his hair as he considered the implications to Earth's humanity. In a week, half the world's population had died; at the rate they were going, they would be lucky to have ten percent survive the year. Then they would face the issues of a population that was getting increasingly older with almost no new workforce for decades to come.

Magic might be able to keep people active for longer, healing the aches and pains and allowing for an older generation to still be relevant in what was bound to be a more physically demanding society than what 21st-century western civilization had required of its citizens. Even then, how were they going to feed their severely diminished population? How many people even knew how to grow a crop? How did you defend a crop from nocturnal bug invasions?

They would have to go back to being nomads.

Suddenly not feeling safe, Drew stood up and cast his buffs. His leg and hands still hurt quite a bit from the day's injuries, but he was reasonably confident he would be back up to full mobility in a week—if he survived that long. Although honestly, if they didn't find a healer tomorrow, they were probably all dead anyway.

Drew reviewed the plan again. Really, it amounted to nothing more than throwing a fireball at the trolls and hoping they chased him like the orcs had. He'd be far enough away that he could cast a storm between him and them, and Daryl said he knew of a good spot where they would be confined between two walls and unable to spread out. Meanwhile, Daryl would throw some Molotov cocktails at the trolls from invisibility; hopefully, the mundane fire would work as well as the magical kind had.

Once the storm had passed, Drew would take out the stragglers. They would hopefully be infuriated by the presence of a red mage. The logic was that the stragglers would think all his spells were still recharging, causing in them a desire to charge him. Fireballs, frostfire cone, and lightning bolts should be enough to take out those last few that remained. As a plan, it sucked. It relied far too heavily on things going the hopeful way and them having not developed any ranged options of their own in the past few days.

He could think of dozens of possible ways for this to go wrong, but he couldn't think of a better solution with their assets at hand. Even if they did win... what then? When they ambush the trolls successfully, then kill more trolls and rescued everyone, then what? Was he going to be responsible for all these people just because he saved them? That's what had happened with the group at HQ. He had come in and because he could fight, they had depended on him. Because of that, Juan and Mitch were dead, and Sarah might as well be.

He began pacing despite the pain in his leg. He was in so far over his head that he didn't even know if there was air up there anymore.

"Nervous?" Daryl asked. Sometime while he had been lost in thought, the man had sat up and was staring at him, visible again.

Drew nodded his head. "Everyone I've tried to help since this whole thing started, they're almost all dead. I'm... I guess I'm just afraid that if we fail tomorrow, I'm going to let down a lot of people. I'm also worried about my friends. They expected me to be back yesterday, and if I don't make it back, they're going to be mostly helpless and stuck."

"Drew, sit down," Daryl said with some emphasis. When he obeyed, Daryl looked at him. "You're getting pre-battle jitters, it's understandable. You were in the coast guard; all of your combat was reactionary. You didn't have hours to think about all the things that could go wrong. When I was in the army, my first couple of weeks in Iraq, I was just like you are now. Eventually, you learn how to deal with it."

"But here's the thing you have that I didn't. You've already been in a ton of fights, and you came out alive. You're not going to freeze up when you realize that your life is in danger, and I'm gonna guess you're one hell of a scrapper." Daryl looked around. "I know the plan has a lot of things that could go wrong, and stuff probably will; it always does. But we're going to rescue all those people, and we're going to be fine. We'll do this together."

"I just, I'm not the guy who should be doing this. I'm a nerd," Drew explained. "My hobbies are Pathfinder, WoW, and playing with my dog."

"Yeah? So what? You fought your way out of a dungeon and then stopped a cultist sacrifice. I think that sounds exactly like what you would do in Pathfinder or WoW. Your experience is relevant here; heck, you're a mage in real life now. Who cares if those were just games? Think of them as battle simulations that all trained you for this," Daryl said with a bit of a laugh. "Hell, I wish I would have played more of them; maybe then I wouldn't be mostly worthless in a fight."

Drew shook his head. "You're not worthless, you're just... specialized in a different way. Against a foe that could be hurt by weapons, you'd be deadly. You're built to be an assassin. Just because this is a paper and scissors fight doesn't mean there won't be fights down the road where you're the rock to their scissors. That's what I learned in Pathfinder; there's always a counter."

Daryl raised his hands in surrender. "I get it." He looked at Drew and then frowned, changing the subject, "What I don't get is why you don't look tired. You can't have slept in at least twenty hours, and you look damn well rested."

"I... might not have been completely forthcoming about what spells that I have," Drew answered cautiously. "I have one called refresh, well, energize now, that keeps me from needing sleep."

"Damn, when was the last time you actually slept?" Daryl asked.

"Other than slotting xatherite? The day before Advent," Drew supplied the answer while studying the other man's face.

Daryl stood back up and walked over to the window, considering what Drew said. "I get why you wouldn't trust me." The night was still dark, but the occasional shriek of a bat could be heard outside. Drew didn't want to consider what a bat that fed on these massive bugs would be like. "I just want my wife back, Drew. I'll do anything to get her back, and... you're my best, my only hope for that."

"Did you just Princess Leia me?" Drew asked incredulously.

Daryl smirked and sat down in the chair. "Can you cast that energize spell on me? Since I'm up, might as well talk a bit more."

Drew nodded. "Sure, I can do that. Just give me a bit. It's still recharging for another fifteen minutes or so."

The two passed the time joking about movies; they both had similar tastes and talked for some time about Shawshank Redemption and The Bourne Identity.

An hour later, the sun was starting to rise and both men, now much more comfortable with each other, set out from the house, getting the bottles of alcohol, rags, and lighters needed for Daryl's portion of the event while Drew cleared their ambush site of the remaining night critters. He was happy to discover that the new lightning bolt could two shot most of the centipedes and other insects that lingered through the dawn.

Once the area was cleared, he made his way to the peak of a roof and began the final bit of waiting.

Chapter Twenty-Three — Burning

Trolls

Wedged in between two roof segments, Drew wished he had taken the time to nail in a board or something. The shingles were loose, and his footing was slightly precarious, but it allowed him to keep a low enough profile that he didn't think anyone would see him before he started launching fireballs. Daryl said the trolls normally came out about two hours after dawn, so he had plenty of time to get bored.

He started aiming his fireballs off towards the Potomac, trying to measure how far they traveled before disappearing. With trial and error, he determined that at around a thousand feet out, it started losing power and then disappeared completely somewhere between fifteen hundred and two thousand feet. It was hard to make accurate assessments of distance without a marked range, but those were his best estimates. He tested his other spells but found the only other one that had a long enough range to be effective was acid dart.

It meant that he was well within the effective range of fireball for this ambush, but depending on how close the trolls guarded the humans, he might have issues with catching a human in the blast. He pushed that thought away and looked around for a spot where he could lay down to take pressure off his leg.

The whole situation was somewhat uncomfortable. The morning sun was incredibly hot, especially reflecting off the black tar of the shingles. The leather vest and dark blue ODU's he wore under it didn't help either. However, they did protect him from the grit on the shingles. He laid down, and his leg twinged slightly in pain as he bumped it a little too hard in the process. "Should probably get shoes instead of boots and a pair of shorts for the heat," he said, thinking out loud.

Running a hand through his hair, he realized that he would need to get a haircut too. Chief would start yelling at him for being out of regs within a couple days at this rate.

He laughed until he realized it was bouncing eerily around the abandoned housing complex. The reverberating echo sounded unnervingly like someone mocking him. How strange it was to have such normal thoughts like haircuts and shoe shopping while he was waiting to ambush a bunch of trolls with magic. It was comforting at the same time to have had such normal thoughts.

Shaking his head at the incongruity, he looked around. He was positioned on a roof back a little way from the road that the trolls took every morning. Between him and the road were two housing units that formed a narrow corridor with a small playground in between them. The trolls would either come straight through the corridor or circle around the two buildings to respond to his attacks. Like most of the plan, it wasn't perfect.

Scanning the road, he poked his head up a little higher and looked over at the DIA building. They hadn't yet exited the big building, but they were due any time now. He then glanced over at the soccer field where the ritual had been performed. He kept thinking that he should see bodies, but they had disappeared either during the night or in the storm. He couldn't tell which he thought was more disturbing: insects capable of eating dozens of bodies, bone and all, overnight, or rain that dissolved bodies in an instant. The fire was also empty, but he could see the reflective shapes of their long daggers in the grass. They were the only thing indicating that a battle had taken place there yesterday.

A flash of light in his eyes caught Drew's attention, and he saw Daryl pointing the mirror at him, their signal to indicate the trolls had left the building. Drew focused his attention on him as Daryl flashed Morse code at him: a short, then four longs, then a pause. One. Three long and two shorts. Eight. Another pause and then a single long. 18T, eighteen trolls. Another pause, and then a short and four long again: one. Four long and a short meant nine.

Then a short, two long, and a short. The letter P. Nineteen people with the trolls. Drew raised his hand to indicate he had received the message, and Daryl disappeared.

Drew realized that he didn't exactly disappear; from his perspective, the body went invisible, but a faint shadow still followed where he must be as it walked to the other side of the road to prepare his portion of the ambush. How did his invisibility work anyway? Did it just bend the light around him? If that was the case, him still casting a shadow made sense. Maybe just a distortion on the ground from where the light had been bent? The shadow was too indistinct not to be affected at all; in fact, against something other than the white pavement of the sidewalk, Drew doubted he would be able to see it at all.

Drew did a quick relaxation technique, tensing and releasing his muscles, trying to limber up for the fight. It would still take fifteen or twenty minutes for them to walk all the way down the road to where he was, and he had a feeling it was going to be one of the longest fifteen minutes he'd ever experienced. He then recast all his shielding spells and hunkered down to wait.

Wiping sweat from his forehead, he waited. Finally, three trolls came into view around the house; they were standing close enough together that Drew wasn't afraid of hitting the humans. Standing up, he launched a fireball slightly ahead of where the three were currently. To Drew, the ball seemed to move in slow motion, and one troll caught the movement out of the corner of its eye. Turning to look, it began to shout but was cut short by the explosion that engulfed all three.

Only fifteen trolls left. Four more had come into view while he took out the first group; they were on either side of a group of humans. One shouted something in a language Drew didn't understand, and all four began to charge towards him. Drew launched a frostfire ball at the first one, but it dove out of the way, taking only glancing damage from a shard of ice that embedded itself in his shoulder.

Acid dart targeted the now prone troll, but its damage didn't seem likely to add much of value to the exchange. He could now see nine trolls, all of which were charging towards him while shouting, and he began to cast frostfire storm. He felt reasonably safe since he was three stories up—that was until one of the trolls in the middle of the pack jumped to the top of the playground in a single bound and pulled something out of a pouch at its side.

Frostfire storm was ready right as the troll drew his arm back to throw whatever he had retrieved. Deciding the one on the playground was the most dangerous of the group, he centered it around him, catching five within the blasts of ice, fire, and lightning. Three, including the one who had fallen prone, were caught behind the storm, but the leading troll was still moving towards him. When he was about sixty feet away, he leaped into the air. His trajectory looked like he would land right next to Drew, but a lightning bolt knocked him back and off course. He landed with a cracking sound on the ground forty feet below.

Switching to cast another storm to get the three stragglers, Drew targeted it near the mouth of the alley, hoping the humans had moved away from it by now. Daryl should have telepathically warned them to back up already, and hopefully, he'd lit a few trolls on fire.

The jumping ability of the trolls had caught him by surprise. He scanned the two surrounding buildings to ensure that they weren't trying to flank him while his fingers went through the motions of casting the storm but didn't see any. When the spell was done, he fired another lightning bolt at the downed troll for good measure.

Twelve of eighteen down. That left six to guard the prisoners. Daryl could probably only take out two or three of them, so Drew backed up to the top of the roof, and with a gulp of air, he began running down the slope, trying to ignore the pain in his leg as he jumped when he was a few feet from the end. The distance between the houses was around fifty feet, which was just past the edge of his blink step range. When he reached the apex of the jump, he triggered blink step, stumbling a landing onto the eaves of the house's roof. He scrambled but lost his footing as his boot caught on a shingle, tripping him.

Rolling off the side of the roof, he reached out to grab the gutter, managing to get one hand on it and arresting his fall but wrenching his shoulder painfully. Kicking off the side of the building, he tried to pull himself up, but the lack of a good handhold prevented him from making any progress. He could feel the winds of the frostfire storm, and he looked down; realizing he was twenty feet up and over a concrete pad, he redoubled his efforts to scramble back onto the roof.

Drew caught movement from the corner of his eye and saw two trolls approaching where he had been from the north side of the house he was currently clinging to. He launched a fireball which caught them both unaware, incinerating them.

Deciding that the fight with the roof was a loss, he used gravitas to lighten himself considerably, then flipped over onto the roof. He then carefully began crawling up until he reached the peak, which he straddled, wincing as his leg banged against the roof. He took a moment to steady himself before standing up; he could feel blood trickling down his leg. Gravitas was still active, so he lightened himself enough that it didn't hurt as he clambered along the roof.

It took him a little under a minute, and he changed elevation five times before he could see the humans he was trying to rescue. There were four trolls surrounding them along with several patches of fire and broken glass. Daryl's aim was apparently not the greatest. He didn't see his co-conspirator, and the trolls were spread out enough that he couldn't catch more than one with a frostfire ball.

"Hey, ugly!" Drew shouted as an acid dart hit the nearest one's face. It collapsed into a kneeling position and covered its face, but the other three immediately jumped towards him. He caught two in midair with frostfire ball, but the third landed next to him with a thump. Cone of frostfire and lightning bolt both shot out of his hands as he turned, throwing the troll off the roof and into the nearly expired storm spell with their impact. He felt rather than heard the fourth troll landing behind him, the force of the blow on his back blocked by his shields as he turned.

The troll was obviously surprised, and blade barrier had done its job well. Drew cast cone of frost and then ducked another fist as it slowed down in the last second, overextending the slowed troll. He returned with a punch of his own, which resulted only in an exclamation of pain from him as he felt a bone in his hand snap from the impact. It had felt like punching a cinderblock wall.

The troll smiled, saying, "Goodbye, Weaver," before throwing another punch. Blade barrier stopped this one as well, and Drew responded by launching a lightning bolt into its face, sending it spinning away from him and off the roof. Turning back to the humans, he looked around but saw no sign of Daryl.

"Behind you!" one of the prisoners shouted as he heard another thump. Turning again, he caught two fists to the side of his head and shoulder, sending him tumbling off the roof and towards the ground below. He triggered gravitas while he fell, keeping him in midair for a heartbeat. He twisted around until he could see a troll with half his face eaten away by acid; the first one he had attacked hadn't gone down, apparently. He launched another lightning bolt and a fireball at it. It disappeared as the air from the explosion buffeted him.

Descending carefully, he landed on his side, unable to move enough to get his feet under him while in freefall. He popped up, looking around. "Did I get them all?" he asked, hoping he had since he didn't think he could take many more.

Chapter Twenty-Four — Chain

Drew didn't see any more trolls, and as the adrenaline drained away from him, he sat down on the curb. "So, hi? Any of you lot a healer? Because I could really use one right now," Drew said while cradling his injured right hand in his lap. As the adrenaline drained out of him, he realized that he had several other sore spots from the scrambling during the fight.

The group of humans just stared at him, then they looked at each other and started shaking their heads silently. Finally, from near the back, a man raised his hand. "Uh, I sort of have a heal." Drew looked at him and raised an eyebrow. He was a few inches over six foot, in his late forties or early fifties, and the exposed portions of his neck and arms were covered in nautical tattoos. He had a mostly yellow and orange aura. The man was wearing NWUs that had seen better days, bearing the anchor rank insignia of a chief on his lapel, although Drew supposed his own newly appropriated ODUs weren't in all that much better shape. The crowd parted to let the Chief come through.

"Hello, Chief, what do you mean you 'sort of' have a heal?" Drew asked. He didn't bother to stand up, knowing that if he did, he would begin shaking from the aftereffects of the fight.

"Well, it's a heal, I just..." The Chief trailed off for a moment and then muttered, "Gotta hug you."

Drew cocked his head to the side. "Pardon? Did you say you have to hug me?" The Chief nodded. "What..._What is the skill called?" Drew asked, confused. He hadn't seen any spells that required anything more elaborate than a hand seal or an incantation to activate.

By now the Chief stood in front of him and was looking down at Drew. "It's called Daddy's Embrace."

Drew looked up, somewhat intimidated by the large man looming over him. With a grunt, he stood up. "Weird, but I'll take it. Hug it out?" he said, spreading his arms for the hug. The

Chief just grunted and hugged him back. Instantly, Drew felt better, the pain in his leg, hands, and the other half dozen minor injuries disappearing. He also felt safe and secure, which he assumed was another side effect of the skill.

"Thanks," Drew said, stepping away from the Chief and stretching out his newly healed leg as he scanned the crowd. There was no sign of Daryl, but the other eighteen people with the Chief were all in a similar state of disrepair—dirty and disheveled, heavy bags under their eyes, and a half-defeated expression on their faces. About half of them wore air force or army uniforms, while the rest were in civilian clothing. "I'm IT2 Drew Michalik. A few others and I just managed to escape Coast Guard HQ. Who's in charge here?"

The Chief glanced at the others. "I guess I am. Haven't seen any of the brass since they led us into the basement." He glanced at Drew. "Where's the rest of your group?"

"Daryl should be around here... somewhere," Drew said, looking around for the invisible man but didn't see him. "He was the one that warned you to get away from the alley. And the other two are back at the St. E's exchange. We had to fight our way out of the building. Only three of us made it. Ensign Rothschild got knocked out and hasn't woken up since that last fight."

"Yeah, it's been rough here too." The Chief looked around. "We should get out of the open, though. Makes me nervous not having something solid between me and those damn monsters."

Drew considered their options. The room where they'd stayed last night wouldn't hold all twenty of them. "Well, to be honest, I hadn't really thought about what to do after I rescued everyone. We probably don't have the manpower to protect the commissary, which is where Daryl said y'all had holed up before. We can make for the St. E's exchange. The trolls might not chase us that far, but it's a fair distance. I need to go back there with a healer anyway to get Katie and Sarah. Is there another building around here we could use?"

The Chief looked around and scratched his cheek, thinking. "I dunno, I guess we could take over just about any building. The only problem is we were chosen for this because none of us have any red skills. So anyone you left behind would be sitting ducks without you."

Drew frowned, glancing at the group, and realized that all the auras had a distinct lack of red in them. The conversation up to this point had been relatively quiet; the group of humans had sort of just sat down while the Chief and their rescuer talked. "Do any of you have any kind of combat or defensive intermediate xatherite?"

He went around the group; mostly they had xatherite that wouldn't help much in combat, at least not without some setup. There was a mostly green guy named Clyde that could tame monsters, a blue girl named Kwincy that had managed to hide the fact that she could summon a medium fire elemental, several oranges that could apply buffs and debuffs, and two yellows with shielding spells that Drew was incredibly jealous of. The rest were things that would make life much, much easier but weren't very useful for combat.

Drew realized that their xatherite had a kind of theme for each person. One woman had three different skills that all focused on her profession as a seamstress. Another had a bunch of woodworking skills. Others had basic spells that would conjure water, clean clothing, or half a dozen other tasks, that while incredibly useful, weren't going to be much use in combat.

The most useful of the group by far was the Chief, whose name was Bill, with his healing and buff spells and two indigos. The second was a seventeen-year-old girl named Jholie who could create headaches and temporary deafness. The other was a nineteen-year-old army private named Trey, who could create stationary illusions and mirror images of himself that would make targeting him incredibly difficult.

The sheer variety of xatherite amazed Drew, and he felt like he knew quite a bit about their personalities just by hearing what xatherite they had received. Bill's healing spell was a perfect example; he obviously had a child whom he loved greatly, and that had caused him to get a skill that would comfort them. Daryl got spells that made him harder to see, and he was always trying to lay low. What did the fact that almost all his xatherite were made to destroy things say about his personality?

While he pondered the ramifications of this new discovery, he cast refreshing rain on the group, their morale visibly improving as the spell renewed their flagging energy. He turned to Bill, intending to ask him a question right as Daryl's aura appeared at the edge of his vision. He ignored it, for now, something telling him not to reveal how close the black man could get before he noticed. When Daryl did fade into existence, he was surprised by the fact that he was carrying several thick green skins.

"Daryl, what... are those?" Drew asked as the entire group turned to look at him.

"Ahh, I was using my resource harvesting xatherite on the trolls, figured we could turn it into armor like the stuff you're wearing," Daryl answered, looking just a bit uncomfortable with the attention he was getting.

Drew wasn't sure how he felt about using the skins of sentient creatures to make armor, but at this point, if it would keep some of these people alive, he would take it. "Alright, Chief, I say we get to the commissary, grab some food and then find one of the nearby buildings to keep most of the group. Then you, me, and Jholie head up to get Katie and Sarah. It shouldn't take more than four hours if we hustle. Meanwhile, Trey will use his illusion to hide the group, Daryl will scout to warn them if anything is coming, and the rest can focus on defense."

Bill nodded his head. "Sounds good to me, Petty Officer." Drew winced as his title was used. In the Coast Guard, you only called someone Petty Officer when they were in trouble or getting an award. He knew that wasn't the common practice in the Navy, but it felt like his mom had just called him by his full name.

Bill began giving orders to everyone, splitting Daryl's load among the others and sending him out to find a place big enough for the group to hide easily. They made their way to the commissary, which was just a few more blocks away.

"Chief, I killed a bunch of cultists yesterday, and they had some long daggers. The Mana Storm last night cleared most of their bodies, but I think I saw some daggers still in the soccer field. Might be a good idea to send people out to grab those while we get food," Drew informed Bill as they passed the soccer field.

Bill nodded his head slowly. "They won't do much against the trolls but might be useful for the other monsters we went up against." He sent three people out running into the field to get the daggers. As they walked, Bill asked Drew questions about what they had faced in the dungeon. "I'm amazed that any of you survived. I was privy to a good deal of the general's planning meetings, and of the hundreds of people on base, we didn't have anyone that came anywhere near your firepower. If we had..." He trailed off, and his eyes took on a faraway look.

Drew could do the math. Bill obviously had a child and odds were pretty good that the kid had died during the first days of the Advent. Unsure of what to say that would comfort the older man, he just let the conversation lull while he dealt with his grief. Drew was frankly amazed that he was functioning as well as he was. He couldn't even imagine what it must be like to watch your child die. He was reminded of King Theoden's line in the Two Towers, "No parent should have to bury their child."

They made it to the commissary without further incident, although most of the former prisoners kept watching over their shoulders to ensure that no trolls spewed forth from the DIA building in retaliation of their escape.

The commissary itself was a creepy structure, the inside dark due to the lack of windows. Drew pulled out Katie's glowrock while the others all seemed to have conjured glow sticks that gave less light but could be used like flashlights to see much further than glowrock allowed in a specific direction. The commissary was empty of any creatures, and they filled up four shopping carts with canned goods and other non-perishable items. Drew began chewing his way through a pound of teriyaki jerky and put another four in his backpack.

By the time they were done, Daryl had found a likely building in the form of the auto shop; its large warehouse would keep them out of sight of the trolls while also giving them plenty of tools to work with in the meantime. They could break into one of the back doors easily enough and have Trey put up an illusion to make it look like it was still intact.

Drew and Daryl went first, clearing the warehouse and front room of a couple of rats, which were as big as the one Sarah killed, that had taken up residence inside the warehouse. The group joined them inside when they announced that it was clear. The troll skins were claimed by the seamstress, who thought she could probably use them to make some armor, while everyone else either found some relatively soft places to sit and wait or began digging through the parts looking for things they could turn into weapons.

Bill stood up on a bucket to get everyone's attention. "Alright, everyone, IT2, myself, and Jholie are going to go get two more survivors. We should be back before dark." Drew winced at that, the exact words he had said the day before to Katie. "We need to figure out a way to get everyone else out of the DIA building, so start looking for weapons that will do fire damage. Also, see if you can all get together and make a map of the place. Anything you remember of where the trolls usually were and where prisoners were would be helpful. While I'm gone, the chain of command is Chuck, then Daryl and Trey."

He indicated the woodworker, who at fifty-seven was the oldest person in the group by a fair margin. Daryl and Trey were working on the defenses. He then turned to Drew and Jholie and nodded. "Alright, let's go save some people."

Chapter Twenty-Five — Traveling

After exiting the auto shop, Drew looked at the Chief. "I was thinking we should head east and walk up the freeway, give the trolls a wide berth."

The Chief nodded. "Same thing I was thinking."

"Why do you keep calling them trolls?" Jholie asked. "Aren't trolls supposed to be short and rock-like?"

Drew laughed. "You mean like the ones in Frozen? No, I guess I base most of my names on games that I've played. In most of those, trolls are immune to physical attacks or have super high regeneration that makes it almost impossible to kill them with physical attacks, but they are vulnerable to fire and acid. The first trolls I killed seemed to take extra damage from fire, so I started calling them that."

"I think I liked the Frozen trolls better. We've been calling them green skins, and I think that's a pretty good name for them." Drew glanced at the Chief, who had pulled ahead of them, and frowned. Jholie had the ability to create headaches in people, and he was pretty sure he understood what aspect of her personality had induced the system to give her that capability.

"Yeah, it'd be nice if we could all pick which enemies we find, but the...creatures that we had to fight in the bunker had green skin too. I called them orcs because they kind of looked like the orcs from my games. But they called themselves the Go'rai, which I think was like the name of the tribe they were from, and the whole race they called," he paused, trying to remember the other name Chakri had called his people, "Nathzim? It was something like that."

Bill spoke from in front, "There was a prisoner that could understand the language they used to talk to each other. He said they called themselves the Ashalla. But we should probably be quiet, don't want to attract any monsters." Drew wasn't sure if that was true or if the Chief just didn't want Jholie to talk more.

Jholie looked a little frightened at that and moved to catch up to the bigger man. Both had an Ashalla dagger at their side, and Bill also had a four-foot-long crowbar he must have picked up somewhere in the auto shop. The route they had decided on was about half a mile to the wall surrounding the base. From there, it was another mile up the freeway to where they would jump the wall and get to the Coast Guard HQ and then a final half mile from that point up to the exchange.

The first monsters they saw appeared suddenly as they came around a blind corner. There in a field to their right were several rabbits. Ranging in size from three to four feet long, they each had a nub of a horn on the top of their heads. The two biggest rabbits were using their horns to bash each other like goats fighting over a mate. The smaller rabbits sat about the field watching the two bash each other. In total, Drew saw more than two dozen rabbits all glowing with a red/green aura. Bill had come around the corner first and had held up a hand to stop them, while Jholie made an "Awww" sound.

Several of the rabbits turned to look at the group as they heard the noise, but none of them seemed interested in pursuing them. Drew pointed closer to the building away from the field, and all three of them moved quietly over to that side, watching as the rabbits continued to bash each other silly in the middle of the field.

Once they were on the other side of the road and a few hundred feet away from the rabbits, Drew looked at them. "We're calling those things bashers. They looked exactly like some monsters I read about in a book."

Bill looked at him strangely. "What sort of books do you read?"

They could see the wall now and headed towards it through the parking lot of the swimming pool. Drew was about to answer, but Jholie spoke instead, "I don't really read books, but I watched Perks of Being a Wallflower, and that was based on a book, so it's like I read it. I also watched the Hunger Games movies, and those are based around books too. I really miss movies; I was excited about the new Jungle Book movie—the live action one that was supposed to come out next month. That's going to be great. My friend Shea says..."

Drew and Bill both turned to stare at Jholie, who didn't seem to realize that they thought it odd how much she talked, then looked at each other and shook their heads slightly. Jholie kept talking, quietly enough that it wasn't really an issue, but Drew tuned her out, nodding and grunting whenever the girl paused. He was impressed with her energy, to be honest. She had probably just had her parents and most of her friends killed, and her world had been invaded by trolls, but right now she was talking about how much she loved Minions and Inside Out.

They made it to the wall without further incident and with Jholie only ceasing her constant flow of words for breath. "We need to be quiet up here. This is where I was attacked by the squirrels, and the trees are thick enough that there could easily be a couple hundred more of them. Bill, I'll help you over first, then you can help Jholie on the other side. I can get myself over." Both Drew and Bill looked at Jholie, who nodded her head and pantomimed locking her lips and throwing away the key while Drew leaned against the wall so Bill could use his legs, shoulders, and hands to climb over the wall.

Bill threw over his crowbar and then took the pre-offered boost up from Drew to scale the eight-foot wall with relative ease. Drew grunted while trying to push him up to make it easier. At the top of the wall, he looked around. "Looks clear," he said before dropping down to the other side of the fence. Jholie watched and then shook her head.

"I can't do that," she said with a frown.

"Sure you can. It'll be easy, and the Chief will catch you on the other side," Drew said, interlocking his fingers together again to help.

"Come on over, Jholie; it'll be fine," the Chief said from the other side.

It took a few more minutes of cajoling before Jholie eventually made her first attempt. Drew had to push her over the top of the wall, but she managed to get up without too much effort. She only let out a small scream as she jumped off the wall into Bill's waiting arms. Drew backed away from the wall and then with a running start, activated gravitas, clearing the wall with ease and sailing over Bill and Jholie and landing far more gracefully on the other side than his first attempt at the maneuver.

He turned around and realized that both were staring at him with impressed expressions. "Did you just jump over the wall?" Bill asked incredulously.

"That was soooo cool!" Jholie exclaimed.

Drew grinned back. "Yeah. Probably one of the most fun xatherite I have." He turned and began walking up the road, the other two moving to follow him.

Drew saw a few squirrels in the trees. He wasn't sure if it was due to the larger group or if they were leery of him having killed the pack that attacked him earlier, but they managed to get all the way to the hill leading up through HQ and to the exchange without being attacked. Jholie stayed quiet for most of the trip. About halfway there, she had been looking tired enough that they took a short break while Drew cast refreshing rain. He also took the time to renew his protection spells.

The highway was relatively boring, but they were able to jump over a chain link fence and up a slight hill to get onto St. E's campus. They passed through the gap between the headquarters building and the parking lot. Drew pointed out where they had exited and watched cautiously but didn't see any Go'rai or wereghouls in the windows. The remains of the barricade looked like it hadn't been fixed yet either. Drew wondered if the manaborn respawned, and if they did, would Chakri become his nemesis like in Shadows of Mordor? He hoped not because that had been a pain.

As they climbed, Drew looked up at the exchange where he'd last seen Katie and saw that the walls were still up. He had been hoping to catch a glimpse of the attractive brunette as they came back. He hoped she wasn't too mad that he was late.

Drew led the others in his excitement to get back and get Sarah healed. As he went around the corner of the exchange towards the front door, he walked straight into what he could only call a swarm of hand-sized mosquitoes which glowed red to his mana sight. A quick fireball killed dozens of them, and he shouted a warning to Bill and Jholie. There were still many of the swarm left, and still more were being drawn in by the heat and light he'd just created.

He looked behind him and then blink stepped back fifteen feet to be right in front of Bill, launching a frostfire ball towards the swarm that was now attacking his afterimage. A few dozen more died to the flames, and others were caught by the flying ice, their wings shredded, causing them to smash against the floor, feebly attempting to return to the air. He raised his hands, waiting for the rest of the swarm to notice him, backing up slowly as the illusion bought them a few more seconds for fireball to recharge. When they came after him again, he dual cast cone of frost and cone of frostfire, his arms spread wide to increase the coverage of the spells. The icy blast took out a large swath of the swarm, leaving only a dozen individuals that had been on the front edge where the cones hadn't expanded.

Drew ducked as one flew towards his head but heard the smack of the crowbar hitting it out of the air as Bill took a swing. Jholie was screaming and had curled up into a ball, waving her hands around her head to scare them away. Drew launched lightning bolts as fast as he could; he missed often, but Bill was doing serious damage with his crowbar.

Seeing one latch onto Jholie's back, Drew smacked it away with his hand. He could feel the proboscises break off inside the girl as he did, and her screaming became even louder. But the fight was mostly over at that point, and it only took a few more swings of Bill's crowbar to drive the rest of them away.

Drew stomped on a few of the still moving mosquitoes while Bill pulled the proboscis out of Jholie's back. She didn't stop screaming until he hugged her, at which point she broke down, crying hysterically. Drew didn't blame her; it was probably the first time she'd felt safe since the Advent began a week ago. He realized that she'd been hiding all the pain and fear underneath that thin veneer of normalcy her constant chatter had allowed.

Drew gave Jholie a minute while he walked towards the door, wondering what had gotten the mosquitoes to swarm there. The outer glass door had been broken open, and inside was what looked like a pure black, enlarged badger and several mosquito corpses. The insects had clearly drained it of blood as it had struggled and killed a few of them, but the swarm had been far too much for it to handle.

He caught a bright red glow of mana from one of the mosquitos and realized there was the smallest xatherite crystal he had seen growing out of its back. He touched it, then with a very mild red glow, a blinking message appeared in the corner of his vision.

The summoned walls inside the exchange were gone, leaving a clear line of vision through the glass door to the back wall, and he could see glowstones spread around the place, but the bedding where he'd left Sarah was empty and there was no sign of Katie.

Chapter Twenty-Six — Reunited

"Katie!" Drew called out after having harvested the red xatherite. He frowned as he realized that his new mana sight xatherite was telling him there were blue and indigo mana constructs in front of him, even though his eyes told him that there was just an empty hallway there. He cautiously walked forward until a finger disappeared like it had been cut off in midair. There was no pain, and he pulled his hand back, his fingertip reappearing.

Indigo aura. An illusion? He pushed his hand through the illusion, but he was stopped half an inch past it, where he could feel the solid surface of a wall. The blue aura must be Katie's summoned wall. He pounded his fist through the illusion, shouting again, "Katie!"

Drew pounded his other fist against the wall, all his frustrations coming to the forefront of his mind. Another fist against the wall; he could feel the pain, but it was a dull and distant thing. He kept pounding, bringing the fleshy part of his hand against the hard concrete of Katie's summoned wall. His hand came down for what must have been the tenth time, and it felt no resistance this time; he just swung through the empty air, throwing him off balance. Then he heard Katie's voice, "Drew?" He pushed through the illusion.

As soon as his eyes passed through the illusion, he saw Katie. She had pulled one of the glass doors on the inside of the exchange open and unsummoned the wall, and he immediately pulled her into his arms. Grasping her as tightly as he could, he said, "I thought... the wall..." He couldn't speak in complete sentences as the adrenaline drained from his body his legs felt weak. Luckily for him, Katie seemed to be in a similar state.

"You're late." It took a minute for both to gather themselves together enough for the nonsense half thoughts to finally graduate to full phrases, but that was the first thing Katie managed to get out. Drew laugh-cried as she said it.

"I'm so sorry, I didn't mean to, but the mana storm hit and then I had to deal with the trolls and…" Drew finally opened his eyes and saw two men standing over Sarah, one of them carrying about ten pistols in various holsters around his body, while the other had a hand on Sarah's forehead. Something inside of Drew snapped, and a lightning bolt flashed from his hand to the one touching Sarah. The smell of ozone immediately filled the room. The man with the guns tried to push the one touching Sarah out of the way, but the bolt impacted along the right side of his back.

"Drew, stop!" Katie shouted in his ears, and he turned to her confused. The gun wielder had pulled out a pistol and held it ready. "They're friends!"

Drew clenched his fists, the emotional wringer of the last minute and a half having completely spent his body. Adrenaline raced through his overly stimulated muscles from the mosquito fight and then the fear of losing Katie and Sarah. He realized just how dangerous what he had just done may have been; he could have hit Sarah, or the bolt could have conducted through the man's skin to her unconscious body. He swallowed, and his legs gave out, landing with a painful thud as his knees slapped the tile floor.

Katie moved to stand between him and the other three people. "Drew, it's okay," she said, putting her hands on his shoulders and pulling him into another awkward hug, his forehead against her clavicle. "It's okay, Drew; we're safe."

The sound of the lightning bolt must have alerted Bill, and the Chief's voice could be heard calling out in the hallway behind them, "IT2, where'd you go?"

Katie pushed him away for a minute, a confused look on her face. "In here, Chief. There's an illusion," Drew said, his voice seeming drained of all emotion.

Bill's hand, followed by the rest of his body, appeared a few seconds later; he was leading Jholie. All three groups stared at each other for a few seconds while Drew managed to reclaim his calm. "Katie, this is Bill and Jholie. Bill is a healer."

Katie hugged Drew tight at that. "You did it," she murmured in the crown of his head. Everyone else looked on awkwardly as the two Coasties had their reunion. Finally, Katie pulled away. Looking at Bill and Jholie, then back to Drew, she gestured behind her. "That's JP and Robbi. They came here looking for supplies and survivors."

Drew looked at the two men. JP was the one with all the guns, and to his mana sight, his aura was almost purple, with a strange intermixture of red and blue. Robbi, on the other hand, was the one sporting a large burn mark across one side of his body armor, and his aura was a weird indigo, green, and yellow that reminded Drew of a half-healed bruise. He was probably the source of the illusion on the wall. Another layer of protection added against the monsters?

He was glad that JP hadn't opened fire on him, and the gun he had pulled out was back in its holster. Drew realized for the first time that both men were wearing blue police uniforms under their body armor, and while he didn't carry as many guns as JP, Robbi had a few of his own. The armor had probably been enough to save Robbi's life; a large, black scorch mark on the back of the vest showed that his aim had been true, despite JP's attempt to save his partner.

"I'm sorry about that lightning bolt thing," Drew said hesitantly. Robbi opened his mouth to say something but was stopped when JP laughed.

"Shit, bro, it makes sense. Katie told me you'd gone out there alone," JP said, walking over to Drew and Katie, leaning down to extend his hand to shake Drew's. "I can't imagine that walking around out there alone is good for a person's mental health."

Drew took the hand and shook it, then putting a hand around Katie's waist, pulled them both to their feet, letting the brunette go as soon as they were back on their feet. "Still, I'm really sorry..."

Bill spoke up then, "Sorry to interrupt, but I should heal Sarah so we can get back to the others."

"Oh right, of course, Bill. She's right there," Drew said, gesturing to Sarah's body. The big Chief walked over to the girl and, kneeling, began to hug her.

Katie tugged on his sleeve and gave him a questioning look. "Bill's healing requires that he hug the person," he answered. Meanwhile, Jholie was staring around at everyone nervously. JP and Robbi were watching Bill curiously.

Katie squeezed his arm, watching, while both held their breath as Bill used his daddy's embrace. Nothing happened at first, but then they saw Sarah wrap her arms around Bill in response. Katie's grip on Drew's arm became tighter, and when he looked over, she was crying. He put his arm around her waist again, and she released his arm long enough to give him a side hug as she watched her friend move on her own for the first time in days.

When Bill finally managed to extract himself from Sarah's embrace, Katie ran over and hugged the Ensign herself. Drew clapped Bill's shoulder. "Thanks, Chief." Bill just shrugged and went over to stand near Jholie.

Drew walked over to where the two cops were standing. "I'm really sorry, Robbi... just a little bit on edge, I guess." Robbi shot him a bit of a glare but didn't say anything as he grabbed a Sprite and stalked over towards Bill and Jholie.

"Give him a bit. It's not every day you're almost killed," JP said, then shrugged, "or I guess, it wasn't every day. It kind of is every day now, isn't it?"

Drew laughed and nodded his head. "Yeah. For me, anyway. How did you guys get here?"

"Well, we were sent out to recruit people. We're set up in Nat's Park with about a thousand people total. There were five in our scouting group when we set out, but we lost two on the bridge to a massive squid that pulled them into the river, and another to what Katie called orcs as we were traveling through the new mental hospital."

Drew frowned. "I'm sorry to hear about your losses." They stood there in silence for a few minutes while they each contemplated those of their companions they had lost.

"Where did you find these two?" JP asked as he nodded towards Jholie and Bill. "Katie said you left alone."

"I did. I went to Bolling. The DIA building on base has turned into a dungeon like the HQ here has, but it's filled with troll-like creatures instead of orcs. I managed to rescue about twenty of them and brought Bill back up to heal Sarah. The plan was to take Sarah and Katie down there and rescue the rest of the prisoners," Drew answered truthfully, hoping the men would join them.

"Robbi and I would like to join you," JP said immediately to the unspoken request. "That's why we came out here, after all, to bring back as many as we could. The guy in charge was a senator before Advent, but he's alright, kept a lot of people alive, and we've got running water and showers up again. There should be plenty of food once we get the five or six people with enhanced farming skills working the playing field. Housing is in the stadium for everyone, and we have enough reds to keep the place safe from the monster attacks." He glanced at Drew. "Not that I expect you're lacking on reds yourself. I haven't seen anyone take out Robbi's shield and still leave enough to actually hurt him."

Drew blinked. JP was certainly trying to sell the place hard. "Does he need healing? I'm sure Chief or Sarah can help him." JP just waved it off.

"When he's ready, he'll ask for it."

"Right, well, I got lucky and got a couple of good red skills from xatherite drops. When did you start setting up at the stadium? I'll be honest, it sounds... too good to be true."

JP laughed again. "Yeah, I know what you mean, especially after what Katie told me of y'alls experience in the HQ building. We'll go rescue those people of yours first and then you'll see." Drew nodded his head. If the dungeons were going to continue sending out raiding parties, having a safe place across the river to keep people was going to be important. How they were supposed to get a whole bunch of people across the squid infested river was a problem for tomorrow.

The two girls were mostly back to normal, and Drew nodded to JP. "I should talk to Sarah." JP nodded in response, and Drew walked back to where Sarah and Katie were. Sarah smiled at him as he sat down next to her.

"I hear you saved me."

"Well, I think Bill's hug did that. I was just Katie's gofer boy," Drew said, and Katie punched his shoulder.

"And you were late too!" Katie said with a frown. "I don't know why I was worried. You have a way of coming out of impossible things intact. I feel like we should start calling you Ethan Hunt."

Sarah smiled at the two. "Well, I'm glad to be awake. Katie told me a few things that happened while I was out. Thank you both for saving me."

"Of course, can't let a shipmate down," Drew said, and Katie nodded in agreement as all three of them thought about Mitch, Juan, Rob, and the others that hadn't made it out of the dungeon alive. Sarah saw his bloodied hands and frowned. "What happened to your hands?" she asked, grabbing them and looking at the split skin.

"Nothing really, just... hit a wall," Drew responded as Sarah sat up enough to cast her spell, managing to target it far enough away that it hit everyone in the room.

"I haven't told Katie yet, but there are some more survivors down at Bolling; they were captured by trolls. I managed to kill a bunch who were sacrificing humans and then rescued twenty people from another dozen trolls, but there are still a few hundred more people stuck in the DIA building over there. Bill and Jholie came to help me get you two, and then we're gonna try and rescue all of them. JP said he and Robbi would help."

Sarah reached down to take the splints off her legs. "Well, I've been laying around long enough. It sounds like we have work to do."

Chapter Twenty-Seven — Setting Off

It took another hour for them to get ready. They raided the exchange of everything of value, mostly the water and protein snacks. Drew also changed into a new set of ODU's after Katie asked him how he always showed up at her door looking like a zombie. Upon reflection, he realized he had collected an amazing array of blue, red, and green blood stains as well as rips and tears. The leather armor he'd taken from the Go'rai had managed to hold up surprisingly well, which was even more reason for them to start putting Daryl's necro alchemy xatherite and Mi Sun's seamstress xatherite to work. If they could get troll armor for everyone, they would be much better off.

Hopefully, no one would be upset by wearing the skin of a sentient being into battle. That had always been a sticking point in his Pathfinder games. It was okay to wear dragon scale and devil skin but not other sentient races like trolls or giants. He had never really understood the distinction, though. If it was better, it was better. Pragmatism beat out any moral issues he had with it currently.

After he was re-attired and restocked, he decided he should check on his notifications.

Congratulations, Midshipman. Your Cone of Frost xatherite has reached level 4. Damage has increased.
Congratulations, Midshipman. Your Fireball xatherite has reached level 4. Damage has increased.
Congratulations, Midshipman. Your Storm xatherite has reached level 4. Damage has increased.
Congratulations, Midshipman. Your Minor Dancing Sword xatherite has reached level 5. Duration has increased.
Congratulations, Midshipman. Your Minor Energize xatherite has reached level 3. Charge requirement has reduced.
Congratulations, Midshipman. Your Minor Lightning Bolt xatherite has reached level 3. Damage has increased.
Congratulations, Midshipman. Your Minor Mana Shield xatherite has reached level 3. Damage absorbed has increased.
Congratulations, Midshipman. Your Major Acid Dart xatherite has reached level 5. Damage has increased.
You have acquired a wild xatherite!
Primitive grade Minor Heat acquired.

Xatherite Crystal Name: Minor Heat
Xatherite Color: Red
Xatherite Grade: Primitive
Xatherite Rarity: Widespread
Type: Magic
Effect: Targeting any object within 10m will raise its temperature by 5% for 1 minute.
Mana recharge time: 14 seconds.

Looking at the list, he realized he must have ignored his notifications after the second troll fight without realizing it. There was no way the mosquitos gave him that many levels. Also, acid dart was likely to upgrade to common any minute now. Still no progress on the rare and higher xatherite, which meant there was a significant growth curve in place.

Minor heat sounded like it could become a very useful spell; it reminded him of the heat metal spell from his pen and paper games. You could increase an object's temperature by twenty percent over a minute. Honestly, it was terrible in its current state, but it was only a primitive grade xatherite. He had gotten his primitive grade xatherite to almost common in a week, and judging by the power increase of mana shield and lightning bolt, it was bound to become far more useful at that point.

Drew glanced over his map. He could put the red in a couple of spots, and maybe it would create a version of dancing sword that was made up of burning swords. But frankly, he didn't use dancing sword much as it was, as it required letting things get far closer to him than he preferred them being. He could also put it over on the left side and open that constellation.

Or he could give it to Katie; she didn't have any offensive spells as it was, and if it linked with telekinesis, maybe she would get pyrokinesis? It would eat up one of her only three red slots though. Sarah also only had three red slots; could she link it with mind sense? Maybe create a skill that superheated someone's brain? Would that be a buff or an attack? He pictured someone boiling his brain from the inside and shuddered; that didn't seem like a nice attack. Still, as a healer, she was better off not trying to get more aggro than she already received.

Did aggro exist in this world? He had successfully kited Chakri away from the group, but that was by being a red mage... and they might target Sarah if they thought she was a red mage too. He brushed away thoughts of Juan being targeted because he was a red mage.

Sarah might be able to use it better, but he didn't like the idea of Katie not having something she could use for offense; if he was being honest with himself, he was more interested in keeping Katie safe. He sent the xatherite her way and watched as she read the notification, then looked over at him and raised an eyebrow.

Drew smiled back at her, and she shook her head, accepted the trade, and inserted it into her map. He walked over and cast minor energize on her to help her deal with the headache.

After everyone was ready, he gathered them together and cast minor refreshing rain, which was much appreciated by the two cops, who clearly hadn't slept much the last few days.

They set off down the hill, Drew leading the group with Katie and Sarah, while Jholie and Bill took up the second row, and JP and Robbi had rearguard. It was an uneventful walk for the most part. The three Coasties talked quietly about what had happened since Sarah went unconscious. They stopped again at the halfway point to rest, where Drew cast refreshing rain again, and everyone took a few minutes to eat something. Drew wandered over to where JP and Robbi stood. "Katie and I were talking, and we were hoping to know what xatherite y'all have so we can plan the rescue a little better."

Robbi snorted, and JP frowned. "What sort of stuff do you want to know?"

"Well, the trolls seem to be pretty resistant to normal weapon damage; the base tried to fight them off with guns but didn't have a whole lot of success," Drew said, pointing to the numerous guns festooning JP's body. "I used spells; fire, in particular, seems very useful against them."

"Fair. Well, I have a blue that fills magazines, and some reds that allow me to change the damage type of my personal guns to be fire, cold, or sonic damage," JP answered, then glanced at Robbi. "Robbi has some indigo and yellow spells that make him mostly invulnerable in close combat, but he's vulnerable to ranged damage." This was, of course, part of the reason why Robbi didn't like Drew after being hit by one of his lightning bolts.

"How long does that fill magazine spell take to cast?" Drew asked, wondering why he would need so many guns if he never ran out of ammo.

"About ten seconds, not really something I can do mid-combat," JP answered.

"Alright, any other utility spells other than that illusion wall and the free refills on magazines?" Drew asked. Both JP and Robbi shook their heads. "Okay, I've got fireballs and some big area spells that I can use up to half a mile away, a couple of near spread spells that I can use, and the lightning bolt spell you guys saw. Pretty much everything I do will affect an area, so I can't use it near friendlies. Katie has a wall spell that will give us cover, but the trolls haven't been using any ranged weapons, and Sarah has a ranged area heal."

"Jholie has ranged attacks, but I don't know how useful they will be against trolls. Mostly good for distractions while someone else kills them. Bill has his heal plus two buffs—one that improves everyone's strength stat and another that improves acid resistance."

Drew looked at the two men as they considered the abilities they had present. "Sounds like our best bet is going to be to try and lure them out. Katie can make some walls, and they'll be lined up like bowling pins," JP said after a few minutes.

"Not going to work. The trolls I saw could jump three stories up and about sixty feet horizontally. Our best bet is to kill them in an enclosed area where they can't jump but where we can see them coming from far away. Daryl, one of the other survivors we're going to meet, should be able to get us some intelligence. He can go invisible." Drew shrugged. "We'll see when we get back. Maybe they'll have some better ideas and maps by then."

They separated again, Drew walking over to where Katie and Sarah were eating with Bill and Jholie. Nodding to everyone, he sat on the concrete, scratching his head. "How many did you say there were in there?" he asked the two former prisoners.

"I think there might have been somewhere upwards of two hundred. You've killed about a quarter of them, I imagine. No idea how that will change their operation, though."

"What about their leadership? Could we take them out and work from there?" Sarah asked.

"Maybe. Not sure I ever saw their actual leader; there were about four or five of the shaman ones that I saw, hard to say because I didn't exactly see them together often."

"Side doors?" Katie asked.

Jholie shook her head. "We never got near 'em; they always led us out the main entrance and then down into the basement."

"So, to sum it all up, we have one hundred to two hundred trolls in unknown locations with possibly a few boss monsters thrown in, and the only reliable way we have to get in is through the front door?" Drew looked around to grim nods.

"Why do we need to go through a door?" JP and Robbi had come up behind them. "Just blow a hole through the side of the building. Heck, if we can find out where they are, we could get everyone out without even fighting any of the trolls."

Everyone turned to look at the gunslinger and considered his words. "Might work, we'd have to figure out where everyone is... and get through the concrete and glass. Maybe need an explosive or two." They all turned to Drew.

"I don't think I can blow a hole in the wall," Drew trailed off, thinking, "but I might be able to melt one. It would take a while, but I don't see why we wouldn't be able to do it. We'd just need to figure out where we want to do it."

"And figure out a way to get everyone freed and out of there," Bill offered, "since I doubt the trolls will just let us walk away."

"Good point... Bill, was it?" JP said, and Bill confirmed his name. "That will have to be where the rest of us come in. Robbi can make illusions, Katie can make walls to prevent them from following, and those we can't confine or confound we'll just have to kill."

Murmurs of agreement came from around the circle. "Alright, well, let's get moving. I want to be back at the auto shop well before dark," Bill said, and everyone began putting everything back in their bags and getting ready to go.

Drew helped Katie into her pack. All of them had packed heavier than was comfortable, trying to bring as many things down to the larger group as they could. She smiled at him. "Thanks, Drew." They got back on the road where Drew pointed a couple of the massive squirrels out to Katie and Sarah.

When they got to the wall they had crossed earlier, they used a similar method to get over. JP went first, then Robbi, the three girls, Bill, with Drew finally jumping over on his own.

"You were either the Easter Bunny in a previous life or have more xatherite than you told us about," JP said as Drew landed.

"Yeah, I have a few more. I mostly just told you the combat relevant ones," Drew said.

Robbi and JP both exchanged a glance that gave Drew a bad feeling. What exactly was their mission out here? What was the goal of this senator who ran Nat's park? In his head, he pictured a Tina Turner type running Barter Town with an authoritarian fist. He thought back to what he told JP the first time they talked about it. "It sounds too good to be true." It probably wasn't true, but did they really have a choice?

Chapter Twenty-Eight — Sleep

Drew watched the two newcomers out of the corner of his eye. Ever since they'd realized he was holding back on how many xatherite he had, they'd been having a whispered conversation with each other. The group had spread out. Drew, Sarah, and Katie had taken the front, the three Coasties only a few feet apart. Jholie and Bill followed a dozen paces behind them, while Robbi and JP were another dozen feet behind the second row.

"What's wrong?" Katie asked quietly, having picked up on Drew's soured mood.

"I'm not sure. Something with JP and Robbi," Drew answered, his voice cast low enough that Sarah, who was on the other side of Katie, had a hard time hearing him.

"You think they're mana twisted or something?" Sarah asked.

Drew considered this for a moment. There didn't seem to be any logical reason why a human couldn't become mana twisted. The wereghouls were evidence that there wasn't something special about their bodies that made humans immune to the ravages of the sudden increase in ambient mana, but it didn't quite fit with what he'd heard in the tutorial. Would the human protectorate have created a system that would allow that?

Katie nudged him in the side, and he looked up, realizing that he'd gotten lost in thought. "I don't think so. Everything else we've seen that's mana twisted physically changed." They were just about to pass the field where they had seen the bashers, and Drew frowned while looking around; all the rabbit-like creatures had disappeared. "You guys feel that?" he asked, turning towards Jholie and Bill.

It was Robbi that answered, "It's a mana storm; we need to move." The fear in Robbi's voice as he answered Drew was evident. JP and Robbi started running to catch up to the rest of the group. They were still a couple hundred feet from the auto shop where they'd left Daryl and the others.

Drew looked out and realized that he could see the storm with mana sight; it looked like a massive ley line floating in the sky miles away. As he watched, he could see it moving closer to their position. Shaking his head, Drew grabbed Katie's hand and began running towards their haven. "We've got to move," Drew said over his shoulder, but everyone was already running.

Bill was keeping pace with Jholie, and Drew could hear his encouraging shouts. The three Coasties in their combat boots moved somewhat slower than JP and Robbi, but as the two of them had no idea where to go, they trailed along behind Drew, who was leading everyone as the fastest person who had been there before. When they rounded the last corner towards the auto shop, Drew's heart sank. Six trolls were walking around the building with a large creature that had a snakehead and a furry quadruped body with bands of bright blue fur running in diagonal stripes across its otherwise off-white fur. The creature was sniffing the ground like it was tracking something.

Drew dropped Katie's hand and began forming the hand seals to cast frostfire storm, hoping to catch the trolls together before they noticed them. He heard Sarah mutter her buff spells, but his focus was on the surviving trolls and the spell he was trying to cast. JP pushed a magazine into his HK-45, and the click as it locked into place caused all seven of their opponents to look their direction.

Making a mental note that their hearing was excellent, Drew finished casting frostfire storm, catching the creature and four of the trolls in its radius. The other two trolls had been lucky in that their bodies were oriented towards them. They'd pushed off the ground, leaping towards the group. Drew pointed a finger at one of them, but before he could activate fireball, a shot rang out. Red traces of energy trailed behind the bullet, and two rounds impacted one troll in the chest. Fire erupted out of the impact points, consuming the affected troll and burning it to ash in half a second. Drew switched targets, launching a fireball at the last one still alive, burning it alive as well.

The group continued to run, the multihued clouds of the mana storm now visible on the horizon. They had to skirt around the frostfire storm that was still raging, but they were inside past the illusion before the first drops of rain hit.

Daryl must have told those inside that the trolls were sniffing around because they were met with a variety of homemade spears and firebombs. "It's okay; it's just us and some friends!" Drew shouted, afraid one of the scared individuals would make the same mistake he made back at the exchange. The former prisoners began lowering their weapons, and JP holstered his gun.

Daryl's voice appeared in Drew's head as Jholie and Bill began hugging their compatriots. "I'm posted up in a building across the way; I'll keep a watch until dark, but I don't think anything will be attacking us during the storm." Drew held his hand up and waved to Daryl in response since there was no way for him to answer back.

"Alright, everyone, a mana storm is hitting, so we're safe for the next few hours. Anyone who wants to can come to see me, and I'll cast refreshing rain on them. But we're going to be planning the rescue as soon as we can." It took a few minutes to sort everything out. Most everyone opted to stay awake to contribute to the plans, though a few, like Jholie, decided they would rather sleep.

As they were discussing sleep, Katie asked him, "When was the last time you actually slept, Drew? Not just passing out from slotting xatherite but really slept?"

"Before the Advent," he said without thinking, and it was loud enough that JP and Robbi heard him. Drew winced internally as they looked at him then each other again. Another piece of information they didn't need to have.

"I think you should sleep too. It can't be healthy for your brain to be going that fast for that long. Besides, with Daryl not here, all the really important planning is going to go on tomorrow morning anyway," Katie said, and Sarah nodded in agreement.

Drew attempted to protest, but the two women refused to bend, and thirty minutes later, he'd taken his boots off and was attempting to sleep on the only couch in the building. It had been somewhat embarrassing how much everyone was willing to accommodate him. He'd saved everyone in the building except for JP and Robbi, and they were all willing to make some sacrifices so that he could get a decent night's sleep.

Before the Advent, he had always had some trouble sleeping, but almost as soon as his eyes closed, he felt like his body had been waiting for this sleep for more than a week.

* * *

Drew smiled. He was warm and comfortable, and they were letting him sleep longer than he anticipated, his body waking up naturally. The soft silk sheets of the bed made almost no sound as he shifted.

Wait, silk sheets? He could feel them around him, and he cracked his eyes open. The view that greeted him was not the one he had fallen asleep to. He sat up to get a better view of the scene. Before him, a massive red and yellow nebula stretched out as far to either edge of the viewport as it would allow before being blocked by massive, metallic wings. He was in a luxuriously appointed bedroom; glowing, polished wood panels and plush carpeting made the room seem more organic, but the viewport and his experience playing space simulators told him that he was on a spaceship or space station.

Was he still asleep? Could this be some sort of dream? He pinched himself but didn't wake up.

Standing up, he realized that the 'form' he was currently in was made of some sort of slightly transparent looking plastic that was visibly shifting to his normal skin tone. A body but not his own. It was a strange realization, reminding him of the replicants in Blade Runner. Before he could delve too far down this philosophical rabbit hole, a chime sounded behind him, and he turned towards the wall, where a drawer slid out, revealing a pair of shoes, socks, and a one-piece jumpsuit with the symbol of a shield and spear crossed on the chest. On the shoulder, a rank insignia of an inverted diagonal line was visible.

Not liking the feeling of being naked, even though this form had no distinguishable private parts, he began putting the clothes on. As soon as he'd finished putting on his shoes, another chime sounded. He turned again to look as a young-looking human appeared from the other side of a door that had opened without a noise.

"Greetings, sir, I'm Themis. I'm here to escort you to the Admiral." He was holding a small blue glass pane in front of him that looked very much like a datapad would in Star Wars. "If I may say so, sir, you've caused quite a stir here. No one expected it to take you this long to arrive."

Drew frowned at the man. The name Themis was familiar to him—one of the minor Greek Gods. But he couldn't for the life of him remember what his portfolio had been. Horses and rivers maybe? Did that make him the god of travelers? As soon as he came near, the man turned and began leading him deeper into the spaceship. He had decided it was a spaceship instead of a station due to the lack of small craft when he was looking out the view plate.

"Themis, where am I?" Drew asked as he rushed to keep up with the secretary? Steward? Drew realized he wasn't entirely sure what the man's job on the ship entailed.

"Oh, sorry, Midshipman, you're on Olympus, the flagship of the Orion-Cygnan Fleet. We're currently near what Earth astronomers call the Ring Nebula. Although we're getting ready to deploy against the ninth Elatrin fleet, which will take us closer to the Deneb system. The admiral wanted to talk to you before we were out of range," Themis replied quite unhelpfully. "Normally, this meeting wouldn't occur for another decade or so, while we waited for you to grow into your powers and be ready to take the Oaths, but the Admiral insisted."

Drew stopped and stared at Themis' quickly retreating form. "What the hell is going on?"

Themis, hearing the distance between them increasing, turned around and tapped on the datapad he held before looking up at Drew. "You were notified that you had been granted membership into the Order of the Dragon, correct?"

Drew nodded his head, confused.

"As the local Order representative in this region of the Milky Way Galaxy, Admiral Ares has opted to take you on as a page until such a time as you are eligible for your training as a squire. Due to the unexpected nature of your emergence on a newly Advent'ed dimensional slice, you have created a rather unusual set of circumstances. But the rules of the Order are clear, and the Admiral has determined to assist you in your training, as is befitting an Order prospect of your potential. However, as I said earlier, we are currently readying the fleet for action against an invading Elatrin fleet. The system prevents the Admiral from doing more to assist you until you have reached the rank of Lieutenant-Commander. What little he can do will occur during your meeting with him."

"Does that answer your question, Midshipman Michalik?" Themis said with a smile, causing Drew to flashback to the first day of Advent talking to Aevis during the tutorial.

"Not particularly, but I imagine that is as much as I'm likely to get," Drew said, and Themis nodded his head to confirm his guess.

"Very well, then please follow me, the Admiral is quite busy."

Drew followed along as the man entered an elevator, and as soon as Drew had entered as well, the lift began moving. Drew could only tell because the auras around him shifted rapidly; there was no sense of motion from the machine itself. They stood in uncomfortable silence for some time, which Drew used to take the time to examine Themis' aura, which was almost completely green. He hadn't seen anyone that was so predominantly one color among any of the Earth-3 inhabitants he'd seen.

Themis frowned as he watched Drew look at him. "You are an interesting specimen, Midshipman Michalik. It's clear you already have some awareness of the mana spectrum and some way to refrain from answering a sleep sync for several days. I'm beginning to understand why Admiral Ares was so insistent on you receiving your introduction before we left the range of the sleep sync."

Chapter Twenty-Nine — Introduction

They had passed a few people in the short walk from the corridor. All of them had given Themis and him a respectful distance. They were all wearing a similar jumpsuit to the one he'd been given but with rank insignia on the right upper arm instead of the shoulder epaulets he and Themis were wearing. Themis' shoulder board held two diamonds and three diagonal lines, significantly more complex than his own single diagonal line. The only assumption he could make from that was that he was clearly a much higher rank than Drew.

"Are you a member of the Order of the Dragon?" Drew finally asked. Themis laughed involuntarily—it was the first time Drew had managed to break the man's calm facade—and then shook his head.

"No, I am a member of the Order of the Scale," the other man answered, glancing at the datapad in front of him. "Admiral Ares is the only assault mage in the fleet, aside from yourself, of course. However, it would be appreciated if you would please refrain from asking any questions. There are rules in place that prevent me from interacting too closely with a newly Advent'ed citizen. We're pushing the limits of what is allowed by bringing you here so early as it is."

That of course, raised more questions in Drew's mind. Who made the rules that these obviously powerful people had to obey? How rare were assault mages anyway? He realized that they must be relatively rare if simply being one had earned him an officer's commission and a knighthood.

Since Themis didn't appear to have any intention of answering his questions, and there was nothing but the quickly passing auras behind the walls of the lift for him to look at, Drew spent the next two minutes pondering the answers to his internal questions. When the door to the lift finally opened, it was onto the bridge of the ship.

It appeared to be more the bridge of an expensive luxury yacht than a warship. Brilliantly glowing wood paneling, sleek displays, and plush seats all focused towards a single man sitting in a throne-like chair in the center of the room. Another thirty or forty people populated the bridge at various consoles, but Drew's attention was caught by the man in the center chair.

It was impossible to guess his age, with a fit frame and young face that contrasted heavily with the shortcut, salt and pepper hair that crowned his head. Most of the people on the bridge had epaulets as well, but the man in the captain's chair was obviously the most ornate. As Themis lead him towards the man, he got a better view of them; each shoulder sported two dragons coiled intricately around each other.

As they got closer, Drew could see Ares' aura, which was a turbulent red with undertones of orange and yellow that made it look like a roaring fire. When they were within twenty feet, the man looked up from the three-dimensional star map he was examining. Seeing Themis and Drew, he quirked an eyebrow at the former. "You finally managed to sync him?"

With a salute, Themis confirmed his commander's question, "Indeed, sir. He finally responded to the sync."

"Excellent!" Ares turned his entire attention to Drew. "Welcome to the Olympus, Drew Michalik!" His voice boomed, and everyone on the bridge stopped what they were doing to glance towards the center of the room. Drew shuffled his feet slightly.

"Thank you, sir. Although I must admit I'm still not entirely sure why I have been... synced," Drew responded, glancing around at all the people that continued to stare at him.

Ares stood up and gestured to another man. "Enyalios has the conn." Another man who had been standing near Ares waited for the admiral to move and then took his seat. "Come, Drew, we have much to discuss and little time." Drew and Themis followed along behind Ares, who led them to a door that connected into a ready room. Ares took the main seat and gestured for Drew to sit at one across from him. Themis closed his eyes briefly, and the room glowed with a green light, though he remained standing near the door instead of joining Drew and Ares.

"I apologize for this highly irregular meeting, but we have never seen an assault mage appear prior to the third generation after Advent. In fact, your split's emergence on Earth-1 was so unexpected that we rerouted a number of assets to Earth to speed up the splitting process," Ares paused for a moment, pulling up a hologram that displayed Earth in triplicate, "and I think you are proof that it was a more than worthy use of our resources." He paused and steepled his fingers; Drew didn't dare interrupt the man who seemed to exude confidence.

"I know you have many questions, Drew. Unfortunately, I am unable to answer most of them. What few I can answer will relate to this," he said, pointing to the globes. "As you know, Earth has been split three times; the first split was only seven Earth years ago. Normally, we would wait longer between splits, usually between ten and thirty years. However, when Earth-1's Drew registered as an assault mage, the Pantheons agreed for the first time in nearly thirteen centuries to dedicate a significant allotment of mana to facilitate a more rapid splitting."

Glancing at Drew to make sure he was following, Ares continued, "Drew-1, the you that originated on Earth-1, was an amazing find. It's uncommon for an assault mage to appear before the fourth generation after Advent. To have one in the first generation... well, as I said, you and your splits are in a unique position." He zoomed in on the third Earth, and as he did so, Drew realized that he was being shown the major ley lines of the planet. There were a few dozen major hubs, each corresponding to a city of some importance to pre-Advent Earth. However, the Washington DC node was considerably bigger than the others; while the others all seemed to be made up of smaller nodes around them, the DC node was fed by these other large nodes, and it was roughly half again the size of the next largest.

"What you are looking at are the ley lines on Earth-3. Each connection of lines creates a node. These smaller nodes," Ares said, pointing to the various major city nodes, "are the secondary nexuses. Your other two splits appeared near the Denver and Miami nodes. While that allows us some exciting opportunities, your appearance nearly on top of the primary nexus is a boon we could not have hoped for."

"You do not know this yet, but it is possible to claim a nexus. When you do so, you are able to influence how the system interacts with the area that feeds that nexus. This comes in a myriad of forms, but a good nexus controller greatly enhances the progression and survival rate of those within the areas near them." Ares tried to say more, but frowned, "With you being near the primary nexus, you could greatly influence Earth-3's progression, even going so far as to..." Ares continued, but Drew could no longer understand what was being said. It was only at this point that he realized that Ares and Themis were not, in fact, speaking English but rather some other language that his mind was interpreting as English.

Whatever it was that had been allowing for that translation was no longer working. Ares looked at Drew's face and frowned. "You could not hear that last part, could you?" He glared at Themis, who shrugged slightly. Drew wasn't sure what the interplay here was, but clearly, Ares wanted to share more than Themis was letting him. The two conversed back and forth several times while Ares grew visibly angry. Themis' tone was adamant, but his entire body held a large amount of tension as if he were afraid of the other man. With a final growl of anger, Ares ceased talking,, and then after a few quick breaths, continued, and the translation magic re-engaged.

"My apologies, Drew. Themis has reminded me that there are some things I cannot tell you. Suffice it to say, that it will be in you and yours best interests to claim the central nexus as soon as possible." Ares paused long enough to shoot Themis one last glare and then steepled his fingers.

"Now, I think Themis told you that I would like to offer you a position as my page with the assumption that you would become my squire when you are promoted to an appropriate level."

Drew nodded his head. "Themis did say that. The way you say it makes it sounds like I have a choice in the matter?"

"Indeed, no one is going to force you to become my squire. As the commanding officer of the fleet which governs your world, I have primacy, but I assume that the others will also make offers when they have discovered I have already done so. Although the others may try to snatch up some of the earlier split versions or wait to see what later splits produce." Ares shifted the hologram, and it zoomed out. Various star systems were shaded in hundreds of different colors. "These are the Protectorate Pantheons. Each color represents a different iron fleet. Eventually, if you survive and rank up as I expect you will, you will build your own fleet and be assigned a territory, as is the mandate to every member of our Order."

"Until then, you should know a little of what we fight. Humanity is the youngest of the known awakened species, but we have some of the largest territory, due in large part to the fact that we are the only race which has given birth to an assault mage. The protectorate is surrounded by older and more established races who are jealous of our power. We are also one of the few awakened races that we know of without allies. There may be more, but our attempts to explore are usually met with stiff resistance."

"Our enemies are numerous; the largest group we face here in the Orion-Cygnus arm of the Milky Way Galaxy are the Daoine. They have several member races, but the main belligerents are the Elatrin, Da Danann, Spyry Jyon, and Piksies. For the most part, we spend our time fending off their fleets, although we do get the occasional Bauk refugee armada or Azura pilgrims." Ares paused, considering. "The fact is, every assault mage we find means we can expand human territory. You and your splits will be the means by which quadrillions of humans will get a chance to live in relative peace."

"You are free to choose your allegiance to any pantheon until you become a squire, at which point you and your mentor will work together to train your fleet. But I hope you will stay here, where you can protect your home planet. In any case," Ares paused and straightened his posture, "I, Cassius Felix Ares, hereby offer you a position as my page on Olympus, and with that offer you the donum duplici. The first represents my faith in you, and it will ensure your integrity in the battles to come. The second is from the Order. It was entrusted to me with a gravity I cannot easily describe. You are to insert it immediately and never utter its name."

A blinking notification appeared in front of Drew's eyes, informing him that Ares would like to trade him two xatherite: one called stricto mentis clypeus and the other simply called aeon.

Xatherite Crystal Name: Stricto Mentis Clypeus
Xatherite Color: Green
Xatherite Grade: Rare
Xatherite Rarity: Limited
Type: Mental
Effect: Creates a shield around the bearer's mind that prevents unwanted mental intrusion.
Mana recharge time: Not applicable.

Xatherite Crystal Name: Aeon
Xatherite Color: Violet
Xatherite Grade: Primitive
Xatherite Rarity: Singular
Type: Divine
Effect: The beginning of the path.
Mana recharge time: Not applicable.

Drew stared at the two xatherite for a full minute. The first was impressive enough, but what on Earth did aeon even do? It was the first xatherite that didn't seem to meet the naming convention he was used to, as a primitive grade without an adjective preceding it. The description was completely unhelpful; the beginning of what path? It was a violet, but it didn't say what it changed. What exactly was a divine type xatherite? He had only seen magic and physical before, and now he had two new types: divine and mental. To buy time, he asked, "What responsibilities will I have if I accept this gift?" Drew kept the frown off his face as he considered what this man, this god, would want of him.

"Your only responsibility will be to survive, to grow so strong that your people are safe, that they need not fear the reapers in the night. To ensure that Humanity Prevails."

Chapter Thirty — Return

Drew accepted the transfer of the xatherite, and another notification appeared.

Drew Michalik-3 has entered into a mana-bound contract with Cassius Felix-9 (Ares). You are never to discuss the xatherite you received from him on behalf of the Order of the Dragon. Doing so will result in death.

Ares smiled at him. "Excellent, we don't have much time, but Themis will take the pain of the slotting from you. Before he does that, I have some words of advice to you as my page." He pulled up the holographic display of the Human Protectorate's territory and zoomed in on a portion of the Orion-Cygnus Arm of the galaxy. "This is my territory. My fleet protects just under two hundred human populated worlds across all twenty-three dimensions, for a grand total of several trillions of human lives. All of that goes away if I die; my fleet would be completely unable to defend against the predation of the Daoine, Bauk, or Azura."

"The life of an assault mage is not an easy one; we are the strength of humanity. My fleet alone contains more humans than lived on the Earth you knew before Advent. I send people to their deaths regularly. They follow my orders, putting themselves in harm's way because they know what is at risk, and all of them would die to protect me." Ares frowned, looking down at his hands. "I tell you this not to brag; they do their duty as I do mine, but you need to realize how important you are. Your life is worth more than those around you."

"I know that where you are from, they believe that all men are created equal, that all lives have equal value. Perhaps there is some cosmic arithmetic where that is true, but as you are the means by which trillions upon trillions of lives will be saved, your life is equal to those trillions of lives. You must change your thinking; for if you die, you are condemning those trillions to die with you. You are worth more than they are. It is not something any of us asked for, but it is a truth that we must live with."

Drew frowned, opening his mouth to argue, then stopped. If there was an argument against that point of view, he didn't know what it was. It had been a long time since he was a religious person, but it still felt wrong to say he was better than someone else. While he had his internal debate, Ares stood up.

"Drew, I look forward to talking to you more, but you should slot those xatherite and go back home. It will be time for you to wake up soon." He came around the table and put a hand on Drew's shoulder. "No life should be spent cheaply, Drew. Just remember the lives you can save, focus on the good you will do—not the bitter path we walk."

And with that he was gone, back through the door and onto the bridge, shouting orders as he went to prepare the fleet for departure. Themis saluted him as he left and then turned to Drew. "If you will be so kind as to remain seated while you slot the xatherite, I will ensure you wake up back on Earth."

Drew sat back down, then looked at Themis' impassive face. "Is what he said true? Am I going to be required to send people to their deaths?"

Themis frowned slightly and then nodded his head slowly. "It is not my place to pass judgment on the actions of the Pantheons, but Admiral Ares is well known for keeping as many of his men safe as possible. But even an assault mage of his caliber cannot save everyone."

Drew nodded his head in acknowledgment, if not understanding. Then, leaning back, he slotted Aeon in the violet slot nearest the origin, leaving him with only one violet left on the entire map and put stricto mentis clypeus in the green just to the left of major blink step. When he clicked to accept the changes, he felt a massive pain flow through his entire body for a split second before he sunk into unconsciousness.

* * *

Drew woke up on the couch. The windows showed that the first rays of dawn weren't far off, and he sat up, rubbing his forehead. "Weird dream," he muttered to himself before he opened his xatherite map to check. To his surprise, the two xatherite given to him by Ares were there. It hadn't been a dream at all. Was he relieved that it had been real?

Now in his early thirties, Drew had been drifting for a long time. Joining the Coast Guard had been an attempt to get direction in his life, and it had mostly worked. He had never really felt like he fit in before; he'd always had friends, and his family had always supported him, but he had never felt... important before Advent.

Was the fact that he was literally the most important person on Earth something he wanted? He didn't think so; he remembered the look in Ares' eyes as he told him about having to send people to their deaths, about not being able to save everyone. Already, he had encountered times when he couldn't save everyone; Juan, Mitch, and Rob had all died when he should have been able to help them... when he should have been stronger.

"What was it about?" Katie asked sleepily from where she sat in a bucket chair near the couch. She lifted her arms into the air and stretched. Drew sat up and did the same with a smile.

"Outer space," Drew said, looking around for Sarah. Katie opened an eye and raised her brows to question it. "We should do a patrol around the building. Do you know where Sarah is?" There were several sleeping forms surrounding them, but he didn't see any with Sarah's telltale curly, brunette hair.

Katie frowned. "Not sure; she might not have gone to sleep." Katie pulled her hair out of the ponytail she had kept it in overnight and pulling out a comb, began brushing her hair.

"Come back when you find her. I should be ready by then... and grab some food if there's anything warm."

Drew grunted and set off to look for the Ensign, not sure how anyone would have made hot food. As he walked through the building, he was somewhat amazed by the level of activity that had continued through the night. Most of those who had taken him up on the rain had been working to create weapons or armor. When he asked around, he was told Sarah was back with Min Sun getting her armor fitted.

Sarah was indeed dressed in troll skin leathers when he found her and was reattaching the spider leg to a spear shaft with Min Sun's help. When he entered, Sarah looked up long enough to smile and then went back to the task at hand. Min Sun, on the other hand, looked up, and seeing him, smiled very broadly.

"Mr. Drew, I fix your clothes. Try on. See if need fix," she commanded him. It took Drew a few seconds to realize she was talking about his armor; the diminutive Korean lady must have picked it up after he removed it before falling asleep the night before. He noticed as he did so that she had changed the position on several of the buckles to make it much easier to get on. She just smiled at him when he commented on it. Drew wasn't sure how much English she understood. He assumed she was one of the soldier's wives and had come back with him after a tour in Korea. It was a fairly common practice, and most of the army towns he had been in had strong Korean communities.

Glancing at the armor, it appeared Min Sun had managed to finish attaching the chitin pieces that the Go'rai had originally used to reinforce the armor. Putting the armor back on, Drew discovered it was indeed a much better fit. Min Sun tsked and made a few alterations with her skill, and by the time she was finished, the armor was much snugger to his frame, which had lost a few pounds with the lack of good food and exercise he'd been getting the last few days. While he was finished getting his armor fitted, Sarah had rewrapped her spear, adding a thin leather grip to the metal pipe they had originally attached it to.

"Come on, I want to take you and Katie on a patrol for a bit; those trolls sniffing around yesterday before the storm have me worried." They retraced their steps to where he had left Katie. She was ready to go, eating a few dry granola bars with some water. She whistled when she saw Drew in his new armor.

"Nice. So, where are we going?" she asked as she picked up her own spear while eyeing Sarah's alterations with a little bit of envy.

"Just out for a quick survey of the area, want to make sure those trolls didn't leave any stragglers behind," Drew answered, while Sarah began casting her buffs on the group. "Leave the knight here. It will be more useful blocking the door than out there; we might need to climb a bit."

Katie nodded, and the three of them set off for the front entrance, but JP and Robbi had apparently heard that Drew was up and about and came looking for him, finding them right as they were about to leave.

"Hey Drew, where you off to?" JP asked with a slight frown upon seeing the two women with their spears.

"Oh, just going to do a quick circuit of the building, make sure there are no trolls around," Drew answered then glanced back. "Stay here and guard the building. We should be back in less than thirty minutes; with the small approach paths, you're a better choice for that than me. I work best in open spaces." JP frowned again but nodded his head in agreement.

Turning towards the open entrance, Drew furrowed his brow. Was it always this easy for him to give orders? Most of the people here had been rescued by him, so they were more inclined to do what he asked of them, but JP and Robbi were another story. Was this part of being a red mage? His mind continued to grind away at the many questions it had acquired since Advent but generated no new answers. When they were far enough away that Drew didn't think anyone could overhear them, he told the two other Coasties about what had happened to him during the night, editing it only so as not to include anything referencing Aeon.

"That's a lot of information, Drew. Somewhere there are other versions of us trying to survive this? Makes you wonder which one of us has a soul or if any of us do," Katie said while leaning against her spear.

"You took all this in stride and just sort of kept pushing forward, which is much more than the rest of us did. Without you, we would all be dead. That includes pretty much everyone we've met since Advent, except JP and Robbi," Sarah said, tugging on her braid. It was something Drew had never seen someone do but which caused him to hide a laugh, as he remembered a book series he had read as a kid where a character tugged on her braid repeatedly.

"But I don't like how this Ares is making decisions for you. You shouldn't have to join the Order of the Dragon if you don't want to," Katie added. "I mean, I know that we've basically been shanghaied here, but they can't force you to accept their morals."

Drew ran a hand through his hair; they were almost back to the entrance to the auto shop and hadn't seen any sign of the trolls. "I guess, but if I sit back and do nothing..." Drew trailed off for a minute, thinking. "I can't do that. I can't just let all those people die if I have a chance to save them. And if it gives me an edge to do that?" That was why he had enlisted. He wanted to help make the world a better place. He had thought the coast guard would help him do that. "Could you? Would you if you were in my shoes?"

Katie and Sarah both shook their heads, but Sarah answered, "No, Drew. We wouldn't. We'll both help you as much as we can, but..." She held her empty hand up an expression of helplessness.

"Well, I was thinking about that, and I think I have some ideas about how all of us can work together a little better to make us more effective at combat." Drew began explaining his ideas. Most of his ideas were for Katie, but he had some ideas for Sarah too; however, those would take either some additional xatherite or pieces of equipment.

Chapter Thirty-One — Murphy

They returned to the auto shop almost exactly... who knew how much later. Drew added mechanical watches to the list of things he needed to acquire. The lack of knowledge about the world around him was beginning to get very annoying; he missed GPS, his cell phone, and hamburgers. The thought of a hamburger made his stomach rumble. Katie and Sarah both laughed.

"I take it you're hungry?" Katie asked, and Drew nodded, digging through his pack to pull out a handful of beef jerky.

"Yes. I really want a breakfast burger with a nice, drippy, sunny side up egg on top."

"Oh gosh, I would really love a honey mustard and avocado salad," Sarah said, her own stomach rumbling.

"I'd like some fresh waffles with whipped cream and strawberries," Katie said. The others nodded in agreement.

"Oh man, remember in A-school, they had that waffle bar every weekend—fresh waffles, any kind of berry you could ask for, whipped cream, and shaved chocolate?" Drew added.

"Yeah, it was basically the only thing that was edible during the entire A-school experience," Katie said with a grin. Sarah just nodded her head, not having spent months in Petaluma suffering the results of students learning how to cook like they had.

Daryl greeted them at the door to the auto shop. He stared at Drew for a moment, then frowned.

"Hey Daryl, how's it going?" Drew asked.

"You can't hear me?" Daryl asked with a frown, and Drew paused for a moment.

"Oh right, one second." He tried to think up an interface—his new xatherite said it would block all unwanted mental intrusion, and it apparently defaulted to blocking everything. Nothing happened, so instead, he thought about allowing Daryl's communication in. "Try now."

'Hello?' Drew heard Daryl's voice in his mind and smiled.

"Okay, I got it that time. Sorry, I had to unblock you," Drew said with a shrug, and Daryl just glanced from Drew to the two girls.

"Did you guys pick up more xatherite out there or something?" he asked. All three of the Coasties just laughed and moved into the building.

"We ready for the planning meeting?" Drew asked between a mouthful of the jerky he'd taken out of his pack after commenting on food. Daryl assented, following along with the other three more out of habit than anything else. They were all as crazy as Drew was.

"What on earth did they do to Coasties to make them so strange?" Daryl muttered under his breath. The Coasties opted to ignore the rhetorical question, although Drew had an urge to belt out some random phrases they had been required to memorize in boot camp about King Neptune. Most of the survivors had collected around a workbench in the middle of one of the auto bays. There were a few papers taped and stapled together that recreated their knowledge of the interior of the former DIA building.

Once all but the three or four people who'd been posted as sentries were gathered, Sarah stepped forward and cleared her throat; the talking immediately ceased. Sarah seemed a little surprised by the suddenness of the quiet. "Excuse me, everyone. I just wanted to get this planning session in order. The sooner we organize everything, the sooner we can rescue everyone." She paused for a minute to gather her thoughts. "First things first, what's our status on weapons, food, and armor?"

Min Sun answered first, "We have fifteen troll armor, two orc armor, and that's it." Sarah nodded her head in understanding.

Bill spoke next, "Ma'am, aside from you and Katie's two spears and JP and Robbi's guns, we've got a half dozen metal bats and other blunt weapons mostly improvised with what was available in the auto shop. We also have five fire axes and about a dozen handmade grenades. As for food, we have about five days' worth for twenty-four people, give or take a few meals."

Sarah nodded. "Alright, so we need to get more food for the prisoners we rescue, and some more weapons wouldn't hurt the cause either. Bill, I want to discuss some logistics with you afterward, but I'll turn the meeting over to Drew to plan the rescue itself."

Sarah stepped back, and Drew took her spot. "So, I guess first thing... Do we think they're going to send another food gathering group out today?"

No one answered, and the silence lingered for ten heartbeats. Bill finally broke it, "Well, they're going to have to feed people somehow. A day or two might be fine, but..." He trailed off, not wanting to say the implications.

"What are the trolls eating?" Sarah asked since the food runs had been for human food only.

"I've never seen a troll eat anything," Bill said, and all of the prisoners murmured in agreement.

"Alright, well, let's assume they're going to send out another team today. If they do, we need to be in a position to ambush them again. We also need to work on how we're going to get everyone else out. Does anyone have any skills that can cut through metal? Even if it's slow—I personally have a small amount of acid I can use a couple times a minute. Anything like that?" Drew looked around, but no one seemed about to raise their hands.

"Okay." Drew turned to JP. "What's your effective range with those pistols?"

"I can hit center mass on moving targets fifty-five out of sixty times at sixty feet."

"Wow, okay. Can you use a rifle?"

"Yes, I'm not as good a shot with one, but all of my skills work on any firearm."

"Any particular reason you aren't carrying one?" Drew asked, running a hand through his hair. Everyone else was pretty much just watching the exchange between the two.

"Lost it on the bridge," JP answered with a glance at Robbi.

The interplay between the two was not lost on Drew, but he moved past it. "Alright, who knows where we can get JP a military grade rifle?"

Looking around the room, Drew got a few shrugs, but no one seemed to know where to find one. "Alright, we'll have to raid the exchange; there should be some rifles in there. We'll send a few people. Arm as many people as you can; not everything is going to be immune to bullets, and we're going to have a lot of people to rescue."

They got into the depths of planning how to rescue the people left inside the DIA building. After discussing the location where everyone was being held and where the trolls inside were, the plan presented by JP ended up being the most popular one. Katie would create a safe location with JP, Daryl, and a few others acting as scouts, and the two illusionists would hide the building until Drew had managed to eat a hole into the wall with his acid dart spell.

If everything went well, they would be able to evacuate about half the people before any of the trolls even knew that they were there. The other half would require Drew to act as a defensive screen from within the building while Bill, Sarah, and the others healed anyone injured and evacuated everyone.

The first major problem was that there was no intermediate safe location before they got back to the stadium. There was no stopping point between here and there, at least, not one that could hold several hundred people. The mana storms had been coming every other night at this point, so that was their deadline to get back to the stadium.

The trip was only a few miles along a paved road, but they would need to find a way to guard against mana twisted creatures like squirrels and turtles harrying them until they got to the bridge. Then they would need to cross the bridge while defending against the squid, at which point it was only a few blocks through the patrolled area around the stadium until they were safe. The difficulty with the first portion was that they really only had JP and Drew that could stand against the creatures; the others would be armed with a few guns, the spears, and other improvised weapons they had made. The only workable solution they had for keeping safe along the bridge was for Katie to create a tunnel. It would take some time, with Drew and JP acting as a rear guard on the near end of the bridge while Daryl went ahead to ask for help from the stadium.

The plan of action decided, the group split up into their various tasks. Drew, Robbi, and Daryl headed north to ambush the trolls if they opted to do another food run. Despite what Ares had told him, Drew wanted to go alone, but even Katie and Sarah had insisted he take Robbi with him in case something got close. Daryl was going to be acting as their forward scout; his invisibility was invaluable for that kind of activity. JP, Sarah, Katie, and all the rest of the former prisoners went to the exchange and commissary to stock up on additional weapons, ammo, and food.

They waited in ambush in the same place he had two days previously, although this time he didn't bother to hide as much. He was too worried they wouldn't see him and would attack the other group. He spent thirty minutes pondering Ares' words and the things that happened to him onboard the Olympus. If they could transfer a mind into another body like that, why would Ares need to send people to their deaths? Couldn't they just transfer them into those fake bodies? Or was it a cost thing? Or a cooldown issue? Did his delaying sleep cause Ares to send some of his people to their deaths that otherwise could have been saved if the spell had been available?

The sound of gunshots to the south roused Drew from his reverie. He glanced south and realized that someone had sent up a flare; where had they gotten flares? He pushed himself up off the roof, blink stepped to the ground, shouting to Robbi, "The exchange!" Hopefully, Daryl heard him as well, but there was no time to ensure the scout was coming with them. Robbi quickly caught up to him and kept pace with him, but his pistol wouldn't be worth much against trolls.

Drew urged himself to go faster but was slowed by his lack of physical training and the heavy combat boots he wore. They were a couple hundred feet from the backside of the commissary. Katie's group should be either in there or in the exchange still, which was another couple hundred feet of parking lot away from the far side of the commissary. As he ran, he continued to hear gunshots, and he pushed through the stitch that was gnawing at his abdomen.

Rounding the southeast corner of the commissary to where they could see the parking lot, they found the source of the shooting. More than a dozen trolls were circling a group of humans. JP was shooting anything that got close, but there were too many people for him to be able to cover all sides, and the trolls looked like they were trying to separate individuals to carry off.

Drew skidded to a stop, slipping on the wet morning grass but kept his footing and began to cast a frostfire storm to protect one side from the trolls. Robbi had stopped with him, but when he began casting a spell, he moved about ten feet out and pulled out another pistol, ready to defend Drew from any trolls that attacked.

The storm spell caught three trolls who had been jumping towards the group and cut them off from the west side of the humans. JP continued to unload his pistols into trolls that came close, but as soon as the spell went off, the trolls disengaged, moving away from their former prey. Drew shouted and launched a fireball at a troll, causing most of the trolls to look his direction as he began casting firestorm. The fireball missed the troll he'd been targeting but hit one behind it as the first jumped away.

They cried something in their own language, and all the ones on the north and east side of the group turned their attention towards Drew, leaving JP to handle the ones on the south side of the group. Drew's firestorm went off while the trolls were still relatively grouped up, catching all but two of them within its radius. Two trolls were still bearing down on him and about one hundred seventy-five feet away from him. Drew cast dancing sword, hoping that it wouldn't get to the point he needed it but not wanting to waste frostfire ball's cooldown while they still were plenty far enough away to dodge the spell.

As they breached within one hundred feet of him, Drew launched frostfire ball, targeting the one that was lagging, where it impacted above the troll, sending icy shrapnel flying. The leading troll's jump faltered as he was impacted from behind by ice shards. Drew launched an acid dart at his face and then figuring that the cooldown was off, launched a fireball at it, causing the troll to disappear in the fiery explosion.

Taking a breath, he frowned, the adrenaline causing his hair to stand on end. Almost on instinct, he blink stepped forward as far as he could, and hearing the deafening crack of thunder behind him told him his instincts had been correct. The shaman who'd sacrificed humans had escaped from his ambush that first day, and he didn't particularly like Drew.

Chapter Thirty-Two — Timer

Drew looked behind him to make sure that Robbi was still standing; he was running forward but was otherwise fine. Drew began running towards JP and the others while scanning around him for the shaman. Where had they come from? How had they gotten out of the DIA building? The west side of that building was open baseball fields and then the river, which would have been nearly impossible to sneak through. Which meant they would have had to go east, along the freeway maybe, and circled back?

Scanning the rooftop of the exchange, the only large building to the south, he didn't see anything out of the normal. They could be lying down, waiting for the spell to come off cooldown? The shaman was an issue, but his late appearance and single attack indicated that he was probably there for Drew. It lent credence to Ares' statements about him being more important than everyone else and explained why the Go'rai had mostly ignored the group back in the dungeon. How could he leverage that? He needed to be able to flush the shaman out.

He was getting close to where JP was fighting off the last few surviving trolls. He launched an acid dart at one of the nearest ones, catching it in the side before it realized he was there. JP had managed to whittle down the attackers until there were only two left, but the problem was that they were too exposed. "Everyone fall back to the commissary!" he shouted as he ran closer. His approach and spell distracted one of the trolls, who exploded in a burst of fire as JP's incendiary shots took it unawares. That left one who started making a hasty retreat, but Drew launched a fireball at it which caught it mid-jump, killing it before it could land.

"There's another one casting lightning bolts. Rooftop probably," Drew shouted, and JP immediately sheathed his pistols and unslung the rifle he had across his back as his eyes darted around the rooftops. Everyone else was making a beeline to the commissary and the safety it provided from ranged attacks.

"Don't see anything," JP shouted as he walked backward, rifle at the ready.

"No idea where it came from, my guess would be rooftops," Drew said, his head on a swivel, looking to the south and west. The eastern approach was wide open, but Drew considered that the least likely source for the troll to be attacking from since there was not enough cover there.

"If it's smart, it'll stay down now that its cover has been blown, attack us again later, or pin us down in the commissary," Robbi said, having caught up with the two of them. Drew stumbled and looking down, realizing that there were small, inch-tall walls in irregular patterns all over the ground near him—Katie's attempt at keeping the troll's at bay. "Careful, rough terrain," he said to JP, who was just about to trip on the small walls.

Drew turned and ran towards the commissary, convinced that the troll shaman was gone, for now at least. Besides, who knew what sort of dangers would be waiting for his people in the commissary? He faltered for a second when he realized he thought of the former prisoners as his people. When had that mental shift happened? Ever since the Advent, he'd been acquiring more and more of these rhetorical questions about the nature of his relationship with those around him and the world at large. However, his answers to those questions were frustratingly few.

Back at the relative safety of the commissary, Drew looked around. Bill was hugging a few people who seemed to be upset but not injured, while Sarah was gathering the injured together to heal them. He looked around for Katie and found her organizing groups to scout out the commissary to ensure nothing had become mana twisted since the last time they were here. Daryl wasn't visible, and Drew hoped he would show up soon and maybe tell him where the shaman ran off to. Robbi and Trey were chanting something near the doorway, hopefully creating an illusion to prevent them from being attacked from afar.

Drew glanced at JP, who had turned a shopping cart on its side and was using it to prop up his rifle as he scanned the parking lot for threats. Feeling slightly useless, he walked over to Katie, waiting until she was done sending a group out, doling out glowrocks and light sticks. Drew really needed to figure out who was making the light sticks. They were more like flashlights than the rocks and could easily light things up at a distance. While he was waiting, the blinking notification appeared in the corner of his vision, meaning he had finally dropped out of combat by the system's reckoning. Hopefully, that meant Daryl had killed the shaman.

Congratulations, Midshipman. Your Minor Energize xatherite has reached level 4. Charge requirement has reduced. Congratulations, Midshipman. Your Minor Lightning Bolt xatherite has reached level 4. Damage has increased. Congratulations, Midshipman. Your Minor Mana Shield xatherite has reached level 4. Damage absorbed has increased. Congratulations, Midshipman. Your Acid Dart xatherite is ready to be upgraded.

He had been looking forward to acid dart leveling up for quite some time now; it was hopefully going to be worth casting soon. He activated the upgrade immediately, wincing as the beginnings of a headache formed, but he was already casting energize on himself, causing it to disappear almost immediately.

Xatherite Crystal Name: Minor Acid Arrow
Xatherite Color: Red
Xatherite Grade: Common
Xatherite Rarity: Widespread

Type: Magic
Effect: Creates two fast moving balls of acid from a finger that travel in a straight line until they impact a target, dealing small amounts of acid damage.
Mana recharge time: 16.1 seconds

Congratulations, Midshipman. Linked skill: "Minor Shocking Acid Arrow" has been obtained.

Linked Skill Name: Minor Shocking Acid Arrow
Xatherite Color(s): Red
Linked Skill Grade: Common
Type: Magic
Effect: Creates two fast moving balls of acid from a finger that travel in a straight line until they impact a target, dealing small amounts of acid damage. Upon contact, each ball will impart a small amount of electrical damage.
Mana recharge time: 16.1 seconds

"Well, that's interesting," Drew muttered under his breath. Apparently, linked skills could not be created with skills that were in the lowest third of the grade skills, or at least, some linked skills required a certain grade before they would activate, even if you had the appropriate xatherite in a linked slot. He had also been correct in that when it upgraded from basic to common, it had gained greatly in effectiveness. He glanced over his map and wondered if there would be a similar upgrade in quality when he went from rare to advanced. For some reason, he didn't doubt that it would.

The apparently nonlinear amount of experience needed to level up xatherite meant it would be quite a while before he got any of his xatherite past that barrier, though, especially

considering that his rare xatherite still hadn't even attuned...
Although Aeon hadn't attuned yet either, so maybe rarity played a
role in how difficult it was to level and attune. However, since he
had no idea how much extra 'rarity' singular or limited had
compared to common, widespread, or uncommon, that wouldn't
help him determine base experience costs much.

Drew really wished he could go back and ask Ares
questions about the basics of the system. There were so many
things he just didn't know and didn't have a good way of figuring
out. He frowned and shook his head, realizing that Katie was
looking at him.

"Drew?"

"Oh sorry, was upgrading xatherite," Drew said
sheepishly. He had taken the system's awarding of XP as a sign to
say they were out of danger, but that clearly wasn't the case. "I'm
sorry, what did you need me to do?"

"Hold these glowrocks and walk around. See if anything
attacks you," Katie said, holding out a mesh bag with about six
glowrocks in it, creating a much brighter light source than an
individual rock would have. "I've told everyone to run towards the
light if they find anything. Head to the canned goods aisle first;
that's our best bet for ready food."

Drew nodded and took the mesh bag. Glancing back out
the door, JP and Robbi standing there staring out at the parking
lot comforted Drew, though. There was something off about the
two cops, but that didn't mean that they both weren't excellent in a
fight. It was nice to have someone else who could deal some
serious damage on his side... If they were on his side? He pushed
those thoughts away since there was no way for him to prove his
suspicions one way or the other, and he didn't doubt it was Robbi
and JP's primary goal to bring people back to Nat's Park.

Walking down the aisles proved to be incredibly boring.
Aside from two-foot-long rats that he killed with a single acid
arrow spell, there were no mana twisted beasts jumping off the
ceilings at the people who were shoving large amounts of canned

food into the carts that they were preparing for the convoy north. Drew wasn't sure if that was a good thing or not, but he was glad for the extra functionality he'd already acquired from the xatherite upgrade. Another cooldown and a big jump in damage, especially the linked version.

After about ten minutes of circling those gathering food without any further incidents, Drew headed back to the front of the store. It looked much the same, although Katie had created a series of walls hanging from the ceiling. He ducked under one and realized that they were a great defense against the troll's jumping ability.

Seeing Sarah, Bill, Katie, Robbi, and Daryl all circled discussing something, he headed in that direction. Sarah and Katie both nodded to him as he approached. Sarah continuing what she had been saying before he got there, "We're in pretty good shape here, but I don't like the idea of being pinned in."

Drew frowned, and Daryl mentally updated him, "*I found the shaman, but he teleported before I could attack him. Odds are we're going to have a significant invasion force here soon.*" That was just about the worst possible situation Drew could think of.

"We'll need Katie to block the other entrances so we don't get flanked—the employee entrance like the side doors and the loading dock," Drew said, and Sarah nodded.

"Good point, Drew. Why don't you take over for JP in a minute, and we'll send him and Katie out to close off the other entrances," Sarah said. Drew wanted to protest but knew that was probably the best option. "We'll keep most of the combatants close to the front door and have all the noncombatants ready to move if we need to."

"JP and I could go and hit them as they come out. We'd be able to see them from quite a ways away," Drew said, glancing at the fortifications. He didn't like the idea of being stuck in here while the trolls slowly ate away at their nerves.

"If we knew how they got around us in the first place, I'd agree with you, but since they got around our ambush once, we have to assume they'll be able to do it again. For all we know, they either found or made some tunnels that they used to get out somewhere in the housing area," Robbi said with a shake of his head.

Drew frowned, "I don't think turtling is going to keep us safe. This is just going to delay our doom. Our sight lines aren't good enough, and if they can tunnel from the DIA building, they'll be able to tunnel in here." Everyone else looked around, but no one had a rebuttal to that. "I think our best bet is to get out into the open; they only seem to have one person that can do ranged attacks."

Sarah shook her head, glancing behind him to where a few of the more injured and scared people had gathered. "I don't think we can move them again so soon after that attack. Maybe we could break out first thing tomorrow morning?"

Drew glanced at the fortifications. "We always knew we would have to deal with at least one night... but if we delay until tomorrow to leave, that will only give us about ten hours of daylight to rescue everyone and get them up to Nat's Stadium before the mana storm hits tomorrow evening."

Sarah bit her lip, but it was Bill who answered, "You're right; we need to get into position up there today. Katie can build some walls to keep everyone safe, but if we sit here tonight, we're never going to make the stadium before the storm. Which means we'd need to put off rescuing everyone until the day after... And deal with whatever retaliation the trolls are going to send. I have a feeling this next attack is going to be a doozy, too. We've beaten them back twice now, so they'll most likely send everything they have at us."

Chapter Thirty-Three — Calm

The group was silent for a few heartbeats as everyone considered the implications of Bill's words. Odds were good that everything the trolls could send at them would be sent at them soon, and they were going to meet them on the open field.

"Also, if anyone has upgrades to be done, now is the time to do them. I'm not sure how much experience you all got from that skirmish outside, but I know I got at least one upgraded xatherite," Drew said, trying to keep everyone's mind off the fact that they were going out to kill a bunch of trolls. "Daryl, did you find any xatherite on the trolls outside?"

"I didn't look. I came right back as soon as the shaman disappeared," Daryl said with a frown.

"Alright, head out now and look. We're gonna need anything we can get for this I think." Drew considered this for a moment. "Also, if you do find some, don't harvest it. I have a theory, and I want to give it a shot. If it's growing on an arm or something that is easy to cut off, do so. Also, harvest as many of their corpses as you can, but you only have ten minutes. Priority is the xatherite."

Daryl nodded and then disappeared, hopefully, to go harvest the bodies of the trolls. Drew turned to Bill and Sarah. "I need you two to get everyone ready to go in ten minutes. Grab as many shopping carts as you think we can easily move, but tell everyone that the second they aren't keeping pace, they need to abandon the cart. Their lives aren't worth a little bit of food."

"JP, I need you to refill as many magazines as you can. I don't want anyone else to be shooting; the trolls aren't going to be hurt by anyone else's shots. Recruit some people to carry magazines or guns and reload for you. Hopefully, we can get something automatic," Drew gave his orders to JP, and Robbi went with him to collect all the firearms and magazines they could. Drew turned to Katie. "I want to get as much flammable stuff as we can, hopefully things that will burn for a while. I'm going to try and cut off their lines of approach as much as possible. When we do finally settle down, I'll need you and as many people as we can creating fire barriers that will hopefully deter them from coming at us from all sides."

"When we do start fighting, I want you to start making a barrier around the noncombatants. If you can seal it off from above do that. Otherwise, just make it at least four stories tall. I don't want them jumping behind us." Katie nodded her head, and everyone dispersed off to do their various tasks.

Drew was left to himself for a few minutes, prepping for what was bound to be the largest single conflict he had been in since Advent. He tried to think of anything he might be forgetting. He could feel the weight of all those lives on his shoulders, not just the hundreds at stake here but the trillions or quadrillions that Ares had told him depended on him surviving.

Drew could escape right now; he could probably fly across the bridge without worrying about the squid ever trying to attack him. It would mean abandoning Katie, Sarah, Bill, Jholie, and all the others to die, though. He could take some of them with him maybe... Katie for sure. He could take all the people he knew. That group, smaller and more capable, would be able to fight their way to Nat's Park. They would be safe, and it would just be the other fifteen people or so he condemned to die.

He wished he hadn't thought of running, that he was the kind of person that wanted to do the heroic thing and stand between the invading trollish army and his people. That was why he had joined the Coast Guard. During boot camp, they had made them recite the Ethos of the Coast Guard. "I will protect them. I will defend them. I will save them. I am their shield. For them, I am Semper Paratus." Semper Paratus, the coast guard's motto, always prepared. He did not feel prepared.

Was he obligated to save these people here? Or should he save himself so that he could save a lot more people down the line? He could sense that if he ran away today, no matter if it was the more strategic requirement, he would always feel like he betrayed these people. They had depended on him. He didn't even stay and fight but ran away and used their lives to buy time for his own survival. He thought of General MacArthur being forced to flee Corregidor in the Philippines after the Japanese surrounded it following the surprise bombing of Pearl Harbor.

If Douglas MacArthur had stayed on the island as he had wanted, instead of evacuating when it became clear that they would lose the Bataan peninsula, the US would have lost its most experienced general. The following years of the war proved that he was one of the few people capable of leading the Allied offensive against the Japanese, but what did that mean to the seventy thousand troops left on the Bataan Peninsula, the men who eventually faced the Bataan Death March, men, who if they survived, then spent the next three years in the most hellish prisoner of war camps the Japanese could devise? Only a handful in every hundred survived to see the end of the war!

Was he supposed to be MacArthur or a King Leonidas? Although, if he remembered correctly, the Battle of Thermopylae had ended with all of Leonidas' Spartans dying. His musing was cut short when he saw Katie heading back towards him with a cart full of charcoal and lighter fluid in front of her. He shook his head, trying to banish the dark thoughts of the past few minutes.

"You okay there, Drew?" she asked, a slight frown on her face.

"No, not really." Drew looked down, frowning. "I was thinking about Ares, about how he said I needed to survive or quadrillions of people would die."

Drew wasn't sure what the look that passed across Katie's face meant; it was inscrutable in its complexity. "Drew, we both know that this is a tough spot. We're severely outnumbered and a bit outgunned. If you need to make a tactical retreat so that you can come back and rescue all of us, then you should do it. It's not going to help anyone if we all die here, and no one knows there are all those people trapped down there. If anyone is going to be able to escape and go get help from the stadium, it's you. In fact, here." A message saying that she wanted to trade him metallurgy appeared, and he shook his head.

"No, Drew. I'm serious. If something happens to me, this goes away. That means that everyone else is worse off. If you die, then either way, we're probably all screwed. This way it's as safe as it can possibly be." Katie fixed her eyes on Drew, staring him down until he accepted the trade. "Now, you'll just have to keep me alive so that you can give that back to me." She grabbed his collar with both hands, keeping him looking at her. "Promise me you'll come back for me or burn these fuckers to the ground if they kill me."

"I haven't even decided if I'm going to leave yet. Who knows? Maybe they'll all come out close together and I can just firestorm them to death before anyone is the wiser," Drew said, trying to force a smile. Katie's elbows against his chest and the closeness of her body was causing him to respond in a way that he hadn't been expecting, and that certainly didn't fit in his ten-minute timeline.

"Promise," Katie said, glaring him down.

"Alright, alright, I promise I'll come back for you," Drew said.

"Or burn the fuckers to the ground," Katie said with a manic gleam in her eyes.

"Or burn the fuckers to the ground," Drew repeated dutifully.

Katie smiled finally and then pulled him close to her, kissing his lips. After what seemed like an eternity to Drew, she let go of his lapel and took a half step back. "There, now you have more motivation to keep me alive." She stepped back again, opening the distance between them more completely and turning towards her shopping cart of inflammables.

Leaving him alone for a few minutes, Drew considered Katie's words. There was a logic to either him or Daryl being about the only ones that could effectively escape. While he liked

Daryl, he understood her reluctance to trust him, but there was also the fact that he wasn't sure he should believe Ares. He thought back to his time in the tutorial. Aevis said that the Protectorate had claimed the solar system, that they had then seeded Earth with humans and waited. Had Earth been an intergalactic Australia? Had they sent all their prisoners here to tame the planet while they waited for the full citizens to be born? Why not just settle here after the mana levels were acceptable?

What did Ares want with him? What was the point of telling him his own importance... of giving him that mysterious xatherite with its obfuscated effect? What was the point of killing off so many people by not preparing Earth-3 for the Advent? Was the system something the Protectorate made or was it something that they just utilized? The fact that they were at war with other 'awakened' species led him to believe that they didn't create the system. But if the Protectorate didn't, who did? And why?

Every interaction he had, they had refused to give him the information he needed. First Aevis telling him he was only allowed to say so much, then with Themis in the elevator, and finally when Ares started to tell him about the central nexus. Drew knew he should have asked a dozen more questions that he simply hadn't even thought to ask when he was there. That wasn't like him.

He had been calm on the ship. Had that been Themis' job, to keep him calm, to control his emotions and prevent certain questions from being asked? He didn't have the shield on until he left, so Themis could easily have been manipulating his mind that entire time. Was thinking about these things now just evidence that they had been pacifying him and that the effects had finally worn off? Themis had said that the system wouldn't let them talk about some things, why? What was the point of the system? What did it want, and was the Protectorate at its helm or just another pawn it commanded? Why did Ares give him that xatherite? Everything about it seemed off. If he was the embodiment of the Protectorate, then it would be against his interests to give him that kind of protection. Or was he a slave to the system and that was his way of giving Drew a warning?

Drew could feel the anger inside of him. Anger at being lied to, at being controlled and manipulated, at the complete lack of caring about billions of deaths. He refused to play their game. He was an American, he had a right to freedom, and he wasn't about to give it up simply because some alien told him that they owned his planet.

He pushed down his doubts about survival. He only felt the cold anger in his stomach that he had learned to control a long, long time ago. He wasn't going to run away. He wasn't going to let anyone tell him what was or was not possible. These were his people. He had saved them from the system's monsters, and he would do it again. It didn't matter what the Protectorate wanted from him—he would do what he wanted.

Looking around, he realized that all the groups had gathered. They were just waiting on Daryl, who appeared a moment later, laden with several thick troll skins and what looked like half a leg. Raising an eyebrow, he turned it around to display the glowing blue xatherite about half again as big as the one from the mosquito coming out of the heel of the foot. He looked over the group of people around him, seeing their auras. Katie and JP both had the strongest blue auras of anyone in the group. But he didn't trust JP; he didn't trust his mysterious senator's motives.

"Katie, collect that xatherite. You just have to touch it." She raised an eyebrow at him, curious. "I have a suspicion that who you are affects what kind of xatherite you acquire. I think you have the best chance of getting a good blue."

"Okay." She walked towards Daryl who held the leg out to her; his clothing was spotted with green blood, his hands stained with it. He managed to keep most of it away from Katie, holding the leg without touching the crystal.

When she touched it, a blue glow surged throughout the room, bathing everyone in its light before fading away.

Chapter Thirty-Four — Initiative

Everyone looked at Katie expectantly. "So, what did you get?" Drew asked. He could have pulled up her map but chose not to. He didn't want to inform JP and Robbi of his additional abilities.

"It's... a familiar?" Katie said with a bit of confusion. "It's called Eyes of the Loon, and it allows me to summon a creature whose eyes I can see through," Katie continued to explain. Drew was circumspectly pulling up her map to look at the xatherite information on his own.

Xatherite Crystal Name: Eyes of the Loon
Xatherite Color: Blue
Xatherite Grade: Intermediate
Xatherite Rarity: Widespread
Type: Physical
Effect: Creates a psychically linked familiar whose vision you can share. Familiar cannot attack but can move up to 1000m away from the user. Lasts until killed.
Mana recharge time: 1 day, 14 hours, 24 minutes.

Glancing over Katie's map, he also realized that she wouldn't be able to slot it currently, but this was the sort of thing that would give them a significant advantage in the upcoming fight; it was obviously something they would need to have slotted into someone immediately. Sarah could slot it, but it would eat into her single white slot. For a moment, he thought about slotting it himself, but he doubted he would be able to fight and use it at the same time. Which made it less useful for him since he wouldn't be able to do reconnaissance during a fight, something that would help prevent them from being flanked or surrounded.

Meeting Katie's eyes for a moment, he could tell she was thinking the same thing. "Daryl?" she mouthed to him, and he blinked. Daryl made a lot of sense, and if he could link it with his invisibility xatherite, he would become an even more potent spy. He turned to the other man. "Hey, Daryl, you got any blue slots linked to your invisibility?"

A moment of surprise passed over the other man's face before he got the semi faraway look in his eye that Drew had taken to mean someone was looking at their node map. "Uh, yeah, I do."

"Excellent, I'd like you to slot it there, the idea of an invisible recon... drone sounds like it would round out your kit quite well." Sarah nodded her head in agreement. "We're gonna need as much intel as we can get for this fight, so I'd like you to stay near Sarah and keep her updated on what's going on." Drew then turned to Sarah.

"I'd like to have you doing command and control with Katie. You two probably have the best experience of anyone here doing that. Use Daryl's mental communication to pass orders if you need to, and you can coordinate defenses and everything."

Sarah nodded her head. "Right, Daryl slot that ASAP. We'll want you back up and scouting as soon as we can. Chief, Chuck, Katie, and Daryl—I want you four near me while we travel." Drew tried to remember who Chuck was but couldn't place the name until the guy who could shape wood stepped forward with Bill and the other two. "We'll have Robbi, Trey, Katie, and Chuck doing defenses. JP, you cover the rear guard while Drew takes the front. Jholie and the rest of you with weapons and armor on the outside; everyone else grab a cart and start pushing."

Drew was amazed that Sarah had learned everyone's names and abilities and wondered when she'd had the time... Probably while he had been sleeping. The young and mostly scared healer he had met a week ago in the Commandant's plot was gone, replaced with this driven leader who ordered actions without hesitation. He wondered idly how she could possibly have changed so much over so short a time frame.

Thinking back on the changes he had experienced himself, he guessed it wasn't that farfetched. After all, two weeks ago, he would never have believed he would be the de facto battle leader of thirty people. Looking around at those people, he realized he didn't know most of their names, only those that had been useful to him. That was something he needed to change, especially if they rescued a few hundred more people in a few hours. Most of the ones he didn't know by name had an air about them, a fear that the others didn't as they clutched their krises and spears. It didn't seem to be paralyzing them like happened to some people, but considering that everyone was military or the family of someone in the military, he supposed that made some sense. Military families learned to deal with uncertainty, or they didn't stay family for long.

Waiting until Daryl had slotted his new xatherite, Drew cast energize on him, removing the headache associated with doing so. He accepted the other man's thanks with a nod of his head and a tight smile before watching him summon what looked to Drew like a fairly large duck, which he guessed was actually a loon. "Let me know if you see anything." He then headed out into the parking lot, scanning around for any signs of trolls.

Not seeing anything, he watched the loon take off and begin flying circles around the parking lot. Daryl was invisible again, although he could see his aura standing off to one side where he was unlikely to be run into by someone accidentally. It only took a few more minutes for everyone else to get organized, and they were off. Drew, in the lead, looked behind him at the sea of green leathered people and then down at his own black jacket and dark navy-blue pants.

It was easy to see the other three main combatants. All three of them were wearing blue; Drew's ODU pants and the police uniforms of the other two. Drew's jet-black, chitin-enhanced armor was even more distinctive than the blue bulletproof vests since at least a few of the others still wore blue jeans under their green troll skin leather jackets. Min Sun had added sleeves to the vest, the troll skin dyed to a color more closely aligned with the original grey leather the orcs had used as a base. He wasn't entirely sure how Min Sun had managed to create so much leather armor in so short a period, but it seemed like at least half the group was currently decked out in at least a green, troll skin leather vest.

Musing on the chance that they would create a new trend, where the warriors wore blue and black as they made their slow progress out towards the main road leading to the north, they could see the DIA building's entrance from here, although it was a little under a mile away from their current location. How fast could trolls run on open ground? He tried to remember how fast they had been during that first ambush with the sacrifices. They hadn't made it very far before his spells had taken them, maybe a third of the way back to the DIA building. That meant they were probably a bit faster than humans. He wasn't sure how fast their jumping ability would make them, but he hadn't seen any of that first group jumping.

His musings were cut short as he began to see green forms filing out of the building. Drew immediately stopped and began casting storm over them, hoping to kill as many as he could while they were still clumped up near the entrance. He heard shouts behind him as his fingers created the seals needed to send death and destruction towards his enemies. Seven or eight were out of the building when the five second cast time went off. Enveloping them in lightning, wind, and water damage, the mist caused by the storm made it impossible to see what effect his spell had caused.

Behind him, the civilians were dragging their carts onto the track surrounding the soccer field, using it to transport the shopping carts full of food and fuel across the expanse of grass. He turned and followed suit, glancing back towards the DIA building's entrance every now and again to check the status of his storm. About a quarter of the way across, the storm's energy dissipated. Drew was slightly ahead of the group of civilians, while Katie, Chuck, and Robbi were running across to the other side where a row of mature trees had been planted as a windbreak.

"Head towards the trees, climb up one, and keep pressure on the entrance," Daryl's voice came into Drew's head. He sped up as much as he could while keeping watch on the doors to the north, waiting for any more trolls to venture out.

Seeing movement out of the corner of his eye, he stopped long enough to cast firestorm about two-thirds of the way across the field. When the spell was cast, he turned back to the east and ran as fast as he could the rest of the way to where Katie and Chuck had begun to build something around a few of the trees. Katie had already created a few walls, while Chuck seemed to be focusing on one of the larger trees, his hand touching its bark and his eyes closed.

Triggering blink step, he jumped just past the halfway mark up the tree, falling half a foot before he managed to catch himself on a branch and cutting his hands on the rough bark. He grunted at the pain in his shoulders as they were wrenched from trying to arrest his fall. He could hear a shout of alarm from below as a branch he knocked loose crashed down through the canopy to land within a few feet of Chuck's concentrating form. "Sorry," he shouted down to the older man and then turned back to look towards the entrance, hooking his arm over a branch and wedging one foot into a y-joint.

Turning his attention towards the entrance, he realized he could hardly see anything. The line of trees that made up the windbreak blocked the entrance of the DIA building. He worked his way around the trunk to the other side where fewer branches would obstruct his vision. As he did, he felt the tree sway a little and, looking down, realized that he was higher up than he had been before by a few feet. Chuck must be growing the tree. Shaking aside his vertigo, he walked out along one branch a few feet until he finally got a decent view of his target. A few dozen trolls had already made it out and were running towards their group.

Drew took a few seconds to ensure he wouldn't fall and then focusing to the north, began casting frost storm. He thought that the cooldown on storm was almost over and planned to switch to that one next, wanting to keep frostfire storm for when he could hopefully get a relatively large group of them together. He finished the last seal of the spell and saw more than a handful of them engulfed within the radius of the frost storm. One, on the leading edge, managed to punch through the last few feet of the frost storm, chunks of ice embedded in his shoulder. He had breached the front side.

Drew frowned, trying to decide if he wanted to reveal his position by launching a fireball at this distance when he heard the report of rifle shots being fired. JP had made his way towards the front and, with his rifle out, shot a few rounds towards the lead troll. The first two shots went wide, launching into the fury of the storm behind it and hopefully catching some of the trolls behind it. But the third shot landed true, and the forerunner burst into flames as JP's combustive ammo exploded on contact.

With no targets immediately visible, Drew glanced down. Katie had not been idle, and several sloping walls had been built around the tree. She was making a diagonal line using the windbreak of the trees as a central point, the first few sections of what Drew assumed would end up being a diamond shape. It would create a choke point for anyone attempting to approach them. As defensive positions go, it wasn't ideal. Drew would have rather had a funnel, but they needed to get as many of their people in a covered area as they could.

He approved of Sarah's decision to put them in the open. With the trees hiding Drew, he would have a decent chance of keeping overwatch and attacking the trolls long before they could bring their melee weapons to bear on his people, and JP could continue to take potshots at them as they approached or switch to pistols when they were closer. He just hoped the man would have enough ammunition for the long fight that was bound to come.

The last few shopping carts were making their way across the fields, most now being pushed and pulled by three or four people each. Others had already begun emptying Katie's shopping cart of flammables spreading the liquids around the area near where he assumed the entrance to their defensive diamond would be.

The sound of new rifle reports caused Drew to glance back up, casting storm before he even saw his first target. Another dozen trolls had spread out, heading east where they could hide behind a building for the final approach. With their jumping ability, Drew assumed they wouldn't be limited by the narrow gap in the buildings, but he and JP would make them pay for any ground they gained.

Another storm lashed out and caught a few of them, making the rest detour around it. JP's bullets had killed another troll. Drew was impressed with his accuracy. They were still eight or nine hundred yards away and running quite quickly. He hoped the two of them would be able to buy enough time for the defenses to be set up. His fingers began casting firestorm as another dozen circled around to the east. More appeared to the northwest, but they had spread out enough that he couldn't catch more than three or four per storm. And he still hadn't seen any sign of the lightning caller.

Chapter Thirty-Five — Rising Action

"There's a large group coming in from the west side by the river; they should be visible to you any moment," Daryl's voice played silently inside Drew's head. He turned to look behind him at the back of the commissary. They must have some sort of hidden exit out that way since they'd come from there twice now. Might be worth investigating it as a possible way into the DIA building that didn't involve cutting a hole in the wall.

Drew wished Daryl would have told him how many were in this 'large group.' A flash of light to the north drew his attention as another troll was ignited after being struck by one of JP's fire bullets. He shifted his weight down to a lower branch that allowed him a better view of the new group's approach path. Glancing back to the north, he considered another storm spell for that direction. Frost storm was probably off cooldown or would be soon, and he still had frostfire storm held in reserve, but the other two still had at least a minute left on their cooldowns.

He counted two dozen spread between the northwest and northeast... Probably at least another dozen coming from the west. Drew swallowed, his mouth suddenly dry. There were already more enemies on the field than he had ever fought at once before, except for a couple of his fights with much smaller and less deadly insects, and there was still the lightning caller to deal with. Drew would feel much better about their prospects when he was dead.

Holding off on more storms for now, he was hoping he could catch them in higher concentrations with such high cooldowns. He glanced back to the west and saw the first troll coming around the corner of the exchange. They didn't seem to be proceeding with caution, and they were still relatively grouped up. He waited a few more seconds for more to appear before beginning the cast for frost storm, hoping that the lightning caller was in this group and unprepared for the onslaught, although he appeared to have some method of surviving his spells; it wasn't a fight he was particularly looking forward to. Maybe JP could just shoot him?

Shaking his head to discard his stray thoughts, he focused on the trolls advancing from the west and cast frost storm. His eyes were on the group as his fingers moved to form the hand seals, counting the trolls. He got to thirteen before it was ready to cast, and then the storm stole them from view.

Looking down, Katie had managed to put up the northwest and northeast side of the fortifications. Tree branches wove above the small holes in the top, creating a barrier even there, and he realized that he was a good ten feet higher than he had been at first. The tree had grown around him. The hair on Drew's arms rose in a sensation he was coming to know all too well, and he shouted, "Lightning!" as he blink stepped as far away as he could to the northeast.

The boom of thunder crashing behind him was the least of his worries as his stomach rolled up into his chest, and he began spinning end over end as he fell, the ground beneath him approaching rapidly. Drew cast gravitas but still landed with a hard roll, his shoulder smashing against the ground as a wave of pain rolled over him.

Sitting up with a groan and then promptly vomiting from the pain, he stared at the chunks of beef jerky that now decorated the grass in front of him. Placing both hands on the ground caused another wave of nausea to roll over him, his stomach clenching. He removed his right hand, and the pain went away, giving him enough strength to push himself to his feet. Looking around himself blearily, he shook his head, trying to get rid of the ringing sound in his ears. Green men were running towards him, though they were still a long way away, maybe a couple hundred feet? He realized there were muffled noises coming from behind him, and he turned around.

JP had braced his rifle against an overturned shopping cart, the muzzle flashes the only indication to Drew that he was still firing. Bill was also waving his hands, and it looked like he was shouting, but Drew still couldn't hear anything over the ringing. He stared at the shattered tree behind JP and Bill, split down the center with two halves still clinging together by the mass of branches and leaves but visibly sagging away from each other. Wait, was JP shooting at him?

That didn't seem right, and he focused back on JP again. No, he should be shooting at the trolls. The trolls! Drew turned around to look behind him, but he spun too fast, and the pain in his arm moved from a dull pounding to a sharp stabbing. The green men, no the trolls, from before were coming closer. Drew raised his good arm, and pointing at the trolls, launched all four of his long-range spells, one each from the fingers of his good hand. Fireballs and acid arrows shot out towards the trolls, and he watched them in a detached manner. Did they seem to be moving faster than normal?

The trolls didn't dodge away from any of the projectiles, and all four of his targets went down. Vaguely, he could hear a voice, though it couldn't quite compete with the ringing in his ears. He probably shouldn't be out in the open like this. He turned back towards JP and Bill more slowly this time, so as not to swing his arm, and began walking back towards the strange, sloped building that was under the trees.

He stumbled a few times; he knew it was because he wasn't paying attention to the ground as much as he should be, but he couldn't really seem to bring himself to care. Bill and another person started running towards him. He should know all his people's names at this point. He should ask them that, maybe after the ringing stopped.

He stopped. It was too much effort to walk, and Bill was coming towards him anyway. He sat down, too tired to keep standing. Bill reached him, and Drew looked up; he was talking, but it was all so muffled that he couldn't make out what he was saying. Then he hugged Drew, and the world came back into sharp focus. The ringing in his ears and the fugue over his brain went away, replaced by the sharp pain in his shoulder from the hug.

Drew grunted like he had been punched.

"Drew?" Bill asked.

"I'm okay. Shoulder still hurts, though," Drew said, moving to stand up, but Bill kept him down.

"Yeah, you dislocated it. Lay down, and I'll pop it back in," Bill said, gently pushing him down while the other man moved to press against Drew's good shoulder while Bill braced his legs against Drew's side and neck and then moved the arm out and towards him. With a sigh of relief, Drew could feel his shoulder slide back into the socket. "Don't move it yet," Bill said, and then he leaned over and hugged Drew again. Instantly, he felt the muscles in his arm knit back together, the trauma of the dislocation being removed.

"Alright," Bill said, and the other man released Drew. Sitting up, Drew glanced back towards the trolls, now only a hundred feet away. He pointed his hands at the nearest and again launched four spells, targeting a clump of three with both frostfire ball and fireball and allowing the four acid arrows to target a single individual each. His spells caught all their targets; the shocking acid arrow targets collapsed and began convulsing while the two normal acid arrow targets merely became staggered for a second. It was just long enough for JP's bullets to take one of them. The three hit by the fireball variants disappeared, a cloud of debris and body parts billowing out away from him in their wake.

He moved to stand up, and both Bill and the other man helped him. "Get back to the shelter," Drew said as he began casting frostfire storm. Bill headed back, but the other man didn't; he just drew the wavy kris from his side and set himself between Drew and the approaching trolls. Drew was slightly annoyed when he blocked his vision, but a half step was enough to see where he wanted to cast.

The seconds trickled by as the trolls got closer. Drew could see their eyes, and for the first time realized that instead of whites, their eyes were surrounded by a bright, neon blue sclera. In their rush to get to him, they had clumped up, the hate visible on their faces. He idly wondered where the manaborn came from—were they conjured out of thin air or transported from their homes by the system? He felt a moment of pity for them if they had been transported away from everything they knew to this new world. He wondered what sort of planet had created these green jumpers.

The spell finished casting, but two trolls were within fifty feet of him and had jumped. The world seemed to slow down for a moment; he targeted the spell beyond where the two closest trolls were, catching many of them within its radius. The blast of air pressure as the storm appeared knocked Drew back half a step, and he could feel the tremors in the ground as the fire and ice bombarded the area so close to him. The blast of air threw the two leading trolls off target, and one of the airborne trolls he shot with a lightning bolt; the kinetic energy of the blast threw it back into the storm and to its certain death.

The second troll sailed through the air unobstructed, and the man in front of Drew moved to attack it. Drew cursed because it was close enough for a cone, but the man had moved to block his line of sight again, meaning it would hit him as well. Drew shifted slightly trying to get a better angle, but the troll had landed gracefully, its thick legs pushing him directly towards Drew and the man in front of him. He could hear the crunch of the impact and the man's scream mingled with Drew's own cry.

A report rang out, and the troll burst into flames. His arms were entangled around the man, causing both to erupt in flames. Drew watched as the man who had tried to save his life caught on fire. The grass around him also began to burn, no doubt treated by the chemicals Katie's group had scavenged up earlier. Drew stumbled away, angry and annoyed that he had another death on his conscience, and this one was completely unnecessarily. If the man hadn't jumped in front of him, he could have easily killed the troll. Angry at himself and at the man, but more than anything at the trolls, he turned back towards the bunker, shielding his face from the heat of the flames.

Reaching a small wall that Katie must have created for him, he turned around with fury in his eyes as he willed more trolls to appear. He heard voices behind him, but he brushed them aside, refusing to allow them even a moment of his focus. "No one blocks my line of sight," his voice rang out loud and clear, the hardened fury causing all the chatter around him to taper off.

Waves of fury radiated off him. He felt something within him stirring, some force being drawn to his rage, a bubbling, burning fire of ice that filled him with clarity and rage he had never felt before in his life. It seemed to fill any cracks in his personality, burning away the pity he had felt for the manaborn just a few minutes ago and replacing it with a cold surety. It was calling for death and destruction, tightly controlled for now, but that was only because there was no target for his rage yet, no outlet for the power that filled his body.

Chapter Thirty-Six — Retribution

With the strange hot and cold energy filling his body, Drew focused his attention outward. The world was moving in slow motion around him; everything crystal clear and within his realm of focus. The flickering shadows of the frostfire storm drew his gaze, their orange and red light reflecting a thousand times off the various chunks of ice. The lightning arcing around within the storm illuminated the elements of destruction before returning them to the ominous darkness.

The timer in his head that told him how long the storm had been raging slowly counted to thirty. When it finished, the world went quiet, the violent fury disappearing in an instant. Immediately, fireballs erupted from Drew's hand, hitting clumps of trolls that had gathered on the far side of the storm while waiting for it to dissipate. The bolts thinned their numbers a little, but there were still dozens of trolls for him to kill.

A grim smile appeared on his face as acid arrows shot from his hand to strike four more trolls. It was only at this point that Drew heard JP's pistols firing. Turning towards JP, he watched as the muzzle flash appeared and, lasting for longer than it should have, disappeared. It felt like he was stuck in bullet time in real life.

With a shrug, he turned back to the trolls that were advancing on his position. Waiting for them to cover the gap between his long-range spells and his short-range spells, he studied the way they leaped at him, watching their leg muscles bunch and then explode down. He counted the distance between them, a lightning bolt striking the first to leave the ground. The next four sailed through the air, and he could see their faces begin to bare their teeth in an unwholesome approximation of a smile.

He felt no fear, even as they crossed the ten-meter distance to him. He waited until all four of them were within a cone and watched as their expressions froze on their faces. His cone of frost impacted them, reversing the course of their flight. Their bodies cracked from the impact. Drew had ceased to pay attention to them as soon as the cone was cast, looking for another target. Another solo troll making his way from the far eastern side jumped towards Drew. He could smell the ozone in the air as his lightning bolt caught it, arresting its momentum.

Losing himself in the fight, Drew threw out lightning bolts, cones, fireballs, and acid arrows until they all merged together, becoming a single dance of destruction. Somewhere in the back of his mind, he could hear a voice screaming at him; was that Daryl again? He ignored it. It was unimportant to the judgment he was passing on the trolls. They had seen it fit to attack his people, to kill them and enslave them, and now, he was exacting the cost of those actions upon them.

Death was their just dessert, ashes their reward. The trolls continued to press in on him, not realizing that their time of judgment was at hand. The world continued to crawl around him, giving him plenty of time to respond to any incoming threats. When he had judged over fifty trolls, he realized that there weren't any left, and he advanced out of the protective bunker he was in. He could see them in the distance making a retreat, causing his anger to flare again. They were too far for lightning bolt and his other short-range spells. He began casting storms at them while fireballs and acid arrows took the smaller clumps of targets.

When the last troll he could see died in an explosion of frost and fire, he looked around. The earth had been devastated. His spells had set one tree to smoldering and had knocked another completely over. Still seething craters marked where fireballs had torn up the ground around the trolls. Everywhere he looked were the green-skinned bodies of his slain enemies.

The energy that had filled him, the anger and hate and need for judgment slowly trickled away. It was then that he could feel the weakness coming over him, the weakness of channeling so much mana through his body in such a short frame. He cast rejuvenation on himself but could sense that it wasn't going to be enough to keep him conscious. He knelt between two craters. The sounds that he had been ignoring since the blood rage had taken him suddenly became clear.

There were voices, shouts from behind him. He turned slightly to look at their source. Katie, Sarah, JP, and Robbi, as well as about half the noncombatants had followed him out of the safety of the shelter they'd created. The rage still wouldn't let him make out what they were saying, but the concerned and scared looks on their faces told him that they were worried about him and maybe afraid of him. He smiled and waved before the rage left him completely and he collapsed on the ground.

* * *

"Sir, I was only able to get a partial lock on him. I'm not sure if he can even hear us. The distance is too far."

"How did this happen, Themis? You know what I gave him. There is no way he should have been able to activate it this soon." Themis and Ares? What were they doing here? Where was here to begin with? His eyes were closed, there was darkness all around him, and he felt cold in a comforting way.

"He is an exceptional talent, which is why you gave it to him. I have no idea how he activated it unattuned, but it is clear he did." A pause. "I think he is mostly here."

"Drew, if you can hear me, don't give in to the rage again. It will destroy you if you use it before you can control it. Every time you use it before that, you risk it taking over for good and losing your humanity." Ares stopped again, and Drew heard something like fear in his voice, which seemed strange coming from the other red mage.

"I am going to make my way to the closest system to Earth that we can. Sol doesn't have enough mana to support the fleet yet, but we will try to protect you. You just painted a huge target on the planet. Grow fast, but don't give in again." Another pause. "Is he still here?"

"Yes, Admiral."

"My brothers and sisters will come; the conclave can't keep this quiet anymore. Trust in the lore you know. Your people remember their nature. You've done something none of us ever have, and they will want you."

"Let him go; he needs to rest."

"Of course, Admiral." The silence prolonged, and then finally, Themis' voice came one last time, "Hades, Loki, Pan, Lilith, Athena, Set, and Isis. Don't trust them, Drew."

* * *

The darkness returned, no longer the comforting cold but rather a growing heat. He slowly became aware that he was not alone in the darkness and that there was something there besides him. It didn't breathe, but he could sense its presence by the power that radiated off it, pure and unadulterated energy that filled him with the same emotions he'd felt during the rage.

"What are you?" Drew asked.

"Retribution," the being answered. Its voice was harsh and cold.

"Are you the xatherite?"

"No, I am a part of you that the xatherite unlocked."

"Why? To what end?" Drew asked, but the voice didn't answer. They sat in silence, Drew too stubborn to talk again in the face of a blunt refusal to answer his question.

"I should not be."

"What?"

"I should not be, not yet. You have called me forth, but I should not be. You should not have called me."

What did that mean? He was a part of him but should not be. Why had Ares and Themis been so concerned that he had used the xatherite before it was awakened? He used plenty of xatherite that weren't awakened yet. Was it because this one was a divine xatherite rather than a magic one?

"Can you go back?"

"No."

"Then what do we do?"

Again, silence answered his question. They stayed like that, and Drew grew more comfortable in his presence. Two companions in the dark. They were the same, but at the same time very different from each other. Finally, the darkness also faded, and there was nothing.

* * *

This time when he came back to consciousness, it was in a world with too much light. He squeezed his eyes shut to try to block some of it out. He was laying down on something moderately hard, wood maybe? There were some distant sounds, but nothing in the immediate vicinity. He felt a warm presence on his shoulder; it reminded him of Zoey, but his memories told him that was impossible. Reaching a hand up, he touched it. Hair, long and loose, met his fingers, and he gently stroked it, enjoying the softness.

"Drew?" The head under his hand moved, and Katie's voice filled his ears. It was tired and worried, spoken softly as if unbelieving. "Drew, are you awake?"

He tried to respond but just emitted a dry croak which caused his throat to burn slightly. So, he simply nodded instead.

"One second, let me get you something to drink." He heard some movement around him, and after a few seconds, something hard was pressed to his lips. He opened them enough to allow a trickle of water in. When he began to cough, the cup was taken away until the fit subsided and then it returned to his lips.

After this repeated a few more times, he felt like his throat was lubricated enough to talk. "What happened?"

"We're not really sure. You started emitting red light and then went a bit crazy, killed a crap ton of trolls and then collapsed. You've been unconscious for almost an entire day." She reached down and grabbed his hand, holding it in both of hers. "You gonna stay awake for a while? Sarah will want to talk to you."

He just nodded his head slightly, and she squeezed his hand before letting it go again. He could hear footsteps as she left whatever room they were in. He tried to open his eyes again, but it hurt too much. He did sit up though and didn't feel any pain like he would expect from a head injury. He assumed that whatever was causing his light sensitivity would go away soon enough. He discovered that he was on some sort of raised platform, but there was nothing to lean against, so he just leaned forward and put his elbows on his knees, his hands covering his eyes.

After a few minutes, he heard two sets of footsteps returning to wherever they were. "Drew?" he heard Sarah ask, and he nodded his head.

"Yeah, I'm here, ma'am." He felt the younger girl pull him into a surprisingly more powerful hug than he had been anticipating. He awkwardly hugged her back.

"We were so worried about you. What happened?" Sarah said when she released him from the hug.

"I'm not sure, to be honest. I think maybe I overused my mana. Why is it so bright in here?"

"Oh sorry, here, let me put some of the stones away. I've been making them nonstop since you went unconscious. Figured we'd need them for all the new people," Katie said, and he heard both of them begin to put the glowrocks away.

"Smart. So, what's our situation? Any more attacks since I was KOed?"

"No, I think you scared them pretty good. Daryl has been doing some scouting. They haven't left since they retreated. JP and Robbi were about to go in with a couple of the other people who got xatherite from that attack," Sarah responded.

"We got some?" Drew asked. That was the second set of good news he'd heard since waking up.

"Oh yeah, a bunch. We already slotted everything. I'm afraid, we were worried you..." Sarah trailed off, and he could fill in the gaps. They had slotted them to defend themselves in case he didn't wake back up.

"Smart, so what did we get?" Drew asked.

"Three reds; JP gathered them, and they all created more gun-related attacks which he gave to three of the former soldiers. It should expand our combat capable group quite a bit. We also got a couple violets. One called blood blade which Robbi got, and I got a yellow called phase armor. That you can look up if you want," Sarah said. The light level was already much lower, and Drew cautiously looked around. It hurt, but more like waking up to a bunch of one hundred-lumen lights in your face.

"That's great. Five total?" Drew asked. Katie had sat down next to him and was looking at his face.

"Yes."

Drew nodded his head, and now that he could see, called up the map UI. To his surprise, it included Daryl, JP, and Robbi on the list. All three of them labeled as SA, just like Sarah and Katie. "Daryl, JP, and Robbi all showed up on my list; I can look at their xatherite."

"What? That's... interesting," Katie said with a frown.

"Looks like they leveled up and got conscripted into the Protectorate Navy too. I bet they have to be level one for me to see their maps."

"Well, that's good news, right? Means we can trust them a little more?" Sarah asked.

"I've always trusted Daryl, the other two..." Drew trailed off as he looked at their grids. Daryl's was shaped like a spider, and he had a respectable number of nodes. He didn't take the time to count, but it was near fifty. Robbi had about the same, but his map was shaped like a man. JPs was the surprise; he had the most of any map but Drew's at around sixty, and his was shaped like a gun.

Finally, he pulled up the information on Sarah's xatherite. She had placed it in the same formation as group cure and mana jump.

Xatherite Crystal Name: Phase Armor
Xatherite Color: Yellow
Xatherite Grade: Common
Xatherite Rarity: Common
Type: Magic
Effect: Activating phase armor prevents all damage to the users for 90 seconds. Allows the user to intentionally phase through objects for the duration.
Mana recharge time: 18 minutes, 43 seconds.

Chapter Thirty-Seven — Fallout

He had a ton of things to do. "Where are we exactly?" He looked around, but all he saw were Katie's walls.

"Still in the field where we fought the trolls. Katie's been reinforcing it when she can, and we've been rotating defenders out to get sleep." Drew nodded and moved to stand up, Katie and Sarah both moving to help him before he waved them off.

"I'm fine. Really. I'll go cast some refreshing rain on the current watch. Any preferences on energize?" He asked Sarah, and she paused for a moment.

"Katie, actually." Drew turned to look at Katie and realized how tired she looked. Dark bags under her eyes let him know she probably hadn't slept since he'd collapsed. Moving his fingers through the motions to cast energize, he touched her hand and watched as the weariness sloughed off her in waves as the spell took effect.

"I'm gonna start calling you insta-coffee," Katie said with a sigh of relief. "Man, I could use a cup right now." Drew and Sarah both laughed.

"How are we on food? What's the plan for the rescue?" Drew asked. They were down to less than a day before the mana storm; his collapse meant that they were in an even worse position. They had limited supplies of food and a narrow gap of time to get everyone up to the stadium.

"Food is good, might be an issue depending on how bad the prisoners are. If we deal with all the trolls, that shouldn't be much of an issue either. We can always get more from the exchange," Sarah said as Drew found his backpack and found a can of chili and the spoon he kept in there. Taking a bite of the cold chili, he grimaced slightly, but he was hungry enough to ignore it. Hopefully the stadium had some sort of method of creating warm food.

Taking the can and spoon with him, they walked to where the guards were watching the entrance to the shelter. There were three people standing watch: JP, Trey, and another kid whose name Drew didn't know. That reminded him of the man who'd died to protect him before the rage took over, and he paused, a frown on his lips.

"What's wrong, Drew?" Katie asked.

"The man that died during the attack. He jumped in front of me when a troll was attacking. I don't know his name."

"It was Frank," Sarah said softly. The look of concern on both women's faces was evident, and it tugged on the part of Drew's mind that desperately wanted to break down and start crying. It was the same part that told him this was beyond his capabilities and he was bound to fail. He was an introvert at heart, and he knew at some point the immediate danger was going to pass and he was going to have to deal with how he was handling the end of the world. But there was still more work for him to do and people that were depending on him.

Drew nodded his head. "Frank," he repeated, tasting the name. "Frank." He nodded one last time, then began walking forward. JP, Trey, and the other guard had been watching them as Drew walked up and stopped a few feet away from the group. He realized that he was going to have to break the silence, and he tried to think of something to say. Finding nothing that seemed to fit, he saluted the three. A little surprised, they gave him shy salutes in return.

"You three look tired. Trey, can you go get the other people with attack powers? I'll cast a refreshing rain on everyone." Trey saluted and rushed off, his former training kicking in. Drew turned to the third guard, who was young as well, probably no more than twenty. "Sorry, I don't think we've met. I'm IT2 Drew Michalik."

The kid blushed, "Yeah, I know." His blush deepened as he realized what he just said. "Sorry, sir, I'm Private Daniel Barnes." He was wearing the same troll leathers as everyone else, although he carried several guns and extra magazines which set him apart. There wasn't much else to identify him; his aura was a mix of colors, no single one standing out as stronger than the other. Sensing that the kid would just get more nervous if he kept talking to him, Drew switched to look at JP.

"Hey, JP. How you holding up?"

"I'm alright. You put on one helluva show back there," the former cop said with a grin.

"Honestly, I don't really remember much of it. I think I might have overused my mana a bit," Drew said with a shrug. JP nodded like that made sense. "Thanks for keeping everyone safe while I was out."

JP snorted. "It's been easy, aside from the lack of sleep. The trolls haven't dared show their faces. So, all we've had to deal with are a few of the scavengers, but that cleared up after Daryl melted the corpses. Speaking of, he's been out scouting, and he thinks you must have killed off almost all of them; said the guards who were blocking him from getting inside are gone now."

"Yeah, we can only hope so. Give me a minute. I need to look at my notifications." He shook both of their hands and then stepped a few feet away and pulled up the notifications that had been blinking in the corner of his vision since he woke up. His hands were mechanically eating the chili while he did so.

Congratulations, Midshipman. Your Minor Acid Arrow xatherite has reached level 5. Damage has increased.
Congratulations, Midshipman. Your Minor Mana Shield xatherite has reached level 5. Damage absorbed has increased.
Congratulations, Midshipman. Your Minor Lightning Bolt xatherite has reached level 5. Damage has increased.
Congratulations, Midshipman. Your Minor Energize xatherite has reached level 5. Charge requirement has reduced.
Congratulations, Midshipman. Your Minor Dancing Sword xatherite has reached level 5. Duration has increased.

Congratulations, Midshipman. Your Storm xatherite has reached level 5. Damage has increased.
Congratulations, Midshipman. Your Fireball xatherite has reached level 5. Damage has increased.
Congratulations, Midshipman. Your Cone of Frost xatherite has reached level 5. Damage has increased.
Congratulations, Midshipman. You have attuned Minor Blink Step.
Congratulations, Midshipman. Your Minor Acid Arrow, Minor Mana Shield, Minor Lightning Bolt, Minor Energize, Minor Dancing Sword, Fireball, and Cone of Cold xatherites are ready to be upgraded.

Drew blinked; every single one of his widespread quality xatherite had leveled up to the point that they could be upgraded off that fight except for blink step, which had at least finally attuned. Those higher grade and higher rarity xatherite certainly took a long time to attune and level up, which didn't give him a lot of hope for attuning aeon or stricto mentis clypeus soon. He assumed they were so far beyond the rarity level of anything he'd encountered on Earth that they weren't going to attune for years.

Which was fine... He wasn't sure what exactly aeon had done to him during that fight, but he wasn't eager to activate it again. As he looked at his grid, he realized that aeon had changed. It was now called, aeon - retribution, but the description had remained the same. He mentally put it aside; hopefully, he could get some more answers from Ares, since it sounded like he was going to be nearby, and Themis could always just pull him there in his sleep.

Having learned his lesson from the first few upgrades, Drew upgraded one at a time. Upgrading fireball, then lightning bolt, and then mana shield. His head started to pound after mana shield, so he took a break while he waited for the other guards to rouse.

Xatherite Crystal Name: Major Fireball
Xatherite Color: Red
Xatherite Grade: Rare
Xatherite Rarity: Widespread
Type: Magic
Effect: Convert mana into a high energy blast of fire that will travel in a straight line until exploding, causing ample fire damage in a 6m radius around the blast.
Mana recharge time: 10.5 seconds.

Xatherite Crystal Name: Lightning Bolt
Xatherite Color: Red
Xatherite Grade: Intermediate
Xatherite Rarity: Widespread
Type: Magic
Effect: Creates a bolt of electricity from any body part to a target no more than 15m away. Deals moderate lightning damage and stuns the target for 4 seconds.
Mana recharge time: 4.2 seconds

Xatherite Crystal Name: Mana Shield
Xatherite Color: Yellow
Xatherite Grade: Common
Xatherite Rarity: Widespread
Type: Magic
Effect: Creates a shield of mana around the caster. This shield will absorb significant amounts of energy and kinetic damage. It also creates a slowing effect around the caster.
Mana recharge time: 4 minutes, 1.5 seconds

Both of his attack spells got significant upgrades; fireball was now up to a six-meter explosion, which made it next to worthless anytime anything was close but would work even better at killing things far away. It had also gotten a damage adjective upgrade, from major to ample. Lightning bolt's stun had doubled in duration from two to four seconds and had also gotten a damage upgrade, which gave him an even more potent close-range attack spell. Mana shield had its cooldown reduced, and the amount absorbed had increased.

All three were significant damage upgrades, although he wished he could have upgraded cone of cold too since frostfire ball hadn't upgraded to the major version of it yet. He suspected it would do so as soon as he advanced the other xatherite. That done, he looked around. Trey still wasn't back with the other guards, but the pounding in Drew's head from the upgrading was annoying him. The cooldown on refreshing rain was only a minute and a half, so he cast it on the group around him, enjoying the effects of the spell's rejuvenating rain.

"So, any of the scavengers look good to eat?" Drew asked, taking another bite from his can of chili.

Everyone laughed. "No, but a couple people have been wanting to give it a try. If any of them had dropped meat when Daryl melted them, we would probably have already had a barbeque," JP said with a grin.

"Well, glad Daryl is here to let us know what is and isn't edible I guess." Drew wondered silently how much if any of Daryl's vegetarian status affected the desired outcome of his necro alchemy spell. He would make a note to have someone try to harvest and cook the meat the normal way next time they killed something that wasn't able to talk.

Daryl showed up on the edge of his aura vision, and he had to stop himself from reflexively casting a lightning bolt at him. When he passed the rain's edge, he turned himself visible. "Drew! You're awake!" He ran towards the other man and gave him a big hug. Much to Drew's surprise, he felt Daryl slip something in his pocket and heard his mental voice in his head, "Look at it later."

"Hey, buddy, sounds like you missed me," Drew said, not sure how to respond to the covert action, so he just went with the obvious response to the physical interaction.

"Well, you haven't rescued my wife yet, and we had a deal," Daryl said, stepping back and letting all levity fall from his face. "But I have good news on that front. I just got back from the tunnel they dug out into the housing area. Got a look through the door, just a couple guards, and those that were there were distracted. I think it's pretty much a straight shot from there to where they're keeping the prisoners."

"Did you see her?" Sarah asked, concern tingeing her voice.

"No, but I did see some others; they have them doing some sort of excavation, I think. They were mostly ferrying dirt, but I couldn't get super close," Daryl answered her with a shrug. "I watched for about twenty minutes. There were only four trolls, so we should be able to take them out easily."

Trey had come back while Daryl was giving his side of the story. He was accompanied by Robbi, a woman in her early twenties that Drew had never seen smile, and another man in his mid-thirties. "Well, when are we going to hit them?" the woman asked, her hand resting on the hilt of the pistol on her hip.

"Soon. Let me just get a refreshing rain on people, and then we need to figure out who goes in and who stays out to protect our people," Drew said.

Sarah stepped in. "Drew, this is Sargent Trista Stirling and DC1 Brady Cooke," she said, supplying him with the new recruit's names. "Trista got an ability that allows her to create a line of fire behind any bullet she shoots. Brady's red is called penetrating shot and is supposed to bypass armor and other defenses. We're hoping it also deals magical damage to the trolls, but we have no way of really testing that."

Robbi had pulled out a wicked looking, red katana that he imagined was the blood blade he'd been told about earlier. "Does that cut trolls?" he asked the former cop.

"Yup, it's cut just about everything we've put it against thus far. Takes a few swings to really do any damage to metal though," Robbi answered, holding the blade up for Drew to see.

"That's awesome; you trained with a sword?" Drew asked.

"Took a couple of years of kendo."

"Yeah, I did some fencing when I was younger. Hopefully, you're better at kendo than I was at that. You gonna be okay going against a troll head on?"

Robbi just nodded his head, and his face grew grim. "Yeah, can't let you and JP have all the fun."

"What did you get, Trey?"

"It's called shatter shot; it turns every bullet into a shotgun with the spread starting wherever I choose. We're also pretty sure it doesn't work on trolls. I shot a few of them before Daryl melted 'em, and it didn't seem to do any damage."

Drew looked at the group and considered. JP, Robbi, Trista, and himself were the only ones confirmed to be able to hurt the trolls. Trey was out, and Brady was a maybe.

"Alright. Daryl, Trista, Sarah, Robbi, and I will head down the tunnel. JP, Trey, Katie, and Brady, you guys stay up here and watch the front door. Don't want them taking all of our people from behind." He could tell Katie and JP were unhappy about being left behind, but he couldn't leave everyone here undefended, and JP had the second most firepower of anyone. "Let's make sure we've got ammo, and I'll cast refreshing rain on everyone a couple times before we go."

Chapter Thirty-Eight — Tunnel

It ended up being closer to an hour before everyone was ready to go. Daryl came back from his scouting mission about midway through their preparation. Refreshing rain had taken the edge off his headache from the upgrades, and with two castings of energize, he had plenty of time to upgrade the rest of his xatherite.

Xatherite Crystal Name: Acid Arrow
Xatherite Color: Red
Xatherite Grade: Common
Xatherite Rarity: Widespread
Type: Magic
Effect: Creates two fast moving balls of acid from a finger that travel in a straight line until they impact a target, dealing moderate amounts of acid damage.
Mana recharge time: 16.1 seconds

Xatherite Crystal Name: Dancing Sword
Xatherite Color: Red
Xatherite Grade: Intermediate
Xatherite Rarity: Widespread
Type: Magic
Effect: Creates a mana construct of a sword that lasts for 60 seconds. The sword will move on its own and attack any target designated for the duration of the attack.
Mana recharge time: 1 minute, 45 seconds

Xatherite Crystal Name: Energize
Xatherite Color: Orange
Xatherite Grade: Intermediate

Xatherite Rarity: Widespread
Type: Magic
Effect: Infuses mana into the target to reduce fatigue and lactic acid buildup. Improves the target's natural healing by 4x normal for 24 hours.
Mana recharge time: 20 minutes, 39 seconds

Xatherite Crystal Name: Greater Cone of Frost
Xatherite Color: Red
Xatherite Grade: Rare
Xatelnrite Rarity: Widespread
Type: Magic
Effect: Creates a cone of cold energy which causes high amounts of freezing damage, originating from any part of your body. Has a chance to partially enclose the target in ice, slowing them down considerably. Cone will extend 6 meters and has an arc of pi/4.
Mana recharge time: 16.8 seconds

Upgrading those four had created a cascade of additional upgrades as the linked skills associated with them finally upgraded as well.

Linked Skill Name: Bladeshield
Xatherite Color(s): Red, Yellow
Linked Skill Grade: Intermediate
Type: Magic
Effect: Creates a barrier of blades around the caster. This barrier will parry 5 melee attacks before disappearing.
Mana recharge time: 4 minutes 33 seconds

Linked Skill Name: Cone of Frostfire
Xatherite Color(s): Red
Linked Skill Grade: Rare
Type: Magic
Effect: Creates a cone of frostfire, which causes significant frostfire damage, originating from any part of your body. Has a chance to partially enclose the target in burning ice, slowing them down considerably. Cone will extend 6 meters and has an arc of $pi/4$.
Mana recharge time: 21 seconds

Linked Skill Name: Frostfire Ball
Xatherite Color(s): Red
Linked Skill Grade: Rare
Type: Magic
Effect: Convert mana into a high energy blast of frostfire that will travel in a straight line until exploding, causing major frostfire damage in a 1.5m radius around the blast.
Mana recharge time: 13.1 seconds

Linked Skill Name: Refreshing Rain
Xatherite Color(s): Red, Orange
Linked Skill Grade: Intermediate
Type: Magic
Effect: Create a localized storm around a target. The storm will have a radius of 10m and will infuse mana into all creatures within its radius, reducing fatigue and lactic acid buildup. Doubles the natural healing of anyone who stands in the rain for at least five seconds.
Mana recharge time: 1 minute 45 seconds

Linked Skill Name: Shocking Acid Arrow
Xatherite Color(s): Red
Linked Skill Grade: Intermediate
Type: Magic
Effect: Creates two fast moving balls of acid from a finger that travel in a straight line until they impact a target, dealing moderate amounts of acid damage. Upon contact, each ball will impart a moderate amount of electrical damage.
Mana recharge time: 16.1 seconds

There were some important upgrades in all that. Acid arrow got a damage upgrade, putting it at the same damage level as lightning bolt. It could probably one shot a troll if he sent both darts at a single target now. The linked skill version of it also got the upgraded damage, making it able to kill a troll with each dart. Energize's healing doubled, making it four times normal, and refreshing rain had also acquired the healing qualities of energize.

Dancing sword's duration had increased from thirty seconds to a full minute. It might be worth casting at this point. The real benefit of dancing sword's upgrade was the extra two melee hits it gave the new bladeshield before he took damage. Cone of frost's length changed from four meters to six, giving him an extra two meters of effect while also improving its damage. This, of course, meant that the linked skill had received similar updates.

That seemed to be all the changes, and he took the time to recast all his buffs to make sure the upgraded versions were active. Daryl had followed the tunnel until he got to a door at the end. The tunnel itself seemed to have been magically constructed. It was a mostly oval shape, wide enough for three people to walk side by side comfortably. The entire thing was perfectly smooth, clearly created by some xatherite skill.

Just shy of an hour after Drew had named the team members, they left the temporary shelter. JP oversaw the combatants left behind, but Bill was in overall command. If the rescue team didn't get back before the storm, they were to set off for the stadium as soon as daylight came. That gave the rescue roughly eighteen hours to find and bring everyone back. The major delay had been to allow Min Sun enough time to sew pockets on everyone's armor. Everyone but Drew was carrying a pistol, at least five spare magazines, two glowrocks, two glow rods, and enough food and water to last three days. Drew carried everything but the gun paraphernalia, while he and Sarah both had included a small first-aid kit among their belongings.

Daryl left first. The scout invisible as he nearly always was to ensure the route was still clear, but the other four members of the party hesitated. Drew and Sarah were hesitant to separate from Katie again. The two girls gave each other a hug and exchanged a few words that Drew tried not to listen in on. When it was Drew's turn to say goodbye, he gave Katie a hug. Aware of the fact that at least a dozen people were watching them, neither did anything beyond that.

"I'll be right back. Just got to run a few errands," Drew whispered into Katie's ear, and she snorted into his chest.

"Sure, I've heard that before. You're gonna go down to the pub and shoot a round or two with the boys, and I'm gonna have to drag your drunk ass home past midnight," she said. Her voice was brittle, like a hint of wind would break it.

"You know, I don't actually drink."

She pulled away from him and raised an eyebrow, "Did I really get saddled with some sort of religious freak?"

Drew laughed. "Well, sort of. I was raised Mormon, even did a mission."

Katie raised an eyebrow. "Well, you'll have to come back and tell me that story."

"You got yourself a deal," Drew said, swallowing down the fear that threatened to break his voice. They were going back into the darkness. True, he wasn't alone in this anymore, but he shuddered involuntarily at the thought of a massive spider queen and the phantom pain of injuries she had given him.

"Alright, go play hero. I'll mind the kids."

Drew nodded, not quite able to laugh just yet. "Alright," he said softly. Then he looked around at the rescue team. Putting a hand in the air, he did the 'spin up' motion with his finger. "Let's roll out."

JP, Robbi, and Trista had been talking off to one side. The two cops gave each other a bro-hug before the three of them separated, with JP staying behind. He looked over at Drew and made eye contact. They both shared a nod. Then Drew turned away from the group, heading out towards the northwest where Daryl had found the entrance of the tunnels.

Forcing himself not to look back, Drew walked about fifty feet away from the entrance before he couldn't take it. He looked back. JP and Katie were still standing near the entrance, while most of the rest of the group had turned back into the camp. He raised a single hand to wave, and Katie returned the gesture. JP gave him a salute. Drew compressed his lips into the closest thing he could make of a smile and nodded his head again.

The rest of the trip to the tunnel entrance passed in uncomfortable silence, everyone dealing with their nerves in their own way. Drew saw a few larger animals, mostly more of those horned rabbits and squirrels, although a crow that looked more like an eagle cawed at them from its perch on a tree as they passed. None of the animals seemed interested in trying to attack, though, allowing them to approach the tunnel's entrance without incident.

"Almost there, the tunnel is still clear," Daryl's voice appeared in his head, and he relayed the message to the rest of the team.

"Alright, weapons ready starting now," Robbi said, pausing at the tunnel entrance. He had a lot more recent experience fighting in enclosed space than Drew. He was also taking point as the only melee fighter of their group. Daryl was ahead of them, at least Drew assumed he was, but the scout was too far away for his aura to be visible. Drew was next in line, positioned where he would be able to bring the most firepower to bear. Sarah came next, and Trista held the rear. Everyone uncovered the glowrock that Min Sun had mounted on their left shoulders. She had created a small lip so that the light wasn't shining directly into their eyes, but it was still a less than ideal situation.

Sarah's spear was held in both hands, her knuckles white from the grip already, while Trista had a Sig P226 held in a double grip. The xatherite she had acquired was more important than any impact the caliber would have imparted. Robbi's red sword glinted strangely in the light, sending ominous red shadows playing across the walls of the tunnel. Drew frowned. He was almost positive the blade had been a katana before, but it was now a more traditional longsword. Drew wiped the sweat from his empty hands on his pants.

The first few steps into the tunnel caused the panic in Drew's mind to come back. He looked behind him to reassure himself that the sun was still shining. The tunnel was pitch black beyond the glowrocks' light. He wasn't even sure how Daryl had scouted this place out. He must have done it by touch. He would have to ask the other man how he did it later.

If they had traveled in silence before, the trip through the tunnel was in something more still than that. The soft scuffing of their boots against the hardened tunnel floor was the only sound anyone heard. Their ears strained trying to pick up any sounds that might indicate the trolls were coming closer to them. Drew wasn't sure how long they traveled like this. The silence grated on his nerves. He felt like they had been traveling in the semi-darkness for hours, but he assumed it was less than an hour.

All his senses were on high alert. Looking ahead of them, under the DIA building, was a glowing ley line, like the one that had been under the headquarters building. He judged their distance traveled by how close that glowing node appeared. When it looked like it was only a few football fields ahead of them, Daryl's aura appeared at the end of the tunnel. Drew held his hand up, and everyone behind him stopped. Robbi turned to figure out what had caused the silence and seeing Drew's hand, stopped as well.

"The door is just a little bit ahead, no movement there yet. We should probably take a short break," Daryl's voice came into his head.

Drew nodded, whispering to the others, his voice too loud after the long walk in the quiet dark, "Daryl says the door is just ahead. Let's take a minute to eat and drink something. We have no idea what's on the other side of that door."

Trista and Sarah both sat down, swinging their backpacks around and pulling some water and snacks out of them. Drew did the same, while Robbi kept his eyes staring forward, the sword in his hands resting against the floor of the tunnel. Drew had no idea how heavy their weapons must have gotten since they had begun their trek through the tunnel, but by the way the two girls were massaging their hands in between bites, it had begun to take its toll. After Drew had a few gulps of water, he swung his pack back on and then relieved Robbi at point.

Drew idly chewed on some of his jerky while he watched the way ahead. He would miss the meat when it ran out. They did still have some canned chili and soups. They really needed to figure out a way to get some fresh meat soon. It would do wonders for the morale of the group.

The break was short, none of them really feeling relaxed enough to do more than mechanically chew food and take a few drinks from their water bottles. When Robbi was done, they began to walk again. The door came into sight in short order.

It looked old, the wood having a darkened quality he associated with ancient church doors. It was clearly something the trolls had created, not something man would have put down here, about five feet across and eight feet tall, its strange proportions marking it out of place for a human building but would have fit with the trolls more bulky frame better. There was no handle or hinges on this side, so Drew assumed there would be guards posted on the far side of the door.

The plan was to blow the door apart and then storm through, hopefully killing the guards before they could sound an alarm to whatever other trolls were still in the cavern. Daryl and Robbi stood behind him while he considered the best way to blow it up. It looked sturdy enough. Drew decided he would use a fireball to break it down, then launch a frostfire ball through the hole. Holding up a hand, he pointed it at the door, and then cast the spell.

Chapter Thirty-Nine — Cage Fight

The fireball impacted the door, and for a half second, Drew thought that it wouldn't be enough to break through. The shockwave from the explosion pushed him back a step even from where they stood forty feet back. Dirt flew through the air, and he covered his face with his arm, his ears ringing. He blinked away the dirt from his eyes and looked up. Smoke and dirt filled the air where the door had been, and he launched frostfire ball into the gap, intending for it to explode a couple of meters past the door.

This time the explosion wasn't anywhere near as potent feeling due to the concussive force having somewhere to go rather than back down the tunnel he was standing in. Robbi immediately ran past him, his blood sword held at the ready. Drew followed, still trying to blink his eyes clear of the dust while his jaw was working to try and relieve the pressure on his ears.

Almost tripping over a fragment of the door, he cleared the dust cloud and stepped to the right of the door, taking a moment to survey the scene. Two trolls lay on the floor near the door; two more trolls still sat stunned at a table. Robbi charged the two at the table, his red sword seemed to grow longer as he held it in a two-handed grip. Drew cast lightning bolt at the farther one, the bolt of electricity hitting it in the chest and sending it and the chair it had been sitting on rolling backward.

Robbi's troll put an arm up to block the sword swing. The red sword bit deeply into its arm, cutting more than halfway through before stopping. Robbi kicked the troll in the chest, ripping the sword out of its flesh as the manaborn tumbled out of his chair. A cry of pain and alarm went up but was quickly silenced by two acid arrows Drew shot at his face. The caustic fluid ate away at his mouth instantly. Robbi raised the sword above his head then swung it down, separating the troll's head from the rest of its body.

Green blood spurted everywhere, pooling on the floor around the two dead trolls, shards of ice from the frostfire ball and shrapnel from the door having opened a dozen wounds. The headless troll's body spurted blood in short intervals. Drew just stared at it until the troll's heart stopped pumping. When he exited the trance, he realized that someone was dry heaving behind him. Turning around, he saw that it was Trista, Sarah holding the girl's hair and rubbing her back. Daryl and Robbi were already examining the room.

Two exits ran away from the small room on opposite sides of each other and away from the tunnel entrance. A few torches burned around the room, giving off a strange purple light, creating an acerbic scent to the air that combined with the smell of troll blood and charred flesh. It made Drew want to sneeze.

"Daryl, check the left tunnel. Go a hundred feet and come back if you don't run into anything," Drew said while they waited for Trista to get over her first smell of battle. Drew wondered idly who cleaned up all the trolls he'd killed before he collapsed. Probably Daryl; for a vegetarian, that man had seen a lot of burned meat lately.

Robbi seemed like an old hand at this. Having taken up a position near the right tunnel, he stared into it with his sword held ready. Drew glanced around the room again. None of the trolls were growing xatherite, and aside from having Daryl harvest them for their skin and their weapons, there wasn't anything worth looting. Sometimes he wished the world was more like video games. He loved pulling two-handed swords out of rabbit loot bags.

There wasn't anything else to do here. While they waited, he walked over to Robbi. Forcing himself not to look at several streaks of green blood slowly trickling down the other man's armor, he looked at the sword. Its clean length still glowed red in the glowrock's light; Drew wondered where the blood had gone.

Sound from the hallway Daryl went down caused both Drew and Robbi to turn their attention in that direction. Daryl's aura made its way into the room, but he didn't bother to remove his invisibility. "They're down there, people, dozens of them," he said, the excitement clear in his voice. "I counted six trolls guarding them." Without another word he turned and headed down the passage.

"Wait!" Drew called after him, but the aura was already gone and didn't reappear. Sarah and Trista had caught up to them, although Trista still looked pale. Drew looked back at the other tunnel and frowned. "Frak," he cursed, "I wish we could block that entrance somehow. Don't like the idea of having unexplored stuff between us and our exit."

Drew was missing Katie, wishing he'd brought her rather than Trista. Logically, he knew that Katie would be needed up with the main group, but it would have been nice to know that there wasn't going to be anything coming up behind him. After about eighty feet, they came to a bend in the tunnel that twisted to go towards the glowing ley line core. He had to switch off his aura sight due to how bright the node was now that they were so close to it.

It felt weird to be without his aura sight; he hadn't realized how much he had come to rely on it, and everything seemed duller, less full of life now. When they got to an open doorway, Drew signaled for everyone behind him to stop while he bent down and poked his head around the corner. He was ready to step back in an instant if it was a trap, although he trusted Daryl to have cleared that far at least.

Drew had no idea what the room's original purpose was; rubble along the far edge suggested it might have once been a cube farm, but it had been repurposed. Thick bars of iron stretched from floor to ceiling, creating dozens of six-by-six-foot cages that each held a captive. Row after row of cages stretched out with eight-foot hallways between them. Drew cursed under his breath. He would have to rely on his three single target spells or risk killing one of the humans.

There was no sign of Daryl—he was probably wandering the room looking for his wife. Six trolls patrolled the room with another four sitting at a table on the far side. Drew pulled back from the edge of the door and looked at everyone. Taking a few steps back from the entrance, he whispered a description of the room. After a brief discussion, they decided to have Robbi go first, Trista behind him, with Sarah and Drew holding the rear.

They tried to be quiet, but they were spotted almost immediately. Drew still didn't have a good line of sight on any of the trolls, but the one that saw them roared, and all ten of the trolls came to alert immediately. Two started down the row they were on, and Trista fired a shot. A line of blazing yellow-gold fire bisected the row following the path of the bullet. One troll cried out in pain as the bullet tore through him, the blazing trail of fire carving flesh as he pulled away in pain.

Drew blinked. It hadn't killed the troll, but the line of fire remained, and the injured troll swiped at it with his claw. It sliced through the hand, sending green blood and fingers flying. The prisoners in the cages around the injured troll began screaming, filling the room suddenly with sound.

Drew launched acid arrow. The already injured one took the acid in the chest, falling to the ground silently. The other troll managed to get a hand up to block the projectile. The acid immediately began eating away its hand, and it fell to its knees, howling in pain.

Trista fired another line of glowing fire at the distracted troll. It impacted at center mass, and he sliced himself in half trying to get away. Everyone stayed where they were, no one wanting to fight where those glowing bars of fire lingered. Drew turned to watch their back. Thankfully, the cells prevented the trolls from converging on them quickly. The captives to either side of him began begging him to open their cells. Swallowing dryly, he tried to ignore them while the fight was still progressing.

Aeon's power began tingling at the base of his spine, and he pushed it down. He couldn't afford to collapse again, not here.

Ares' warning also lingered in his mind. There was danger in using that power. Besides, there were only ten, no, only eight, trolls, he corrected himself, and the rising power subsided.

Behind him, two more trolls had rounded the corner and were advancing on the group. With a thought and a flick of his wrist, shocking acid arrows impacted their chests. The lightning caused their muscles to seize while the acid ate their hearts. They died before their bodies could hit the floor. Six trolls left.

The trolls were shouting to each other over the din, their words spoken in a guttural language that sounded like it would rub his throat raw after two sentences. He glanced over and realized that one of them was making for a second entrance on the other side of the room. "Going after the runner!" he shouted, as he blink stepped through the cages, ending up on a row right next to two trolls. He immediately rolled and shot a cone of frostfire towards the ceiling, catching both trolls head on but hopefully not hitting anyone in a cage.

The runner was directly ahead of him, too far away for lightning bolt. With a curse, he jumped back to his feet and began running after the troll. Just as he was getting in range, it turned down an intersection in the cages. He cursed and pushed his legs to give him more speed. He was running full out now, his right hand held out as he grabbed a bar to swing him around the corner without killing his momentum. He blinked, confused as the yellow aura of his mana shield flared for a moment, and he felt a sharp pain in his shoulder.

Another troll had come around the corner, a double barrel shotgun in its hands. Drew blasted it with lightning bolt without thinking. The concussive force of the shotgun blast against his mana shield threw him against a cage; the blow reverberated against Drew's skull. He pushed the pain away, and with the fleeing troll in his sight, he launched an acid arrow at its back. The troll ducked right before it would have hit him, and it splattered on the iron bars of a cage instead.

"Get back here, you green bastard!" Drew shouted, and the troll turned to look at him, fear evident in its purple eyes. The prisoner whose cell it was passing pushed out an abnormally long leg, but it managed to trip the troll, sending it sliding along the floor. It was enough for Drew to close the gap and another lightning bolt ended its life.

Drew turned around; he couldn't remember how many were left, but he looked for the rest of the group. Trista's glowing fire lines were easy to find, and he followed them to the source. Robbi was dueling with a troll. The red sword seemed to be sucking in crimson lines of power from the cop's body, while the troll was leaking green from several cuts all along its body. It appeared to be the last troll standing. Even as he watched Robbi charge the troll, swinging his sword wide, it jumped back directly into one of Trista's fire lines. It burned a hole halfway through the troll's skull before it collapsed on the floor.

Drew scanned the room. He didn't see any trolls, but he held his ready stance. The humans in the room were divided into three groups. The first two groups were easy to identify, either screaming in terror or hovering close to the edge of their cages, watching the fighting with anticipation. He only realized the third group existed after a second. They were usually sitting in their cage silent and staring off into nothing. "Search the bodies, and see if we can't find a key. We'll get these people out!" he shouted while he turned to loot the bodies of the trolls in his sector.

Trista ended up finding the key on one of the two that died first. She began unlocking the cages, while Drew stood near the far entrance, looking to see if more trolls were coming. As he passed the cage where the captive had tripped the troll, he paused, and then cast acid arrow on the lock, opening it after a few seconds of metal sizzling.

"Thanks," he said, looking at the teenager inside. He was short, a few inches shorter than Drew even. With unruly, black hair showing a lighter color at the roots, several piercings dotted his face.

"Who are you?" the boy asked.

"IT2 Drew Michalik USCG," he said with a mock salute. "Go help Trista and Sarah organize the captives. We're gonna need to move out as soon as possible." He turned away from the kid then and walked to the doorway, peeking out to ensure they were alone. His fingers found the note in his pocket that Daryl left there. He glanced around to make sure no one was watching, then pulled it out.

Chapter Forty — Battle Lull

The paper was faded. Drew wasn't sure where Daryl had scavenged it from. There were splotches where it looked like it had gotten wet, which ruined the lines. Whatever he had written on it was written in pencil, so Drew held it up to his glowrock to see better. The handwriting was feminine with a lot of unnecessary flourishes.

> *Robbi is using a device to communicate with someone he is hiding it from JP I heard him talking about bringing a bunch of people in soon and to meet him at the bridge said the senator wouldn't notice. - Kara*

Drew frowned. Who was Kara? If the note came from someone other than Daryl, it made more sense that he would give Drew the note with its warning, so that he could get it from the horse's mouth so to speak. This was another instance where Drew's lack of interest in the non-combatants was coming back to haunt him. First with Frank and now with Kara. Who were these people? Drew vaguely recalled that there were three or four more women with the group, but he couldn't recall a name for any of them.

Glancing around to check their progress, the group was a third of the way towards releasing all the captives. The kid that Drew had released now had the key and was in the process of unlocking cages. Several others were helping people out and bringing them to Sarah and Trista, who were organizing them into groups and casting heal on those who had been injured. Robbi had a few of the stronger looking kids gathering the trolls' weapons and armor. Daryl was nowhere to be seen.

Drew watched Robbi and considered what he was going to do about him. The note made it sound like he was conspiring against the senator with another group, and that they were going to what? Steal people? Attack Drew's group? Help them across? There wasn't anything particularly damning about the whole thing, other than the fact that Robbi had some sort of cell phone like device he was keeping hidden. The other problem was that he didn't really have a way to do anything about it. They needed Robbi. They needed another dozen people like him, to be honest. Drew was just now beginning to realize the scope of what they were trying to do. They were going to need to escort hundreds of people with six combatants.

The group they were in the process of releasing right now? They looked to all be about the same age, which meant there was bound to be a bunch more groups of people. How was he going to protect everyone on the way to the stadium? What was he even going to do with the people in this room while he went to get everyone else? Hoping that Sarah had a solution for that, he headed back towards the main group, freeing four more people with his acid darts without a word. The four teenagers followed him nervously.

"Does anyone have any combat xatherite? Healing, attacks, or buffs?" Sarah asked a group of about ten teenagers.

Drew mostly ignored the responses; they added a couple of situationally useful skills and spells between them. His focus was on Robbi and the group he was doing quick training with on how to hold the long daggers they had recovered from the trolls. Feeling the paper, it was like a hot coal threatening to burn its way through his pants.

Trista walked over to stand next to him. He glanced over and gave her a nod. "What are we going to do with all these kids?" she asked quietly.

"Still trying to figure that one out myself. Any ideas?" Drew responded in kind.

"Hole 'em up somewhere and have them sit tight until we get back."

"Could work, if they have enough xatherite to create a barricade or fight back, so it wouldn't be suicide for them. Wish I had Katie here. We could use some more lights and walls."

Trista laughed. "Yeah, no joke."

It would be easy to ask Trista who Kara was, but he wasn't sure he wanted to draw attention to his anonymous source. He would just wait and ask Daryl when they had a minute. Drew turned. "When you were here, were you ever kept in this room?"

Shaking her head, Trista looked around, "No. Nothing like this. They had us separated. But we only had a couple hundred people total. There looks to be a lot more teenagers here than we had in our original group. I don't even recognize any of them."

Another problem then. The trolls had been gathering people the entire time, which meant that there were probably more tunnels out of this place. Were there tunnels into Anacostia, Berry Farm, and Congress Heights? He didn't imagine they would go much further than that, but if there was a tunnel under the river to Reagan Airport, that was only a mile from home. The idea of searching for such a tunnel was appealing to him.

"Daryl said he saw people transporting stuff. They must have been down the other tunnel," Drew said. Looking around, there didn't seem to be a point of the captives here. What were the trolls doing with them other than trying to sacrifice them to the mana storms?

Drew made eye contact with the kid that had tripped a troll for him and beckoned him over. The kid immediately dropped what he was doing and ran over to them.

"Yes, Mr. Michalik?"

"Please, just call me Drew. How long have you guys been here and where did you come from?"

"Most of us have been here for a few days, I think. Hard to tell time down here. I used to live off Iverson Street on the Maryland side. A group of about fifteen of us were heading to Bolling, hoping the military was doing better than everyone else..."

He trailed off and glanced around. Drew and Trista both had remnants of military uniforms on.

That was a good distance away. "What happened? Where did you guys get captured?"

"We were sleeping in a church off MLK Ave when the trolls broke in. They killed a couple of the adults and took the rest of us. Until a couple days ago, we were in a big group with a bunch of other people, but then there was a bunch of commotion, and they put us in here. We've been here for a night, maybe? A lot less of the green guys here than there used to be."

They had been with a larger group but separated everyone into individual cells right about the time the attack happened. Easier to guard them this way maybe? Drew pulled at his stubble as he considered the information. "The rest of the kids the same?" The goth kid just nodded his head.

"Did you guys hit them recently, sir? Is that why we got moved? Did you kill all those bastards?"

Drew blinked at the vitriolic nature of the kid's words. "Yeah, we killed a lot of them. Don't worry; we'll get you all somewhere safe." The kid seemed satisfied, and he sent him back to what he was doing before. But Drew wondered how true his words were; was the stadium going to be safe? He was beginning to warm to JP and Robbi, but Daryl's note ensured that he wouldn't trust Robbi for some time yet. As representatives of the stadium, was he leading these poor people into danger?

"Penny for your thoughts," a female voice said. Drew looked up, realizing that Sarah had come up to him while he was lost in thought.

"Just trying to figure out what to do with all these people."
"Any good ideas?"

"Trista suggested we hole them up somewhere. If they have some decent xatherite, they could defend it pretty easily."

Sarah bit her lip and looked around. "Well, they've got a bunch of decent attack skills. They could probably do it, although I'd feel safer if they were up with Katie and JP."

"We'd need to send someone to escort them at least," Drew said, glancing at the kids.

"Daryl?" Sarah asked, looking around for their scout.

"I mean, he would be the obvious choice, but I don't think he'll be leaving until we find his wife. Plus, I haven't seen him since we came in. Do you know where he went?" Drew asked.

"No," Sarah said. Trista shook her head as well.

"Alright. Let's head back to the entrance; we'll post them up there, have them make some barricades or whatever they can use to defend it. Hopefully Daryl will be back by then." Drew looked around and raised his voice to get everyone's attention.

"Alright everyone, we're heading out to the tunnel we came in through. We need you guys to hold that position while we search for the rest of your friends and family. I'll go first. Robbi, Trista, and Sarah will be the rear guard. If you have ranged attacks, come with me near the front. The rest of you stay back, keep together, and we'll have you somewhere safe as soon as we can."

It took more cajoling and shuffling than Drew would have liked, but they eventually got all the teens moving. They set up a base camp where they had broken in, and Drew saw several of the kids start to fashion walls and barricades out of thin air. One of them created walls of ice, and he saw a few others try out some weak attack skills, swinging flaming swords. A particularly nerdy kid held what looked like a lightsaber. Although he clearly had no idea how to use it; his neighbors kept yelling at him to put it away before he hurt someone.

Shaking his head, Drew wondered how these kids still managed to be so... normal. The kids had started to gather in groups, and it was obvious the lines they had drawn around each other. Having been through a literal apocalypse and then captured and enslaved by a band of human-sacrificing trolls, they still segregated into jocks, nerds, and cool kids.

From the tunnel they had come down, they heard one of the kids shout, "Something is coming!"

The four adults pushed through the crowd of kids who were trying to move in the opposite direction, Trista's gun out and lining up a shot before Drew managed to slide into a spot next to her. Down the hall, they could see a form stumbling towards them.

Passing next to a torch, it became obvious that it was Daryl. Covered in blood and clutching his arm close to his chest in obvious pain, the smile on his face seemed very out of place.

Sarah and Drew rushed out to meet him. "Stay here, guard the kids," Drew shouted back to Trista and Robbi before they left.

When they got to Daryl, Sarah cast a heal, and immediately, Daryl regained some of the color that had been missing from his face. He still cradled his arm though.

"I found her, Drew. I found my wife," he said with a weak grin.

"That's great, Daryl... What happened?" Drew asked, gently lifting his arm and probing it with his fingers. There was an obvious fracture, his forearm bent at a significant angle. They led him back to the group. "Tell me when your cooldown is up, Sarah. I'm gonna put this back in place, and then I want you to heal it," he said while he cast energize on the wounded scout.

"I found them," Daryl's voice was breathy, punctuated by grunts of pain. "Twenty trolls in a pit. Prisoners digging. My wife, digging. Hundreds more. Tried to get her. I slipped, landed wrong. Barely got out. Can't focus on invisibility." They were back with the rest, and Drew had Daryl sit down.

"Here, bite this," he said, giving the man a folded-up shirt he pulled from his backpack. "This is gonna hurt." Glancing at Sarah, she nodded her head, and Drew placed Daryl's arm on the table, the only flat surface they had, then with a crunch, pushed the bone back in place. Sarah immediately cast her heal again, which cut off Daryl's muffled scream.

"There, you're right as rain. We're gonna go rescue her in a few minutes, so get your strength back," Drew said, patting

Daryl's uninjured shoulder. He then turned to the group around him. "Get the kids ready; we're leaving in ten minutes."

Chapter Forty-One — Duty

Sarah wandered off to go deal with the kids. Trista stayed nearby while Robbi had only gotten halfway across the room before turning back to give basic pointers to the kids holding the swords. "Trista, can you give Daryl and I a minute?" Drew said without looking up from Daryl.

"Sure thing, IT2," she said before heading out to talk to one of the groups of kids.

Drew crouched down next to the other man, his voice soft. "Two things, Daryl. One, you shouldn't have gone off on your own like that. If we lost you..." Drew trailed off, trying to think of a way to explain to the other man how important his intelligence was. "We'd all be sitting ducks." Daryl was still gingerly holding his formerly injured arm, and he just nodded. "Especially now that we know you can't hold your invisibility when you're injured. I know your wife is important to you. I promised you I would help rescue her, and we will, but we both have more obligations than just our personal preferences." He gestured around to the kids around him.

Daryl looked suitably chastised, so Drew let that section of their conversation drop. "Next, I need to know more about what you gave me. Who's Kara?" Daryl looked confused by this.

"Kara? She's one of the girls in the group." When nothing registered on Drew's face, Daryl shook his head. "You know, the brunette that isn't Katie?"

Drew blinked again. Was there another brunette in the group? "Okay. Let's pretend I'm not a terrible person and know people's names. How reliable is she? What do you think this other group Robbi is talking to is up to?"

Daryl's switched to his telepathy. A glance at Robbi indicated his preference was not to be overheard. "*Kara is pretty reliable. I mean, I don't know her super well. As for the group, who knows? It could be another faction in the stadium that's working against the senator, or they could have a different origin and objective completely. When we get back, you can ask her yourself."*

Frowning slightly, Drew gave a furtive glance around the room. "Alright, we'll figure this out when we get everyone rescued. How are you feeling? You sound a lot better."

"Better. I'm sorry for running off like that. I just... I needed to know. I needed to know that she was still alive, Drew."

"It's okay; like I said, I get it. When we get out of here, I'm going to tell you a story about what happened when I was asleep. Let's just say there's more to this whole Advent thing than we realized," Drew said, helping the other man to stand.

Three kids were standing off to one side, clearly waiting for their one on one conversation to be over. Drew noticed that goth kid who had tripped the troll seemed to be the group's leader. "We want to go with you." His brave words were ruined slightly by the fact that he gave an almost audible gulp before saying anything.

Drew blinked, then looked at Daryl, who shrugged. "Hey, what's your name?" he asked, while his eyes searched the room for Sarah. The Ensign did much better at these kinds of conversations.

"I'm Gary. This is Mike and Lewis," Gary said, pointing to the two boys on either side of him. Mike was the lightsaber kid from earlier.

"You can call me Juice, though," the kid Gary had introduced as Lewis said.

"We've got red xatherite. We can help," Gary continued after shooting Juice a glare.

"Gary, how many people in this room have effective red xatherite?"

"Uh, I dunno. Like five of us. Kim and Nora are staying behind to protect the others, though."

"And how many trolls can Kim and Nora kill if this room gets attacked?"

"I dunno, like two or three?"

"And how many more can you three kill?"

Gary gave the two guys backing him a look as if considering them. "More than that," he said reluctantly, "but, that's not the point. We want—no, we need to help rescue our families."

"I get that, Gary. I want to make sure my family is safe too. The problem is that if I did that, you and all of your families would be stuck here with the trolls." Drew shrugged softly. "I need to be here. This is my duty. Just like you need to stay here and protect these people so that I can go rescue your families. I won't be able to fight as well as I need to if I have to keep worrying about if they're safe or not." He let the three teens think about his words for a moment. "Besides, I need someone to be in charge here. You're the only one I can trust to do that, the only one who helped in that fight. Stay here, and I'll get your families back, I promise."

Drew immediately wanted to take those words back. He had no idea if those kids' families were even still alive, and he had just promised them he would bring them back. There was no way that wasn't going to come back to bite him. He tried to cover the wince he wanted to display with a tight-lipped smile before turning away from the kids.

"Alright, team, let's get going. We're burning daylight," Drew said, and everyone drifted over to him. He turned back to Gary. "Alright, Gary, you're in charge here. Make sure everyone stays safe. If we're not back in a couple of hours, head up that tunnel." He pointed at the exit tunnel. "Head east to the soccer field. You'll find the rest of our group there." When Gary gave him a quick nod of understanding, he looked at the rest of his group. Daryl seemed eager to leave, while Sarah and Trista looked nervous. Robbi didn't look nervous, but he held a white-knuckled grip on his longsword. Wait, longsword? Wasn't it a katana earlier? Drew shook his head and cast refreshing rain on the group, giving the kids the benefit as well.

One blonde girl in the corner started to complain about getting her hair wet, but everyone else seemed to take it in stride and enjoy the cool rain. When the rain finished, everyone looked ready for action, and Drew mentally kicked himself for not casting it earlier. He took a moment to recast all his buffs and let Sarah do the same; then they were back down the tunnel.

Daryl walked invisibly ahead of the group, the rest of them trailing along behind him. Drew tried to use mana sight, but the brightness of the nearby ley lines made his eyes hurt if he used it for more than a few seconds at a time.

They walked down the tunnel, passing the room where all the kids had been kept. As they progressed, they passed several more rooms full of empty cages. There was enough room for hundreds of people. Where were they? How big was this pit they were going to? Why did the trolls need so many of them?

The trip down the tunnel was filled with that same tense silence that Drew was beginning to associate with dungeon dives. That had never been in any of the books or games he used to enjoy. His shoulders itched from the tension. After what seemed an eternity, the silence was broken by the sound of shouting and digging ahead of them. Daryl appeared, holding a finger to his lips.

"They're just ahead. There's room for one person to get a look at everything, but you'll have to be careful." The group nodded, and by silent agreement, Drew went first to get an idea of what was ahead. Drew hoped that Daryl's telepathy would be able to project images soon; that would be highly helpful.

The entrance was wide, a strange, almost organic looking substance framing the door and webbed across the ceiling. Whatever it was, it clearly had great structural support. The pit was massive, looking to be several hundred feet across and nearly a hundred feet down, dug in a spiral until it reached a strange, shiny, blue, metallic structure. A massive gate was partly visible on the building, almost entirely excavated at this point, although there was clearly significantly more of the structure still buried. A quick pulse of mana sight told him that the ley node for the building was housed in that structure.

Hundreds of humans were digging to expand the pit. Trolls walked among them using long, thin whips and shouted curses to hurry the work along. It was exactly like some dark age period piece, to a level of similarity that made Drew wonder if he hadn't fallen into some video production. There were only about twenty trolls, but that was more than enough to keep everyone in line if none of these people had offensive xatherite or the will to use them. He almost missed the ledge near the top of the pit in his survey, which was at least twenty feet above the spiral down. The troll shaman he'd seen sacrificing people a few days ago was pacing across its surface.

The cold indifference on its face sent a chill down Drew's spine. He backed out the way he came. When he got back to the group, he described the room to everyone else. "I need to take out that shaman before he can escape again. I'd like to try to sneak as close as I can, and then I'll blink step up to him. While I'm doing that, you should be able to free some of the prisoners and take up a defensive position near the entrance. The trolls are spread out enough that they shouldn't be able to come at you more than a couple at a time."

"After I kill the shaman, I'll snipe the trolls from the high ground. I didn't see a way up there, so they'll have to jump if they want to get up. Should be easy enough if they come after me." Left unspoken was, of course, the issue with how long it was going to take him to kill the shaman. When he'd fought Chakri, it had taken him a few minutes of wearing the orc down, but he had more spells at his disposal now, and they were much more powerful. He should be able to alpha strike the boss to death if he opened with everything he had.

They went back and forth on some of the various ideas, trying to find a better way to eliminate the shaman and the threat his elevated position presented. They briefly discussed alternative objectives; the structure at the bottom of the pit was clearly important to the trolls, but it would be easier to secure after they'd cleared the room. The discussion only lasted a few minutes, and by the end, everyone was convinced the original proposal was the most likely to succeed.

They all crept back towards the entrance to the pit, Drew leading the way. After he passed the gateway, he crouched low, trying to hide behind the mounds of dirt that were piled haphazardly around the upper rim. The others followed in after him, and once they were in position, Drew began creeping forward. He would have to travel about sixty feet before he would be close enough to blink step up to the shaman.

Moving from cover to cover, he made it about halfway before a troll turned right as he was moving between two piles of dirt. They made eye contact for a split-second before the troll bellowed a scream of anger. Immediately, the report of a gun echoed throughout the room, and a line of fire traced from near the entrance into the troll's chest, carving away green skin as it burned the beast.

Drew cast acid arrow and shocking acid arrow, targeting four more trolls to weaken them as he started running full speed towards the shaman. More gunshots and lines of fire exploded throughout the room, Trista's skill in action. The narrow confines and echoing nature of the room made Drew's ears ring a little louder with each report. Sarah was going to have to treat all of them for tinnitus after this.

About halfway to his target, a troll jumped in front of him. Without thinking, he launched a lightning bolt, which sent the troll crashing down a level of the pit. Drew hoped he didn't land on a human. Five ragged breaths later, he was close enough to trigger blink step.

It took him half a second to reorient himself. When he did, he launched his full complement of spells at the shaman. Blasts of superheated plasma balls and shards of ice struck a shadowy shield around the shaman, followed by a bolt of lightning and two cones, one of pure frost and the other of sticky frostfire that clung to the shield and kept burning.

Drew was pushed backward by the force of the explosion, losing his footing and saving himself from falling off the ledge by a last-second grab for a big rock. Luckily, the shaman wasn't completely un-fazed by the alpha strike. He had been pushed back as well against the wall, the shield around him now visibly leaking black umbral energy. He quickly cast another spell while Drew struggled to stand up. The shield seemed to recover some of its shape, becoming more solid.

The shaman held up a hand, palm out. "Hold, Deathweaver. I wish a parlay before we attempt to kill each other once more," his voice cracked like dry parchment.

Drew glanced down at the conflict between his team and the other trolls. Robbi was slashing through a troll with a massive, ruby greatsword, while lines of fire kept the trolls at bay. "Okay, you have thirty seconds."

Chapter Forty-Two — Pyrrhic

"You have obviously talked to humans from the greater population. That divine xatherite you used to kill my people on the surface is proof of their interference. Tell me, Deathweaver," the troll spat out that title, animosity dripping off his tongue, "did they tell you that you were special? That you were their best hope of survival?" He snorted and turned around.

"You are nothing but a tool, a means by which they can destroy their enemies. You cannot create. You cannot heal. You can only obliterate. You are a blunt instrument, designed only to destroy. That is what they need you for. They don't want you to think. They don't want you to stop and consider the consequences of your actions. They need a loyal soldier who will kill in the name of Protector and Senate."

"I can save lives," Drew rebutted. "Human and troll alike. I can use my powers to protect people from suffering," Drew said, circling the troll, wary for a trap. He needed information about the universe, about Ares and his siblings, and about the system. "We don't have to fight. There could be peace between our peoples."

The troll snorted. "At what cost? You save others, and they will reward you. They'll give you anything you want: women, drugs, physical pleasures you cannot currently comprehend, but only so long as what you want is war and death. The system does not want us to make peace with each other. It feeds on our blood. It stole my people from our homes and deposited us here, and then promised that if we sacrificed enough of your kind, we could go home. Why do you think it did that?" He paused, giving Drew a chance to think but not long enough to answer.

"It wants to foster war, to create a never-ending conflict. Whatever the system's purpose is, it wants our blood. My people were powerful once, like yours. We eradicated hundreds of weaker species and created an empire that ruled across the cosmos. Then at the height of our power, we too thought to create peace, an alliance that would foster learning and growth for every awakened species." He paused, his words remorseful, "We had such dreams. The system would not allow it. It gave quests of sedition. It turned us against ourselves, and for that salacious promise of power, we turned cannibal. We killed our brightest children, craving the power they would give us, fearing that they might outshine us."

"Too late we realized the error of our ways. We had already ruined ourselves. Those of us that were left gathered together the scraps of our once great civilization and fled. We fled to the furthest reaches of the known, to places where no mana engine could reach. We became vagrants, wanderers of the stars. The system could not let us escape its clutches so easily, though. We fled for millennia, for generations, afraid of the day the system would find us again." He turned and looked at Drew, his violet eyes glowing with emotion.

"Find us it did, and it brought us here. It promised us freedom, real freedom, if we would only sacrifice ten of your people for one of mine." The troll smiled a wicked grin. "So I gave the system the blood it desired. A thousand dead humans for a hundred of my people, finally safe from the system." As he said that, the blue building below them flashed, shedding a bright light throughout the pit.

The color drained from Drew's face as he looked frantically down at the pit, the captives that had been digging were now mostly dead. His group had managed to save thirty or forty, but the trolls hadn't been trying to fight, their efforts had clearly been on killing as many of their captive humans as they could. Red blood stained the dirt. He turned to look at the troll shaman and saw him in the process of casting a spell. Immediately, a fireball erupted from Drew's hand; it exploded against the weakened shield around the troll. It was only the first impact. Within a second, frostfire ball, acid arrow, shocking acid arrow, cone of frost, and cone of frostfire were all launched again. He could feel aeon's power struggling for the surface for control, crying desperately to be let free, to punish the wicked.

Drew tamped it down as his spells ripped through the troll's shield and then sent it flying, landing with a crack against the far wall and then sliding down with a wet thump. Drew stalked over to him, anger coursing through his veins. The troll just looked up at him and smiled. "Your people die, Deathweaver." And then he kicked out with his legs, sending Drew tumbling. A blast of fire transferring heat into his side where the blow was stopped by blade barrier, but the energy it imparted still cracked the cockroach shell embedded in the armor. Drew cast lightning bolt, but the shaman managed to get an arm up, whatever was left of the shield bouncing the bolt up and into the ceiling where it dissipated harmlessly.

Rolling for cover behind a table, Drew began casting dancing sword. He wasn't sure if the sword would cut as well as Robbi's, but his other spells were on cooldown. Once it was cast, he peaked around a corner, launching another lightning bolt at the shaman, who had to jump to avoid the blast.

Hair standing on end, Drew rolled over the top of the table he was hiding behind. Feeling a jolt of electricity bind his left hand to the ground, the smell of burned flesh filled his nostril. He cried out in pain, but his momentum saved him, rolling over the table before more damage could be done by the pillar of lightning that had erupted where he had been hiding.

Dancing sword slashed into the troll, cutting deeply into its right arm. Drew tried to focus on another spell, and lightning bolt was almost up. The pain in his left arm was incredible, the shaman's attacks having already burned through his mana shield, leaving him vulnerable. He jumped towards the shaman, trusting in blade barrier and dancing sword to do the work for him. Impacting with a thud, he slid back, the troll's superior strength preventing him from being able to complete the tackle.

Dancing sword struck again, cutting deeply into the troll's neck, and green blood fountained from the wound, soaking Drew immediately. A last lightning bolt flickered from his fingers, catching the troll straight in the chest and sending him flying back against the wall again. Drew kicked him once in anger then turned back to the edge of the ledge.

Robbi and Trista were fighting off the last of the trolls, a mere handful that seemed almost eager to die, rushing into the battle without a thought for their safety. Drew launched acid arrow and shocking acid arrow. One troll saw them coming but dodged into a slowly fading line of fire, decapitating itself immediately. His other globes struck true, and Robbi scythed through the rest with powerful swings from his glowing red... nodachi? Drew shook his head; trails of blood flowed up from the slain humans around him, filling the sword with a malevolent energy that Drew could feel from here. The sword shifted as he watched, becoming a claymore as he turned to block a strike from the last troll.

Trista claimed the last kill. She had begun firing not at the creatures themselves, but rather where they would be. Evidence of the effectiveness of her attacks adorned the area around them, severed limbs and diced trolls. Drew shook his head. The last of the trolls taken care of, he stalked back to the shaman, where three xatherite crystals grew from his chest: a yellow, blue, and indigo. He briefly considered having someone else come up and grab them or throwing the body down but opted just to harvest them himself, causing three bright flashes of color.

Drew kicked the dead shaman again for good measure and then jumped off the ledge he was on, activating gravitas to land lightly on the ground next to two dead bodies. He coughed as the stench hit him. Dead bodies, blood, viscera, and bodily waste created a miasma of odors worse than any he had encountered before. Putting his good arm to his nose to block out the smell, he picked his way through the bodies and trails of fire until he was next to his team.

Robbi was in the process of slicing the heads off several trolls who despite being less than half together still clung to life. Trista was sliding a magazine out of her gun, checking to see how many bullets it had left in it. Three of her holsters were empty; Drew didn't see the other two guns. Sarah was holding a woman who was crying loudly. Aside from the thirty or so people huddled behind where Robbi and Trista had made their stand, there were another twenty or thirty that were slowly making their way up the spiral to join them. Drew didn't see Daryl.

"Everyone, I know you're scared, but some of the people might still be alive. Ensign Rothschild is a healer." He said pointing to Sarah. "Bring the injured to her, and she can heal them." He received blank stares from the group looking at him incredulously. "Move it before more people die!" he shouted. They broke then, moving with haste to find those who were still alive. More than a few of them had to stop to vomit.

"Where is Daryl?" Drew asked.

Trista didn't answer, but she did pull on his good arm and point. When he turned to see where she was pointing, he saw Daryl about two spirals down, kneeling next to a woman, their foreheads pressed together.

"Sarah, I need you," Drew shouted, and he ran towards Daryl and his wife, forgetting for a second his own injured body. Sliding down the side of the pit, he reached Daryl with a grunt of pain. The man looked up as he approached, his eyes bloodshot with tears streaming down his face.

Drew got his first look at Daryl's wife and swallowed. It looked like a troll had hit her in the stomach. She was still alive, but her lower half was a mess. Drew paused when he got to her, wondering where to start with this kind of mass trauma. "Daryl, what's the status? Is she awake?"

The man just shook his head, his face a twisted mess of emotions. Drew felt for a pulse, reaching first with his injured hand before gasping and letting it hang at his side. Using his other hand, he pressed it against her neck. "She's alive; it's weak, but she's alive." He turned to see where Sarah was, but the pit prevented him from seeing up too far, "Sarah! I need you." Others were calling out as well, calling for help, but Sarah's head appeared over the pit. Her face was pale she looked at Drew, Daryl, and Daryl's wife and then cast heal, encompassing all of them in the effect.

Drew's felt the pain in his arm diminish, but his attention was focused on Daryl's wife. He tried to remember her name but couldn't think if Daryl had ever actually told him what it was. How could they not have discussed what his wife was named? He glanced down at her. The pulse was stronger, but her injuries were extensive. He could see some of her flesh knit itself back together, but he knew it wasn't going to be enough. Like the broken bones, Sarah's spells wouldn't be able to heal this wound.

Drew swallowed and looked at Daryl who looked back at him, pleading in his eyes. Drew cast his mind around, trying to think of something, anything he could do. Energize was too slow, but he cast refreshing rain, knowing that it would hit some of the others injured by the trolls and help Sarah's energy level through what was bound to be a large amount of healing soon. Aside from that, what could he do?

The yellow xatherite! He checked his notifications.

Xatherite Crystal Name: Major Mental Blow
Xatherite Color: Indigo
Xatherite Grade: Basic
Xatherite Rarity: Common
Type: Magic
Effect: Strike a blow against the psychic energy of the target, dealing small amounts of mental damage.
Mana recharge time: 21 seconds

Xatherite Crystal Name: Sacred Shell
Xatherite Color: Yellow
Xatherite Grade: Undeveloped
Xatherite Rarity: Uncommon

Type: Magic
Effect: Shields the caster in radiant energy which will block
against all profane attacks.
Mana recharge time: 31 minutes, 30 seconds

Xatherite Crystal Name: Major Volley
Xatherite Color: Blue
Xatherite Grade: Basic
Xatherite Rarity: Common
Type: Magic
Effect: Launch a multitude of arrows that fall from the sky,
dealing small amounts of piercing damage to enemies in a 4m
radius for the duration.
Duration: 8 seconds
Mana recharge time: 14 minutes

Drew cursed under his breath. The words of the shaman
came back to him, when he said he could never heal. Looking at
Daryl, he shook his head. "I'm sorry. There's nothing I can do."
Daryl's entire body seemed to deflate, and his head rested near his
wife's. Drew stood up, awkwardly patting the man on his shoulder.
"I'm so sorry, Daryl." He stumbled away from the man, leaving
him the last few precious minutes he could have with his wife.

Looking around, he began doing the same thing as the
others still walking—checking for survivors. He was soon covered
in blood and gore, his boots steeped in filth. He cast refreshing
rain as often as he could to renew the people around him while
trying to clean the mess around him as much as he could. It took
them nearly an hour before they had checked everyone. Trista
had gone to tell the kids, and some of them had come to help as
well, speeding up the process considerably. In the end, everyone
was mentally drained, if not physically exhausted. They relocated
almost everyone to the entrance room with the kids.

Luckily, if there was such a thing, there had been two more healers among the survivors. Everyone that lived would be healthy again before the morning. Daryl's wife, Angela, was not among the survivors.

Chapter Forty-Three - Ranks

It was well past dark. Drew was able to keep everyone awake with refreshing rain, but the fact of the matter was that his people weren't in any position to move. A small leadership meeting was held. Drew, Sarah, Trista, and Robbi were joined by an air force major named Tracy Hoffecker and a naval captain named Matt Snyder. They were the highest-ranking people among the survivors, and while there were a lot of civilians, everyone seemed content to have the two senior officers represent them.

"Final count is two hundred twenty-eight people. One hundred twenty-three of those are the kids rescued from the cage room, seventy-three more from the pit. Scavenging for food turned up another twenty-two individuals in various rooms around the building, and Ensign Rothschild's team of five. Of those, we've got about three dozen military or former military that we've got organized into a loose command structure composed of small groups of six to seven, with the senior NCOs in charge of two to four groups each, depending on combat capabilities. Our four JO's are each assigned six NCOs under them," Major Hoffecker summarized their position. Drew was a little put off by the immediate return to a military structure that had happened when the two senior officers had realized they were free.

Hoffecker was a middle-aged woman who might have been pretty in her youth. To his aura sight, she glowed with a mix of yellows and oranges underscored in green. She exuded an aura of confidence and competence, despite her rather frayed appearance. Both officers had been among those first captured by the trolls and were rather worse for wear. Snyder was in his late forties with salt and pepper hair, a strong jaw, and piercing eyes. His aura was blue and yellow with some sickly looking indigo and violet highlights.

"How many numb do we have?" Captain Snyder asked, breaking Drew out of his reverie. The numb were the third group of kids he'd noticed. The ones that had mostly given up. They would follow along with someone if supervised but tended to stare off into space and do nothing if left to their own devices.

"The adults fared better. Only one in ten of them succumbed to Numbness. The kids, well, it's more like one in five. The exact numbers are nine adults and twenty-six kids. We've split the groups into two different types: caretaker groups and work groups. The caretaker groups have a person with minimally effective combat skills assigned to each numb member. All our people with more effective combat skills are spread between the workgroups. Most of them aren't anywhere... combat ready, but they should be able to hold long enough for our big guns to show up," Hoffecker said, inclining her head towards Drew's group.

"Good, what's our food and water status?" Snyder asked, and this time, Sarah spoke up.

"We've sent a few of the work groups out scavenging. We're not sure what the trolls were feeding everyone, but we haven't been able to find any large stores. We have enough for one more meal, and then we're going to be out." Drew's group had come in with backpacks half full of food, but that wasn't anywhere near enough to feed more than two hundred people. "The only reason we have that much is that we have a couple people with food-related blues. Otherwise, we'd all be hungry already."

"Alright, well, we'll need to rendezvous with your group topside as soon as we can and hope the stadium can solve that particular problem when we get there," Snyder said, scratching at his stubble.

"We should be able to, Captain. When I left, we had more production capabilities than we would need for twice this number," Robbi offered as the only one that had been to the stadium. Snyder just nodded his head then glanced over at Sarah.

"Alright, Ensign, I'd like to split your team up a little bit, spread our experienced people out among the groups. I'm going to keep you in charge of all the combatant teams, though, so figure out distribution and skills so we can be as effective as we can," the captain announced. "Major, I'd like you to start getting everyone ready to move out at first light. Sergeants Montgomery and Stirling," he said, indicating Robbi and Trista by using their last names, "grab the combatants when Ensign Rothschild is done with them and get them practicing what drills you can. We'll need them as ready as we can get them. Petty Officer Michalik, help with the combatants, but I also want you going between the groups and casting your rain spell. We need everyone sharp for the morning. Get your teams ready, and we'll reconvene in two hours."

"Excuse me, Captain, but there are still a couple of things we need to do here. We need to take care of the dead and get into that structure the trolls were excavating," Drew said. He felt that itchy sensation between his shoulders that he was coming to associate with doing some incredibly stupid things that were bound to get him in trouble.

"I understand your concerns, petty officer. You said your friend didn't turn into one of these... wereghouls until a few hours after he died, so we should have plenty of time before they start turning, and quite frankly, we don't have the manpower to deal with all those bodies," Captain Snyder said with a shake of his head. "As for the structure, we'll just have to come back for it."

Drew frowned; from what he had been told by Ares, he knew that there was bound to be some sort of mechanism for him to be able to take control of the node in the building, But he didn't want to tell the captain about his time with the Protectorate admiral. "I don't think that's a good idea, captain. It was obviously important to the trolls, and there could be something in there that gives us an edge."

"While I appreciate the rescue and all the hard work you've done, I disagree with your tactical assessment, Petty Officer."

"But Captain-"

"That will be all, Petty Officer; you have your orders."

Drew really hated being called petty officer. It was common slang in the Navy, but the Coast Guard tended to call each other by their rate. Petty officer was the equivalent of his mother calling him his full name. It grated on his nerves. He had never been great at respecting the chain of command, and luckily enough, his command had been pretty good about listening to him. But it was clear that the O-6 thought a mere E-5 was too far down on the command chain to take seriously. He gritted his teeth, especially when Sarah shot him a look that told him to shut up.

With a grunt, Drew turned away from the group and headed down the tunnel back towards the structure. Sarah caught up to him almost immediately.

"Drew, are you alright?" she asked, touching his arm.

"Yes, I'm fine. Just... pissed," Drew answered, not slowing down.

"Drew, stop and look at me. We need to talk about this," Sarah said, pulling his arm. Drew let himself be stopped and turned to look at her.

"Drew, he's a captain. I know we've been on the edge of survival for the last bit here, but there are too many of us to keep doing things the way we've been doing it. Heck, you don't even know half the people in our old group's name. You know as well as I do that you don't want to manage the logistics."

"That's not the point, Sarah," Drew said, stepping closer and lowering his voice. "The node is in that... thing. Ares said I needed to take control of the nodes. If I did, I would be able to shape this world into a better place, but I can't do that if I'm stuck being a glorified water boy for some captain that got captured two days into the Advent."

"I know, I understand. Look, I'm in charge of the combat groups. Take some people with you, and head down there. We'll call it a training exercise. Daryl's already down there, and you need to pull him away from his wife... help him bury her at least."

The reminder of his failure to protect Daryl's wife was sobering. Drew took a deep breath and let go of the anger that dealing with the captain had filled him with. "Fine. I'll try to deal with as many of the dead as we can while I'm down there. Just because it took Juan a few hours to turn doesn't mean that it's always going to take that long."

"Yeah, I don't think he realizes how... terrifying they are. Honestly, I'm not sure he even really believes it's going to happen," Sarah said, shaking her head. "Look, we're still in this together, right? You're not going to go do something stupid?"

Drew snorted. "Right, nothing stupid here. I'm not going to abandon you." He glanced back at the room. "I just, I can't go back in there. Sarah, I feel like they're all blaming me for not being fast enough. Like it's my fault that all those people are dead. And maybe there is something in there that can prevent that from happening again."

"Drew, you didn't kill those people. The trolls did, and without you, all these people would be dead. You're the linchpin that is keeping us afloat. The captain will figure that out soon. I think he's just scared and relying on his previous experiences."

Drew nodded his head. "I know, well, my head knows that anyway, but my heart still keeps telling me I could have done better." He sighed. "When did you get so world wise? Where was the scared little Ensign who saved my life back at HQ? The one who didn't want to leave her safe room?"

Sarah shook her head and laughed. Drew wasn't sure he had ever actually heard her laugh before, but it was a nice sound. "Well, I'm pretty smart, you know? That's why they accepted me into the academy and made me an officer. We're all much smarter than you dirty enlisted." She pretended to dust off her hand that had been on his shoulder, and Drew laughed.

"Yeah, well, I prefer to work for my pay, thank you very much."

"Alright, there is a ton of stuff I need to do. Wait here; I'll get some people to go with you," Sarah said, giving Drew a final smile before she headed back into the main room. Drew sighed, and putting his back against the wall, slid down to rest his feet. He ran his hands through his hair; it was getting long, out of regulation. Soon it would be turning curly. He hadn't told anyone about the three xatherite that he'd gotten from the shaman. He glanced at his map and decided that he really wanted sacred shell to round out the last spot in his mostly full constellation.

For one, it was another element, which meant that he could theoretically add a considerable amount of firepower, especially if his fireball, storm, and cone of frost all linked with it. He wasn't sure what radiant energy was, but he imagined it was sort of like sacred damage type from his Pathfinder days, and umbral was probably the profane equivalent. The other reason was that he was pretty sure there was going to be an added bonus for completing an entire constellation, and he wanted to know what that bonus was.

Slotting sacred shell into the yellow slot, he barely felt it as it was such a low-grade xatherite, and the headache just seemed to fade into the general haze his brain was in after the emotional trauma of the past few hours. He waited for a few heartbeats but didn't get any indication that he had done anything. It would probably need to be attuned before it gave him any of the bonuses. Another plus of using such a low-grade xatherite. It would attune much faster than his other ones. He glanced at the other two xatherite.

Mental blow would be amazing for Daryl. He wasn't sure why it was an indigo instead of a green, but the system did weird things. This would give the scout something to use as an attack skill and a way to defend himself. He glanced down the hallway, concerned for Daryl. He wasn't sure what the man would do now that he'd lost his wife. Rescuing Angela had been his primary objective ever since they met all those days ago.

Hopefully Daryl didn't blame him for the failure. Drew swallowed. He'd never been good at helping grieving people. His only real experience was with a cousin that died in college. He pushed those thoughts away as something to deal with later. Who would he give volley to? JP seemed the obvious choice. The power of putting area of effect spells in links was becoming more obvious to Drew with all his storm spells. They had been a massive force multiplier. And JP was currently the only one in the group that had anywhere near the amount of elemental xatherite to take advantage of it.

There were a couple of decent spots for JP to slot it in too. He frowned, thinking about how he was going to have to tell the three men that he could access their maps soon. It felt a bit like an invasion of privacy, knowing exactly what xatherite they had and how they connected. Drew tried to put himself in their shoes and knew he would be offended if he wasn't told that someone had that kind of access to his map. Vowing to tell them the next chance he got, he pulled his last water bottle and some jerky from his backpack, snacking to relieve the emotional pressure of the day.

As he ate, he pondered the shaman's words. He said that Drew was built to kill. All the xatherite he'd gathered had been made to kill or to defend himself from being killed. Even the non-combat colors like blue and indigo. What did that say about him exactly? Was the shaman right? Was the captain? Was he just there to kill things, to be a good soldier? Ares didn't seem to think so. Ares called him a leader. A savior for humankind. A protector.

Katie would probably tell him that he was being stupid. The troll was obviously trying to unbalance him, and he should ignore everything it said. With a pang, he realized how much he missed the brunette. He had hated having to split the party but knew that it was the most logical course of action. Inside, he realized that he didn't want to explore another dungeon without her. He was growing to depend on her ability to call him on his crap, not to mention her very useful skills.

Several pieces of jerky later, he saw three people heading up the tunnel towards him, and he stood up to greet them, glad for something to distract him from his thoughts.

Chapter Forty-Four — Core

The three people came to a stop a few feet from Drew, who greeted them with a wave, "Hey, guys. I'm Drew." He neglected to give his rank, and he wondered if it was because he was purposefully trying to distance himself from the captain. All three of the people were adults, and he vaguely recognized them from their time in the pit looking for survivors.

"Hello, sir. I'm PFC Kyle, and these are Airmen Jones and Wilson," the lead figure said. They were all young, probably early twenties, and Drew nodded his head to each as they were introduced.

"Alright, nice to meet you. First off, what are your first names and what combat xatherite do you have?" None of them had weapons, so Drew assumed they had other skills.

"Ah, first name is Dak, sir. I have an orange that turns my skin into stone. Tires me out something fierce, but I can't really be hurt in that form." That was from Kyle, and from his accent, he was from somewhere in the Great Lakes area.

"I, uh, don't really have any combat xatherite, but the Ensign said you'd need my help clearing the gate. I have a terrakinesis violet," Jones said. "Oh, and my first name is Adam."

"Glenn," Wilson said with an up-nod that made Drew think he hadn't quite been acclimated to the military before the Advent. "I got two, a blue that allows me to summon throwing daggers and a yellow that can deflect projectiles."

That made sense; none of them would have been able to fight against the trolls, as they didn't have any elemental attacks. He turned to Adam. "The trolls didn't use you to clear the dirt?" he asked the airman with a quirk of his eyebrow.

"No, sir. They didn't ever find out I had it. I read about how the emperor of China used to have his workers killed after they finished digging stuff up. These guys reminded me of how he ran things. So I sort of used it to make it take longer." Adam looked a little ashamed at his inability to do anything productive against the trolls.

"Good, no telling how many people you saved. If the trolls had been able to get into the building earlier, we might not have been here before they went all trigger happy," Drew said with a nod, and then he turned and began walking down the tunnel. "We don't have a lot of time; I'd like to get this done as quickly as possible." All of them had been in the pit, so they understood what they were getting into.

The smell hit them before they ever came close to the pit. Drew put his sleeve up to his mouth to block the stench. It had been bad before, but a few hours of decay hadn't improved the situation at all. The first step into the room was nearly overwhelming. Pushing down an involuntary gag, he surveyed the room. Dark shadowy things seemed to crawl around the corners of the room at the edge of his vision; he was sure that it was just his imagination playing tricks on him, but as they made their way down the spiral, Drew cast fireball and frostfire ball whenever he saw more than two bodies together, cutting down on the number of possible wereghouls.

"Ideally, I could do a couple of firestorms, clear the whole place out in an hour or so. But I'm not sure how it will work on the relatively broken terrain here," Drew said to the other three. They had likewise created masks from their shirts, but all of them tried to breathe in shallowly. Drew decided he would do that on the way out. When they were midway down the second spiral, Drew stopped at the spot where Daryl's wife had died, but she was no longer present. "Daryl?" he called out questioningly.

No response came to his query, and the node made using his mana sight to detect the scout impossible. They continued down the spiral until they got to the blue, metallic structure. Up close, it was clear that it had a pyramid shape. The topmost section was flattened, leaving two or three feet exposed on more than half of its surface. The gate was at least fifteen feet tall and twenty across, and a split down the center seemed to indicate that at least one side of the gate should be able to operate.

"Alright, Adam, you're up." Drew stepped aside, and the other two did likewise. Adam held out his hand and closed his eyes. Nearly immediately, Drew could feel a vibration through the ground; it wasn't particularly strong, just noticeable. The earth and rocks that had been blocking a good seven feet of gate moved like a wave away from them, up the side, and then formed into a more solid wall. Drew blinked. He'd moved enough earth to fill two pickup trucks ten feet in about twenty seconds. "Holy crap, that's impressive."

Adam nodded; turning around, he wobbled a bit, his face white and sweaty from the exertion. Drew rushed forward to help him sit down. "You alright there, Adam?"

"Yeah, just a little tired, never tried to move that much that quickly before," Adam said with a slight shrug.

"Alright. Glenn, you stay with Adam. Shout if anything comes," Drew instructed the others while he and Dak advanced on the gate. There was no access pad or doorknob. Drew was sort of hoping it would just slide open when he approached now that it was clear, but he had no such luck. He reached out and touched the blue metal. It felt cool and so smooth that it almost felt slimy. However, he could feel something resonate inside when he touched it and pulled his hand back.

"Do you feel that?" Drew asked Dak who put his hand on the gate and then looked back at Drew, shaking his head.

"I can't feel anything, sir."

Drew rolled his eyes; the sir thing was going to get old quick. "You know I'm only an E-5, right? No need to call me sir," he said and put his hand back on the gate, concentrating on the feeling inside him as he did so. It felt a little like when aeon wanted out, although nowhere near as potent. Now that he was focusing on it, it felt like... the start of a spell, he realized with a start. Then he began the process of pulling mana through his body; it was awkward at first, as he'd never tried to do it without xatherite to guide him. However, the familiar sensation from casting so many spells made it so that his body knew what to do. Like manually breathing, only awkward because you were so used to your body doing it on its own.

As he channeled mana, lights began to appear on the surface of the gate, red lines that turned to purple on their edges creating a door frame around him, slowly filling in until the three by six rectangle was blazing a perfect red. The next instant, Drew was no longer at the gate but inside. The entire structure appeared to be made of glass, and everywhere he looked, he saw security camera-like footage of the DIA building. It felt like a guard station.

With a pop, Aevis appeared next to him again, the AI standing at attention. She gave Drew the same salute he had seen Ares' people give him. When he returned it hesitantly, she spoke, "Greetings, Midshipman Drew Michalik. I am the artificial intelligence assigned to Earth-3. You may remember that my name is Aevis. As you have met the criteria to control this node, I am here to facilitate the expedient transfer of ownership to your command."

"This facility is currently designated as PN-SN83. It is currently operating as a fourth-tier node function. Would you like to change the name of PN-SN83?"

"Who designated it PN-SN83?" Drew asked, a little overwhelmed by the entire procedure.

"PN-SN83 is an acronym. The facility's full name is Primary Nexus-Sub Node 83. As a previously unclaimed node, this was generated by the system in accordance with standard operating procedures for the newly created dimensional slice. Does that adequately answer your question?"

"Oh, holy shit, I totally forgot about that. Yes, gods, yes it does. And yes, I'll rename this to the DIA node."

"PN-SN83 will be renamed to DIA Node, in accordance with the new ownership transfer protocol." The area around Drew shifted, going from a bright blue tinge to a glistening ruby.

"Warning, download of AI database is incomplete. Your claim of this dungeon is significantly earlier than projections. Please be aware that some functionality will not be available. I have taken the liberty to request an emergency update due to these unforeseen circumstances."

"As the owner of DIA Node, you are able to set its designated purpose. The node is currently designated as a dungeon training center or DTC. Would you like to change the designated purpose?"

"A couple of questions: First, how much earlier am I than the projections? The second question is what are my options?" Drew asked, and immediately, a list appeared in front of him.

"Your ownership is fifty-three local years earlier than the previous record for a primary node's occupation and three local years earlier than the earliest node claimed on a new split. As this is the first node that you control, options are limited. Controlling multiple nodes will increase the options available to you."

1. Dungeon Training Center
2. Xatherite Concentrator
3. Mana Funnel
4. Biological Growth Accelerator

Drew frowned as he looked over the list. "What exactly are the differences between those four? And is there a way to see what else I can unlock by controlling multiple nodes? Also, what does a fourth-tier function mean?"

"A dungeon training center is designed to advance the combat capabilities of the locals near it. Manaborn or mana caught creatures can be designated as enemies. As a fourth-tier node, intelligent creatures with a danger rating of three or below can be generated. While a DTC acts as a closed circuit for all mana within its sphere of influence, they do, however, grant a .5

multiplier on all controlled adjacent node's mana generation facilities."

"A xatherite concentrator will take the ambient mana in the area and create a chamber where xatherite crystals will grow. Type and rate of growth are dependent on the mana generation of the facility. They do not grant any bonuses to adjacent nodes. As a fourth-tier node, you can select a preference as to what color of xatherite crystal will be generated."

"A mana funnel will cause all nodes within a radius to receive a multiplier based on node tier. As a fourth-tier node, you will grant all nodes within three adjacent links a .75 multiplier."

"A biological growth accelerator or BGA will convert its mana generation capabilities towards developing the growth of all designated biological organisms within its field of influence. As a fourth-tier node, the generation of grade three results is highly likely."

Aevis finished her recitation. "Does that adequately answer your question?"

"No. I have some follow up questions. The DTC, you said it only affects friendly nodes, whereas the funnel will affect all nodes, is that correct? How many nodes would setting DIA node as a funnel affect?"

"You are correct. Currently, there are eighty-five nodes that would benefit from the funnel's area of effect."

Drew shook his head, eighty-five nodes with more mana? That would undoubtedly make the DC area completely inhospitable to human life. BGA would be great if he could leverage it so that they could feed everyone. There were still a lot of questions that needed to be answered, though. "Aevis, what are my responsibilities as a node owner?"

"As the node owner, you will be responsible for the protection of the node. You are also responsible for keeping the node in good working condition. However, due to the current lack of database and the earliness of your occupation. I, as a representative of the system, will maintain responsibility of the good working condition of the node until after the first oversight review has been completed."

"I see, and when will that review happen?" Drew asked Aevis.

"The first scheduled review will occur in ninety-one years, eleven months, eighteen days, and six hours by the local calendar. However, as part of my emergency update request, an emergency oversight review will be scheduled within the next local decade, pending review authority availability."

"Right, so not something I'm going to worry about soon. Okay, so let's go back to it being my responsibility to protect the node. What resources do I have available to do that?"

"The node currently has six thousand one hundred forty-three mana stored. You are able to purchase any upgrade available to you for the mana cost contained in the database records," Aevis said.

"The database records that you don't currently have?" Drew said with a frown.

"That is correct. You have demonstrated a flaw in the system. Please wait while I attempt to determine the proper workaround." Aevis became as still as a statue. Drew waited, but after a minute, he got bored, so he began watching the screens around the room. There was a seat near the center of the room, and he took it, not sure how long it would take Aevis to determine the proper course of action. He watched as his people went about the business of getting ready to leave the tunnels.

Searching for the people that he knew, he saw that Sarah was hip deep in the middle of managing a dozen people, and there was a hive of activity around her. Drew smiled; she had really come into her own these last few days. The Major was similarly occupied, while Robbi and Trista were doing weapons drills. Daryl had found a small room off to the tunnel towards the pit and was in the process of burying his wife. Drew looked away, not wanting to intrude without the other man knowing. The last person he found was the Captain, who was sitting in a dark corner and crying. Drew wondered what the man was like before the Advent, wondered just how terrified he must have been over the last few weeks stuck in the pit digging while people disappeared or died around him.

Drew sighed. The stupid system was making him feel empathy for that asshole. He turned as Aevis began talking again.

Chapter Forty-Five — One

"It has been determined that through improper planning and through no fault of your own, you have been placed in circumstances where the completion of your duties has been deemed irresponsibly difficult," Aevis said with her typical emotionless voice. "As such, you have been allocated a mana stipend to contact a superior officer. As there is only one superior officer within range, we have contacted them, and they have agreed to speak with you. Would you like me to connect you now?"

Drew blinked. "Sure. I guess."

Instantly, one of the main windows before him shifted from displaying a section of the building to view a throne-like conference room like the one he had seen Ares using. Sitting at the command chair was a man wearing a long, well-worn, leather trench coat. His hair was short, and he had a full-length beard. He was looking back at Drew with a predatory glare that spoke of many battles. What was most surprising was that under the scars and glare were familiar facial features.

"Go tsao de, you must be Three," Drew's own voice spoke from the other man. He remembered the curse he spoke from back when he was really into a TV series called Firefly that cursed in Chinese.

"Three?" Drew asked, confused.

"Yeah, Drew Michalik-3, the third iteration. You move fast. Two just barely got online last year." The other man, who Drew decided to call One, used some sort of interface to pull up some information. "Shiong mao niao, you conquered a Primary Nexus sub node? How old is your slice? We haven't been able to get past the Appalachians yet."

"It's only been two weeks or so. I was sliced in a bunker in DC and have sort of just been trying to survive since then." It was surreal talking to himself. The other man had similar mannerisms.

However, there was something about him that seemed just enough off that it broke the uncanny valley.

One whistled softly, glancing down at the info screen he was looking at. "Well, sounds like you're in for a rough ride. What took you to DC?"

"I joined the coast guard four years ago. Was stationed here after school," Drew said.

"Oh yeah? Two said he was in the process of trying to join up when the slice happened. We both started up here in the intermountain region. I'm set up in Colorado Springs, and Two is down in Vegas. He's gonna get a kick out of this. But anyway, mana is burning, what's this garbage about an emergency protocol enactment?" One said, flipping from social back to business like abruptly.

"Well, I took over this node, but apparently, they hadn't downloaded the database yet. They assumed it would take longer, so I guess it wasn't a priority. So now I have the facility but no way to know what everything costs. They figured that was a breach of my responsibilities to protect the node and put me on with a superior officer."

"Ahh, yeah, the system is a little backed up around here, although the speed got kicked up a notch a week or so ago. I'm assuming that's your doing actually now that I know your situation." One paused, considering the situation. "Alright, so, you've got like a couple thousand mana to work with, and you're trying to build a defense?"

"That's about the size of it, yeah," Drew said, wondering what his other self was considering.

"Well, a couple things. One, you're probably the only person on the planet that can even try to take control of the node. An awakened race must have officer rank to enter the command structure. There are only sixteen of us officers on Earth-1, and last I heard, Earth-2 only had a handful. So, the odds of someone being able to ninja it from you are slim. And you'll have a little bit of time before the WBs start showing up. Two and I compared notes, and they didn't start spawning until midway through the first year."

"Sorry, what is a WB?" Drew knew the term from gaming but was really hoping it wasn't the same context as he understood it.

"World bosses, big monsters that take over territory. That's what's keeping us out of DC and, well, most of the major cities. They claim nodes which gives them more strength, and once they get entrenched, it's a long, hard slog to dislodge them. As far as we know, that's the only thing that can claim a node other than another officer," One said, looking down, considering things. "Look, right now you have a DTC that no one else is going to claim. It is going to take more mana than you have to reconfigure it into anything. I would suggest you set it up with some sort of beast you feel okay eating. Giant chickens or pigs. Plant a few people there and use it to get your people experience and xatherite.

"You're going to be in a world of hurt once the WB spawns, and you're gonna need a massive cadre of people who can fight. You're probably better off running southwest if you can get to another population center out there. Charlotte probably would be best. You can set up there and have a chance at creating a power base that will survive the WB spawns. But hey, if you can hold on to the primary nexus," One trailed off, thinking, "Earth-3 would be... well, it would be a good thing."

"I don't think I'm going to run away," Drew said after a few seconds of thought. "Ares indicated that I needed to stay here to gain the most benefit."

One quirked an eyebrow, scratching at his beard. "Sorry, who is Ares?"

"Ares is the Order of the Dragon Admiral that contacted me."

One went still, and Drew could see him rapidly considering that information. "You've already had your Accolade ceremony?" His voice was devoid of emotion. Drew recognized it as the voice he used when anger was threatening to overcloud his judgment and blinked, trying to determine what had caused it.

Drew shook his head. "No, they just contacted me due to the high difficulty level of my starting area. Told me that as a valuable asset, I would need extra assistance, or it was unlikely I would survive." He had gotten a lot better at half-truths in the military. Part of not being able to talk about his work was that he needed to be able to deflect questions in a believable way. One never had that requirement, and although he was sure the other version of himself could win in a fight, he hadn't had to develop his social skills to the level that Drew had.

One's voice had a little bit more emotion to it as he responded, "Well, that makes a certain kind of sense. I can't imagine having to start off with that much ambient mana." Drew wasn't out of the woods yet, but he still needed One to help him with the node system.

"Anyway, so how do I configure the monster type the node creates?" Drew asked, trying to distract One.

"Once you select the purpose, it will give you a list of what kind of monsters you create. You can sort them by a number of different options. With your mana levels, you probably won't be able to deviate too much from what it started out with, which according to this was something called Ashalla, whatever those are."

Drew frowned. If the system wouldn't let him change it from the trolls... he wasn't sure he could deal with more intelligent monsters that were capturing humans in the area. "We called them trolls; they were an intelligent bipedal race that were... well, a lot like trolls."

One nodded his head. "Huh, pretty rare. We didn't get a lot of intelligent creatures out here in Colorado, although one of the guys who set up down in El Paso said they had some goblin critters." He scratched his beard again, thinking. "Probably because it's already a fourth-grade node. I just barely got my first fifth-grade node setup here, and I've been fighting for eight years. You have some kind of luck to start in the primary nexus. High risk but great rewards."

Drew nodded his head. "Yeah. Let me see what I can do with the options while you're still on the line." He touched the option to keep the node as a dungeon training center.

> You have selected Dungeon Training Center as this node's primary function. As that was the previous function, no additional mana must be spent to convert it. What creature type would you like to populate the dungeon?

What followed was a massive list of creatures ranging from squirrels and rabbits to dragons and leviathans. Almost all of them were grayed out, requiring a higher tier node. He clicked the buttons to only display those that would require less than ten thousand mana to convert into.

"Alright, I have a list of stuff that shouldn't take too long to make. How do I figure out how much mana I generate in a day?"

Aevis answered him, though she had otherwise been silent throughout the entire conversation, "DIA Node is currently generating five hundred mana per day, not counting additional bonuses from mana usage within the facility."

One whistled. "Shunsheng duh gaowhan, the perks of a primary nexus node. That's a lot of mana. Most of my nodes generate a third that much. With that much wiggle room, I do have some suggestions for you. First, you'll want to buy a remote monitor interface. It's three thousand mana but well worth it. It will allow you to control the node from your interface instead of having to be in the control room to do it. A week's worth of mana well spent, especially since you probably aren't going to want to live in a DTC and this is your first node."

Drew glanced over the screen in front of him. "Alright, let's do that. How-" He was interrupted by Aevis.

"Please confirm that you would like to purchase a remote monitor for DIA node," she said.

"Yes, I do," Drew said, and a new notification appeared at the edge of his vision.

"Alright, next. Like I said, pick a food animal to populate the dungeon. That will give you a source of food which will otherwise probably be rough in a metro area like DC," One said. Drew nodded and changed the options on the list of possible creature types to include only quadrupeds. Each of the options had a small image next to him, and he scrolled down until he found one that contained a cow-like creature.

"Oh yes, beef is gonna be back on the menu," Drew said, selecting the cow-like creature, which had a mana cost of eight thousand to convert the facility. "Alright. Got it all locked in." He glanced up at One and smiled.

"Thanks, One. It was nice talking to you."

"Likewise, Three. You probably won't be able to call me back for a bit, but once you get a communications node, you should have plenty of mana to start a call. I'd recommend your next couple nodes be either DTCs or BGAs until you have five linked nodes. That will let you set up a habitat; everything gets easier after you can get a system recognized habitat node. You'll definitely want at least one of those and an armory before the WB spawns. Comm nodes are great, but they're a luxury you won't need for a bit since odds are there won't be another officer on Earth-3 for years. But me and Two would be happy to share our knowledge if you get one up and operating."

"Anyway, the mana stipend is about up. Try not to die. It's super hard to find people to talk to. Oh yeah, that reminds me, Two is gonna want to know if you and Melanie ended up working out?"

"Melanie? Nah man. She married her dance partner and has a kid and two ferrets," Drew said. Melanie was a girl he had dated before joining the coast guard. They broke up due to the distances involved.

"Dang, Two's not gonna like that. He's been pining after her for years." A countdown appeared on the screen, telling them they only had thirty seconds remaining.

Drew laughed. "Yeah, wait 'till I tell you about Emily. It's a good story."

One perked up. "Emily? Redhead Emily or blonde Emily?"

"Blonde. It's a good story. I'll tell you as soon as I can," Drew said, and the countdown hit zero, causing One's image to blink out of existence. He looked around the room, watching his people work. The three guys outside the pyramid had backed away and looked nervous.

"Aevis, is there anything else I need to do?" he asked the AI.

"Negative, the facility will convert to use the Korath as its base monster type. It should take between nine and ten days before conversion is complete. You can check the status of it at any time through your remote monitor interface."

Drew nodded and with a last glance around, said, "Alright, so how do I leave this room?"

Aevis gestured to a small square near where he appeared. "Simply stand in that location, and it will transport you out of the facility. Have a pleasant day, Midshipman Drew Michalik-3."

The AI's projected form disappeared, and Drew walked over to the square. In the blink of an eye, he was back on the ledge in front of the gate. Looking around, he waved at his three companions who started shouting at him. However, they were all shouting at the same time, so it took him a moment to realize what they were saying. Turning to look at what they were pointing at, he saw one of the bodies shaking, hair having grown all over its form.

As he watched it sat up, feral eyes and a fanged mouth opened to scream at him.

"Shit, we need to leave," Drew said, launching a fireball at the wereghoul, which killed the beast, and he started running towards his team. "Out! We need to get all our people out now!"

Chapter Forty-Six — Sub-Lieutenant

The three kids were already halfway up the first spiral, so Drew merely ran towards them and activated gravitas, flying to land next to them. They stopped to stare at him 'flying' through the air. "Stay behind me! Whatever you do, don't stop moving!" The spiral was long, although it didn't cover all that much ground. The fact that they had to go all the way around to gain a few feet of elevation meant that they would be traveling hundreds of feet just to get out of the room that was fast becoming a deathtrap.

Lightning sprang from his fingers, catching a rising wereghoul and sending it back to the earth. Drew wasn't sure if it was dead, re-dead, or no longer undead, whatever it was that you called killing undead creatures. But they moved past its smoking form and continued up the spiral. Only about one out of thirty of the bodies were turning, but that still meant that they were going to have a dozen wereghouls on their tail soon.

A fireball crashed into two newly turned wereghouls that had died close together. Engulfing them in plasma added the smell of burned hair to the miasma of noxious smells already filling the pit. Around and around they went, following the spiral up and out. The first wereghoul that dropped down from a level above might have killed his three young teammates, but their screams arrested his forward movement. With a thought, a lightning bolt altered the trajectory of its fall to make it land on the next spiral down. Dak had turned into his stone form, and it took a few seconds for him to shift back into normal so that he could move.

The delay was long enough for another couple of wereghouls to drop down on them. Glenn's daggers took them in the throat right before a cone of frost froze them solid. They landed with a tinkle of shattering ice, and the group moved on.

They were all covered in sweat and gore when they finally made it to the exit. Ten minutes at a double-time march would have been draining to Drew a few weeks ago, but the Advent had done wonders for his fitness. The other three were keeping up, although they were slowing down. At the entrance, Drew slipped from the lead position to the back. "Alright, move. We're gonna make a short detour when you get to the first left turn, otherwise don't stop unless I start screaming, then come save my ass."

The three kids in front of him kept moving down the tunnel as Drew turned and faced the rear. A wereghoul appeared, and he shot it with lightning bolt before it got out of range. Next, a head appeared around the corner watching Drew but ducked back before a hastily launched acid arrow could kill it. Drew heard a growl that varied in tone as it continued. Were they communicating? The only other wereghoul that had done that was Rob. He mentally created a second tier of the undead creatures that he called wereghasts. If he was right about that, then wereghasts would be even more intelligent and able to control their lesser brethren. This was just becoming an even worse day.

The wereghast poked his head around the corner again, locking eyes with Drew and twisted its head slightly, almost questioningly. Its eyes weren't as feral as the others; there was a sense of awareness in them, just like the wereghast Rob had become. Could they learn to communicate? He shook his head as the head disappeared beyond his vision again.

No other wereghouls appeared down the tunnel, although they soon lost sight of the pit exit. The kids stopped at the first left as he had asked them to do. "Daryl?" Drew shouted into the room,

"Daryl, I know you're in there. We've got wereghouls chasing us you need to come with us. We're going to be evacuating soon."

Daryl appeared seconds later, looking at Drew with bloodshot eyes. "Daryl, your wife would have wanted you to survive. I own the node now, so we'll be coming back, and we'll build a proper memorial." Daryl's eyes had never been so vacant before. He simply nodded and turned invisible, heading down the tunnel and away from the node.

Drew turned on his mana sight to make sure the man was following them. To his surprise, the ley line underneath them no longer blinded him; it had taken on a muted coloration, although it now blazed like a fire of shifting reds, oranges, and yellows, unlike every other set of nodes he was near, which remained white. More stuff to figure out later. Daryl went ahead of the group. The three kids were next, and Drew held up the rear. The angry blinking of notifications in the bottom corner of his vision was new, a response to enemies in the node maybe?

They managed to get all the way back to the entrance room where Sarah and the others were without further incident from the wereghouls. However, they were followed the entire time by the creatures' angry howls echoing down the tunnel.

They were met at the entrance by Robbi, Trista, Sarah, Hoffecker, and Snyder. "What did you do?" Snyder shouted angrily.

Everyone looked at him, surprised at his outburst. Hoffecker put a hand on his shoulder, and he turned to look at his defacto XO as she whispered something into his ear.

"We need to get everyone out. I was down in the pit, and the bodies started to turn. I killed at least a dozen, but then a wereghast, or a pack leader turned, and they all hung back. I think they're amassing for a bigger attack. I don't think we can protect both entrances at the same time."

"But it's still night out there." Gary had come up while Drew was looking at the officers. Gary had far more experience with the night than most, having traveled above ground for some distance before getting captured. The fear in his voice was evident; at this point, they all knew what sort of monsters existed out there.

"I know that, Gary, but I'd rather take my chances with the bats and the bugs than wereghouls. They're intelligent," Drew frowned, looking around at the group, "and I'm hoping at some point we'll figure out how to communicate with them. I think they remember something of their previous lives." Nearly everyone in the room had lost someone they cared about in the pit, and the idea that they could someday be able to communicate with their loved ones again was a powerful motivating force.

"Fine, we'll evacuate. What's our status, Major?" Snyder asked, the anger in his voice still evident.

"I can have everyone moving in fifteen minutes," Hoffecker answered.

"Make it so," the Captain said, causing Drew to roll his eyes. A Star Trek reference? Really? The captain turned back to Sarah. "Ensign Rothschild, I need your people to secure the exits until we can leave. We also need a scout to move ahead of the group." He turned away from Drew and stalked away.

"Guy has a stick so far up his ass he can probably smell it," Gary said softly. Drew bit back a chuckle; the goth kid was growing on him.

"Alright, Drew, you and your three stay here. Robbi and Trista, take some of your people over to the other tunnel. Daryl?" Sarah said, looking around, then focusing on him when the scout reappeared. "Daryl, are you up to scouting ahead, or should I send someone else?"

Daryl looked at Sarah then glanced over at Drew. "I can do it." His voice was raw, and he turned away.

"Daryl, wait," Drew said. He cast refreshing rain, then opened his interface and traded mental blow to the other man. "Take this; it'll keep you safe."

Daryl blinked as he read through the xatherite information and immediately slotted it. Drew cast energize on the other man when he saw him do so.

"Thanks, Drew. It'll be nice to be able to fight back finally," Daryl said before turning and heading up the tunnel, looking much readier than he had just a few minutes before.

Sarah touched Drew's shoulder and smiled at him. "Thanks, Drew," she said, squeezing his arm, "I've got a ton of stuff to do. Drew, you've got rear guard. Robbi and Trista, you'll be first out the tunnel when we start moving." With a nod from everyone that they understood their jobs, she was off to organize the rest of the action.

Drew turned to his tunnel, but nothing was coming out of it, so he pulled up his notifications.

Congratulations, Midshipman. You have conquered your first node. You are awarded bonus experience for being the first person on Earth-3 to do so.

Congratulations, Midshipman. You have conquered a primary nexus node. You are awarded a bonus level experience for being the first person on Earth to do so.

You have reached level 2. You are now a Sub-Lieutenant. Interface options have expanded.

Congratulations, Sub-Lieutenant. You have attuned your Sacred Shield xatherite.

Congratulations, Sub-Lieutenant. You have attuned your Major Mana Sight.

Congratulations, Sub-Lieutenant. You have attuned your Major Gravitas.

You have completed a six linked section of xatherite. All xatherite abilities and linked abilities inside the linked section will receive double your mana discharge bonus.

You have completed a constellation.

Beginning constellation analysis.

Analysis complete. Constellation has been renamed: Elemental Tempest.

All xatherite abilities and linked abilities within Elemental Tempest will have their elemental effects doubled.

Congratulations, Sub-Lieutenant. Linked skill: "Gravity Tempest" has been obtained.

Congratulations, Sub-Lieutenant. Linked skill: "Cone of Binding" has been obtained.

Congratulations, Sub-Lieutenant. Linked skill: "Grav Ball" has been obtained.

Congratulations, Sub-Lieutenant. Your Sacred Shield xatherite has reached level 5. Damage absorbed has increased.

Congratulations, Sub-Lieutenant. Your Sacred Shield xatherite is ready to be upgraded.

Congratulations, Sub-Lieutenant. Your Acid Arrow xatherite has reached level 5. Damage has increased.

Congratulations, Sub-Lieutenant. Your Acid Arrow xatherite is ready to be upgraded.

Congratulations, Sub-Lieutenant. Your Dancing Sword xatherite has reached level 5. Duration has increased.

Congratulations, Sub-Lieutenant. Your Dancing Sword xatherite is ready to be upgraded.

Congratulations, Sub-Lieutenant. Your Energize xatherite has reached level 5. Charge requirement has reduced.

Congratulations, Sub-Lieutenant. Your Energize xatherite is ready to be upgraded.

Congratulations, Sub-Lieutenant. Your Lightning Bolt xatherite has reached level 5. Damage has increased.

Congratulations, Sub-Lieutenant. Your Lightning Bolt xatherite is ready to be upgraded.

Congratulations, Sub-Lieutenant. Your Mana Shield xatherite has reached level 5. Damage absorbed has increased.

Congratulations, Sub-Lieutenant. Your Mana Shield xatherite is ready to be upgraded.

Congratulations, Sub-Lieutenant. Your Storm xatherite has reached level 5. Damage has increased.

Congratulations, Sub-Lieutenant. Your Storm xatherite is ready to be upgraded.

Linked Skill Name: Gravity Tempest

Xatherite Color(s): Red, Orange
Linked Skill Grade: Advanced
Type: Magic
Effect: Create a localized gravity tempest around a target location. The storm will have a radius of 24m and will cause major amounts of gravity damage within its radius. Secondary results may occur.
Complete Linked Skill bonus: Double benefit from your mana discharge stat.
Elemental Tempest Constellation: Elemental effects doubled.
Total effect: Create a localized tempest around a target. The storm will have a radius of 24m and will cause substantial amounts of gravity damage within its radius. Secondary results may occur.
Mana recharge time: 1 minute, 45 seconds

Linked Skill Name: Minor Cone of Binding
Xatherite Color(s): Red
Linked Skill Grade: Advanced
Type: Magic
Effect: Creates a cone of gravity, which causes all objects to be bound to the ground with significant force. Cone can originate from any part of your body. Cone will extend 10m and has an arc of pi/4 radians. Secondary results may occur.
Duration: 10 seconds.
Complete Linked Skill bonus: Double benefit from your mana discharge stat.
Elemental Tempest Constellation: Elemental effects doubled.
Total effect: Creates a cone of gravity, which causes all objects to be bound to the ground with major force. Cone can originate from any part of your body. Cone will extend 10m and has an arc of pi/4 radians. Secondary results may occur.
Mana recharge time: 21 seconds

```
Linked Skill Name: Grav Ball
Xatherite Color(s): Red
Linked Skill Grade: Advanced
Type: Magic
Effect: Create a ball of gravity at the target location within
100m. Causing major gravity damage in a 1.5m radius around
the blast. Secondary results may occur.
Complete Linked Skill bonus: Double benefit from your mana
discharge stat.
Elemental Tempest Constellation: Elemental effects doubled.
Total effect: Create a ball of gravity at the target location within
100m. Causing substantial gravity damage in a 1.5m radius
around the blast. Secondary results may occur.
Mana recharge time: 13.1 seconds
```

He was slightly disappointed that he only got three links
out of gravitas attuning, that was until he read the results. They
were all considerably more powerful than he could have hoped
for. Also, they all had that ominous line at the end of their effects,
"Secondary results may occur." He was itching to cast them to see
what those results may be but didn't think the cave was the right
place to try. Grav ball was amazing, though. It didn't have to pass
through the intervening area, which meant it could be cast
anywhere he could see, within range.

Drew immediately clicked the option to upgrade storm
and lightning bolt.

```
Xatherite Crystal Name: Major Storm
Xatherite Color: Red
Xatherite Grade: Rare
Xatherite Rarity: Common
Type: Magic
```

Effect: Create a localized storm around a target. The storm will have a radius of 12m and will cause high amounts of wind, water, and lightning damage within its radius.
Complete Linked Skill bonus: Double benefit from your mana discharge stat.
Elemental Tempest Constellation: Elemental effects doubled.
Total effect: Create a localized storm around a target. The storm will have a radius of 12m and will cause ample amounts of wind, water, and lightning damage within its radius.
Mana recharge time: 1 minute, 17 seconds

Xatherite Crystal Name: Major Lightning Bolt
Xatherite Color: Red
Xatherite Grade: Rare
Xatherite Rarity: Widespread
Type: Magic
Effect: Creates a bolt of electricity from any body part to a target no more than 20m away. Deals moderate lightning damage and stuns the target for 4 seconds.
Mana recharge time: 4.2 seconds

Congratulations, Sub-Lieutenant. Your linked skill Frostfire Storm has been upgraded to Major Frostfire Storm.
Congratulations, Sub-Lieutenant. Your linked skill Frost Storm has been upgraded to Major Frost Storm.
Congratulations, Sub-Lieutenant. Your linked skill Fire Storm has been upgraded to Major Fire Storm.

Storm's radius had increased by two meters. It had also upgraded damage to high. However, the bonuses from completing a linked chain and for being in a named constellation, boosted that to what must be the next stage of damage, ample. The linked skills had likewise increased. In fact, fireball, cone of frost, and all the linked abilities looked like they all jumped two levels of damage. Which meant that each level of damage must have been double the previous level.

Lightning bolt was another amazing upgrade. With a five meter boost in range, it was quickly shoring up the major flaws that it had as a close-range attack spell. Its quick cooldown and newly extended range was only diminished by its relatively low damage modifier. He had the feeling that most of his spells were going to be a bit overkill for most things anyway, especially the ones in Elemental Tempest.

He had leveled up and gotten additional interface options; a quick glance told him that he could now get a status report for each of his teammates. It consisted of a general health status including how tired they were and how hurt they were, consciousness status, and something called mana fatigue level. There was another window that represented his own status, and pulling it up gave him more detailed information.

Sub-Lieutenant Drew Michalik-3's status

Physical: Intermediate.
Resistance: Common.
Pain Threshold: Intermediate.
Speed: Undeveloped.
Mental: Advanced.
Mana Receptivity: Intermediate.
Mana Discharge: Rare.
Mana Charge: Advanced.

He wasn't entirely positive, but he was pretty sure both his physical and resistance stats had been one stage lower during his initial evaluation, although the other stats hadn't changed. The last function of his new interface was the ability to designate positions under his command that looked like they would provide bonuses to those individuals in them.

Drew was pulled from his examinations of his new interface options when someone cleared their throat behind him. Turning back again, he saw that Major Hoffecker had returned. She reached out a hand to shake Drew's. "I just wanted to personally thank you, IT2. I know you've put yourself in harm's way to rescue us. I also know the Captain isn't handling this whole thing very well. He wasn't exactly prepared for this kind of thing. Hell, I don't know if any of us are prepared for this, except you. I don't know how you do everything you've been doing, but keep it up." She then saluted him.

Drew felt weird. He'd never had an officer saluting him first before. He returned the salute. "Of course, ma'am, that's the coast guard's unofficial motto. You always have to go out, but you don't have to come back."

She shook her head. "I think we need you to stick around for a bit. I imagine there will be a good deal of fighting left to do before all is said and done, and we're all counting on you."

With a nod of his head, Drew accepted the rebuttal, "Of course, ma'am." Hoffecker smiled and turned away, immediately shouting orders to her people to keep everyone moving. He watched her leave and shook his head. The world that he had known before was clearly gone. The new world wasn't anywhere near as safe as the previous one, but it wasn't all bad.

Epilogue

The bridge was quiet and dimly lit, just the way he preferred, his people quietly going about their tasks in whispered conversations. The bridge was calm, despite the battle being waged outside. Battle was hardly the correct term for it. A Tuatha ship had landed on some backwoods planet. Hopefully, it was young enough that his men could kill it and bring its xatherite back. Otherwise, he'd be forced to obliterate the planet. The other pantheons would complain if he did that, even if it was only in class five space, and then he would be forced to make an accounting.

One of the Eumenides appeared at his side. Turning to look at her, he raised an eyebrow.

"Pardon Lord, but we have detected a use of divine mana in the Sol system of the Orion-Cygnus arm," she said with deference.

"Ares?" he asked, knowing that the Eumenides wouldn't have brought this to his attention if it was.

"Negative, Lord. It was unattuned." That caused both eyebrows to be raised, and he turned to give the Eumenides his full attention.

"Typed?" he asked.

"Yes, Lord, Retribution," she answered, anticipating his next question.

"Assets in Sol?" he asked.

"None, it's a class nine space but only recently activated. The detection originated from the third slice."

He pursed his lips and, with a thought, brought up the display for Sol. He frowned. "The third slice is only a few weeks old."

"Affirmative, sir, I queried HP-ONI, but all information about the third slice was listed as restricted to the Enclave of the Dragon."

The man leaned back in his chair and considered the system before him. As he did, he mused aloud, "What has my brother been up to?" After a moment of consideration, he turned back to the view screen. "Command all troops to disengage and return to the fleet. Prepare the fleet to travel to the nearest sustainable system to Sol and have Tisephone meet me in my ready room. Alert me when all troops have departed and prepare for planetary dissolution."

"As you wish, Lord Hades."

Afterword

We hope you enjoyed Advent! Since reviews are the lifeblood of indie publishing, we'd love it if you could leave a positive review on Amazon! Please use this link to go to the Red Mage: Advent Amazon product page to leave your review: geni.us/Advent.

As always, thank you for your support! You are the reason we're able to bring these stories to life.

About Xander Boyce

Xander is a USCG veteran and lifelong sci-fi/fantasy reader. Having begun creating worlds for his pen and paper roleplaying games more than a decade ago, he has always been fascinated by what can be done when people are pushed beyond normal boundaries. He was drawn to science fiction as a way to explore the human condition, and his debut book, *Advent*, is an extension of that desire.

Connect with Xander:
Facebook.com/AuthorXanderBoyce
Facebook.com/groups/AuthorXanderBoyce
Patreon.com/dmxanadu
Discord.gg/h243sg4

About Mountaindale Press

Dakota and Danielle Krout, a husband and wife team, strive to create as well as publish excellent fantasy and science fiction novels. Self-publishing *The Divine Dungeon: Dungeon Born* in 2016 transformed their careers from Dakota's military and programming background and Danielle's Ph.D. in pharmacology to President and CEO, respectively, of a small press. Their goal is to share their success with other authors and provide captivating fiction to readers with the purpose of solidifying Mountaindale Press as the place 'Where Fantasy Transforms Reality'.

Connect with Mountaindale Press:
MountaindalePress.com
Facebook.com/MountaindalePress
Krout@MountaindalePress.com

Mountaindale Press Titles

GameLit and LitRPG

The Divine Dungeon Series
The Completionist Chronicles Series
By: Dakota Krout

A Touch of Power Series
By: Jay Boyce

Red Mage: Advent
By: Xander Boyce

Ether Collapse Series
By: Ryan DeBruyn

Bloodgames: Season One
By: Christian J. Gilliland

Wolfman Warlock: Bibliomancer
By: James Hunter and Dakota Krout

Axe Druid Series
By: Christopher Johns

Skeleton in Space Series
By: Andries Louws

Chronicles of Ethan Series
By: John L. Monk

Pixel Dust Series

By: David Petrie

Artorian's Archives Series
By: Dennis Vanderkerken and Dakota Krout

Bonus Side Stories

Mission District, San Francisco, California

Shelly used her sleeve to wipe the sweat off her forehead. She had managed to climb up to the top of the building, but the bay breeze wasn't quite strong enough to cool her down after the exertion. She paused as she activated mental scan, searching for a sign of her prey. She was dressed in the thick, black, leather armor she had stolen from one of the horde, and whatever it was made of, it somehow managed to stay clean despite the copious amount of green blood that had soaked it.

The scan extended outwards, slowing when it was more than fifty feet away from her. It took another two minutes for them to catch up to her; they were slowly walking up Florida street. She was crouched on the roof of three buildings that had been joined together decades ago, creating a strange amalgamation of rooftops that merged into a flat outer edge, a perfect place to lay an ambush. She stretched her limbs, getting ready for the attack.

From the stories, she would have assumed gnomes would be better at this hunting prey thing. After all, the ugly things were supposed to be part beast. She couldn't see their shape, not with mental scan—which showed them as small orbs of mental energy, but she knew there were three of them. They were all that was left of the two-dozen strong patrol she had been slowly tearing chunks off for the past three hours. It had been a good chase throughout a large portion of the mission district as she used her skills and xatherite to take out the stragglers and the weak.

She was army crawling to the edge of the roof so that she could look at them. These last three were the strongest. One stood about four and a half feet tall. His bright pink hair looked silly, but the strange, wickedly curved khopesh blades it dual wielded were no laughing matter. The other two were a few inches shorter. The blue haired one carried a shield and short spear, while the one with green hair gripped a glaive in both hands, which he had almost killed her with earlier.

Shelly intended to save that one for last—his death was going to be slow. They finally got to the intersection of Florida and 20th Street and stopped, looking around. The blue one had some sort of scent ability. He'd been the one tracking her most of the night, but he didn't seem to understand how her trail had just disappeared. When the pink one started arguing with the blue one, she activated her drake jump xatherite. She spun through the air, reveling in the freedom of movement as she fell the three stories to the street below.

She landed on the blue haired one. Her foot braced against the nape of his neck, and she could feel the snap of his spine as the skill transferred the force of her fall to her target. He smashed into the asphalt with an audible crunch, and she wasn't sure how many bones he had just broken, but she knew from experience it was enough to take him out of the fight. She grinned at the other two, who were stunned by her sudden entrance. She flicked her wrist, and the pink one sprouted a dagger four inches into his skull via his left eye. She hadn't even needed to activate a skill to kill him.

The green one screamed as he tried to swing the glaive at her. She stepped into the weapon's arc, one arm raised to block the swing. The bone armor growing out of her forearm caught the pole of the weapon, pushing it even further off target. She flipped the grip on her other dagger and activating power thrust, stabbed it into his stomach. He was wearing armor, but the xatherite enhanced strike parted the leather like a hot knife in butter. She only stopped when the blade cracked against his vertebrae, severing the nerves and causing him to fall to the ground, the lower half of his body no longer connected to his brain.

His bigger than life anime eyes went even wider, and blood came out of his mouth as he tried to open it. Shelly flipped off him, rolling away just in case he still had some fight in him.

She came up in a combat pose and smiled down at the dying gnome. "Fucking gnome horde comes to my town? Kills my boyfriend and expects me to just take it in stride?"

She kicked the glaive away from him, even though his hands were more focused on trying to keep his innards inside him. She circled around to the side, then kicked his torso, driving the blade deeper inside him. She then activated blade call, and all her weapons returned to their sheaths, sparkling clean. "Now, I'd really like to just let you bleed out, but there's a chance you have a xatherite behind those big fucking eyes. So, sadly, this is going to be faster than I'd like. She pushed her foot against his windpipe and slowly pressed down.

"You motherfuckers invaded the wrong goddamn town." The dying gnome's hands feebly tried to push Shelly's leg away, but he was powerless. The celery crunch of his windpipe breaking was enough, and she turned away from him to look at the other two. "Oh look, your friend already gave me some. Guess that means you won't have any on you, and I can let you die slowly!" She touched the red crystal that had grown between the eyes of the pink haired gnome. The street, littered with green blood and viscera, glowed red briefly, and she smiled as the notification blinked into reality in the corner of her vision. With a shrug, she left the gnome to slowly suffocate, then activated shadow of death and disappeared into the darkening gloom.

The fog was rolling in, and she had plenty of hunting time left before the sun came up. She wouldn't rest until she had killed every single one of the green horde.

I-70 West of Edwards, Colorado

Erik looked down the ridge to where he could see a town. It had been called Edwards a week ago, but there probably wasn't anyone still alive down there. Still, he had to check. His armor kept him warm as it took on a strangely reflective quality from the snow around him. It was still early April in Colorado, and this late in the day, it was getting back down to the mid forties. He looked behind him at the nineteen people he had managed to convince to follow him.

All of them had been through a harrowing six days. He frowned. At this rate, he wouldn't make Denver for months. Advent had started while he was overnighting in Gypsum just a few miles to the west of here along I-70, and he was grateful that God had given him the xatherite he needed to save as many people as he had, but he'd left far too many graves along the trail. He gestured everyone forward, his hand resting on the handle of his war hammer.

Cutting a far more imposing figure than the rest of the group, Erik was encased in his conjured armor. It resembled that of the old knight's templar but wasn't anywhere near as heavy as their plate mail had been. He could barely feel its weight and it didn't restrict his movement at all. It still did a fine job at stopping attacks, though. The massive demon possessed bears, rabbits, elk, and wolves that had attacked the weary travelers had more than tested its worth.

Picking up the heavy war hammer, whose head glowed with an inner light, and throwing it over one shoulder, he began to walk down the road to Edwards. His people followed him. The three young children he had managed to save that first day were riding his summoned charger. The xatherite he used to summon it was a godsent reward he had received after he killed the biggest bear he'd ever seen. He glanced back at the kids and waved, though they didn't respond. He didn't expect them to. He hadn't been quite quick enough to save their parents from the wolves, and none of the three had said a word since.

The rest of the group was just as ragtag. Most of them were young, under twenty, and all had lost someone they loved. The only one older than twenty-five was a former diner waitress who had taken to caring for the kids after he'd pulled her out of the burned remnants of her diner back in Eagle three days ago.

It was only a couple miles to Edwards, but they probably wouldn't make it until midday tomorrow, so he'd have to have Ross dig them another cave to sleep in for the night. Realizing that light of faith's cooldown was probably up, he activated that prayer, and yellow light surrounded all twenty of them. The shivering stopped immediately, and everyone picked up the pace, wanting to make as much distance as they could while the buff was in place.

They made it halfway down the hill before they heard the howling. It originated from further down the road, but Erik immediately swung his hammer up. "Defensive positions!" It was a well-practiced maneuver at this point. Ross dug a pit, and they began putting all the unawakened children into it. Then he shifted the earth around them, creating a slope as steep as his powers would allow. Meanwhile, Rose used her xatherite to create long forks along the top of the ridge, and Ross buried them until just their razor-sharp tines were visible.

Erik commanded the horse to come to him as soon as the children were off it. At twenty-one hands tall, it was a massive beast. Without the strength enhancement of his armor, he doubted he would have even been able to mount the charger. He patted the beast's flank to comfort it. It was a worthless gesture as the conjured horse had no feelings, but it felt right to him. He watched their preparations as he circled the fortification. As he circled, he thanked God that they had the right abilities and the people to keep so many alive, despite the growing difficulty in doing so.

When the entire bulwark had been created, he nodded to Rose and Ross, then tilted his visor down and hefted the hammer into a readied combat position as he nudged the charger forward. The wolves would be here any moment now; it never took long. He took this chance to pray, his deep voice reverberating throughout the canyon, echoing into the wilderness around him.

"O Lord, we ask for a boundless confidence and trust in
Your divine mercy
and the courage to accept the crosses and sufferings
which bring immense goodness to our souls and that of
Your Church."

The wolves appeared before he could finish the prayer,
but he merely raised his hammer. The light within its head glowed
brighter as he activated his divine light xatherite. It was his only
red skill, and the hammer flashed red, causing the wolves to cry
out as they were blinded by the Lord's grace. He motioned the
charger forward and shouted, "For God and Freedom!"

With the battle joined, the charger used its heavy hooves
to crush wolves while he swung the war hammer with far more
ease than the heavy weapon should have allowed. The wolves did
manage to pull the horse to the ground, but it disappeared in a
blink of blue light as Erik jumped from its back. He sent two
wolves flying with the impact of his landing, managing to keep his
feet. He began swinging the hammer around him in wide arcs
while the wolves tried to nip at him, but aside from the force and
weight of their attacks throwing him off balance occasionally, they
couldn't do any damage to his holy armor.

Nine wolves were dead from the combination of his
hammer and the charger before he managed to kill the alpha, the
hammer connecting solidly with its head, sending brain matter
flying. The remaining five wolves turned and fled, their sense of
self-preservation reasserting itself over the Satanic corruption that
had caused them to show such growth and aggression.

He looked back to the fortification to ensure that the
children had been delivered safely through the conflict with the
demon beasts. Seeing Rose and Ross standing atop the
embankment unharmed, he knelt down among the bodies of the
slain wolves, praying to St. Michael for his safe deliverance
through the battle.

When he was done, he stood up, calling out to the others, "Let's make camp here for the night. The light is almost gone anyway."

North End, Boston, Massachusetts

Nick stepped on a twig, snapping it with an audible crack. He ducked back into the alley as a two-ton dog turned her head to look for the sound. He was hoping she hadn't seen him. He'd already cast bond on her five times, so odds were that she wouldn't attack him, but he didn't want to risk her getting angry, especially this close to the final casting.

He kept out of sight, counting twenty heartbeats before he began to slowly move back to where he could see the courtyard. He caught her tail flashing by just past the Paul Revere statue as she ducked into her den in the Old North Church. Nick glanced back at Hanover Street. It was unlikely that anything would follow the undisputed ruler of the North End, but he wanted to be sure. He made his way into the church, pausing at the entrance to allow his eyes to adjust to the dim light.

She had made a den at the far end of the church from the entrance, and he realized that he could see the red glow reflecting off of her eyes as she watched him from her bedding. She was no more than a few days from giving birth, her belly swollen with the pups, but otherwise, she had the shape of an overly large hound dog. Her coloring was beautiful, the coat a gorgeous blue merle, with tan trim and glacier blue eyes. Nick had no idea what breed she had been before she was changed, probably a great dane or a catahoula.

Nick crept forward under the expectant mother's watchful eyes. He pulled out the meat from his backpack and held it in front of him. He'd had to kill a rabbit, a simple enough matter with his mesmerize skill. Fish was even easier to get, but she refused to eat any the one time he'd brought a couple cod. He had stuck to red meat after that, mostly rabbits and squirrels. His target was completely capable of hunting on her own of course, but she seemed to accept these small snacks as payment for letting him get closer. Since bonding required that he be less than a meter away from her when he cast it, he would take whatever he could get.

Throwing the rabbit meat towards the hound, she snapped it out of the air, chomping down on it once before swallowing it whole. At nearly twelve feet long and seven feet tall, the small amount of meat he was able to carry wouldn't be able to do more than put a dent in her hunger; it was more the act of providing her with food that was important. It turned him from prey into an annoyance, and hopefully in a few minutes, a friend.

Inching forward, Nick kept his demeanor calm despite the sweat dripping down his back. She was lethargic after having just returned from hunting. He assumed she wouldn't hunt again until after the pups were born, but it was hard to get an accurate guess, given that he had never worked on a two-ton dog before. She looked at him and growled, indicating he had come close enough. It was a soft growl for such a massive beast, yet still loud enough to make his chest rattle from the reverberations. He stopped but kept his eyes locked on her red glowing ones. He stood there and waited; she eventually got bored and began grooming herself.

He took several cautious steps forward, and when she didn't growl again, he took a few more. Repeating the process until he was a meter away, he activated bond for the sixth time. The skill had a massive cooldown, twenty hours, but it allowed him to form a bond between himself and a beast. As soon as the skill finished, she sat up, looking at him while cocking her head slightly to one side, considering him. For the first time since he had begun following her, there was no malice in her eyes, just curiosity, excitement, and significantly more intelligence than before the bond. Her tail began wagging, her ears were back, her mouth parted slightly, and her tongue lolled out a bit. All good signs.

Nick crossed the distance between him and the big dog, reaching up to dig his fingers into the hair behind her ears. She pressed her head against him, leaning into the scratching. He used both hands; her fur was almost three inches thick and difficult to penetrate, a great protection from the other predators around.

After several minutes of scratching, he stopped. She turned to look at him and licked his face. Her massive size meant she also licked most of his chest. Nick laughed. She carefully tackled him and began licking him clean, even as Nick tried to protest. There wasn't much he could do to fight off his overzealous new pet, however.

When she was satisfied, she curled back up and sighed contentedly. Nick lay down next to her front legs and put his head against her shoulder. It had been days since he'd gotten a good night's rest. Now that she was his, he could finally sleep, trusting in her instincts to protect them both.

"I'm going to call you Lupa, after the She-Wolf that birthed Rome." If she responded, he didn't hear it, as he had already fallen asleep curled up beside her.

Perdido Key, Florida

Lee was running. It was honestly a bit like a bad recreation of Forrest Gump.

He could see his destination ahead of him, a strange block of metal, slightly rounded and very organic looking. It had taken him almost two days to grow it from the shed that had been there before.

He could hear the creature behind him gaining speed. He cut to the left. The thing could really build up some steam, but it couldn't turn for crap. Another few seconds and he adjusted his course again, moving for the entrance to what he affectionately called his gatlopp. Lee still couldn't see the creature behind him, but from the sounds it was making, he knew it was going to be close.

Another course shift, slowing the beast down just a little bit more, and then he was past the entrance. Six feet in, he slapped his hand against the wall, causing a two-inch metal sheet to drop behind him. The beast squealed in pain as the corresponding one at the entrance to the gatlopp slammed down, cutting the creature in half with its sharp bottom. It was sharper than a razor, as his new talents allowed him to make things that science would never have been able to create a week ago.

Leaning forward, Lee placed his hands on his knees as he tried to catch his breath. The monster behind him still squealed, it's sharp tusks raking against the metal behind him even though its spine had probably been severed by the door. He placed his hands on the wall and metal melted away, giving him a handle and footholds to grasp. Then the holes slid most of the way up the wall, allowing him to see over the door where the mana twisted boar was slowly bleeding out.

After a moment of consideration, Lee caused another wall to fall, cutting the boar's head off in an instant. He patted the gatlopp and descended, resetting the inner door as he did so. "Wish I had as much control over all metal as I do over the stuff I've grown," he muttered to himself as he began raising the floor and started to cut the pig into portions. It was a big beast, but with a few hundred people to feed, he knew it wouldn't last long. He'd pay his tribute to Kira and her thugs; that should get them out of his hair for a few days at least.

He cut off a portion for his own meal, and putting it on a spit, he lit the fire to cook it. He didn't take advantage of Kira's protection or her communal food pot, but he was also one of the few people bringing in meat. If he had a way to keep his food fresh, he'd be long gone. Nothing in the swamp could hurt him; he'd just have gatlopp march along until no one could follow him.

Well, as soon as he could figure out how to get gatlopp marching. Until then, he'd have to deal with Kira. Her thugs would come by soon; they always did after he lit his fire. They'd probably be happy he killed something other than gator this time.

He glanced over at the boar and frowned. It had been bigger than any of the rest of them, but he still hadn't gotten another xatherite. Jacobs, one of Kira's stupider thugs, had told him that Pensacola had managed to pick up three now. He knew that the stuff he was fighting was harder than whatever Jacobs could kill. Even if he was mostly red, his attacks were weak compared to the kind of damage Lee's traps could dish out.

Another problem... All he had was traps, things that he could create with his lifetime of swamp hunting and the violet xatherite that allowed him to grow steel and shape it however he wanted. He sat musing over his options for almost an hour. His mouth was beginning to water from the aroma coming off the haunch of meat on the spit.

Banging came from the side of gatlopp. "Lee, open up. It's Kira."

Lee frowned. She came personally? She hadn't done that since the first day he'd been found when they tried to get him to come back to Pensacola and grow protections for the town. He opened the outer door. "That's your portion," he shouted, and he could hear several of Kira's people beginning to transport several hundred pounds of pig meat.

"Lee, come talk to me, or I'm going to tell your mama that you're being rude."

Lee frowned. While his Ma and Pa had survived, he felt no need to join them. With a grunt, he opened a door large enough for Kira to walk through. Jacobs was the first to appear through the doorway, and a spike of steel shot up, stopping him in his tracks before he impaled himself on it.

"I didn't invite you, Jacobs. Go make yourself useful and pick up something heavy," Lee said with a wave of dismissal.

It took almost five seconds for Jacobs to realize that Lee wasn't joking, and he could see the big man's face turning red in anger. Lee prepared a few more spikes in case the stupid lout decided he wanted to try to start something again. They hadn't gotten along since Lee had forced the bigger boy to pee his pants in fear back in elementary school. It honestly surprised Lee that Jacobs could even remember that long ago.

His spikes were unneeded, though. Kira laid a hand on Jacobs' shoulder and whispered into his ear too quietly for Lee to hear. The big man turned around and began helping the others carry the meat back.

Kira stepped through the portal and waited for Lee to remove the spike, which he did with a wave of his hand, and he then created a stool for her to sit on instead. She was a pretty woman with dark auburn hair, freckles, and a plump body that most men would have called curvy. "What can I do for the new gang lord of Pensacola?" Lee asked, grinning as he saw Kira barely restrain her rolled eyes.

"I'm not a gang lord, Lee. Just trying to keep everyone safe."

"Sure, sure. What can I do for you?"

"Look, I know you said you were only interested in helping us get food and otherwise had no intention of affiliating with the rest of humanity." She paused, looking around at the barren metal room he had created for himself. The lines were all wrong, slightly curved and bent instead of straight, like something robotic trying to look organic. "But we really need your help. With your skills, we could easily keep everyone safe."

They had been friends, once, back before... Lee's eye twitched, and he shook his head. "Not interested."

"Lee, it isn't safe out here on your own." She was switching tracks. "What if you get hurt and can't make it back here? You'd be a sitting duck," Kira said, but Lee refused to meet her eyes. He cut off a portion of the meat and blew on it for a second as he shifted it between his hands before biting into it.

"No. Not if he's there," Lee said, dismissing Kira by turning away from her and back to his fire. He heard her sigh and then stand up, walking to the hole he had created for her. They'd had this argument before, and he refused to go near that man.

"Thank you for the meat. I really wish you would reconsider."

Lee said nothing; he knew she would go away soon. She was too busy saving the whole town to spend too much time on the outcast.

As she left, the metal folded back into a seamless wall. The thought occurred to him as he heard the last of the transporters leave—was he trying to keep them out or something else in?

Appendix

Adam Jones – A member of the third group of survivors Drew rescues. Adam has a terrakinesis xatherite.

Admiral – A high rank in the Human Protectorate Navy.

Advent – The process of introducing mana into a dimensional slice.

Aevis – The AI Assigned to Earth-3.

Angela Swaze – Daryl's wife.

Anthony Jacobs – A survivor in Florida, a subordinate of Kira's.

Ares, Admiral – Cassius Felix-9, known by his Pantheon name of Ares is the leader of the Orion-Cygnus Ironfleet, which is assigned to protect the Sol system. A red mage and member of the Order of the Dragon. His flagship is the Olympus.

Assault Mage – Another term for a red mage.

Athena – A member of the Order of the Dragon.

Azura – An awakened species. Invading Azura are known as Pilgrims. Main enemies of the greater Orion-Cygnus branch of Humanity.

Bauk – An alliance of species. They are referred to as refugees.

Bill Mather, SKC – A member of the first group of survivors Drew rescues. Chief Bill has a heal spell called daddy's embrace.

Brady Cooke, DC1 – One of the first group of survivors Drew rescues. Is given the penetrating shot xatherite.

Chakri – The chief of the orcish clan residing in CGHQ.

Chuck – One of the first group of survivors Drew rescues. Can grow trees and control wood in various ways.

Clyde – A member of the first set of survivors, mostly green xatherite.

Conclave (of the Dragon) – The ruling body of the Order of the Dragon made up of the most respected Knights.

Da Danann – A group of awakened species, they are considered to be main contenders in the Orion-Cygnus arm of the galaxy. A member species of the Daoine.

Dak Kyle, PFC – One of the third group of survivors Drew rescues. From the Great Lakes. Dak has a xatherite that allows him to turn into stone.

Daoine – A group of awakened species, consisting of the Da Danann, Spyry Jyon, Piksies, and Elatrin among unspecified others.

Daryl Swaze – A survivor that finds Drew on JB Anacostia-Bolling. Indigo specialist the main group's scout.

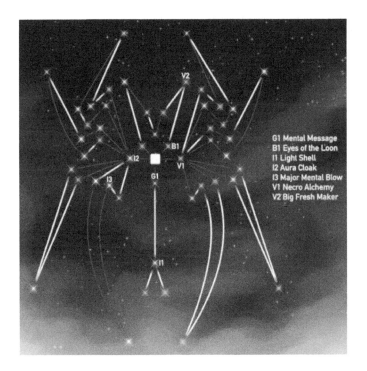

G1 Mental Message
B1 Eyes of the Loon
I1 Light Shell
I2 Aura Cloak
I3 Major Mental Blow
V1 Necro Alchemy
V2 Big Fresh Maker

Daniel Barnes, PFC – One of the first group of survivors Drew rescues. Proficient with guns.

Deathweaver – A derogatory term for a red mage.

Dimensional slice – The process of splitting physical space into distinct dimensional slices that can still communicate with the Alpha timeline.

Donum duplici – Gift given to a squire when they are offered a squireship.

Drew Michalik-3, IT2 – A coast guardsman from Idaho, currently stationed at CGHQ in DC. A red mage and Order of the Dragon. Drew's current Human Protectorate rank is Sub-Lieutenant.

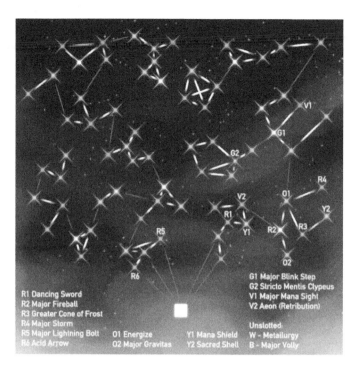

Earth-1 – The first-dimensional slice of Earth. It split off from the alpha timeline 8 years ago.

Earth-2 – The second-dimensional slice of earth, it split off from the alpha timeline 4 years ago.

Earth-3 – The third-dimensional slice of Earth and the primary location of the red mage story.

Elatrin – The main combat forces of the Daoine. It is unclear if Elatrin is a title or a species. All that is known is that they are one of the few things that can go up against the full might of a Knight of the Order of the Dragon.

Enyalios – A high ranking officer on the Olympus.

Erik – A paladin survivor in Colorado.

Eumenides – A name for Hades' attending officers.

Frank Hambelger – A member of the first group of survivors Drew rescues.

Gary Kramer – A member of the second group of survivors Drew rescues. Gary was a goth before the Advent.

Gatlopp – Lee's metal house.

Glenn Wilson – One of the third group of survivors Drew rescues. Glenn can summon throwing daggers.

Gnome – A species of manaborn seen in San Francisco.

Go'rai – See orcs

Hades – A member of the Order of the Dragon.

HP-ONI – Human Protectorate Office of Naval Intelligence

Ironfleet – The deadly Human fleets. Each Ironfleet is responsible for a section of space, the leaders of each fleet are known as Pantheons.

Isis – A member of the Order of the Dragon.

Jholie – Seventeen-year-old member of the first set of survivors Drew rescues.

JP White, Sargent FPD – One of the cops sent by the Senator who has set up in Nat's Park to gather survivors. Mostly blue xatherite. Level 1 - Seaman

R1 Sonic Gun
R2 Fire Shot
R3 Chill Shot
B1 Full Mag
B2 Armored Uniform
Y1 Chill Shield

Juan Cabellos, IS3 – A coast guardsman from Puerto Rico. Currently stationed at CGHQ in DC. Mostly Indigo xatherite.

Kara Daniels – A member of the first group of survivors Drew rescues.

Katie Sabin, OS1 – First name is actually Kathryn. A coast guardsman from Vermont, currently stationed at CGHQ in DC. Mostly blue xatherite.

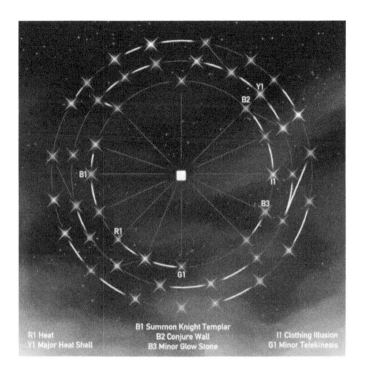

R1 Heat
Y1 Major Heat Shell

B1 Summon Knight Templar
B2 Conjure Wall
B3 Minor Glow Stone

I1 Clothing Illusion
G1 Minor Telekinesis

Kim Purvis – A member of the second group of survivors Drew rescues.

Kira – A survivor in Florida, and leader of the survivors in Pensacola there.

Korath – A cow like species.

Kwincy – A member of the first set of survivors Drew saves. Mostly blue xatherite.

Lee – A survivor in Florida with the ability to grow metal objects that respond to his will.

Lewis "Juice" Patrick – A member of the second group of survivors Drew Rescues.

Ley Line – Magical conduits that spread throughout an area.

Lilith – A member of the Order of the Dragon.

Linked Skills – Skills created when two or more xatherite in a linked node system synergize.

Loki – A member of the Order of the Dragon.

Lupa – Nick's tamed mana-twisted dog.

Manaborn – Creatures created by mana.

Matt Snyder, CPT USN – One of the third group of survivors Drew rescues.

Midshipman – The first officer rank in the Human Protectorate Navy.

Mike Wallace – A member of the second group of survivors Drew rescues.

Military Ranks (US) – American Military ranks are split into three groups called paygrades. Enlisted (E-1 through E-9), Warrant (W-1 through W-4) and Officer (O1-O9). Each branch can have a different name for each pay grade. For example, a Navy E-1 is a seaman recruit (SR) while the Army calls their E-1's Private (PVT). The USCG and USN use similar naming conventions. The other three branches have distinct names.

Min Sun – An older Korean woman among the first set of survivors Drew rescues. An accomplished tailor turned armorsmith.

Mitch Windsor, OS2 – A coast guardsman. Currently stationed at CGHQ in DC. Mostly red xatherite.

Natren – A tribe of orcs

Nick – A beast tamer survivor in Boston.

Node – When two or more ley lines connect they form a node. Nodes can be conquered and provide benefits to their owners.

Nora Storm – A member of the second group of survivors Drew rescues.

Olympus – The flagship of the Orion-Cygnan Fleet

One – The split of Drew from the first-dimensional slice. Has taken up residence in Colorado Springs. Current HP rank is Sub-Lieutenant.

Orcs – A race of creatures that populate the CGHQ building. Squat and heavyset, the orcs are ferocious warriors but cannot jump.

Order of the Dragon – The Knightly order to which Drew belongs. It consists of red mages.

Order of the Scale – A knightly order of the Human Protectorate, to which Themis belongs.

Orion-Cygnan Fleet – The Ironfleet commanded by Admiral Ares

Pan – A member of the Order of the Dragon.

Pantheon – The Ironfleets of humanity are run by a cadre of officers known as a Pantheon.

Piksie – A group of awakened species, they are considered to be main contenders in the Orion-Cygnus arm of the galaxy. A member species of the Daoine.

Primary Nexus – The area around Washington DC on Earth. It consists of the largest collection of ley lines on the planet.

Rob Amako, IT1 – Drew's partner who is on a lunch break when the Advent happens.

Robbi – One of the cops sent by the senator who has set up in Nat's Park to gather survivors. Tank skills, skilled with a sword and his signature xatherite: Blood Blade.

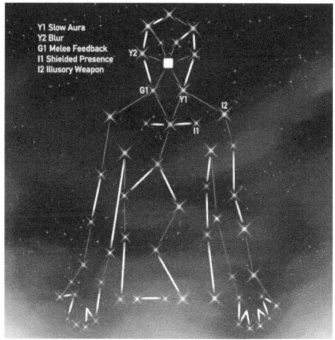

Sarah Rothschild, ENS – A coast guardsman. Currently stationed at CGHQ in DC. Mostly yellow xatherite.

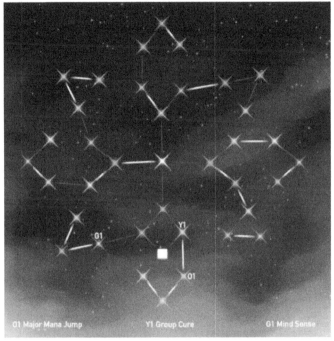

Seaman – The first enlisted rank in the Human Protectorate Navy.

Set – A member of the Order of the Dragon.

Shelly – A ninja survivor in San Fransisco.

Spyry Jyon – A group of awakened species, they are considered to be main contenders in the Orion-Cygnus arm of the galaxy. A member species of the Daoine.

Sub-Luitentant – The second officer rank of the Human Protectorate Navy

Tartarus – The flagship of Hades' iron fleet.

Themis – A high ranking officer on the Olympus. Ares' mental mage. A member of the Order of the Scale.

Tisephone – A subordinate of Hades.

Tracy Hoffecker, MAJ USA – One of the third group of survivors Drew rescues.

Trey Smith, PVT – Nineteen-year-old member of the first group of survivors Drew rescues. Illusion skills.

Trista Stirling, SGT – One of the first group of survivors Drew rescues. Is given a red xatherite.

Troll Shaman – Also called the Lightning Caller for his propensity to call down lightning. His name is unknown.

Trolls – Also called Ashalla, long-legged green species that occupies the DIA building.

Tuatha – A member race of the Daoine.

Two – The split of Drew from the second-dimensional slice. Has taken up residence in Las Vegas. Current HP rank is Midshipman.

Wereghasts – More intelligent versions of wereghouls. Also called alpha wereghouls.

Wereghouls – Humans that die in mana dense areas have a chance of coming back to life as a wereghoul. Nearly feral, wereghouls are pack animals.

Xatherite – Crystalized mana that can be slotted into someone's map. Xatherite comes in seven different colors: Red, Orange, Yellow, Green, Blue, Indigo, Violet, and White. Each color has a general theme, although there does appear to be some overlap between the colors.

Zoey – Drew's Dog